After the War

a novel
by Libby Sternberg

This book is a work of fiction. Characters and places are either made up or, if real, used fictitiously. Any resemblance between fictional characters and real people is entirely coincidental and not intentional.

———————————————

Visit the author's website at www.LibbySternberg.com
Or her blog at www.LibbysBooks.wordpress.com

Copyright 2013 Libby Sternberg
Copyright 2017 Libby Sternberg
ISBN: 978-0988472556 digital
ISBN-13: 978-0615763132 (Custom)
ISBN-10: 0615763138

Publication date, first edition: June 6, 2013
Publication date, second edition (this one): March 2017

———————————————

*To the Leroy sisters: Lillian, Helen, and Beatrice,
beloved aunts and mother*

PROLOGUE
Tempest

Saturday, July 30, 1955

BACK AGAIN?

Blue veins shading those deep, rounded eyelids, skin as pale as ivory, mouth dry and chapped, shorn hair of dark reddish straw—the nun looked like an angel fallen to earth after a rough struggle. Nurse Kate McClaren stared down at Sister Francis Marie on the white stretcher just wheeled into the room.

"Here, help me move her." Betsy Watson, the other nurse on shift that afternoon, stationed herself on one side as they maneuvered the nun onto a bed. Efficient and grim, Betsy didn't like to make mistakes or take too much time with any one procedure.

"Why is she here this time?" Kate asked.

"This time? Stomach pumped. Overdose of Phenobarbital. Dr. Remy's ordered electroshock."

A shiver coursed through Kate. Oh, dear, Sister. Electroshock. So the doctor thought—no, not that, poor woman. Not a nun. She stroked Sister's hair, still dry and coarse from the starch in her wimple. How young she was—looking more like a girl than a woman.

"Shouldn't she be at Mercy or St. Joe's?" Betsy

asked, holding Sister's wrist to check her pulse.

Kate shook her head. "Her convent's doctor doesn't have privileges there. Or if he does, he prefers Hopkins." Kate remembered him from her previous chart. An old general practitioner operating out of an office in the basement of a pharmacy near the convent. The nuns had called him first, then shipped Sister here, for Dr. Remy's care.

Poor Sister—she looked like a portrait of a dead martyr, lying so still. All that was missing was a lily on her chest.

"You say she's been in before?" Betsy asked, writing her findings in a chart.

"Mmm-hmm. In the spring. Fell down the stairs at her convent. Collapsed from nervous exhaustion. Nothing broken, just bruises and a twisted ankle." And a wounded psyche. Dr. Remy had treated her then, too. He'd prescribed the Pheno. She'd stayed for several weeks before being discharged, supposedly whole and new again, but with something missing from her eyes. They had been as dull as her hair was now. She'd looked so frightened when she'd left that Kate had wanted to go check on her. But she never had, of course. Now she felt guilty for forgetting. Out of sight... Maybe she should have tried harder. Nursing was supposed to be about caring for patients, not just doctoring them, wasn't it?

"When she wakes up, Dr. Remy says she can have liquids."

"I can get her some broth and tea if she needs it. I'll keep an eye out," Kate said, standing by the bedside, stroking Sister's arm, feeling as if she had to make up for her previous lack of follow-up.

"What caused her collapse before?" Betsy asked, hanging up the nun's habit in the wardrobe in the corner. "Fasting? She looks thin as a bird."

"No, no. Something to do with—well, I don't know exactly. Her sister had passed away. From polio. And she'd been ill and...I guess it just became too much to bear. They're human, you know."

Betsy came over and peered at the wraith before them. "If you ask me, she probably just needs a few good meals and some sunshine."

With that, Kate could agree. She would ask about taking Sister out for walks. The air would do her good. And if she helped her improve—well, then Dr. Remy wouldn't have to jolt her with electricity. Kate might work in Hopkins's Phipps clinic, but that didn't mean she liked all the methods the doctors employed. Sometimes it seemed as if they were torturing patients, a modern-day version of the Inquisition, forcing them to endure pain until they confessed to their disabilities.

Kate managed to take Sister's temperature, poured some water into a glass on the bedside table, and then, after Betsy had left the room, found Sister's rosary in her belongings. This she placed next to the glass of water, in case Sister would want it when she awakened.

Overdosed on Phenobarbital—surely it had been an accident. Why had Dr. Remy prescribed that anyway? Such a strong drug.

Betsy came back in with a light blanket she folded at the end of the bed. Although it was summer, some patients complained of drafts.

"Good news for her—she won't have Remy for long. He's leaving for his honeymoon, remember?"

"Oh, yes."

"And he's not coming back."

"You're joking!" Kate looked over at Betsy, who was grinning. Dr. Remy was not her favorite, to say the least.

"Nope."

"Thank goodness."

"You can say that again."

After a moment's pause, Kate spoke again. "If she doesn't have a doctor, do you think I can make a suggestion?"

Betsy smiled knowingly. "Go ahead. He'd probably get the assignment anyway."

Blushing, Kate continued, "Oh, I don't know. He's kind of low man on the totem pole."

"That might be precisely the reason he'd get it—not interesting enough!"

Kate felt oddly wounded by that remark, both for Sister's sake—that Betsy trivialized her pain—and for the sake of Dr. Aaron Kaplan, the man she wanted handling the case. She and Dr. Kaplan had started seeing each other recently, despite some initial reservations on Kate's part. He was Jewish, after all, and she was Catholic.

Kate looked up at the other, unoccupied bed in the room. "Do you think we can keep that free?" She gestured to the bed.

"We're not jammed, so I guess."

"It's just that a nun... Well, she'd be used to her privacy." Kate had managed to let her stay in a room by herself the last time she'd been in. It was the least she could do.

"I'll make a note of it. But no promises." Betsy pulled the blinds so that the late afternoon sun didn't cut into the room. "Does she have family here?"

"Her Mother Superior will be the contact. But she does have a brother in town. And a sister-in-law." Kate remembered the sister-in-law, a very stylish woman with blond hair and blue eyes. She'd visited Sister when she was hospitalized before. She had been expecting a baby then. Kate wondered if she'd had the child yet.

Sister stirred, turning her head but not opening her eyes, and emitted a soft moan.

"Welcome back, Sister," Kate said in a loud, cheery voice. "Don't worry about anything. We'll take care of you. I'll go get you some tea."

CHAPTER ONE
Afraid

THE BOMB has dropped. That's all right. We'd practiced for this at school. It must have knocked me out. Dear Lord, please let everyone else be fine. Am I the only survivor?

I am very quiet, and by my quietness, very small, unworthy of notice, good or bad.

I know someone is in the room who can give me a sip of water, but I don't ask. I'm so tired, and my lips are so dry that they no longer feel a part of my body.

I'm very quiet now and everything is very calm, only the softest breeze flowing from the window caressing my perspiring brow as I lie in this warm bed alone in the universe. If I break this silence, everything will change. I don't want to be noticed. So I remain silent and drift and rouse and drift and rouse...and my lips stay dry....

❧

Someone's murmuring in the corner

"I thought you worked yesterday!"

"Yup—but now I start my morning shifts. Nell needed somebody to change up with her."

"Kate, you're such a Goody Two-shoes."

"I just like the work!"

"I swear, every day I show up—day or night shift— you're here. Do you sleep?"

A chuckle. "Of course, I do."

"You don't have time for much else is my guess..."

Those are the voices and that is what they are saying.

Zdrowaś Mario, łaski pełna Pan z Tobą

That is my thought. A prayer in my parents' native tongue.

I don't know where I am. No, I know this—I am in a white room. White sheets, white bed, white furniture, white white white.

Haec Dies quam fecit Domino.

I have so many prayers, all in different languages. Is this heaven? Disappointment. Why is it so unremarkable? And where precisely is He? In my mind I see myself tapping my foot.

Didn't I tell you I wanted to talk to you? You took her from me – from me, your faithful servant who had worked with humility and sacrifice and a complete surrendering of will!

And yet you took her from me.

Dear Lord.

"Is she waking up? Should we call Dr. Kaplan?"

"Let's order a breakfast tray, too...."

Yes, I am really rousing now, swimming from the deep pool where I slept, up into warm light. From the sounds of it, this awakening should be occasion for a celebration. My eyelids sputter like a film on the wrong speed. Everything blinks into focus. A window to my left, a door to my right, a fan whirring somewhere out of sight.

It is hot. Unusually hot. Too hot for March. March is...

The worst season of the year. A trap of a month – bare, spindly March where winter clings, jealous of life, to raw, wet days, and spring is still too timid to advance beyond a few apologetic crocuses amidst a sea of mud in the convent yard.

That day when Rosy was buried.

A tear escapes my eye. Now thoughts construct into memories, but at least they're whole, so I cling to them even as they scrape raw a grief.

Why is it so hot this early in the season? It is a portent. I only seem to understand His messages in retrospect. I see only the past and myself as an actor in it. I see that day. Or is it this day? That day…

"Do you know where you are?" He looked like a mariner, with short, thick beard hugging his jaw and chin, curly hair that hid the sweat creeping around the edges, stocky build, hands behind his back, one with a folder. This is Dr. Kaplan. She remembered the nurses saying he'd be by. She opened her eyes, refreshing her newest memories.

She'd been dozing, and for a moment when she'd awakened, she hadn't been able to remember where she was. Her mind had run through the catalog of the rooms she could be in, her panic growing as she'd negated each possibility—her bedroom at home, her dormitory at the novitiate, her first room at St. Elizabeth's, other convents after that, and finally her tiny room at St. Benedict's. It had taken a deep breath, another closing of her eyes and opening them again, to remember. Just in time to answer this question of his, posed, she knew, as a test.

She nodded. Phipps, the nurses had said yesterday when the kind one had brought her some tea. Baltimore was her home. She knew what Phipps was—the part of Johns Hopkins Hospital reserved for lunatics. She'd been here before….

She must be here by mistake, or perhaps because the rest of the hospital was too full. Perhaps the nurses were shielding her from the fullness of the story. Perhaps if she looked out her window she'd see rubble and barren streets, the result of the bomb.

Surely then the hospital would be full to bursting, though. But her room, large enough for two, only had one occupant—herself. Maybe the tragedy had been so great that there were few survivors.

"Phipps," she managed to whisper. Her throat scratched as she spoke. He offered her a glass of water.

"Do you know what day it is?"

She tried to remember, but the days were a blur. "Not yet," she murmured.

"Sunday," he offered, satisfied with her attempt.

Sunday—had she had Communion? Had anyone thought to offer it to her?

"And why you're here?"

Only the truth would pass this test. "No."

"Do you remember being here before?" he pressed, sitting in the chair by her bed.

She inhaled. *Yes. No. What was the right answer?* "I— I'm not sure."

"In March, you were here."

She didn't say anything, afraid if she gave away too much of her memory lapse, he'd be angry with her, as if she'd not studied hard enough.

He looked at her with great intensity, as if weighing how much to reveal, how much to wait for.

"You fell down the stairs that time," he said, tapping a file on his lap. "And you were prescribed Phenobarbital."

"Pheno—" she said slowly, trying to remember.

"It's a sedative. You were diagnosed as suffering from anxiety."

"It was after my sister's death," she whispered in self-defense. Of course she had been anxious. She still felt that pain. Who had prescribed it? Was it this doctor? If she couldn't remember, would it mean staying here interminably? Her breath came fast, and her hand clamped the rosary in a fist.

"You remember her death?"

She closed her eyes. "Yes."

"The fact that she died? Or more?"

"She died of polio. I went to the funeral." She remembered that day—the one day she'd like to forget. The pain and anger surfaced anew. Polio! When it was now cured! Rosy among the last to… She swallowed. She couldn't bear to think about it.

"That's good," he said with enthusiasm. "You went to her funeral, yes. To your brother's house after… "

The smoky living room, everything feeling like soggy cardboard from the rain, the smell of damp overcoats, Karol and Bernard arguing, Paula interfering.

"I fell down their stairs?" she asked, trying to piece together that story at least.

"You fell at your convent. Back in March, that is."

Standing at the top of the stairs, her head spinning… She remembered nothing more of that adventure.

"Did I break anything?" She opened her eyes, looking at her arms, opening her fingers.

"You were remarkably unscathed," he assured her, smiling. "No physical injuries to speak of, just a few bruises. But you were found to be suffering from a nervous anxiety."

"You were my doctor?" she asked, inwardly wincing as she couldn't remember him.

"No. A Doctor Remy tended to you. But he's no longer at the hospital."

That was a comfort, that she didn't have to struggle to remember this new doctor.

It was Dr. Remy who had prescribed the sedative, Dr. Kaplan explained to her, but his notes were not very comprehensive, so Dr. Kaplan himself would like her to fill in many blanks about her past. She yawned and sighed. Fatigue was like a hand pressing her to the bed. She'd never felt so tired. Or rather, she couldn't remember ever feeling so tired.

She tried to think of something to say, something that would satisfy him while at the same time allowing her to rest with no more pressure to talk about such intimate topics—her family, her life. She wanted to ask why she was here this time, but that would alert him to more of her memory lapse, and she just wanted time for it to come back, without being interrogated.

She looked away, her face warm. Sister Fulgentia would be so angry with her. Another setback. Her life in the convent had been filled with them—and she'd hardly been a nun at all, only a decade. The disastrous alternative she'd just imagined upon wakening—the bomb dropping—seemed better.

How long ago had her sister's funeral been? It was cruel for no one to tell her. The panic returned, making her heart gallop. She looked around. She wondered if it was dangerous here, if violent patients roamed free. She remembered that fear from the previous visit! That was her punishment for such stupidity—to live in fear.

"Your...supervisor...had you brought in after you collapsed." He sat back, smiling but not moving his gaze from her, analyzing her reactions.

Not her supervisor. Her Mother Superior. He wasn't Catholic.

"You mean...this time?"

He nodded.

"We've been giving you some medicine. They can make you very sleepy. And, of course, some other therapies have helped." He spoke slowly and loudly, as if she were hard of hearing. "Your sister came to see you yesterday evening, with your brother, but you were asleep."

No. He'd just mentioned her funeral. But maybe she'd imagined that.

A thousand years passed in the next instant. Rosy alive... *just an awful dream!*

Rosy, afflicted by a disease about to be eradicated for sure. She'd remembered the news—Sister Barbara had spoken of it. Salk and his vaccine. Of course, Rosy was alive! She must have misheard Dr. Kaplan earlier...still waking up, still half dreaming....

Dr. Kaplan stood and talked of getting her

something to eat, of seeing her the next day, of other things, but she heard only the beating of her heart. She needed to be alone. She needed to confess to not believing, for having so little faith...surely the Phenobarbital was somewhat to blame...why did Sister Fulgentia let her take it....why had she even gone to the doctor in the first place...her weak constitution, it had plagued her since her early days in the convent when she no longer had to care for her younger sister...it was as if her own body had collapsed, given up, or maybe rested...

Dr. Kaplan stared, tilting his head. "Is something the matter?"

"Will she come see me today?" she whispered.

Dr. Kaplan shook his head. "The heat is hard for her in her condition, so I don't know."

"Her condition?"

The benevolent yet judgmental stare returned. "She is nearly at full term now."

"Rosy is...with child?"

His benevolence vanished, replaced by furrowed-brow confusion. "I thought her name was Paula." He looked down at his notes, embarrassed.

No, no, no. *Not Paula. Paula was...who? Karol's girl.* Seeing her distress, he hurried to give her more water, standing by her bedside.

Paula was not her sister. A memory. Paula on the walk home to the convent after the funeral, confiding that Karol and she had eloped. Paula was her sister-*in-law.*

Her *sister* was dead—dead, dead, dead! And he, a psychiatrist, a healer. He'd stumbled into her sorrow and ripped it open afresh.

Her lips quivered. The gentle tears of gratitude that had watered her lashes just moments before now changed to a torrent of anguish. Rosy had been stolen from her again—*again!* No need to beg the Lord's forgiveness. He still needed hers. She sucked in her lips

16

to staunch the flow. She gasped for air.

"Tell me what you are thinking," he said, almost in a whisper, as if afraid it wasn't the right thing to say.

She shook her head, wiped her eyes and blew her nose. *No, Mr. Mariner, I won't be tricked again. You made the mistake, yet I am the one judged lacking.*

She fidgeted, twisting the sheet between her fingers, shaking her head, clucking her tongue, all because she couldn't accuse him outright of boorishness. He was her captor now, and she had to learn to behave.

One of the nurses, the red-haired one, who apparently had been standing in the background during Dr. Kaplan's visit, quickly appeared to retrieve a used tissue she wasn't even aware of holding and dispose of it. He murmured a command to the nurse; she nodded and disappeared. He pulled up the chair next to the bed and sat again.

"Losing your sister must have been a terrible blow," he said softly. "Maybe you'd like to tell me about her."

"No!" she groaned. This she would not bear.

He sat back, as if he were slapped.

She clamped her mouth shut. She knew how to be silent.

CHAPTER TWO
Heaven

THERE WAS no sleeping now. Consciousness grabbed her by the scruff of the neck and yanked her awake with such violence that every muscle in her body ached, and her head throbbed from the effort to stifle tears. First she held her breath. Then she sucked in her lips. Then she blinked fast. Still the tears came, stinging dry cheeks.

She had so few memories, why had he awakened that one?

Wind whistled into the room. Thunder cracked in the distance. The smell of wet concrete perfumed the air. Soon all would be fresh from a storm. Was it summer?

She remembered only March. The crumbs of winter.

The worst season of the year. A trap of a month— bare, spindly March where winter clings, jealous of life, to raw, wet days, and spring is still too timid to advance beyond a few apologetic crocuses amidst a sea of mud in the convent yard.

That day when Rosy was buried.

Another tear escaped, its salt dampening her parched lips.

That day she had awakened in the dark to the patter of rain on the window, rain that blew in gusts as if a hoodlum child were throwing handfuls of fine pebbles at the glass to taunt them.

She had to hurry if she didn't want to be late for

morning prayer and Mass in the chapel. As her eyes adjusted to the shadows, she noticed the bed on the opposite wall was already empty and neatly made, no trace of a living thing left in its flat blanket and tidy pillow.

And still she could not stir herself. Her teeth ground together and her eyes stung. Too late. Tears slid down the side of her head to the pillow. It would not be tidy now, like Sister Imelda's.

Sitting on the edge of the bed, she thought of the blessing she should offer for the day. No time. She dressed quickly and rushed to the tiny bathroom at the end of the hallway to relieve herself and wash up. There, she tugged on the wimple and pinned the veil. Feeling the hem of the veil uneven, she reset it. And reset it again. And the tears started to build as her frustration grew. Finally, she used the mirror.

It wasn't really a mirror. It was merely a corner of one, barely a half inch of reflective surface showing beneath a coat of beige paint the same color as the walls. Because looking at one's reflection was a show of vanity, the medicine cabinet's mirror had been painted over when the convent was built.

But over time, a chip of paint had fallen away, revealing a tiny window in which they could view themselves, and she often wondered if their Mother Superior, Sister Fulgentia, never had it repaired because it presented them with a daily test of their willpower, a perpetual reminder of the need to be vigilant against the temptations of the flesh. She had never used it before. She wondered if others had. Now, she bent and peered with no guilt, adjusting the veil until it was even on either side, but still not seeing her face, her image, herself until she was finished.

Then she saw—her eyes, wide, hollow, watery, and

frantic. Her chest ached. Was she having an attack of some kind?

Moving away from the mirror, she covered her face with her hands and sat on the toilet.

A soft knock on the door and Sister Imelda's voice. "Sister Francis?"

She cleared her throat. "I'm washing up. I'll be right out." She stood and ran water over her fingertips, staring at the flat beige of the painted mirror, seeing nothing, feeling nothing....

The rain spattered on the window now as then, rousing her to the present.

A nurse scurried in to cheerfully close it.

৵৶

When she opened her eyes again, orienting herself didn't take as long as before. The light told her it was still high daytime. The heat told her it was close to midday.

She knew immediately she wasn't alone. Perfume. Something too sweet and floral. Paula. She turned her head to see her sister-in-law, paperback book open on her distended stomach, perspiration on her upper lip. But still she was beautiful, with soft blond curls damp at her temples, blue eyes, a rosebud mouth. Of course Karol had fallen for her. For a split second, Sister was glad she was here. She needed to talk to someone. She needed to have holes in her memory filled in so that she could escape, so that she could satisfy Dr. Kaplan.

The seconds ticked away, and she sank into herself, realizing that Paula couldn't be that confidante. Sister remembered distrusting Paula. Paula wasn't telling the truth about something. What—?

"You're awake!" Paula said in her honeyed southern accent. "You need me to be gettin' you anythin'?" She stood, looking around for something she could do. She fixed on the water pitcher and poured a glass, offering it to Sister. She eagerly took it. Her throat was still dry and sore.

"I'm so sleepy," she said, handing the glass back. "How long have you been here?"

"Not long." Paula stretched and walked to the window and then to the wardrobe, which she opened. Seeing Sister's habit, she pulled the garment into her arms. Sister recoiled at the thought of Paula handling her clothing.

"I can take this home and wash it up for you. All fresh." She turned and smiled again, seemingly happy to have found something useful to do. She walked with the habit back to the chair.

"I came after your breakfast—you didn't eat anything, which is no way to get your strength back, Sister. Do you want me to fetch you a snack or something? I can call the nurse." She turned toward the door, ready to start on the next good deed. Sister sensed she'd just been waiting for an audience.

"No. Thank you."

"Well, I reckon lunch is about ready. I thought I heard a food cart down the hall." Paula sat, keeping her smile in place. "Karol and I went to early Mass, and he went on to your mother's to visit after dropping me off here. He sends his love."

So it was nearly noon. Sister was glad she hadn't had to ask.

But if food were around the corner, there wouldn't be much time to ask Paula the questions she needed to have answered. Her sister-in-law wasn't likely to stay through the meal because…

…*because they didn't eat with anyone but their own*. A fresh memory! In her Order, sisters didn't eat with lay people. Dining was an act of communion, and they shared it only with each other. If they had to, they deferred a meal. If they couldn't, if it was an emergency, they could sup in public.

Paula wouldn't know those rules. She might stay. Nonetheless, Sister felt the pressure of time. Who knew when Dr. Kaplan would return? But she didn't know where to begin, how to ask outright without seeming obvious. Instead, she latched on to a memory that still burned.

"They keep calling you my sister," she told Paula, not looking at her. "In my confused state...I..."

"Oh, dear. Oh, my." Paula immediately understood and seemed genuinely agitated. "I know that must be painful. I'm so sorry."

The apology soothed her, even if it was from the wrong person. It was as if Paula were saying she was sorry she wasn't Rosy. That was precisely how Sister felt—so deeply wounded that Rosy was gone and Paula was here in her stead.

"I fell again?" she prodded. "As I did in March?"

She watched Paula's brows crease. "Well, yes, you did take a tumble. They found you in your room. Another sister called the doctors."

Found her—what did that mean? She hesitated, not wanting to give away too much of her lack of insight. She felt as if the world were waiting for her to stumble again.

"And it was good thing, too, because she found the bottle right away and knew what had likely happened."

The bottle. Despite the heat, a chill cascaded over her. She went still. The Phenobarbital bottle. She didn't need to ask. She guessed.

"It was empty."

As if realizing the seriousness of this admission, Paula leaned in and stroked Sister's arm. "Lordy, when I take a pill or a spoonful of somethin', I hardly remember an hour later if I'd had it or not. And that Dr. Remy had you takin' it somethin' like three times a day. I'm so glad he's not your doc anymore, Sister. When Karol told me you had a new one, I said, glory, hallelujah. Not out loud, but in my heart. I'm sure this new doctor will be better. He already stopped the shocking."

Her hand scratched rather than soothed. And her

voice—with its dripping accent as she grew more verbose—made Sister wince and close her ears. Paula was making excuses for her. Sister knew what that meant. They didn't think it was an accident at all. No wonder Dr. Kaplan had been so coy.

ન્य

"Your sister is doing better today," Kate told her when Paula hauled her heavy body around the corner of the Hopkins corridor. *Lordy, when this pregnancy ends, I'll finally be able to feel my belly's a part of me again.* She patted the babe in her tummy with her free hand, a smile spreading on her face. This baby was everything to her. Everything. Honey on the comb.

"Not my sister," she corrected Kate. "Sister-in-law."

"Are you taking that home?" Kate asked, pointing to the habit in Paula's arms. "I think she might be able to get dressed soon."

"That's wonderful," Paula cooed. "I'll wash it first thing." Paula shifted her weight, her ankles throbbing. "Do you know when she'll be gettin' discharged? Going back to the convent, I mean?"

"Dr. Kaplan will start seeing her regularly now and let you know her progress."

Paula smiled at her, pushing a damp lock of hair from her temple, her face moist from the heat. She would stop in the ladies' room to refresh her makeup. Karol was picking her up in a little while. She always liked looking her best around Karol.

Before Kate headed off, Paula stopped her, patting her arm lightly. "I was wondering, Kate, if you could help me with something…." Paula took a deep breath. Just like the makeup, this was another task for Karol's sake. "I want to talk to a priest about converting," she said softly, hoping no one else would hear.

Kate's face transformed, her fingers finding her Mary medallion—the one that had tipped off Paula to her religion—every muscle beaming happiness as a grin lifted her lips. She took both Paula's hands in hers.

23

"That's wonderful, Mrs. Wojehedski! The Catholic chaplain here might be the place to start. Father Dalton. Aloysius Dalton. You can call him Father Al. He comes in every morning for Communion and has a small office he shares with other ministers. I can find out his hours for you. He's a dream, a special guy..." She stopped, tilting her head, her eyes now narrowing a little. "But why not go to your home church—I mean, Sister's church? It's in your neighborhood, right?"

Paula looked down, not liking the lie she was about to tell. Oh, not that telling a little white lie now and then bothered her much. It was lying about something like this that pricked her conscience.

"My husband doesn't know," she said, which was definitely the truth. "And I want it to be a surprise." Which was definitely not the truth. If anything, she didn't want him to find out at all.

When she'd married Karol, it was at a civil ceremony, at City Hall. They'd talked about doing it right in the church after the baby was born. And there'd be the baby's christening and all to contend with, too. She didn't think she'd be able to hide her non-Catholic status then, filling out all the papers and whatever else was required.

Everybody—Karol included—had just assumed she was Roman when she'd started working and teaching at St. Benedict's over a year ago. She was a fast learner, so she'd picked up on the kneeling and praying parts pretty quickly when she had to take class to Mass. She'd already known about the not eating meat on Fridays and a couple other things that non Catholics knew and sometimes made fun of.

Paula had grown up in the south, a little North Carolina town, where Catholics were "papists." She'd played organ at a tiny church and sometimes at the nearby Lutheran chapel. They were an acceptable type. Not those Romans, though. Her Daddy—bless his soul— would die all over again to know she'd married one and

24

was thinking of converting.

But it wasn't as if Karol talked about his religion a lot. He didn't seem to be what she'd call a churchy type. Oh, he went every Sunday and on the holy days—she cringed, remembering how she had almost slipped on that, not catching on that Ascension Thursday was a church day—and his mother, she prayed the rosary to beat the band. And then there was Sister Francis...but nobody sat around talking about the pope or the bishops or anything at all like that. She wished she could tell Daddy all this, so he could change his mind about them.

Kate had turned to a nearby desk and was writing something on a piece of paper. She handed it to Paula, her smile a bright ball of sunshine in the dim hallway.

"This is so exciting," she said. "It gives me goose bumps."

A pang of guilt coursed through Paula, but she mentally shook it off. *Why should I feel guilty? I'm a God-fearing woman, after all, and I'm just trying to make things right.*

"Thanks," she murmured. And then, feeling she had to change the mood so Kate wouldn't think more highly of her than she deserved, Paula said, "About Sister Francis and me—do be careful, now, not to refer to me as her sister. It upsets her something awful, since Rosy died just this year...and she might not always say something about it." No, she'd just brood.

Kate reddened and bobbed her head. "Oh, yes, I'm so sorry. It's just that you're so...loyal...coming yesterday and today. More like a sister than a sister-in-law."

Paula held a smile back at this, not wanting to encourage those false assumptions too much.

No, I'm not trying to be a good sister-in-law as much as I am trying to be a good wife. This wonderful baby is the reason my husband married me, and I want to make sure he realizes a good wife comes with the bargain.

Oh, she knew Karol loved her—or, rather, she knew

he'd once loved her—but he was a careful man with his feelings, more stingy than he was with money. He was a good provider, generous with her household budget.

A twinge of regret creased her brow. She could have seen to his feelings earlier, if she'd not let things get all jumbled up for a while. Now she needed to fix a mistake she'd made with him early on. If she tended to his wayward sister, that was a way of showing him she was all in.

That's why she was correcting Kate on the sister-in-law business. No need upsetting Sister. She knew mentioning Rosy was salt on the wound.

Salt on Paula's wound, too, come to think of it. Rosy and Paula had been friends, the best friend she'd had outside of Ginny, her cousin who'd been the reason she'd come to Baltimore more than ten years ago. But Ginny had married, and then…they'd drifted apart.

Rosy had filled a big hole in Paula's life, even though the woman had been several years younger than Paula and they'd only known each other less than a year.

And then she'd gone and died. Polio, of all things. It hardly seemed fair, coming on the heels of the news the disease was going out. At least she'd been spared the iron lung for long. That's what Paula kept telling herself. Told Karol that, too, and it seemed to comfort him some.

"Thanks again for this," Paula said, waving the scrap of paper with the priest's name and number on it. "And thanks for looking after Sister here. I'll bring this back tomorrow!" She hefted her arm, laden with the heavy habit. She'd have to wash it first thing when she got home, if it was to dry on the line that afternoon.

&❧

While one hand continued to finger her rosary beads, Sister's other hand reached up at last to touch her head. Coarse straw prickled her hand, shorn hair made stiff from the starch in her wimple and veil. She must look a fright. Dr. Kaplan had stopped by that afternoon, asking more questions, but she'd given him few answers.

She couldn't find the strength to say things, even things she knew and remembered, because she'd been afraid he'd find something lacking in them, something that painted a picture that wasn't the right picture. She needed to unravel her thoughts, to plan a strategy, to decide what to say.

She felt hollowed out, aching in her head, behind her eyes, in her chest. She was sick, all right. But she shouldn't be in this part of the hospital. *Ave Maria, gratia plena...*

The city reeked of industrial perfumes that drifted through the open window. Baltimore could be cruelly stifling in summer—she'd at least figured out the time of year from Paula's advanced pregnancy. Swampy humidity trapped everyone, rich and poor, sinner and saint, equalizing them all. *Zdrowas Mario, laskis pelna Pan z Toba...*

The words had changed from Latin to English to Polish, the language of religion in her youth. The nuns at St. Bridget's had taught religion in Polish and she had prayed in her parents' native tongue for many years. She was too tired to force herself away from it.

Zdrowas Mario, laskis pelna Pan z Toba, blogoslawionas Ty miedzy niewiastami I blogoslawiony owoc zywota Twojego Jezus; swieta Mario, Matko Boza, módl sie za nami grzesznymi teraz i w godzine Smierci naszej.

What had Rosy said after their father had died? She struggled to remember. All memories were hard work. Pulling them from their hiding places was as tiring as dragging out an old suitcase.

It had been in February over a decade ago, two and a half months after their father had died. They'd been sitting on the marble steps of their home in the blue shadows of a February thaw. It had been four o'clock and Margaret—she had been Margaret back then, not Sister Francis Marie!—could smell fish frying somewhere.

A Friday. No meat that evening. She would make potato gnocchi and onions. And only a half day's work the next day, and church on Sunday. She'd smiled, tired and content.

Rosy had wrapped her hands around her knees and stared at the dusky sky, filled with blushing clouds and a royal blue backdrop so beautiful that it had made Margaret feel as if God had painted it just for her.

"This must be what heaven is like. Papa's there," Rosy had said.

Margaret had agreed, and she'd thought of the painting in back of the altar at St. Bridget's, of the saint herself on billowing mists with fat cherubs shepherding her into the holy gates.

"This is the best time of day, don't you think?" Rosy had asked her, not waiting for an answer. "When everything stops. When people come home." And then Margaret had realized that's what she'd meant by heaven.

Heaven isn't a time of day, silly. Heaven is the splendor of God's presence.

Heaven is...a kitchen so bright with light that it feels as if the sun is sitting on the table throwing its rays outside the room instead of letting them steal in. Rosy had said that, too. A year before she'd died. She'd written it in a letter describing their brother's new home.

Karol's home. She'd seen it. When had she seen it? Oh, yes, after the funeral.

Margaret's lips moved slightly as the words of the prayers tumbled one upon another until she could not think.

But she did think. The thoughts crept in. So she let them flow, following the rhythm of the prayers, two twin rivers of thought consoling her, taking her somewhere.

She had been ill, not ill enough to stay away from her teaching duties, at least not every day. She had gone to the doctor. Sister Fulgentia had been irritated. Too many days off. And then there was Karol, living in the same parish. That wasn't allowed. To be in the same parish as family.

She'd looked in the sliver of mirror; she'd dressed.

She'd followed Sister Imelda's petite figure down the stairs and into the cramped chapel. Sister Fulgentia must have sent Sister Imelda to see if she was all right. A flush of anger had colored her cheeks, but she'd lowered her eyes and slipped into place, her elbows touching those of the nun beside her, who'd already been murmuring prayers.

Her fingers had searched her cord belt. Nothing. She'd forgotten her rosary beads.

Nothing.

Psalms, Hail Marys, the Mass itself—they passed as time passes, with no effort on her part. After this, it was on to the dining room, another too-small room in that too-small convent, with chairs that pressed against the walls when they were all seated. At the end of meals, they all had to wait—out of necessity, not Rule—for the sisters on the end to finish and leave before walking out of the room.

After breakfast, Sister Fulgentia beckoned to her in the hall.

"See me in my office."

Sister Francis followed her there. Before Sister Fulgentia went behind her desk—set diagonally because it wouldn't fit across the tiny room any other way—she motioned for Sister Francis Marie to come closer.

"Kneel down."

Sister Francis Marie obeyed, closing her eyes, waiting for the blessing. Instead, she felt Sister Fulgentia's pudgy fingers pull at her veil, resetting it farther forward, repinning it.

"There," the Mother Superior said.

Still, Sister Francis waited. No blessing came. Sister Fulgentia was already sitting behind the desk, her hands folded in front of her, when Sister Francis opened her eyes.

Slowly, Sister Francis rose. Without asking permission, she sat in the chair in front of the desk.

"I can spare Sister Rose for the morning. To accompany you." Sister Fulgentia said.

"There's no need."

Sister Fulgentia stared at her, as if trying to tell if what she'd said was true, that there was no need to send someone with her as she attended her sister's funeral.

Sister Francis Marie held her breath. She wanted to go alone.

"Well..." Sister Fulgentia reached for the phone with one hand and a thick directory with the other. In a few seconds, she was on the line with a taxi service, ordering the cab that would take Sister Francis Marie to the funeral home that morning. To Sister Francis's dismay, Sister Fulgentia told the driver to be there at eight. At eight. The funeral was at nine. That would hardly give her enough time.

Enough time to what? To sit and pray? To stare, to talk to her family?

To be. Just to be there. To breathe the same air. To exist.

Her hands searched for the missing rosary beads. Glancing quickly at Sister Fulgentia to see if she'd noticed, Sister Francis blushed. Her veil. The rosary beads. What else had she done wrong?

The mirror. She'd looked in the mirror.

She stared at her hands, twisting over each other in her lap. She'd looked in a mirror the night she'd found out her sister was ill. Of course. And now this.

Sister Fulgentia was opening a drawer, pulling out a change purse.

"Here. This should be enough for the fare." She handed Sister Francis a few bills and some change, and Sister Francis knew it was probably enough and no more, and she would have to be careful in tipping the driver, in order to leave enough for the return trip.

But in her mind there'd been nothing beyond that morning, only a void of error, of mistakes she'd always feel sorry for, that every prayer she now voiced would start with "please forgive me for…"

For looking in the mirror.

Sister Fulgentia stood and raised her hand in the air, sweeping it as she murmured the blessing. Unprepared, Sister Francis felt the breath of the gesture breeze over her and stood as Sister Fulgentia moved past her toward the door.

She waited by the door for the taxi. The house was quiet. Just the bump and creak of the furnace as it settled back. Sister Fulgentia always turned the heat back during the day. When they all returned in the afternoons, it would take a good hour before the convent warmed up again, and even then it would feel like an autumn day.

Better the cool than the heat. That little box of a building trapped the heat.

Opening the front door a crack, she stood leaning against the hall wall, her hands clasped in front of her. Her chest still ached, and she still thought that perhaps her young life would be plucked away like a flower, joining Rosy's in an early spring bouquet. She felt at peace then.

She watched the rain splattering on the concrete walk. She saw cars pulling up, fathers and mothers waving and kissing their children goodbye. The children rushing into the school under scarves and hats and umbrellas, rubber boots splashing, searching for puddles, not trying to miss them. Yellow slickers, blue jackets, black overcoats.

Rain and more rain. Sorrow and more sorrow. Please forgive me for…

"Sister Francis?"

She jumped at the sound of Sister Fulgentia's voice and turned to see the older nun staring at her from the kitchen. She'd returned for something.

"Close the door, Sister Francis. You've been sickly enough this year already."

Without a word, Sister Francis closed it. But not all the way. A tiny sliver still let in a piercing arrow of a draft aimed right at Sister Francis's heart. Sister Fulgentia left as silently as she'd appeared. A ghost. They were all ghosts.

And eventually the street in front of the convent and school had cleared and fallen silent, becoming a ghost neighborhood with the noise of the rain shutting out any noise of life. She fell into a trance, staring straight ahead through a slit of window by the door, and the trance became the journey when the cab arrived, the journey back in time, through her old streets, her old neighborhoods.

Her posting to St. Benedict's had been a mistake caused by the post-war building boom. No postings in a Sister's home city was the Rule. But her Mother Superior had looked at the pinprick on the map that indicated this little parish outside of Baltimore and thought of it as a separate town, not realizing it was a suburb, a community of city workers who thought of themselves as Baltimoreans, not as residents of some idyllically named community set apart from the city they'd grown up in.

She had no connection to the city's history. Her family had not fought its earlier wars or debated its future. Her family had arrived a scant thirty years ago, interlopers, foreigners interested in fortune, not philosophy of government. Yet she herself felt as rooted to this city as a descendant of the Ark and Dove. A mere mention of a street name would send her spiraling back in time to her youth. She could close her eyes and smell the city and know she was home. She could hear it and know. And now she could see it.

The taxi smelled of cigarette smoke, stale and poisonous, but she breathed deeply to remember what this smell was like, this smell of men and things and action.

"Anything the matter?" the cab driver asked her, twisting a little to see if she was okay. He was about Karol's age, dark-complected, with a moustache and curly hair. She guessed he was Italian and wondered if he'd served in the war.

"No," she said softly. A lie. Rosy was dead, and she was headed to her funeral.

The funeral home...at the end of the hallway, as if waiting for royalty, her family stood. Karol was dressed in a dark blue suit that had looked a little too big for him. Still handsome, though. Dark wavy hair. Well-proportioned features. Tall stature. Next to him, their mother. Shorter than Sister remembered, she was obviously in a new, black dress with its store-pressed pleats and folds still intact. Sister wondered if Karol had bought it for her, and she worried, for a fleeting instant, that her mother might have forgotten to take the price tag off.

And on the other side of Mother was Paula, Karol's girl and a teacher at St. Benedict's, who looked uncomfortable. At the end of the line was Bernard, now returned after so many years away, returned for visits, but living in New Jersey, a job on the docks, she knew. A huskier version of Karol, he was in a double-breasted brown suit that made him look a little dangerous. His hands were crossed in front of him, and he stood with his legs apart as if guarding the place.

No bright slice of heaven here, Rosy. Only stabbing pain, held at bay by holding her breath. Her whole body ached as she contained her grief, her anger. What a cruel joke, polio.... She overheard the comments, *how sad, how sweet she'd been, how unbelievable it was to have her taken when that doctor had been on television telling them all...*

The miserable funeral, the uncomfortable gathering at Karol's after. She just wanted to go home and sleep and forget.

At last, in the twilight, after it was all over, she

opened the convent door slowly, without any noise. From the dining room, she'd heard the quiet sounds of the other nuns eating dinner, spoons scraping against bowls, teacups rattling in saucers. Chairs squeaked, and a few seconds later, Sister Fulgentia appeared in the hallway.

"I was worried about you," she said, her voice tight and angry. "Come into my office."

Only a thin wall separated the dining room from Sister Fulgentia's office. The other sisters would hear whatever was said there. Obediently, Sister Francis followed her Superior there, already flushing from embarrassment as she braced herself for rebuke.

"What took you so long?" Sister Fulgentia asked before she'd even made it to her chair behind the desk.

"No one was there to drive me home. I ended up walking," Sister Francis replied, using her rehearsed excuse. It was so easy. Lying.

"Why couldn't you walk home earlier?"

"I—they had planned a wake. They wanted me to stay."

"You were supposed to go to the funeral and come home. If you wanted to stay longer, the least you could have done was to notify me."

Yes, she should have.

"I am very disappointed in you." She said it sadly, not in anger.

"I'm sorry, Mother. Please forgive me." Sister Francis sighed it, not sure at all how sorry she was.

"You're not looking well again, Sister, and I have no one to take over for you tomorrow." The nuns in the dining room would have been able to hear everything clearly. "If you are ill, you will see the doctor."

And she did see the doctor, after falling on the stairs. All those memories now flooded back. All the memories except one—the day that had landed her here now.

CHAPTER THREE
Remembrance

"WOULD YOU like a cup of coffee, Dr. Kaplan? Betsy's brewed a fresh pot in the lounge." Aaron looked up. Kate stood in the doorway, her nurse's uniform crisp and clean, looking as bright as the new morning itself at the start of her shift. Every time he saw her, he couldn't help smiling. It was as if she'd opened a curtain in his heart.

She was so fresh and beautiful, her red hair pinned under the white cap, her pale skin as soft as cream. Since arriving at Hopkins, he'd relied on her help—help she'd eagerly provided, showing him where offices and labs were located, telling him about good restaurants nearby, warning him of certain regulation-bound administrators. She was a kind soul. The world was filled with unkind people...or rather, thoughtless people, who needed reminders to be kind. Kate did it instinctually.

"Oh, thank you, no," he stammered, looking down. No matter how much he fought it, he continually feared giving away his feelings through his glance. Discipline overcame fear, and he looked up again quickly. He didn't much like coffee, but ... maybe that was his kindness, to let her bring it to him.

"Well, just one cup," he said, smiling. There, that relaxed him.

She smiled, too, making him feel like sunshine had returned after a long rain, and turned to get him his coffee. They'd only been out together a few times, but the more of Kate he saw, the more he liked. Despite vast differences in their backgrounds, they shared some key attributes. They both were hard workers—he noticed she often stayed late and happily filled in for nurses who needed to switch a shift—and they both tried very hard to listen to the patients, not just hand out treatments like interchangeable linens on the beds.

Although she'd been extremely helpful to him as he'd settled in at Hopkins, her real help was in an intangible, a mood she brought with her. She believed in him, in what he could do. And lately, he wasn't sure if he believed in himself or psychiatry in general.

Every day he read of studies showing breakthroughs with drugs. Thorazine had had marvelous effects on patients in France. And more medicines were being studied, tested and put into use at breakneck speed. Had his training been for naught? Was the landscape of the human mind nothing more than mechanics and gears? When they got rusty, they needed oiling, perhaps, but not existential discussions and analysis. Maybe this explained why evil flourished. It was just bad chemistry, not free will.

His confidence had been shaken the past ten years, and these new advances only served to unsettle him more. Kate, however, provided a safe, warm harbor from these inner storms. With her, he seemed able to believe...in something, maybe just in the possibility of them. He and Kate were still in that early stage of a relationship, where discovery exhilarated and teased.

Breathing easy now, he settled back into looking through Sister Francis Marie's file. Dr. Remy had been notorious for his shorthand notes, and, in the case of

Sister, he'd done no follow-up after her initial hospitalization.

English hadn't been Remy's first language, but he'd been a proud man. So he had covered his inadequacy by constructing a philosophy around it—one should spend one's time dealing with the patient in the present rather than with writing what happened in the past, he would say. Thus, his notes read like telegrams: Patient confused and nervous, stop. Patient eager to recover, stop. Patient agrees to take Phenobarbital as prescribed, stop.

He scratched his head and then tugged at his beard, a nervous habit of his own that probably arose from a strong desire to be doing something—anything at all—to solve a puzzle.

Dr. Remy had been Sister's physician when she'd been brought in this March. And his therapy had been continued before Dr. Kaplan had officially received the case this time. Already Sister had received electroshock therapy—so fast, it had made Dr. Kaplan's head spin. The woman had barely been admitted, and that very evening, before he'd seen her, taken down to electroshock. Why so quick—were they automatons with no ability to make decisions? Is this what psychiatry held for them in the years to come—shocks, shots, pills?

Dr. Kaplan suspected that the electric shocks were partly to blame for her memory loss and her dazed stupor-like countenance. *Patient confused and depressed, stop.*

Dr. Kaplan frowned.

"I wouldn't have shocked you," Dr. Kaplan whispered under his breath. "I would have talked to you first." Maybe because of his fear of the future or maybe because of what he'd seen of a barbaric past, he wanted, desperately, to find treatments that were…human.

"What?" Kate breezed into the room, steaming mug

in hand. She looked around for a place to set it, but his desk was covered with file folders—he was reading up on the cases he'd inherited from Remy—and the room was hardly larger than a closet, just a place to grab some quiet while he wrote notes, not his larger office on another floor where he actually saw patients. Kate, in fact, had helped him secure this little nook before it was taken over by others for supplies.

"I put a drop of cream and sugar in it."

"Oh, here, thank you." He took the mug from her, nearly burning his palms as he scooted some papers out of the way to make space for it. A file fell to the floor.

"Do you need some help in here—straightening things up, Dr. Kaplan?" Kate bent to retrieve the papers.

"Please, call me Aaron here. I don't think we need to worry," he said. They'd been meticulous about keeping up a professional demeanor at work.

He found himself holding his breath as she stood and handed him the file. To regain his composure, he took a sip of the coffee, stifling a gag at the strong, sickly sweetened brew. She'd put too much sugar in it, more than "a drop." Since he'd not corrected her the first time she'd served it thus, he didn't have the heart to do it now. Small price to pay to be with her.

"I could see if there's a secretary who could help out—or I could stay a bit after my shift. . . Aaron."

She said it timidly, and this, too, thrilled him, how she wanted to please, to make sure he was comfortable.

"That would be wonderful," he said, placing the mug down, afraid his hand was trembling from the vibrating attraction in the air. "I'm trying to catch up with Dr. Remy's files. As fast as I can."

"Dr. Freeman—when is he coming?"

So, she knew why he was hurrying. The psychiatric staff had been informed that the great Dr. Walter

Freeman was bestowing a visit on them in two weeks. His bile rose just thinking about it. The lobotomy pioneer had his acolytes at Hopkins, and Aaron was sure some patients would not survive his visit unscathed. Families devastated by a loved one's descent into madness sometimes grabbed at the promise of peace. And lobotomies promised that, all right. A cold, emotionless, restrictive peace.

The procedure sickened Aaron. Getting rid of what was "undesirable," outside the norm, what was different. Didn't he know where that led?

"The Thursday and Friday after next." Despite his personal feelings, he felt the need to be tactful. He was still new to Hopkins, having moved here just a year ago to be closer to his parents. They'd lost a lot of relatives in Europe's camps—aunts, uncles, sisters and brothers, as well as countless cousins who'd failed to emigrate years before the war. He knew they wanted to hold their own now-small family close, so he, the only son, had left a practice in New York to be nearer to them and his sister, who'd settled in a new suburb west of the city.

As these thoughts flitted across his mind, he mentally shook his head and corrected himself, forcing a more honest evaluation, just as he expected his patients to do when considering decisions made in the past. No, he'd left New York for a purely personal reason, too. To start over after the dissolution of his marriage. Although the divorce had been final since '48, New York was his wife's hometown, and he'd become painfully aware of how small it could seem when you moved in the same circles and supported the same charities. He'd left it to flee those ghosts. And found himself surrounded by others.

"You don't like him either, do you?" she probed, bringing him back to the present.

"I don't know him, so I can't say if I like him or not," he answered. How cowardly that sounded. He added, "The man himself—I don't know him. The procedure is horrible. It's too permanent. Much can be done with analysis still, and, of course, the other treatments— electroshock therapy, and some new drugs that will soon be available." How easily he said it. Maybe if he said it enough, he'd believe it...or at least accept it.

"I've heard he's like a missionary," she said, "acting like you're a heretic if you don't believe."

Yes, he'd heard that, too. He still needed to go through his patients' files, to see if any among them would appear to be candidates for the procedure. He didn't want Freeman near them. Unfortunately, he'd already seen some notations from Claude, indicating he thought various cases should be presented to Freeman.

"He won't see Sister Francis Marie, right?" she asked. She dropped her hands in front of herself, clasping them. She had a soft spot for the nun, probably because of their shared faith.

He rubbed his brow but didn't respond directly. Any case that seemed chronic—and this was Sister's second hospitalization, possibly a suicide attempt— would probably be presented. He'd have to fight to keep her from being visited in rounds. Aaron didn't want to stir up trouble or appear self-aggrandizing, though. He despised self-appointed heroes, who could do more harm than good. Just because Freeman was one didn't give Aaron the right to be one, too.

"She's eating. Talking a little. Who knows how long she'll be here?" he said, not convincing himself, let alone Kate.

"Dr. Kap—Aaron—shock therapy really puts patients through the wringer, you know. We nurses see it all the time. And she was so. . . fragile when she came in. Like a broken bird. Wish she hadn't gone down for that therapy when they brought her in. It was awful fast."

"Yes, well, the attending..." The nurses were so protective of their patients, sometimes seeing the doctors as the enemy from whom the patients needed to be guarded. But he shouldn't criticize a colleague in front of her, so he changed the subject. "I know nothing about her...code, how she lives. It might help to learn about it."

He glanced around, wishing there was a chair, but she leaned against a table jammed near the door.

"Well, as a nun she was probably taught to be quiet and to listen and be polite and not draw attention to herself," she explained. "So if she thinks someone might think she's done something wrong, she'd clam up and probably hope they'll forgive her."

They both knew what the "something wrong" was. She'd overdosed on Pheno. Had it been deliberate? It usually was.

"But she'd be willing to 'confess' to something she did wrong, wouldn't she? Wouldn't that be part of her code?" He wondered if Sister knew what she had done but wouldn't admit to it, that perhaps her memory loss was selective.

"Well, yes. Confess to a priest, though."

"Not to someone like me?"

"You mean because you're a Jew?"

Kate was so refreshingly direct, without guile. "No, a doctor. A psychiatrist. Rather than a priest."

"I think if she knows it's what's expected of her—if her Mother Superior tells her to, in other words—she'd be obedient. Obedience is a big part of their Rule. It's called a 'Rule,' by the way. Not a code, Aaron." She chuckled softly, a pleasant musical sound.

He grinned, and they both stared at each other for a

few minutes, wishing they could find something else to say to prolong the moment. Finally, he broke the mood.

"Thank you, Kate. I appreciate your help."

"No problem, Doc. Anytime." She stood up straight. "Guess I better get back. The head nurse is probably wondering where I've been."

She turned to the door, then back.

"Are we still on for tonight?" she asked with the barest trace of tentativeness in her voice.

"Yes—seven-thirty. You choose."

She smiled again and left. It bothered him, that little bit of fear in her voice.

✎✒

Sometimes Paula grew tired of thinking of ways to jolly Karol into good humor. Today was harder than most. She first had to lift her own spirits.

On this day, thirteen years earlier, she'd learned her first husband, Tom DiGiacomo, had been killed. Not in battle, but in an automobile accident just off his base, probably carousing and womanizing.

On this day, thirteen years earlier, she'd learned that Tom DiGiacomo hadn't loved her and hadn't bothered to even pretend to love her.

"Karol?" she called out, sitting on the edge of the bed. She rubbed her stomach, waiting for the friendly kick that always gladdened her heart. She heard the rush of the shower in the hall bathroom. He'd risen early. What was on his mind that made him wakeful?

Paula was keenly aware of men's moods. She spent an inordinate amount of time, in fact, not thinking of how she viewed the world, but of how the world— mostly its men—viewed her. This preoccupation wasn't vanity so much as habit. When she had transformed from gangly duckling into curvy swan, men noticed her. And she hadn't realized, growing up with an adoring widower father, how much she craved being noticed and being told how beautiful she was. It had been an everyday thing with her father—his compliments and drenching affection. She'd expected it of the world.

Had she not met Tom, however, flirtation, with its addictive reactions, would have been a harmless game she surely would have outgrown. Tom had robbed her of innocence, in every conceivable way. He had stopped her clock at that hour when she'd discovered that, to be loved, she had to give men something they craved.

She shook her head of bad memories and went through the list of things that could have irritated Karol.

The paper hadn't been delivered yesterday morning. A neighbor had awakened his after-dinner nap with a whining lawn mower. The radio had taken so long to heat up, he'd missed the ballgame's best play. She'd overcooked the roast, but she would set that straight by making hash with the leftovers. Or maybe it was something at work getting him down. He sometimes complained about a coworker who took credit for his work at the gas company. Was he brooding about that as the work week began?

She caught her breath as the baby pressed against her lungs. Hugging her stomach with her right hand, she stared at her face in the mirror above the dresser. She looked puffy and haggard. She'd have to powder her nose and put on a little lipstick before making the coffee.

It was the heat. Even though it was early morning, the house was already warm. A swift breeze tantalized the curtain and then receded. She smoothed the seersucker bedspread and stood.

Pink chenille—that had been her bedspread in her Percy, North Carolina bedroom. And a blue-and-rose print wallpaper that had made her feel like spring. On this day thirteen years earlier, she'd stared out the window at the peaceful street—sun-speckled, quiet, with the smells of breakfasts—bacon, coffee, toast—wafting through the small town.

She had been home when she should have been at work. Her father had already been off on house calls, but she'd been running late, trying her hair in a different style that wouldn't quite stay in place. She'd seen it in a movie magazine, hair swept off and up the sides, pinned in large curly rolls near the forehead, rams' horns they were called. It was hard to get it so the part on the side wasn't too wide. The page had lain open on her dresser. That's why she had still been home when Tom's friend Ralph had stopped by with the news, the awful, life-shattering news.

Later, she'd sat on the bed, dry-eyed at last, and penned a letter.

"Dear Mrs. DiGiacomo," the letter had said in her sloping, good-girl handwriting. "We've never met, but I married your son, Tom, on December 7, 1941. Sergeant Ralph McGroarty, Tom's friend, came by today to tell me Tom . . ."

And there she'd stopped, not knowing whether to write "died," or "passed away," or the more accurate "was killed in an accident." And what would she say after that anyway?

With an animal moan of despair, she'd pushed the magazines and paper away, fresh tears streaming down her face with a rush of wind outside, as if one triggered the other. She'd opened the top drawer in her dresser, angry that it stuck, that she didn't have new furniture but some old beat-up thing that had been in the family a long time. Her father was the town doctor, but he'd not buy her new furniture while they had perfectly usable old things handed down through generations. From inside, she'd pulled a small stack of letters, tied with blue ribbon and scented by her rosewater sachet.

She had opened them, one by one. All love letters, overflowing with affection.

"Dear Paula, I wish I could write more but we're always on the go...."

"Dearest sweetheart, you're always in my thoughts even if I don't get a chance to write...."

"Dear Honey, do you remember when we danced at the holiday Canteen? I think of that time often but I'm not good with words like you...."

And she had torn them all up, making herself curse him with every forceful split of paper. In half, and then in quarters, and then again, separating them into smaller piles as the pieces multiplied. Until finally, there was nothing but confetti, sprinkled with handwriting.

Her handwriting. When Tom himself hadn't written, she'd penned the notes herself. After all, he loved her but couldn't say it well, and he certainly wasn't good at writing anything down. So she had done it for him, filling lonely hours after work writing what she knew was surely in his heart.

His heart was dead. And it had never beaten for her.

Grabbing the pen, she'd pulled out a fresh piece of paper. "Dear Mrs. DiGiacomo, I loved your son Tom and I thought he'd loved me, and we thought we were going to have a baby when we got married but there was a miscarriage. Tom loved . . ."

Tom loved to dance.

An image, a scene from a movie with no sound — Tom at the Canteen, mouth open wide in a friendly laugh, bending her back, dipping her close to the dance floor, his eyes saying what his lips wouldn't. Tom, making her feel special and glamorous like a movie star, too pretty for this hick town, born for better things. *I'll take you out of here, honey. I'll take you home to New York.*

Never seen New York? You ain't lived. We'll dance every night of the week.

Good old Ralph McGroarty, thin as a rail, with a long face and carrot hair. So shy and embarrassed, but a good boy. He'd stood up for Tom at the wedding, the only friend from the base to attend.

He couldn't *not* let her know, Ralph had said, standing at the door holding his hat in his hand earlier on that morning.

"Not let me know what?" Paula hadn't asked him to come in, because, even then, she'd known something bad was about to happen.

He'd looked at the floor. "Tom's dead. Car accident a month ago."

The army hadn't notified her because Tom hadn't told them he was married, but Ralph had come by, using up a day of leave.

So many things stolen in a moment. No future. No chance to try again to make him really love her. No past.

No, she'd had a past, a past as an innocent, well-loved girl in a sleepy Southern town, happy but yearning for something more. She remembered ...

....years before the war, before this bad news, skipping, lighthearted, along an uneven sidewalk for half a block, her right saddle shoe untied, her pleated skirt bouncing, before catching herself and stopping. At seventeen, she was too old for skipping. But a doting father had kept her younger than her years, at least in heart if not in body. She had a shapely figure and fashionably mysterious face, with dark blue eyes and pointed chin, and thick wavy hair the color of the cornfields beyond the town.

Gosh, it was warm. Indian Summer in Percy was still as hot as high summer. She breathed deep. The smell of dried leaves and faraway wood smoke tickled her nostrils. She walked at a steadier pace, reminding herself she was no longer a girl, but a young lady. Besides, she didn't want to soil her new powder-blue sweater with perspiration.

Her thoughts had drifted back to the movie magazine she'd been reading earlier, a story about the latest love of her life at the time—Clark Gable.

He'd shown up at the premiere in Atlanta. Why not a showing in Norfolk? And maybe he'd take a long drive in the country, over the border into North Carolina. It was mighty pretty country, flat land stretching to the shore, just waiting for a hurricane to rush in, farms not busted up because of dry heat like they were in Oklahoma, small towns like hers filled with pretty little houses, and, why yes, pretty girls. Just like her. Blond hair glinting in the light, shining from the fifty strokes before bedtime, cheeks pinked by the sun, a figure that made more than one boy look twice.

He always looked so sad. She could make him happy.

She rounded the corner toward Drake Street, straightened her posture and held up her head. As she stepped onto the front porch, her hand glanced the swing, setting it in squeaky motion. One squeak followed another as her father opened the screened door on the side of the porch.

"Where you been, Paula? It's near on time for supper."

"Sorry, Father. I was delayed." She spoke with exaggerated enunciation, as if she were in a play.

"It is a nice day," he said by way of accepting her excuse.

She breezed past him into the large living room, crinkling her nose at the smell of his pipe smoke. She'd bought him some fine English tobacco for his birthday that summer, but he'd only used it once before going back to his old brand.

From the living room, she turned left, hurrying through the bright dining room with its bay window on

47

the side yard that turned the space into a glow of yellow light, and then into the more shadowed kitchen on the back of the house. She threw her purchase on the kitchen table and sat down to stare at the picture of Clark Gable on the cover while their Negro maid, Adelaide, finished the pork chops.

After dinner, in the quiet living room: "Play the Beethoven; that's the one you do so well."

Her father sat back in his chair and closed his eyes while he waited.

She accommodated him, sliding onto the bench, not bothering to open the music because she had memorized the Moonlight Sonata long ago. She didn't think she played it all that well, or rather, any better than anyone else, but he liked it so much and they were both so content, full of a good dinner and warm from the waning glow of the sun. She couldn't introduce a "no" into this evening that whispered so many sweet "yeses."

She looked out the window as she prepared. The light was oddly yellow, as if the sun were covered by gauze. No one stirred. Neighbors were probably settling down, just as she and her father were, for quiet entertainments, a good book, or the radio, or, as was her case, some music performed by a talented child. She sighed. She had the feeling it would never be so perfect or still again. This tinged her contentment with melancholy, which only heightened her enjoyment of the moment. She was at an age when melancholy, with its pinch of yearning, was a sophisticated emotion, something that only afflicted the worldly and mature.

The music flowed from her fingers like a lullaby. She hoped others could hear her through the open windows. She hoped her playing sparked a beautiful melancholy in their breasts.

When she finished, she thought her interpretation had been so successful that her father had fallen asleep. But he slowly opened his eyes, which now had such a sad look in them that they doused her dreaminess with real sorrow. He said to the room, more than to her, "Your mother wanted to be a concert pianist. I think she was good enough for it, too." Her mother had died in childbirth, a doctor's wife unable to be saved by the science of her husband.

Irritated that the mood had changed, she turned toward him. "Could I go to the movies with Ginny next weekend, Father? We want to see *Gone with the Wind*."

He blinked and folded the newspaper in his lap. "Your Aunt Claire is visiting next Sunday, to hear you play in church." Her Aunt Claire—her father's sister, married and moved to Atlanta, a sophisticate in her eyes. She liked seeing her Aunt Claire, but she wanted to see the movie more.

She knew from past experience that this merely meant he wasn't prepared to offer a decision right now. After all, she wouldn't be going to the movies on Sunday but on Friday or Saturday. It wasn't a "no," however, so she left the room happy.

"I'm going to telephone Ginny," she said over her shoulder, heading to the kitchen.

"Don't stay on the line too long, dear." A doctor's household meant keeping the phone available for patients.

She mumbled her agreement, knowing she'd stay on as long as she wanted, until he came in the room to remind her to get off in that gentle voice that would signal she could stay on five minutes more.

And finally, that weekend…

How could Rhett *not* still love Scarlett? He'd waited all that time, only to walk away into the mist with a muttered curse? Ginny was full of reasons why, articulating them in her know-it-all voice over ice creams at the drugstore. "My goodness, Paula, he put up with far too much nonsense as it was. He would have been better off with Belle."

As close as Paula felt to Ginny, as many secrets as they shared, Paula sometimes found her cousin extremely…unlikable. Ginny could drift from shy into sanctimonious in an instant, passing fast judgment on wayward souls whom Paula often felt sorry for. It chilled Paula's heart to think Ginny didn't believe Rhett and Scarlett would get back together eventually. Didn't she believe in True Love?

Ginny's brother had ended up driving them to the movies Saturday afternoon and she would walk home from downtown. It was the perfect compromise. No late-night walk alone and no need to have her father take her. His protectiveness made everything both difficult and too easy. Why should she try to arrange rides or walk home when she knew her father would move heaven and earth to be her chauffeur? Sometimes she hated herself—and him—for this.

The front door to the drugstore jingled open and Paula and Ginny both wagged fingers in the air at a schoolmate, chubby Angel Baker and her date, George Criswell, a farmer's boy, all awkward and lanky with dirt under his nails.

"It belies belief that Angel would be the first among us with a steady boy," Ginny said, trying to sound worldly.

"I'm not sure I envy her," Paula said, staring at the couple from the corner of her eyes. "There just aren't any decent boys in this town. I want to move to the big city as soon as we're finished with school. Atlanta. Or maybe even New York."

This set them off on a half hour's dreamy conversation about how they'd move together and share an apartment, working at glamorous secretarial jobs during the day, wearing all sorts of gorgeous suits and dresses, and going out at night with a string of handsome—and wealthy—beaux.

It was a dream they returned to often but with different pleasurable variations. Sometimes they'd concentrate on how they'd furnish the apartment, the precise styles and fabrics of the various pieces they'd collect. Sometimes they'd focus on their wardrobes and how they'd meticulously buy only expensive clothes, even if it took a long time to build a wardrobe, and what colors they'd construct these marvelous collections around. Sometimes they talked about the vacations they'd take together.

"Dad says plenty of fellows will be filling up the camp nearby soon enough," Ginny said, scraping the last of her sundae from the bottom of the fluted dish. "He says Franklin will be having us bail out Churchill if we're not careful."

Paula knew only that Germany was making trouble again, but being an optimist at heart, she always expected it to be over tomorrow when reasonable people decided enough was enough. Nonetheless, she wouldn't mind if a threat lingered long enough for the nearby army camp to fill up. She immediately began to think of the new dresses she would buy for the dances...

New dresses of blue silk and dark green satin—those were the ones her father bought for her as the camp filled up. She received one, wrapped in fine, blue tissue paper in a huge box, for Christmas, another for her birthday that January. She'd admired both in a window of Trelaine's Dress Shop downtown. And these were just the ones she could get locally. Ginny and Paula both bought new suits of gray wool on a Saturday trip to Norfolk, chauffeured by Ginny's new friend, Frederick Williamson III.

Frederick was one of the "boys in the camp," a dashing lieutenant, training other boys in the art of war. His chiseled movie-star looks were only marred by a scar on his right cheek from playing lacrosse as a child. He was from a well-to-do Virginia family and had already finished college in three years. He wanted to be a doctor, which made him a big hit with Paula's father.

But it wasn't Paula's father who mattered here. It was Ginny's, and her parents both accepted Fred with cautious courtesy. Ginny was only eighteen, after all, and they weren't quite ready to let her go. They saw, even before Paula admitted it to herself, that they were losing Ginny to Fred, that he was The One their daughter had chosen.

She and Paula talked less and less of their plans to move to the big city. He even came to their high school graduation that spring, a handsome figure in his uniform, making Paula envious of her good friend and cousin. Although Paula had gone out with a few local boys, she'd still not lit on any she felt worthy of her attention.

After graduating, she thought of moving to Atlanta on her own, but her father had already shrewdly tempted her not to.

"Mrs. Gilbert is leaving," he'd announced one winter evening as he sat in the kitchen reading the newspaper. Paula had been at the sink, washing the dishes, since it was Adelaide's night off. He often sat with her on winter evenings as she finished up. It was warmer in the kitchen, and they both enjoyed their silent companionship. "She's moving in with her sister over in Duck."

She turned to look at him, trying to judge the depth of his dismay. Mrs. Gilbert had been her father's receptionist and secretary for as long as Paula could remember. But his face was placid, with even the hint of a smile at the corners, something only she would notice. In an instant, she knew what he would suggest, and, sure enough, he came out with it.

Not looking up from his newspaper, as if it were an impromptu thought, he said, "You know, it's not a bad job. Interesting work. Something different every day. Do you think you could help me out until I find a replacement? Just part-time, that is—Saturdays and a week night or two." Now he looked up and his smile twinkled. "I'm an easy boss. You can ask Mrs. Gilbert."

Paula had always known a job in her father's office was hers for the taking. And it wasn't as if it were unpleasant work. She'd worked there one summer, when Mrs. Gilbert had gone on vacation—to visit the very sister she was now moving in with. Ginny herself, meanwhile, had started working in her own father's legal office as an assistant to his secretary. At least Paula could claim the full title if she worked for her dad. Besides, it would only be temporary, until she found something better.

"I'd be happy to help out, Father," she said, drying a dish and placing it in a stack. "Just until you get a replacement."

That job had paved the way for other jobs, especially the one she'd landed when she'd moved to Baltimore…

"*Paula!*"

Not her father's voice, not Ralph's voice, not Tom's voice. Karol's voice. Her husband.

He appeared in the doorway in T-shirt and pants, his dark hair shiny wet and a tuft of shaving lather on the strong line of his chin. "You all right?"

She must have looked awful for him to stand before her like that. He rarely let her see his naked arms, the left one with its scars and the twisted fingers looking like melted wax. No matter how hot, he wore a long-sleeved robe to the table in the morning, if he didn't dress first.

She smiled, happy that he asked her. "Just tired. You're up early."

Standing, she swayed with light-headedness, but Karol wasn't looking now, so he didn't fuss. These last months were hard, especially with the heat. Karol was at the dresser, bending and squinting at himself as if he didn't like what he saw when he combed his hair.

"Anything the matter?" she asked, grabbing her robe. "I'll put the coffee on."

He grunted and said no more, so she shuffled off to the kitchen, forgoing the beauty touch-ups she'd meant to make before he saw her.

A few minutes later, with the smell of fresh coffee filling their bright kitchen on the back of the house, Karol came in, dressed in white shirt and tie. He kissed her quickly on the cheek and grabbed a coffee cup from a shelf, then poured some from the electric percolator on the table. When he was in a bad mood, he didn't like it if she tried to serve him, so she always waited to see what his disposition was before determining whether to let him fend for himself.

"You didn't answer me," she said. "Is anything the matter? You were up early."

"Naw. Nothing. Just got up, that's all."

She buttered her toast and thought of asking if he wanted her to butter his but decided against it when he lost himself in the paper. She stared out the open back door into their tiny yard. She wanted to plant more roses but was too big and tired to do it this year. Maybe they could put in some tulip bulbs in the fall, though, after the baby came. These daydreams made her happy and took her mind away from this melancholy anniversary, her husband's moods, and her own physical discomfort. She took a last long sip of coffee.

"I guess I better get dressed. I'm going to see your sister today."

When he didn't respond, she continued. "I'm taking her habit to her, so she can take a walk. I washed it." A tiring job it had been, too. The cloth was so heavy, she'd been panting by the time she'd clipped it to the line, and it had barely dried by the time she'd taken it in at twilight.

Karol snorted in derision. Aha—this was it, the source of his annoyance.

"A walk would be good for her," Paula said defensively.

After folding the paper and placing it aside, Karol

grabbed some toast from the plate in the center of the table. "She'll worry Mom half to death. After Rosy..." Shaking his head, he buttered his toast by securing it with the palm of his bad hand and scraping the knife over the rest of it.

Yes, this was the heart of it. He was angry at Sister for causing Mrs. Wojehedski distress. She relaxed. On this she could agree. Paula now wondered if he'd even told his mother about Sister when he'd seen her yesterday. She guessed not.

"She might be discharged soon, Karol. Your mother doesn't even need to know," she reassured him.

He didn't say anything but ate his toast as if he'd not eaten in days. She remembered the burnt roast the other night and how she'd fix something later that would make him forget the bad dinner.

"You're awfully far along," he said at last. "You have to take care of yourself."

"It's a little cooler today. And my doctor is there, you know. At Hopkins."

"Margie needs to stand on her own two feet." He still called his sister by her given name—Margaret—but Paula only knew her as Sister.

"I'll take her her habit and not stay long."

Karol wiped his mouth and swallowed the last of his coffee. "I'm leaving in five minutes."

Taking that as her cue to get ready, she left the kitchen and rushed to wash and dress. As she pulled on stockings and skirt and top, applied makeup, and brushed her hair, she thought of the mistake she'd made in asking Karol if she should go to visit his sister.

She had to go—she'd promised she'd bring the habit. And she knew that if she didn't show this level of care, he'd resent that even more, see it as evidence of her lack of care for him. She had to go. She just shouldn't have asked him if it was all right. She should have just told him she was going, and that was that.

It bewildered Paula why he was so resentful of Sister to begin with. As far as Paula could tell, Sister had never done anything to hurt him. It wasn't like their older brother, Bernard, who'd run away when Karol was just a boy, forcing Karol to drop out of school so he could help in the store. There she could at least understand the always simmering resentment when they reunited.

But Sister—she was harmless. If anything, she was almost nothing, leaving virtually no imprint on their lives, and none on Karol's that she could distinguish. Sister was shy, quiet, timid, and mildly annoying. When Sister had fallen in the spring, right after Rosy's death, Paula had been more irritated than concerned. Rosy had fallen due to illness, but Sister—why, Paula had assumed it was more a conscious decision on her part, a martyrdom of sorts she had decided to try on, the way Paula liked to try on new dresses.

The phone rang, startling her. Who'd be calling? Only bad news came in unexpected calls. She rushed to the kitchen to answer it. Karol was in the bathroom.

"Mrs. Wojehedski?" a smooth male voice said, a voice with a British accent.

"Yes."

"This is Father Aloysius Dalton. Kate McClaren suggested I call you. I hope it's not too early."

Nurse Kate—she'd jumped the gun. Paula had intended to call the priest herself when Karol wasn't around. Now she nervously lowered her voice. Karol couldn't overhear.

"Yes, I was wanting to talk to you about converting. I'm kind of in a hurry now, though." She heard the water in the bathroom turn off. Oh, Lordy... "Are you at the

hospital today? I'm comin' in to see my sister-in-law…"
Hurry, hurry.

"I'm already here. I'd be happy to talk to you. I'll be here until midday."

"That's fine. I can come then. Noon. I'll…I have to go now, though."

"I have an office. It's on the —"

"Not to worry, I'll find you. Really have to run!" Heart pounding, she hung up the phone, just as Karol came around the corner, his jacket over his arm.

"Who was that?"

"Nobody. I mean it was the hospital. Wondering if I was bringing in the habit. For Sister to take a walk."

He nodded, and she breathed a sigh of relief.

"Are you ready?"

"Almost!" She hurried back to the bedroom, where she finished getting ready, dabbing some perfume behind her ears, grabbing her purse and the hanger with the long, black habit on it, and heading for the door.

Karol grimaced and rushed to help her, draping it over his bad arm while his right hand held the car keys.

"I'll have to park the car and help you in," he said as they walked out and down the two flights of concrete steps from their bungalow to the curb.

"You'll do no such thing! It's hard to park around there. I'll be fine. It's not heavy."

Karol didn't say anything in response, nor on the drive in. Paula, on the other hand, was too tired of worrying about what would cheer him and focused on enjoying the drive instead. She loved drives — the feeling of motion, of the air rushing in the window, of the sights. Of life experienced but free of pain.

She would help Sister with her walk today and then go find this priest. And after that, maybe she'd head into town to window shop. She was eager to look at clothes that would fit her after the baby was born. Maybe she'd even buy a few baby things. She still needed a christening gown and some crib sheets. She'd been careful with her household money that month and had a little left to splurge on herself. She'd been thinking of having her hair done. This was a special day—the day that Tom had died in her heart.

CHAPTER FOUR
Muddled

AFTER HE dropped his wife at the hospital, Karol headed to the gas-company office farther in town, where he worked in bookkeeping. Rosy had urged him to go back to school, to study accounting. Maybe he should still do that. It wasn't that they were hurting for cash—Paula was good with her food and house money, and he'd learned early on how to stretch a dollar. It was a niggling itch inside him that kept irritating his peace of mind. Maybe just being a bookkeeper wouldn't be good enough one day. Maybe being an accountant would mean more security.

He was in an irritable mood to begin with that morning. Paula visiting Margie—sheesh, Paula didn't have to do that. Yeah, she had to take in the habit, but she didn't have to offer to wash it. Why'd she think that was necessary? It wasn't like she and Marge were close. Marge wasn't close to nobody, being in the convent and all. Marge had never been close to a single soul. Just Rosy.

"Sort of like me," he snorted, turning a corner toward the harbor. He fumbled for a cigarette in his pocket and lit it at a stoplight.

He had to admit he missed Rosy an awful lot, more than he'd ever expected. Of course, he hadn't expected her to die. Nobody had expected that. So young. Just goes to show, you're never safe.

As he drove, he dug further into the roots of his

irritation. Rosy—she'd told him not to give up on Paula. "Don't you think you should give her more of a try? I mean, c'mon, Karol, you're going to die a lonely old man. A lonely old *Polish* man." She'd thrown that in to tease him. Their parents had grabbed for "American" names for the girls, and Bernard, well, he'd changed his Polish first name to something close enough to be pronounceable, while Karol had stuck to his, raising his dukes to anybody who gave him trouble over it.

"No, I won't," he'd teased back. "I'll have my sister to keep me company."

"Ha! I'll die first, just to show you."

You sure showed me, Rosy, he thought, biting his cheek so he wouldn't get all emotional. Dammit. Dammit. Dammit.

He had to tell Ma about Marge. He hadn't done that. He'd thought: Ma don't talk to her, and Marge can only write once a month anyways, so why does she even have to know? After Rosy, Ma didn't need no more worry. It had made for a strained visit with his mother yesterday. He'd been on edge, wondering if she'd ask about Margie, if he'd seen her in church lately. He'd kept her talking about her friends, the weather, even went on a bit about his job and Paula and the pregnancy.

But he didn't know how long it would take for Margie to recover. And who knew what his mother would hear at her own church? Things got passed around in the convent and made their way to the parishioners even at other churches. He wouldn't want her hearing something from anyone but him.

Dammit. He'd call her from work. He blew out a plume of smoke.

Deeper still, he ferreted out more worry. His mother would be alone now. Rosy had lived with her in their old basement apartment in Highlandtown. He didn't like her being alone. Rosy had done her shopping for her, kept her spirits up. He'd counted on that when he'd moved away. Hadn't realized how much he'd counted on it.

Now he had to step up. Just like when Bernard had run away from home, and he'd dropped out of school to help in the store. Why was it always him?

He wiped sweat from his brow. Maybe he should ask her to move in with them. Paula wouldn't like that. Not that his mother was difficult, but he knew they put on for each other. Or at least, Paula did. His mother didn't hide her resentment of their quick marriage. She didn't do nothing outright. She just held back.

More digging. Yeah, that was what really bothered him. A part of him didn't want to ask Ma to move in. A part of him wanted to do what Rosy had said. Give Paula a chance. Like it or not, he had to.

Well, like it or not, he couldn't let his mother just sit there and suffer by herself. *It's what you signed up for when you signed on with me, Paula.*

That thought stopped his exploration. Calm descended. He took one more drag of his smoke and found a parking spot outside of the Gas and Electric building, right in front. Lucky day.

It was as if this were part of not giving up on Paula, telling her he'd ask his mother to move in. Depending on her response, he'd feel settled, one way or the other.

∝৩৩

"Yes, I understand. Thank you for your time. This has been helpful. Please, don't worry. It wasn't your fault at all. Not at all. I'll keep you updated." With a sense of nervous excitement, Aaron hung up the phone, stood and…stopped. What should he do?

Aaron was scheduled to see Sister early afternoon, but now that he'd gotten off the phone with her supervisor—her Mother Superior—he felt eager to talk to her, armed with new information to prod her memory. He looked at his watch. An hour before his first appointment. He'd intended to check on some other patients during that time, answering mail, doing paperwork. But this was perfect—he could use the afternoon instead to think through his campaign against

Dr. Freeman. He was still weighing whether it was best to speak personally to the chief of psychiatry or write him a note...

What would Kate do with Sister? He smiled. She'd burst in, all elbows, and probably say just the right thing, with the perfect balance of well-intentioned frankness wrapped in compassion. There'd be no hidden messages, no secret agenda. Her bluntness would both provoke and reassure.

Yes, he needed to talk with Sister now. The sooner the better. This Dr. Freeman—his visit was like a sword hanging over all their heads.

He stretched, squared his shoulders. With determination, he turned and walked down the hallway, approaching Sister's room, file in hand. As he strode past one room, he caught a glimpse of Kate talking with a patient. She had already changed him. He usually was meticulous and slow to adapt. She was quick and adjustable. As her face turned toward the doorway, it brightened. She nodded a hello, and he reciprocated, without slackening his pace. No distractions.

At Sister's room, he was pleased to see her awake and finished with breakfast. With her short hair and angular features, she looked a bit like a young boy on the cusp of adulthood, with scrawny arms and timid movements.

After knocking politely on the open door, he stepped in and stood beside her.

"It's good to see you eating," he said, nodding toward her tray.

She looked surprised, as if she hadn't realized she'd eaten.

"Now that you're doing better physically, perhaps your memory will start returning. Sometimes that happens." He was improvising, a bit unsure how to start now that he was in the room. There was a reason he relied so heavily on planning, after all. But he couldn't lose his nerve.

"I remember many things. Just not that day." She fidgeted and didn't look at him.

That day. The day she'd collapsed again, due to the overdose.

"Nothing at all surrounding the day you were brought here? Not waking up, going to breakfast?" he prodded.

"Nothing! But that nurse told me this isn't unusual, memory loss, after shock treatment."

"Your memory loss is somewhat selective," he said softly. "I just want to make sure..." He stopped himself, not wanting to place ideas in her mind that she might not have. Kate made it look so easy, this kind of honesty. Why was he struggling with it, when he was the psychiatrist?

Fully committed now, he pulled up a chair and leaned forward. This should be a simple case, really. If not for Dr. Freeman coming, he'd be taking his time with it. But now...he had to hurry the poor girl along.

"I spoke with your Mother Superior. She said it was all right for you to talk to me."

She'd told him other things, too, about how St. Benedict's was Sister's fifth transfer in more than ten years in the convent, and although she'd not said it outright, she'd hinted that this was unusual. Sister Frances Marie had been transferred back to her "Mother House" several times, each one after a stint at a parish school where she'd fallen ill and been unable to fulfill her responsibilities. And on the day of Sister's overdose, her Mother Superior had informed her she'd be transferred back again. Sister Fulgentia suffered a bit of guilt over that. He'd reassured her she was not in any way to blame for what had happened.

When he looked at Sister now, he saw a young lady with a history of mental illness, undiagnosed and uncared for, shunted back to her home convent, each trip acting as something of a rest cure before she was discharged to the world again, only to collapse and start the cycle over. She truly was a chronic case. Now she'd been pushed to the limit. Why?

"I told you that I was forgetful about the medicine. Sister Fulgentia had to remind me to take it. Maybe she gave it to me—gave me too much, I mean." Her tone was childlike, as if she were trying to find the right thing to say to please him.

His awareness sharpened. She knew about the overdose. And she was accusing her Mother Superior of being an accomplice in that action? Her obfuscation overwhelmed him, pulling him down, as if they were both sinking. It happened often with his patients. It made him want to leave the room, to angrily say, *I can't help you if you lie to yourself, if you've gone to a place...where I can't follow*. As always, he mentally shook those feelings off, reminding himself that this was why she was here—her lack of honesty with herself—and decided to tackle the question of her antipathy toward her Mother Superior first.

"Do you like Sister Fulgentia?"

Her gaze shot to him and away, troubled. "It's...it's a...I love her."

"Love but not like?"

"We love each other. I love her." Her voice softened to an almost sing-song rhythm.

"We can love people, yet they can still annoy or irritate us," he said, trying to get her to trust him. She refused to own up to the smallest indiscretions, the tiniest of sins. Surely she'd confess such things to a priest. Did he need written permission to hear them?

"Don't be afraid, Sister. I won't tell anyone what you tell me—not even Sister Fulgentia. You can tell me anything. Memories, dreams…"

When she didn't respond, he tried again. "You say she might have given you too much medicine that day. Why would she do that? Did *she* dislike you?"

Again, her head swung back to him, her stare dark and now angry. "What a hateful thing to say." He could see tears welling in her eyes.

Now she wouldn't admit to a possible sin by a fellow sister. So many barriers…

"Did you hate *her?*" he asked, cuing off the word she'd used.

"No!" She chewed her lip and looked toward the window. "Why can't I go? I'm fine. Much stronger. It's just the one day I can't remember. Just one day."

"You remember the overdose, though. You suggested Sister Fulgentia was responsible."

"I…I…I have vague memories. No details."

Or did she remember it all in vivid detail and was unwilling to admit it?

"Where would you go if you were released?" he asked, knowing the answer already from her case files and his talk with her superior.

"Back to St. Benedict's," she said, still not looking at him, her voice taking on a resigned quality. "To my students. To teaching."

His heart raced. Either she didn't know or she was lying again. "But you won't go back there."

She paused and sighed, then looked down at her hands, as if accepting her fate. "You'd commit me?"

"No, no, nothing like that," he said. "It's just—Sister Fulgentia has informed me you were to be transferred back to the convent in Glendale, in Pennsylvania." He wished he could repeat it in a gentler tone. It sounded as if he were barking out an accusation…or an order.

She stared at him, confusion on her face. "The

Mother House? No, I'm fine. I can start teaching again."

"You received the news the day of...the incident."

She shook her head. "You must be wrong. Transfers are done earlier, in late spring. I would have had my lessons planned. I would have...they wouldn't have had a replacement for me...I would...." She narrowed her eyes. "You're testing me."

"No, I am not. I assure you, Sister, I'm trying to help. Sister Fulgentia has given you permission to talk to me," he reminded her, frustrated. These were simple questions, not difficult at all, and he was trying so hard to be patient and appear nonthreatening. The clock was ticking...Freeman was coming...yet he couldn't tell her that was the reason for haste.

"You must have something wrong, then. We don't do it that way."

What way did they do it? He felt at sea. All he knew was she'd been scheduled to go to this other convent, and once she was well, that would be her home. He knew the Mother House was where they received training. Did it mean other things? Was it like a prison? He'd have to ask Kate. No, Sister Fulgentia. He'd have to ask her. But Kate was so easy to talk to, and Sister Fulgentia like a foreign country.

He needed more time!

"So, you don't want to go to Glendale?"

"I told you," she said, shaking her head, "we don't do it that way." She even smiled now, as if he were a stubborn student refusing to understand. "I'm going back to St. Benedict's."

"You don't like Glendale?" he tried again.

She laughed, but it sounded artificial. "Why do you want me to dislike everything? I'm going back to St. Benedict's. The Mother House is beautiful, but I'm going back to St. Benedict's."

"You don't think it's possible you've forgotten you were to go to Glendale?" He had been so sure this would jog her memory, even if it just triggered snapshots of the day. But nothing. It was as if she willfully blocked the memories.

"I don't think it's possible that I was being transferred there this late."

"Perhaps you knew of it earlier and have forgotten those days." Had she suspected, he wondered, known of Sister Fulgentia's plans?

"If I were to have gone back to the Mother House, it would have happened early in the summer, maybe even late spring, right after school was finished." She said it patiently and securely, on comfortable ground. Ground he knew nothing about.

"Besides," she continued, now even more confident, "there would be nothing for me to do at the Mother House. I'm not the type they would choose to lead new novices or postulants, and I haven't any administrative skills. They prepared me for teaching. They need teachers. If I were to be transferred anywhere, it would be to another school."

"What did you do at the Mother House the other times you were transferred there?" Maybe this would be more comfortable to talk about.

She looked down and pursed her lips, embarrassed, he thought.

"Small things," she said in a small voice. "I helped new novices sew habits. I worked in the garden."

"You enjoyed that?" She was hiding from him, just as she was hiding from herself.

"Yes. I mean, sometimes, like all work, it was boring. But mostly, yes."

"If you're not to go to the Mother House, would you want to go to another school to teach?"

She swallowed. "It doesn't matter what I want. I go where they send me."

"So if they were sending you back to Glendale, say, and it wasn't a mistake, if they did have something for you to do, say, more gardening, or sewing, you'd be happy with that?"

"They weren't doing that, Doctor," she said. He heard a nervous question mark creep into her voice, making it waver. "I already told you. Any transfers would have occurred earlier in the season."

"But if it were true…"

"It's not!" She struck her fist on the bed. Visibly reclaiming control, she closed her eyes and sighed before continuing in a tired voice. "It simply doesn't work that way." She looked at him with desperation in her eyes.

Before he could continue, he noticed her gaze shifting, now staring over his shoulder into the hallway. He turned and saw her sister-in-law, a quizzical look on her face, as if wondering whether to come in.

He stood, feeling both satisfied and unsettled. He'd learned something, but he wasn't sure precisely what.

"Are you up for a visitor? Your sister-in-law is here," he said, proud of himself for remembering the correct relationship.

"Yes," she said quickly. He wasn't fooled. He knew she was eager to be done with him.

He motioned for Paula to enter, then turned back to Sister. "I'll be back tomorrow. We can talk more then." He'd plan that session better.

CHAPTER FIVE
Confession

"SO...I guess I better be going or Karol will worry," Paula said after a miserable hour. Her legs itched under her stockings, her head had begun to pound, her ankles were swollen and her face stiff from trying to keep a pleasant look on it while she scrounged for things to say.

Can't she make more of an effort? She's probably said all of a dozen words while I've been here. Thank you when I hung up her habit and a question or two about Saint Benedict's. Like if any new sisters have shown up. How would I know?

"You don't need to come," Sister said, turning to Paula, those big, sad puppy eyes already starting to water. She looked like...a lost little waif, so pitiful.

Goodness, she cries at anything now. You could say the weather's mighty fine, and her lip will start to trembling. It gets tiresome having to be so careful about what you say.

Paula stared at her. She was really a pretty woman but probably didn't know it. Paula almost hadn't recognized her when they'd first seen her here in the hospital. Without the veil, her face was more filled out, and you noticed her fine cheekbones and nose. She had big brown eyes and red-gold hair, even if it was a bit dull now. Once it started growing out, she could be a beauty. So different from Rosy. Well, it wasn't that Rosy wasn't a beauty. She'd been a pretty thing, blonde like Paula, and full of fun and spit. But she'd been rounder and only seemed to care about her dress when they were going out someplace special. She would wear the shabbiest things to church on Sunday, dresses shiny from use and stockings with runs. Paula had kidded her about this, and Rosy had said she had to save her good clothes for the weekdays when people saw her. People—as if those in church weren't among them. She would have looked good in a brown bag, though. Her smile could light up a room. That was her real attraction. She was one of those girls you'd hear a lot about and then wonder what all the fuss was when you first met her, seeing as how she was a bit on the dowdy side. Then she'd open her mouth and start to talking and all was clear. She'd been a firecracker of a girl, the kind everybody wanted to know.

"I want to come," Paula lied. Well, not really a lie. She wanted to come because she wanted Karol to know she was looking after his sister. Oh, he protested when he dropped her off, worrying about her in this heat, with the baby. But if she didn't come, somehow she'd feel he'd hold it against her. And besides, she also needed to see the priest.

Paula stood. Her appointment with Father Al was in a half hour. Maybe she could grab a cool drink or even a sandwich.

Sister's skeletal hands fisted the sheet. Oh, no. She looked panicked, the way Paula had seen her once in front of the little children's choir. The poor thing—she was such a nervous soul. Despite her impatience, Paula couldn't help but sympathize. She stood closer and stroked Sister's arm.

"There, there. You'll be leaving soon; I'm sure of it. You're looking better today. A lot better."

Wide-eyed and frantic, Sister turned toward her. "But where will I go?"

"I—I'm not sure." She'd not given much thought to that at all. Back to the convent. Some convent.

"Dr. Kaplan says...he says..." She took big, gulping breaths as if she couldn't bear to tell Paula the news. Was it secret, something she shouldn't share?

Now worried, Paula bent over and whispered, "It's all right, Sister. What does he say?"

Sister grabbed her arm with such force that Paula almost fell over into the bed.

"He says I'll be going back to the Mother House. I'm supposed to be teaching...I should be at St. Benedict's...He doesn't understand."

It was nearly summer's end. Paula was no doctor, but she doubted Sister would be up to teaching in the fall. Oh, maybe if she managed to get some real rest, a real break. But that was unlikely at St. Benedict's. Paula knew that August would be full of planning and scheduling, preparing for the new school year.

"You'll have to explain it all to him then. Maybe he's just confused," Paula said, trying to sound reassuring but feeling uneasy. She was treading into foreign territory here. "Look, maybe one day this week we can take a walk," Paula said slowly, trying to soothe her by changing the subject. "The weather should be fine. Just like today." Fine and hot.

This seemed to calm her, and her grip relaxed on Paula's arm.

"We'll take a stroll, and you'll be getting your stamina back in no time. I'll talk to Nurse Kate about it."

"Would you?"

"Of course, I will. Now, you take care and get yourself some rest. Make sure you eat a good lunch, ya hear?"

Lunch—she'd not have time for it herself. She'd content herself with a quick iced tea in the cafeteria and then off to Father Al.

And she'd see what she could find out about where Sister would go once she was released. It was the least she could do. Hmm...she genuinely felt like doing it, too. Not just to please Karol, but to really help this poor, suffering spirit.

☙✍

As it turned out, Paula barely had time to gulp down a cool tea in the crowded cafeteria before hurrying to find Father Al's office.

When she finally stepped into his room, she was sweating to beat the band and tired and wondering how long it would all take—*please, Lord, let it be quick.* She'd told him she wanted to convert—shouldn't he be hurrying her to the font before she changed her mind?

But Father Aloysius didn't seem the hurrying kind, she thought during their polite introductions. He reminded her a little of the older men from Percy—not that he was an old man himself—slow and very precise with his words. She got the impression he didn't say a word he wouldn't be willing to go to the stake for.

He was tall and lean, wearing that long, black dress that high-church priests seemed to favor, a wide sash around his waist. He ushered her in with a broad smile, gesturing to a seat, a hard wooden thing upon which he'd placed a pillow. He'd probably done that special, seeing as how she was heavily pregnant, and that put her in a good frame of mind that he'd think of her comfort. She couldn't remember if she'd told him she was expecting; maybe Kate had put in the word.

When he talked, the sound of his soft British accent was soothing. "You must be tired. Let me get you a cup of coffee or tea," he said as she sank into the chair with a heavy sigh. She couldn't seem to do anything these days without it being heavy.

"No, thank you. I couldn't bear the thought of anything hot." She fanned herself with her hand. The room had one window, letting in bright, hot sunlight. He stretched over his desk to pull down a dark shade, leaving only the screened part open. And then he pulled a bulky electric fan from the side of his desk, angling it so it faced her. When he flipped the switch, papers started to dance, and for a moment, they had a good chuckle as he arranged books and knickknacks on the sheets.

That was an ice-breaker. When he finally sat across from her, they were both relaxed.

"I'm so pleased to meet you," he began. "Filled with new life, you desire to start a new life for yourself, too—it makes one happy to contemplate it."

She was glad Kate had sent her to this priest. Some of them were so distant. She had to admit the long, black robe seemed sinister at times.

"Well, like I told you on the phone, I've been wanting to convert for some time now, but the moment never seemed right."

She just wanted to blurt out: What do I do, where do I sign, when will you commence with the holy water pouring and all? But she knew that would seem eager in a bad way. So she sat, her hands on her purse on her big stomach, and waited for him to tell her what to do.

He didn't begin with instructions. He started with conversation. All right, she could chat if that's what it took.

"If I understand your story correctly, your husband and his family are Catholic." He smiled. He had gray hair but a youngish face. She pegged him as in his forties, maybe, prematurely gray. He had brown-green eyes that looked right through her.

"Your husband, however, does not know of your intention to convert—you want it to be a surprise." His tone was friendly enough, but she was on edge. She'd prepared answers as best she could, but one never knew what to expect, especially since she still tended to think of these Catholics as a bit heavy on the mystery side of things. There was that whole Inquisition thing. They might be skilled at interrogation.

"That's right, Father. I go to church with him on Sundays—have been for some time now, even before we got married. And I teach at St .Benedict's, a Catholic school, so I've become somewhat familiar with how things are done."

He nodded and smiled, but she could tell he was

fussing mentally with something. She squirmed a little in the chair.

"Naturally, I assume your husband will be pleased by your conversion?"

"Oh, yes, real happy, I'm sure."

He paused. "Then might I suggest that you surprise him with the news now so that he can witness your baptism? Might he not be disappointed not to have been there at the moment?"

Of course this made perfect sense, assuming her husband knew she wasn't Catholic. But Karol didn't know. He'd just assumed—as had the good folks at St. Benedict's—that she was R.C. when she'd listed her "home parish" as the Cathedral in town. When she'd filled out the application for work, she'd assumed the nuns just wanted to know what area of town she lived in, and that's where she was living at the time. She knew she should have corrected this misunderstanding, but time marches on, as the newsreels said, and it didn't seem to be hurting anyone. Besides, now she wanted to make it right.

"I've thought about that a lot, Father," she said, her gaze flickering away from his penetrating eyes. "And with his sister sick and all, I'd rather not burden him with a big to-do."

He considered this as he lit a cigarette—first asking if she'd mind—and she expected him to point out it needn't be much of a big to-do, but he didn't. Instead, he smiled again, a sad sort of grin that told her he might know she wasn't telling the whole truth, but he wasn't going to push her away because of it.

"Were you raised in a particular faith?" he asked.

"Oh, yes, Southern Baptist."

"How will your parents feel about your conversion?"

"If Daddy were alive, I suppose he might be bothered. He wasn't much for the Roman way." That was putting it mildly. He thought they were a superstitious, secretive bunch and called their Latin Mass a bunch of "mumbo jumbo." "And I never knew my momma. She died when I was born."

"Oh. Oh, dear. So sorry. He never remarried?"

"No, he didn't. I don't know if it was out of respect for Momma's memory or just because he was a busy man—he was a small town doctor—and he never got around to it. Not that there weren't prospects. I'm sure Ida Mae Burnside or Reba Carlisle—two women from our church—would have loved to step into the job. He just wasn't interested."

"He must have loved your mother very much."

"Mmm-hmm. Was a broken man when she passed, my Aunt Louisa told me. Could hardly stand it. Didn't even take me in for a few months after."

He sat up a little straighter. "That seems rather cold."

"I was a baby and didn't know better, so it didn't matter to me. Momma passed giving birth to me, and since Daddy was a doctor, I think he felt a heavier burden of responsibility in that regard. He not only lost his wife, he failed her as a doctor."

"I see." He paused, and she breathed easier, thinking she had the name of his game. He was going to keep asking her about her past, thinking she'd eventually get around Robin's barn to explaining why she didn't want Karol to know she was getting baptized.

She squared her shoulders. All right then.

No racing to the baptismal font for her. But she'd take her time wandering to the point, and maybe Father Clever here would get to holy-water dispensing eventually. He was foreign-born. He didn't know Southern women. She could talk a blue streak that would fog this room heavier than the smoke from a whole pack of his weeds, and he'd be choking for the good, clean air of salvation—and its holy waters—before you could say "Amen."

"You've had your fair share of difficulties," he said

75

at last. "Your sister-in-law is ill, and you lost your other sister-in-law to polio just months ago."

Ah, Kate again. She'd probably thought she was setting the stage for this wondrous conversion.

"They're kin, but not blood kin." As she said the words, her hand flew to her mouth. She'd not wanted to sound so lacking in compassion.

He chuckled, though. "Don't be troubled. I know what you mean. I'm sure your affection for your husband's family is appropriately strong."

What a fine way he had with words, creeping up to the truth without stepping on any toes.

He cleared his throat. "So, you were raised Southern Baptist…"

"Yes, that's true. I wouldn't call it high church so much as high-tide church. That's how we did our baptisms. In the drink with you. I was mighty relieved to hear you don't favor such practices." The fan provided a delightful breeze. She'd have to ask Karol if they could get another one, for the living room.

"You were baptized in that church?"

"Well, that's an odd story, see? My daddy, being broken up and all after Momma's death, he kind of stopped churchgoing for a while. And my Aunt Louisa, well, she began to fear he wouldn't be raising me in a holy state and getting me to the tank at the appropriate time—she just kept imagining me growing up in some sort of heathen state, wild and full of sin. She couldn't tolerate this situation, knowing her sister had been a God-fearing woman. She took it upon herself, she told me, to do a sort of informal baptism at her kitchen sink. Even though we don't do the infant baptism. She felt a powerful strong calling, she said, like an angel's voice in her ear, she said, to do it, so she overcame any reservations she might have about the practice. She saw it as a preventative measure, she confided to me later, in case Daddy couldn't see to it and she had no control later when I was old enough."

"And you never made it formal?" he asked, a smile in his voice.

"Well, no. You see, Daddy found out about Aunt Louisa taking it on herself to do this—truth be told, she gave him the news herself when they were arguing about how she thought he was too easy on me—and they ended up having quite a few theological discussions, really, more like arguments, certainly lively talks, over the years about whether it had been a valid baptism and whether I should be dunked in the church, and I think he got to be a bit embarrassed about the whole thing, or maybe he was just being stubborn with Aunt Louisa, and we all just sort of put it off...."

"But your mother was a Baptist, too?"

"Yes, she was." She smiled. He waited. She let him wait a few more seconds. She knew what he was after—an explanation for why she didn't want her husband at her baptism. She'd give him everything but. Let him wait a bit for it, though. Let him get a little eager. At last, when she felt he was sufficiently curious, she began:

"I didn't know my mother, except through my daddy and my aunt Louisa. My aunt Louisa told me about her mostly, since Pappy was so broken up after her death. As a doctor, he tended to everyone in our town and beyond. He was always on the go seeing to people or in his office taking appointments. I worked for him for a while during high school and after. He was the most admired man in our county, no joking. Beloved by everyone. He even tended the Negroes from time to time when their doctor fell ill for a spell.

"But he was out all day and all night when I was born, Aunt Louisa said. Seeing to a cholera outbreak on a farm outside of town. Fixing a little girl's broken arm beyond that. My goodness, I think Aunt Louisa knew every one of his stops that day. Then again, she was my mother's sister, and I came to wonder if she, too, thought he should have been home tending to his wife...

"June was her name. June Elizabeth. People called

her June-Beth or June-Bee. Aunt Louisa said I got my looks from her. She said she was as sweet and kind as the day was long."

"But your father had a hard time taking to you after that?" he prompted.

"Daddy wasn't what you'd call a complicated man. He was honest and tell-what-he thinks, whether you like it or not. Me looking like my mother wasn't what put him off, I'm sure of it. He was tired and sad, that's all. Horrible sad.

"Aunt Louisa and Uncle Bill cared for me for only a few months, that's all. My father couldn't bear the sight of me, Aunt Louisa said. But not because of my looks— my baby pictures show I was just like any other infant back then, all puffy and pouty and the twin of anyone else's babe. No, seeing me just reminded him his June-Bee was gone and how she'd died. I coulda had a birthmark covering half my face and a stunted leg, and he'd have felt the same. I was a reminder of his omissions. I'd set him into a grief so deep, it would take weeks to set himself aright. So said Aunt Louisa. He had patients to see still after it was all over....

"Anyways, it was raining and storming that night, Aunt Louisa told me. And my momma must have gone into labor. She knew she could have called him—there was a telephone at one of the farms he was calling at, and he'd told her quite clearly to phone if her time came, and someone would come fetch him so he could be on the road.

"But Momma, she apparently was mighty proud of his work, and she didn't want to be the cause of anyone thinking poorly of him. She knew she could be laboring for hours or even days. So she waited and didn't call, thinking he'd be home before midnight...

"He didn't get home till nigh on dawn, Aunt Louisa said. By that time, Momma was in bed, not much able to do anything but whimper. Aunt Louisa was with her by then, too. She'd tried reaching Pappy, she said, but he was on the road. Turned out a tree had fallen in the storm, blocking his way. He'd had to drive clear around the county to get home.

"He was so mad at my aunt, she'd never heard him so mad. He didn't speak much to her for months after that. He wanted Momma to go to the hospital, but she'd not been keen on a hospital birth. All her mother's children had been born at home, and she wanted to have her child at home, too. My mother had had three sisters and a brother, but Aunt Louisa and June Bee were the only who'd made it past childhood.

"My father gave in and let her stay at home. Aunt Louisa said that was another thing he blamed himself for later—that he'd not insisted on going right away. He was tired from that long night, you see, and he always thought he might have let that fatigue settle into his decision-making.

"Even so, he only let her labor another hour or so before he put his foot down and said they were leaving for the hospital even if he had to call the police to help him take her to the car, that he wasn't going to stand by and watch the Lord take his June-Bee away from him because he was too yellow-bellied to stand up to a harridan like Aunt Louisa.

"I do think Aunt Louisa must have memorized his speech that night, so stung was she by being called a harridan.

"So they bundled Momma into his Ford and made their way to the town hospital, a little thing that did little more than care for women giving birth and the occasional bad gallstone. All the big cases went to Norfolk up the road in Virginia, after all.

"And, of course it took longer than usual because the rain was coming down in sheets, muddying the roads and making driving slow.

"But get there they did, much to the relief of everyone, including Momma at that point, who Aunt Louisa said was near crazy out of her mind with hurting and ready to have the whole thing behind her.

"Well, that came soon enough I expect because I was born by cesarean but two hours later, and then Momma just slipped away on the operating table they tell me. And Daddy, why, he howled like a wolf at the moon, Aunt Louisa said. She said it was terrible to behold, she didn't like to think about it. He told the doctors they were dunces who never should have been let out of medical school and the nurses were no better than kitchen maids. He yelled at everyone and everything, including himself. He saved the worst of it for himself, in fact, screaming to the heavens that maybe he should have let her have me at home after all, that maybe moving her here was against her will and she'd needed all the will in the world to live, and he'd taken it from her, broken it...Aunt Louisa told me this story more than once. I think it did something to her, that night, and she just couldn't let go of the memory.

"Anyways, even I can see why he'd not want to set eyes on me right away after that. He was embarrassed by his hollerin'—he's a quiet, serious man most times, not a joker or a crank.

"He had a bad spell after that, Aunt Louisa told me, taking to drink for a while. No two-day spree for him, no, sir. He did it up big, downing moonshine liquor even the Negroes wouldn't touch. He stayed like that for weeks, until Aunt Louisa took him to hand and said he had to think of his daughter and do right by me.

"He threw out the booze, didn't touch a drop after that. And he saw to some patients who needed help bad—a poor farmer got run over by his tractor that year and lost a leg. Aunt Louisa even thinks the ailments and breaks and cuts and bruises of everyone served a higher purpose those months, keeping him upright and living each day by day.

"He got right with the world and with the Lord, Aunt Louisa said. He took me home that Easter because she was with child herself by then, with Ginny, my cousin and best friend.

"But when Daddy took me back, he must have decided then and there that he'd keep me safe in ways he didn't keep Momma safe.

"I was a bird in a gilded cage." She laughed, but Father Aloysius didn't laugh with her. He just smiled and nodded his head. She noticed his fingers were stained, and she told him it was okay if he'd like another smoke since his first one was gone by now. He lit up, and the room filled with the strong smell, one that had never bothered her, that took her back to childhood days.

"Sunday's child, that was me—bonny and blithe and gay. Not a single thing in my childhood troubled me. Daddy gave me all I needed and then some. He only held back a little when I got older, not wanting me to be too extravagant with clothes because he knew it would set tongues to wagging and earn me no friends but plenty of envy. I suspect Aunt Louisa set him right on that score. She and Uncle Bill did fine by Ginny, but it didn't escape my notice that I wore cashmere and Ginny wore cotton. And Uncle Bill was a lawyer."

"Is Ginny still in Percy?" he asked, blowing a plume of smoke toward the window.

"No, she's not far—in Virginia—but she was here in Baltimore with me early on. I'll get to that quick enough—"

"No, no, don't abbreviate on my account. I'm enjoying your story. And your voice. I don't hear that southern drawl very often. Baltimore is something of a northern town I'm told."

Well, this wasn't working as she'd planned. She'd hoped to have him bored and restless by now. She soldiered on. "Yes, it is, which is why it caused a ruckus when Ginny and I headed here. But that's getting ahead of myself." She resolved to talk more slowly, so her story now poured out like cold molasses.

"Like I said, I was a pampered girl, hardly having to

lift a finger for anything—we had a maid who cleaned up and cooked, and Daddy was generous with my allowance. About the only thing I applied myself to was music lessons, and I think I was drawn to it because it made me something of a local star. I could about play anything on the piano. I had my mother's gift, Daddy would say, and he'd listen to me playing piano in the evenings."

Even though her talk was part of a strategy, it was good to remember those peaceful times back in Percy, before the war, before everything. Sitting in that parlor laughing and jabbering, so excited to come home with the latest hit tune from the store or the post office where a special order had come in. Daddy being happy, too, to see Ginny there with her, sure of her good influence. Daddy sitting in his chair, eyes closed, paper on his lap, just listening to her play piano on slow, cool evenings when hardly a breeze stirred the curtains, and the world crept in through the wide open windows...

"Or sometimes he'd listen to me and Ginny sitting and talking on the porch swing. Once when I caught him sitting in the living room with the paper on his lap, I accused him of eavesdropping on us.

"'No, Paula,' he said, 'I couldn't make out a word you lambs were saying. But I dearly liked the music of your voices.'

"I played for our church and sometimes for the Lutheran one down the street, you see. Everyone always complimented me to beat the band after I'd play. It made me feel like the best girl in town."

"How did you end up in Baltimore?"

She hoped this question meant he was getting tired. Good. Maybe they could move on to the baptizing lessons soon.

"Well, men started filling up the army camps, and me and Ginny started going to weekly canteens, helping set things up and all.

"And she met Freddie Williamson III and fell in

love. And for the first time in my life, I didn't feel special anymore."

"You were losing your best friend," he said, tapping ash into a tray on his desk. "It's only natural."

"Yes, I suppose. Jealousy overcame me for a bit, but soon enough I met Tom DiGiacomo, and he swept me off my feet. Tom and I got married."

"Oh. I hadn't realized. I—"

"We didn't divorce," she added quickly, knowing the church didn't look well on that. "He died."

"In the war?"

"Well, I suppose you could say that. Technically, he died during the war. Just not in it.

"We married on the very auspicious day of December 7, 1941. And he and his unit had to ship out right away. We didn't have any honeymoon to speak of. Freddie left, too. The camp nearly emptied before it started filling up again with new recruits.

"I got word months later he'd died in a training accident."

There was so much more to tell, but she couldn't bring herself to confess it all, not even to this priest used to hearing confessions. She was the one growing tired just thinking about it! This sly priest had outfoxed her. And no matter how wise and kind he might seem, she was not willing to share just anything with anybody. Like how upset Daddy had been that she was marrying so quick. How angry he'd been that she'd had to get married. With dismay, she realized that she'd made a habit of that.

"I'm so sorry," Father Aloysius said. "So many losses during the war. It's unfathomable."

"Well, Freddie wasn't lost. He asked Ginny to marry him before he shipped out, and she nearly made herself sick waiting for his letters to come. My goodness, but she turned into a skeleton and she'd already been a willowy girl with pale skin and dark hair. I worried about her. So did Aunt Louisa and Daddy. Aunt Louisa even sent her to Daddy's office—I'd started working there—to get some vitamins.

"She needed only one vitamin, and that was Freddie. She got word in late '43 that he'd been badly wounded. He was in Walter Reed Hospital in Washington, and there was some question as to whether he'd walk again or whether he'd even be able to keep both his legs.

"When Ginny got word, she was beside herself. Both sad and happy. She couldn't contain her joy at knowing he was out of the fighting for good, but then when she thought of why—him possibly losing his legs—she'd become morose with shame. It was terrible to see her swing back and forth like that. She was just as bad up as she'd been waiting for his letters. It was fearsome how gaunt she looked. I know Aunt Louisa heard from more than one helpful soul about it, telling her how poorly her Ginny seemed to be faring. And I knew the only thing to set it right was for her to go see him.

"It took lots of convincing—not of her but of her momma and of my father—to let us go. I think Aunt Louisa might have even helped persuade Daddy to give his permission for me to travel with her because she was so afraid for her daughter traveling so far alone, and north on top of it all. And I know Daddy wasn't keen on me going because, well, I suspect he knew once I went to the big city, I'd not be coming home."

She'd only realized that later, of course. At the time, she'd thought her father was just being overprotective, and she'd resented him for it.

"Fred's momma, Mrs. Williamson, called us with good news days before we left. We'd not have to go to the expense of renting rooms if we didn't mind a little travel each day. A friend of the family had an empty flat in Baltimore, just up the road from Washington. We could stay in it for free and come in on the train to see Freddie every day. She herself had a hotel room in town, seeing as how they lived a good three hours away in

Virginia.

"Now, I came to realize that Mrs. Williamson's generosity of spirit was mixed with another less merciful inclination. If we were nearly an hour away, it was easier for her to control how often Ginny got to see her son.

"And she did try to control that—at first at least. But we didn't know that was afoot when we arrived here in town. All we knew was that we were dead tired, and we had the good fortune to have a lovely little apartment in a good section of town—just north of here in Roland Park—at our disposal. Why, it was like the dreams we'd talked about growing up—the place we'd imagined renting together as women of the world. The first morning, we giggled through breakfast discovering every little thing we liked about the place. It even had an electric percolator!

"We went to see Freddie right away. It was pitiful. He looked half his size in that bed, and the smell in the room was such that I couldn't help thinking something was dying there. Maybe his legs. Maybe his soul. Something. Ginny had to bite her lips something awful to keep from crying, and I had to go into the hall to pull myself together.

"Seeing each other revived them both, though. You could tell. He must have been afraid she wouldn't want him all beat up because when it was clear that she did, he sat up straighter in bed. Even the nurse noticed it.

"Mrs. Williamson was a different matter. You have to understand something about Southern women, Father. We can be all charm and sugar, but sometimes it's as thin as ice in a spring thaw. And that's how Mrs. Williamson was with Ginny and me. She and me and Ginny would smile and hug and kiss each other on the cheeks each morning when we got to the hospital. We'd step back and admire each other's clothes and say a few words about the weather or some news of the day. She'd ask us about our family, about Ginny's momma and my daddy. She'd even tell us how nice it was to have company since Mr. Williamson could only come up on weekends, and it got mighty tiresome being alone for so long. And not a word of this was untrue.

"But underneath all that sweetness was another truth. Mrs. Williamson didn't have a shred of desire to share her battered son with anyone right then. I think she was like Daddy after Momma died once he took me to his bosom, clutching on for dear life to that what was left. I've come to realize she was battered herself, afflicted with a powerful fear that made her want to grab on and hold tight to that which was precious to her, and that meant batting away anyone who wanted to come near, even if that person was offering succor.

"So, day after day, we'd show up and she'd tell us that Freddie was sleeping after a bad night, or he was being seen by the doctors, or the nurses were giving him exercise. And we'd have coffee with her, then she'd go check on things and come back to tell us it wasn't a good day to visit. And she felt just awful with us coming down for the day, but maybe tomorrow, and she'd be happy to take a note to Freddie for us so he'd know we'd been by. Oh, poor Ginny, she always sat there writing those notes with tears in her eyes. Surely Freddie saw those tear stains when he read her letters....

"We'd only planned on staying a week, and the days were drifting by. Poor Ginny didn't know what to do.

"So I told her she would get to see Freddie by hook or by crook. I came up with a plan.

"The next morning, after we did our little dance with Mrs. Williamson, with me telling her how much I just adored the way she combed her hair and she complimenting me on how I wore my hat and all three of us saying how happy we were to see each other again, she once again gave us the bad news that Freddie wasn't up to a visit.

"I gave her a big smile and said that was fine since I wanted to talk to her alone anyway about whether or not

Baltimore was a good place to settle. This was no lie. I was beginning to like it on my own, away from the smothering affection of my father. I told Ginny to go on next door to the flower shop and pick up a nice bouquet for Freddie that we could have Mrs. Williamson take to him with her note that day.

"Of course Ginny took the flowers to Freddie herself, just as we'd planned, while I talked up a storm to Mrs. Williamson in the cafeteria.

"When Ginny came in to fetch me hours later, she was beaming like the sun itself shone from behind her eyes. She told Mrs. Williamson she'd not wanted to interrupt us when she'd seen us talking so amiably, and she'd gone to see if Freddie could take a visitor.

"Of course he could and did. She told me later that he'd been hoping she'd come by, that he'd been afraid she'd had a change of heart and had been writing the letters just to assuage her guilt at not coming in person. No change of heart for her. She was already wed to him in her soul.

"And the next day, Mrs. Williamson didn't play any more games with us. She knew she'd been beaten fair and square, and she gave in with grace.

"Freddie couldn't bear the thought of Ginny going back to Percy, and truth be told, he was improving at a rocket's speed with Ginny around, sitting up in a wheelchair even, and eating more. I swear you could see the pounds coming back on every single day.

"So Ginny agreed to marry him right there in the hospital, and we called home to Percy and told them all we'd be another week or two gone. Aunt Louisa cried a river knowing she'd not be there for her girl's wedding, but Ginny promised she'd be home for a visit with Freddie as soon as he was able.

"What a wedding it was, too! Right there in the hospital room, with Freddie's roommate, some poor sailor with a leg missing, standing in for a groomsman—although he didn't really stand, mind you. And me as matron of honor. Mr. Williamson was there, too, with his wife, and the hospital chaplain performed the honors. Have you ever performed a wedding in a hospital room, Father?"

"No, I haven't. It seems as though it would be quite nice."

"It was more than nice. It was, well, I've thought a long time for a word to describe it all, and the only one I can come up with is 'heavenly.' But that word's used for so many things now it hardly conveys what I truly mean. I mean 'heavenly' in that it just took you out of yourself, you know? Like time standing still. I remember seeing a cascade of dust in the sun coming through the window and thinking we were like all those little floating specks, just hanging there in that beautiful glow, all warm and happy and without a care. It felt like every word and thought was being recorded somewhere, somehow, that it meant something...."

She looked down and sucked in her lips. Even now, it was a powerful fierce memory, Ginny trembling in the early sunlight, holding a small bouquet of daisies, wearing her best powder blue suit and Paula's white charmeuse silk blouse (something borrowed). Freddie in his bed—the nurses didn't want to move him that morning because of his dressings or something—and the chaplain intoning those words that meant so much to the two of them but had meant so little to Tommy and her.

"Mrs. Williamson had paid for a photographer who took pictures to beat the band, so many that my eyes were running for an hour afterward. It was irritating at first. But later I found out she'd sent a whole mess of them with a long letter about the ceremony to Aunt Louisa. She'd wanted her to feel she hadn't missed it all. Mrs. Williamson is a good mother-in-law.

"We did go back to Percy after that, so that Ginny could pack up all her things. And I told Daddy that I wanted to go back to Baltimore with Ginny, to be her companion while she waited for Freddie to heal and be released, and that I'd even found a job—which I had by then—working for a bone doctor. Daddy gave me the sorriest look. Oh, I think he knew I'd not be returning, like I said. It would have broken my heart if I'd have let myself think about it. Think about him being older, that is, and the possibility that he might not live forever. Funny how we think our parents will live forever, isn't it? Anyhow, I came back with Ginny.

"That's how I landed in Baltimore," she said simply, skipping all the details of that first job, of saying goodbye to Ginny when Freddie, healed and whole, finished his medical studies and they moved to Virginia, of starting her new life.

"And then I met Karol eventually, and we got married at City Hall because his mother was kind of her own version of Mrs. Williamson and…well, here I am."

There was a lot left out of this part, too, but she'd told him enough. All the good parts at least. And she'd not slipped, as she was sure he was hoping she would, and told him anything more about not wanting Karol to know of her conversion.

He stubbed out his cigarette and looked at her, his eyes troubled. She hoped she hadn't misjudged him. She hoped he wasn't going to come up with some reason not to baptize her.

"So what do we do now?" she asked, with a smile.

"We set up another appointment. I'll go over some catechism items with you. And we can talk about who you would like to have stand up for you. For infants, there are godparents. For adults, they play the role of sponsors." He picked up some booklets and gave them to her.

"Oh." Maybe Kate would step in.

When she got up, he stood, too, holding out his hand to help her right myself. Despite the fan, her legs felt sticky hot. And she felt unfairly bamboozled. That wouldn't do.

At the door, he said, "Thank you, Mrs. Wojehedski. I

hope you don't mind if I tell you that I enjoyed your story. And I learned something about Southern women that I won't forget."

He gave her a wicked, mischievous grin. And she knew he was seeing through all those holes in her story, but, like Mrs. Williamson, he wouldn't be voicing any objections. Not yet, at least.

With a little irritated shrug, she decided to turn the tables on him. "I've spent quite a bit of time telling my story. What's yours, Father? How'd you end up here?"

He remained unruffled, just raising his eyebrows before he spoke. "My story is as long and complicated as yours, Mrs. Wojehedski. But I can see that you are tired. To summarize, I lost my family in the war, went to seminary, became a Jesuit, and am here in the States to study and teach. I intend to stay."

Feeling bested, she left.

CHAPTER SIX
Regret

AFTER PAULA Wojehedski left his office, Father Aloysius stretched. He reached for another cigarette but stopped himself. Cut back on the smokes, his doctor had told him in his last appointment. He fought the urge to rationalize "just this last one," and closed up his office instead, moving away from temptation.

A few minutes later, he was in the battered old car owned by the congregation at Loyola, making his way north to the college campus and its rectory. He'd been in the States for over a year now, but still a mantra went through his mind as he sat behind the wheel: *right side of the road, right side of the road.*

His windows were wide open, yet the heat blasted him, sending sweat trickling down his neck at every red light. When he'd first encountered the heat here, it had left him reeling, often lying on his bed at the Jesuit residence with a cold cloth on his forehead. But a kind fellow priest had assured him he'd adapt, as long as he stopped waiting for the heat to go away. Embrace it, in other words, accept it. That simple lesson had lifted him out of his bed and to work.

Restless, he drummed his fingers on the steering wheel at a stop. He knew Paula Wojehedski's secret. He smiled. Charm hadn't hidden it. She'd obviously lied to her husband at their marriage. Oh, perhaps it was the lie of omission she'd owned up to already. Or perhaps it was an outright lie. Did it matter?

Am I aiding her in sin, he wondered.

Did it matter?

But her desire to convert—how could he not aid her in that quest, even if it was motivated more out of love or respect for her husband than true faith? Perhaps faith would grow from that love and that loving act. Although he'd chosen a disciplined path for himself, he was well aware of how the small step outside the prescribed route sometimes ended well. He'd not be sharing the particulars of her "conversion" with his fellow priests, some of whom took a medieval delight in the angels-on-a-pinhead minutiae of Catholic doctrine and ritual.

He wiped his brow as he drove forward. By the time he reached the campus, he felt a headache brewing and a nervous inability to stay still. A cigarette would soothe both. Now his rationalization was the smoke's medicinal effect.

Once in the Tudor-style rectory, he gave in and grabbed a smoke from a pack in his room, taking a long, calming drag while surveying the green quad, the small chapel at its far end, through his second-floor window.

The campus tightly snugged into a corner of a well-to-do Baltimore neighborhood. At high summer, trees arched over streets and lawns providing sweet shade, and quiet reigned. He wondered how parents in this area managed to keep their children so quiet.

He had nothing more on his schedule today. He'd planned on reading in preparation for the theology class he would teach when the semester began. But it was such a warm day to stay inside. And his thoughts were rambling even if he were not. Perhaps he should allow his feet to catch up and take a stroll.

Grabbing his camera from a shelf, he walked into the hall filled with determination, nearly running into Father Peter Dalton.

"Glad I caught you, Al," he said, holding out a white envelope. "This was in my mail slot."

"Thanks." He and Peter occasionally received each

other's mail—they shared a last name but no relations or other characteristics. While Al was tall and lean and introspective, Peter was a clear-eyed athletic man, originally from Indiana. He'd served in the war as an army chaplain. That was the one thing he refused to talk about, saying with a sad smile to any inquirer that it had been too sacred a time to share in conversation, that its memories were between him and God. Al suspected Pete didn't share the stories because they would have revealed his own heroism, and he wasn't a braggart.

After Peter walked away, Aloysius looked at the envelope. From England. His heart chilled.

Cramming the envelope into his pocket, he hurried down the stairs and out into the warm, sunny day. He walked north toward the wooded area that separated the all-male Loyola campus from the women's College of Notre Dame until his heavy breaths and aching chest told him it was time to rest. He sat on a tree stump, seeing in the distance a shrine to the Blessed Mother.

Help me, his inner voice cried without prompting as he stared at her outstretched arms.

After stubbing out his cigarette, he pulled the envelope from his pocket, ripped it open and read. It was from Benson Galworthy, the caretaker of his aunt's estate.

"Dear Rev. Dalton, I'm sorry to inform you that your Aunt Beady has died. Despite her past, I was sure you'd want to know. She died peacefully at the sanitarium a week ago. As her sole surviving relative, you have inherited her small property. It is probably worth a goodly sum now. I can settle it all for you if you provide instructions, or, if you prefer, you could come to discuss the matter...."

As he read, his throat constricted, his brows crept into a frown, and his eyes began to sting.

When he was finished, he let them fall. Tears of rage. He looked at the distant statue. His heart screamed: *Why won't you let me go?*

His eyes closed, he calmed his thoughts. He said a Hail, Mary. He asked for forgiveness and strength. Swallowing hard, he stood. He forced himself to put the letter away and raise the camera to his eyes to take a picture of the woods, capturing its play of light and shadow, its blessed beauty. He walked for a half hour thus, stopping to photograph a glistening leaf or a still life of fallen branches.

By the time he was finished, his heart had stopped racing. He could think.

But he couldn't decide. Should he go home to settle the estate? Or could he simply write to Benson with instructions on how to handle it? The money would go to his congregation, not him personally.

He wanted nothing to do with it.

I have been so happy here, he thought to himself as his gaze, unblinking, landed on a squirrel scampering up a tree.

Why should I have to face this again?

He thought back to his snapshot history he'd given Mrs. Wojehedski in his office: *"To summarize, I lost my family in the war, went to seminary, became a Jesuit, and am here in the States to study and teach."*

*I lost my family in the war...*it always comforted him to put it that way. While they'd not perished in battle or in the bombing raids unleashed on his native London, they'd still died because of the war. Without the war, they never would have been in harm's way—the specific harm that had led to their demise.

That was the reach of evil, he thought. It touched the lives of far more than those who stared it down outright. It oozed as well as marched to claim its victims.

Again, he closed his eyes.

If only he could have served, could have fought that evil outright. Maybe then it wouldn't hurt so much, or feel so meaningless.

He'd wanted an RAF commission. But he'd inherited his father's bad ticker. They'd rejected him.

He'd tried other branches with the same effect.

It had all been part of his extended youthful rebellion, though, he realized now. His parents had been devout upper-class strivers, his father the head of a small insurance agency. They'd been comfortable, and he'd felt privileged, even if he weren't a member of the privileged class, even if they were members of a small minority, Catholics. Such were the delusions of youth.

He'd stopped going to church at nineteen. His mother had wanted him to go to university. But he'd insisted on working in his father's insurance business while buying cameras and taking pictures on the side, sure he'd become a famous photographer at some point. Some had been published in a local community paper, feeding his dream.

In his off hours, he and his friends raised a pint or two at the local pub, talking with great seriousness about the mistakes their parents' generation had made. Hadn't they been responsible for the Great War, they argued? And all for what? For naught, for death and heartache and not a bit more peace.

Peace through pleasure became their motto. Their parents had been too rigid, too moral, too averse to the hedonistic drive within them all. They'd been too serious. And that seriousness had obviously led the world down the path to peril. The key was to take life less seriously, more wryly skeptical. How sophisticated they'd felt!

But his friends and he hardly adopted the hedonism they espoused. Except for the occasional gin hangover and the unfortunate dallying with a loose woman or two, their rebellion was limited to the known borders of their comfortable lives. The pub. The dance hall sometimes. The raucous talk and pretend cynicism, the tamping down of hope so as to appear worldly.

Yet after their boozy meetings, they all retreated to the enemy camp—those prudish unsophisticated parents. Not a one of them lived on his own.

Outside of the fake bluster of his clique, he'd lived a quiet life. He, his younger sister, Anne, his father and mother, in a small townhouse in a respectable neighborhood. He contributed to the family till. He worked. He took pictures. He dated numerous women. He drifted.

By the time the war came, his sister had grown into something of a beauty—hair like wheat, a rosebud smile, a personality as sweet as her looks. He limited his friends' visits to his house—he hadn't trusted them with her. His sophistication had its limits.

"If Mum and Dad don't have to send you to university, perhaps they'd consider it for me. What you think, Al?" she'd asked him one summer afternoon in her eager, trusting voice. She'd wanted to study veterinary science. It had stunned him. He couldn't imagine her as anything but a housewife—wasn't that what all women were? That had begun his transformation, he realized later. That question made him question his own devotion to his hedonistic principles. He wouldn't want them applied to Anne.

The war—it ended his drifting. He became one of those men who suddenly felt the invigoration of having something to believe in. He believed in Britannia. He was a patriot. He wanted to do his duty even before duty called.

And then, when he was rejected for medical reasons—why, he began thinking of that as the first in his Job-like travails.

To begin with, there were the doctor's visits to ascertain just how serious his condition was. He was loaded up with vitamins and a regular schedule of medical appointments. He felt unjustly cursed and, for quite some time, believed all the doctors were quacks.

His friends succeeded where he failed, landing commissions to a man. He was the lone exception, and he'd felt quite the disappointment. No white feathers for him, though. He'd do something useful, doctors be damned.

So when his father volunteered for some local fire brigade, he'd gone with him and signed up, too. They thought they'd just be filling in for the chaps who'd joined the military. But that was before the bombs fell.

One moment there was talk of war but no war, with some people treating it as an elaborate hoax, and the next minute, they were running for their lives.

But for him, the drifter, the rebel, the disappointment to his parents, well, it had been strangely liberating. After he'd lived through his initial fear of being killed, he felt exhilarated as he rushed to smoldering buildings collapsed into rubble. He'd run into any building, any opening to rescue someone.

"I was compensating, you see," he said to an unseen Mrs. Wojehedski. "I felt I was making up for being kept out of the real battle and that I had to prove myself. I enjoyed proving myself."

He never thought of how his father viewed this recklessness. He knew the man was proud of him. But once, when he'd been in the basement of a burnt-out shell that had started tumbling while he looked for a little girl, he came out of the ruins to see his father's eyes closed as he stood in the shadows, silent and still, his hands clasped before him, his head bowed, a sculpture of intense supplication. He'd been praying.

After some particularly bad nights, his father made what seemed to him a wise decision. Mother, and his sister Anne, would go to the country. They'd stay with Aunt Beady, a distant relative—really a second cousin— at her farm. Anne was ecstatic. She'd have a chance to tend animals. His mother had been less exuberant, and only partly because she'd not wanted to leave her son and husband behind. She'd never been that keen on Aunt Beady, and for good reason. The woman was a raging eccentric.

Again, he smiled remembering his mother. Her theory had been that Aunt Beady had lost her way after her husband had been killed in '17 in France and had destroyed her mind with too much drink.

They went off, though, and then it had been just his father and him, living the bachelor life.

None of these experiences made him into a churchgoer again. He'd been proud of the fact that he didn't go. It wasn't that he'd not been spiritual. He just hadn't been... religious. Not a day went by that he hadn't been murmuring some prayer in his head, usually to keep his family safe, but also to watch over another person who'd entered his life—dark-haired, irreverently funny Charlotte.

Charlotte was a young nursing student he'd met right before joining the brigade. He'd been becoming quite serious about her, and, for the first time in his life, he'd thought of settling down. He'd been waiting for the right moment to ask her and was considering selling one of his cameras to buy the ring, but, as usual, things happened.

"No, she wasn't killed," he said to the cool forest air. "She merely slew my heart, breaking up with me before I was able to pop the question. She'd met a doctor, whose charms obviously outranked mine."

No, Charlotte didn't die, but his father did, before Charlotte had had a chance to wound him. Perhaps his father's death had delayed her action; she seemed ever more distant after it.

His father... Heart attack one night as they were leaving to tend a fire. He collapsed near the front door. He could see him now, crumpling to the floor in the most ordinary way, as if he'd run into an invisible wall and just...stopped.

It had taken him hours to believe he was really dead. It made perfect sense, of course, that his father's heart would be bad, too. Had he known and not said anything? It was at this moment that Al learned his own heart condition was inherited.

Devastated, his mother and sister returned from the

country for the funeral.

An absolutely stunning day. Blue skies with hardly a cloud. And Father McAllister could hardly have done a better job with the service, although he did lose his place in the prayers for the dead. Even that, though, seemed fitting. His father had been such a stickler for such things. It had cheered him to think of his father at St. Peter's gate, wagging his finger and saying, "You see, that's exactly what I've been telling you about."

Mother and Anne stayed on a full week until he assured them he was fine and that he would absolutely not retreat to the country with them. He still had that fire brigade to work with, and felt it his responsibility to carry on now that his father had perished—in some way—for the cause. He'd been filled with a sense of noble sacrifice bidding them farewell, stonily turning from their tear-streaked faces, filled with the haughtiness of a puffed-up patriot who knew the way to salvation was through Great Works of Heroism.

If only…

In the distance, he heard a bell. He should get back for supper and evening prayers. The woods were so pleasant, though. They made him want to stay there, to rest, to find peace…

But he turned and quickened his pace, heading back to the rectory. He was fortunate enough to enjoy all his fellow priests' company. They were a solid group of good men, an elite battalion of intellectual spiritual warriors.

❧

Hello, Jake. Good evening, Al. Warm day, Rob. Does anyone mind if I turn on the fan?

Their friendly voices filled the dining hall as they sat down to eat. First, the grace, then soft murmurs as soup was ladled—soup in this heat, complained Father Robert, but everyone smiled because he among them always managed to say what they were all thinking.

Their talk was like balm, and it refreshed as surely

99

as the soup, the salad—well, at least that's cold, muttered Rob—the bread and the late summer berries for dessert.

By the time dinner was over, he felt calm and ready. Ready to think again of Aunt Beady and whether he should go home.

Instead of joining others in the small study for smokes and talk, he went quietly to his room, pulling the envelope out and straightening it with his hand on the desk before him.

He picked up a pen and found his stationery, but before he could write back to Benson, he heard the chapel bells. Evening prayer. He should go....

He should go....Was this letter a calling to reconciliation, to forgiveness? Should he go home?

When he'd first looked into coming to the States, he'd been filled with the energy and excitement of someone who's finally lit on a plan he knows will be best for everyone. He'd enjoyed seminary, finally going to university as his mother had dreamed of. He'd enjoyed the rigor and discipline of the priesthood. Most of all, he'd enjoyed its quiet, its reverence.

He'd wanted, like many a young priest, to throw himself into missionary work. There was adventure and the possibility for real offerings of body and spirit.

But his mentor, old Father Gregory, had advised against it. "Your heart isn't good. Now, why would we invest all this time in you just to send you somewhere that will tax that heart even more than normal life? No, I'm afraid your sacrifices will have to be more prosaic, my son. But sometimes those are the hardest."

How disheartened he'd been at that news! It had felt as if he were being rejected again by the military—no, worse, as if even the Fire Brigade of the Jesuit order were rejecting him!

But he'd learned something about acceptance since the war, so he'd kept his disappointment to himself and asked eventually if he might apply for a fellowship and teaching position in the States, after reading of the opening in a Jesuit newsletter.

As soon as he'd been accepted, he'd felt ecstatic, eager to tell the world the good news.

The world? No, he'd longed instead just to tell his mother, his sister, his father...even silly Charlotte, now a wife and mother in London.

He'd visited his family's graves then and told them he was leaving. He told them that he probably wouldn't come back, too. That he thought this was the path that called out to him, and he wanted to do God's will.

"I knew I was running away," he whispered to the twilight air.

But he'd believed that, too, was God's will, reward at last for his chronic grief, physically removing him from the island where it had occurred, the "scene of the crime."

His Aunt Beady, it had turned out, was more than eccentric.

Anne had called her "daft," but she'd laughed about it, telling him before they'd left after his father's funeral, that the time Anne spent helping with the farm made up for their aunt's "insanity."

An apt word, Anne, he thought. Aunt Beady was insane, criminally so, it turned out.

Upset that Anne and his mother had left her for a few days, Aunt Beady had plotted her revenge. It had been a simple, but effective plan—to set the house ablaze at night.

They'd died mercifully, he'd learned, from smoke inhalation. Aunt Beady had been sentenced to the sanitarium after being found in the nearby caretaker's shed.

It was actually at that time, he'd learned of Charlotte's infidelities. He'd truly felt like Job, without the nasty skin conditions.

He was utterly alone. The evil of the war had touched him with the thinnest of tentacles, like the almost invisible threads of a jellyfish stinging a hapless victim.

The war ended. The fire brigade no longer needed him. He remembered feeling quite angry about that, tossed to the side like old garbage.

The insurance company, run now by a friend of his father's, was bringing on veterans from the war, who were treated with a respect and admiration he could never have hoped to engender with his lowly at-home service.

He discovered some taxes Mum and Dad had neglected to pay. He sold most of his camera equipment to settle the debt.

The world was changing, and all he'd felt like doing was running backwards to enjoy that which he'd not realized had been so wonderful. Still attracted to high drama, he tried a two-day drunken spree—just like Mrs. Wojehedski's father after her mother's death. An easy therapy. The hangover was so ghastly that it served to keep him away from overindulging from that moment forward.

He'd cleaned himself up and set about living, thinking that perhaps his path would be made clear if he could just put one foot in front of the other long enough. But now all that cynicism he'd tried on as a young rebel fit snugly and became his own skin. Hope vanished from his life. He stayed to himself, not going out, not dating, not looking up old friends returned from war.

Every day he'd walk to the office and pass a little Catholic church. He'd liked to watch one of the nuns shepherding her class of ten-year-olds inside. For some reason, it warmed him to see this, it reminded him there was warmth in the world, and he would stop and watch, enjoying the glow, even though he was unable to feel it shine on him.

One day, the nun turned and looked at him.

Oh, no, she didn't look at me in any welcoming kind of manner at all, Mrs. W. She rather glowered. I suppose she thought I was one of those men up to no good. With lightning speed, she hurried those children into the church.

But that just made him angry. After all, the church was supposed to be a welcoming place, wasn't it? So he'd marched right across the street and flung open that door after the last uniformed lass had crept inside.

He'd hunched in a corner in the shadows, daring someone to cast him out. *Come get me,* he'd snarled inside. *Come, toss me onto the streets like the bum I am.*

He had a plan. As soon as he was tossed out, he'd show them. He had thought about it already, so many times it haunted him, constantly in the back of his mind. No one would miss him. Just a few neat slashes, and rest and peace would be his. Oh, yes, he had a plan. And here, at last, was the "when," which had eluded him each time he'd considered this final option. When should I do it? When they toss me out. Come, toss me out.

But no one did. And he'd sat there for hours, succumbing to angry sobs when the church was empty, finally dozing until the soft thwump of a closing door roused him.

He hadn't been thrown out. He'd been…accepted, with his grief, his bitterness, his anger.

He'd left that church with no clear idea of where he should go, only that burdens were being lifted from his heart.

Now he stared into the glimmering twilight, the letter before him on his desk under the window. A soft knock made him turn. Peter stood there.

"I hope it wasn't bad news," he said, referring to the misdirected letter.

"I'm afraid it was." He told his fellow priest about his aunt's death, sparing him the rest of the tale.

"You should go home. I'm sure Don would let you." Father Don Berringer was the head of their congregation.

"I'm not sure what I could do. I'm her only living relative, after all. No one to comfort, in other words." He smiled uneasily.

"You never know, you never know. It could mean the world to someone. Don't be afraid to ask for the leave. I could take your first classes for you."

"That's kind of you." Now his smile was genuine and heartfelt. Peter meant well, he knew.

"And the visit might do you some good, too. You've been away a long time, right?"

"Nearly two years." He shook his head slowly. "But I'd never intended to return."

"Then maybe this is your chance to really say goodbye." Peter paused. "Sometimes these small things can mean a great deal to someone we don't even know."

CHAPTER SEVEN
Lost

"YOU KNOW, as I think on it some more, I'm not sure it would be very wise, honey," Paula said softly after a long pause. She stared out the car window as Karol drove them home, the air finally cooling now that twilight approached.

She'd gone into town to shop after meeting with Father Al, then called Karol. He'd been in a good mood and suggested they dine out, in town, so she'd mentioned a nice little restaurant near his office and met him there. After a good steak and even better dish of ice cream, he'd revealed the reason for his generosity—he had proposed his mother move in with them. Shocked, Paula had quickly masked her disappointment and heard him out, politely nodding her head. She'd said, "I can understand how you feel. Let me think about it some, sweetheart. Let's take a walk and window shop."

Well, she didn't need time to think about it. She only needed time to think of an alternative. Mrs. Wojehedski would put a strain on their already fragile relationship. Paula was working so hard to make it grow. Mrs. W's critical eye would surely impede any progress. The first time she'd met the woman, Mrs. W. had pointed to Karol's good suit and said, "He won't have money to buy fine things with a wife."

"She's all alone. I don't want her all alone."

"But I was thinking—I wanted to talk to you about

it—that maybe we should be inviting Margaret to stay with us." She never used Sister's real name. But this occasion surely called for the familiar, to remind Karol of her desire to help.

"Marge'll go back to the convent," he said in a tight voice.

"Well, yes, she will. But there's this period of time, you see, where she'll be better but not better enough to go...home. And she's mighty upset at the idea of going to the Mother House, I gather. I think if we offered, she'd snap up the opportunity in an instant."

Oh, it wasn't that Paula relished the idea of having Sister—Margaret—under her roof. She'd not even thought of the idea until this evening as she'd mulled her response to Karol's news. And then she'd thought back on Sister's—Margaret's—questions about the next steps and how upset she'd seemed, and it all fell together in her mind. Margaret's illness was a perverse blessing.

Margaret wouldn't stay forever, she was sure of it. Margaret would be a temporary annoyance, not a permanent burden. Margaret would give Paula time—time to have the baby, time to make Karol love her again.

By his brooding silence, she knew she was on the way to victory. In the car, she waited a little while, as he was pulling onto Old Philadelphia Road and passing the St. Benedict's convent, and then said, "It will only be for a little while. Then we can talk about having your mother stay."

By then, Paula hoped, Karol would be so devoted to her, he'd not want to entertain the idea of having his mother live with them.

✥

"There you are!" Kate breathed a huge sigh of relief, hoping he didn't notice as he approached the small booth near the back of Beck's Tavern, a few blocks from the hospital. She was still new enough to going out again—going out seriously, that is—that she thought it might disappear in a blink.

After a day shift made longer by a tardy afternoon nurse, she'd rushed home to change and had been afraid of not making it back in time. Then, as she'd waited, she'd worried that he wouldn't show up. Oh, because he'd been delayed by a patient, but still... What would she say, how would she act when she saw him the next day?

He'd suggested seven-thirty because he had so many things to do at the hospital. She normally ate much earlier with her mother, usually around five or so.

He grinned and looked down as he approached. Aaron was so timid, she sometimes felt like a tugboat nudging a big ship. She knew he wanted to see her, but was she being too pushy? She felt out of practice.

He'd kissed her at the end of their last get-together, an outing to a concert, music she didn't know and had been intimidated by. She'd enjoyed his explanations, and she'd known that they'd relaxed him. He'd driven them—my, he was a timid driver, too, but Baltimore was still relatively new to him, and he'd confessed to not driving at all in New York—and walked her to her door, held her hands in his and planted the sweetest kiss on her lips, tickling her cheek with his beard.

"I'm sorry I'm late," he said, easing into the seat across from her.

He smiled directly at her, and she was glad she'd changed. She wore a pale green cotton dress, with a light, white sweater draped over her shoulders and big gold earrings and matching necklace her mother had given her last Christmas and she hardly wore at all—only to church every once in a while.

"I never expect a doctor to be on time," she joked. "Burgers are good here. You hungry?"

"Yes, very." He nodded, then reached for a menu, propped against the wall behind the sugar container.

"Burgers, you say?"

"Or pork barbeque, whichever you prefer. Best barbeque north of Charlotte, I've been told." And immediately, she warmed with blush. *Pork – really, Kate?* "I mean, the burgers are really the best. Everybody loves 'em."

The waitress came by and they both placed orders for burgers. She ordered a beer, and he followed suit. She knew he had to head back to the hospital after their dinner – that's why she'd come in to meet him. He had a new admit that he wanted to see this evening when the family visited.

"You look lovely," he said, smiling.

"Why, thank you, kind sir," she joked. They were still in the getting-to-know-you stage, and Kate had determined she'd find out more about his history tonight after someone at the hospital had told her he was divorced. Oh, she didn't hold that against him, but it had made him a rarer creature than he already was. In her circles, people didn't divorce. Catholics didn't, at least. There was still so much to learn about him...and lately, it had been making her afraid. He's Jewish, her mother had said when Kate had told her about him. She knew that didn't mean her mother wouldn't like him. It meant she was telling her daughter that it wouldn't be easy should they become closer. But nothing was easy, was it? Kate had learned that the hard way.

"I took your advice and talked to Sister's superior," he said, leaning in. But even that hadn't helped much, he went on to tell her, outlining the conversation he'd had, before asking if she knew if it were true that Sister wouldn't be assigned back to the Mother House so late in the summer.

"Hmm, I'm not sure. When I was a kid, it did seem we knew when a nun wouldn't be back the next year –

before the school year ended."

"You were taught by them?"

She nodded. "Twelve years. And then I went to nursing school at St. Joseph's and had a few there, too."

"So you know a great deal."

"Yup. But not just from that. I actually thought of being one."

He straightened.

"You can relax," she said, smiling. "It's quite common among Catholic girls. We all dream of wearing the habit one day. It's romantic-looking. And we all dream of being the Little Flower — that's Saint Teresa — being loved through the ages."

"But with you, it was something more?" he prodded.

Their beers arrived — tall, frosty glasses with foam skimming the top. After taking a sip of the malty brew, she answered.

"Yes, I looked into it seriously. I considered it twice, actually. Once when I was in high school and then — well, about five years ago."

His eyebrows shot up. "So recent," he said and then sipped his own beer.

Oh, that was good, Kate, giving him the impression you're not interested in anything but the single life. Best correct that misperception quickly...

"I — I was going through a bad time. My husband was MIA in the war. I found out he was really dead." She remembered how it had appealed to her right after finding out Brian was gone, for sure. Oh, how nice it would have been to lose herself in a white habit, in anonymity. She felt so exposed in the world, so foolish for cherishing the hope he was alive for so long. She had wanted so badly to hide.

She had planned on telling him about Brian, as a

way of getting him to tell her about his marriage. She'd share her story, and surely he'd share his. It was the nice thing to do, and he was very nice hidden behind his passive mask, his dark beard. It was what had attracted her to him. He wasn't like the other doctors — imperious and dismissive.

"Oh. I'm sorry."

"And I thought maybe I should dust off that convent dream. But it's not something you should do to run away from problems. You should be running toward it."

He smiled. "Like everything in life really."

She eagerly agreed. "Yeah. Like everything in life." She felt him relaxing, so she relaxed, too, the tension easing out of her shoulders as she looked into his eyes. They were very dark eyes — a deep, earthy brown. She realized this was the first time they'd had a chance to really look at each other, not just talk. Besides the concert, they'd been to the movies once, and to an art gallery — none of them occasions for deep conversations about their lives.

"So tell me about your life, during the war, after," he began, looking back into her eyes, as if he were realizing the same pleasure as she at this chance to deepen their relationship. She couldn't remember him doing that at the hospital — that kind of straight-on stare. It made her feel giddy, almost light-headed.

And afraid.

"Spoken like a psychiatrist."

He grimaced, and she reached for his hand. "Oh, I'm sorry. I didn't mean to offend…you must get that all the time."

"I don't want you to think my interest is clinical," he said. "I'd really like to know. Tell me about your husband. He was MIA? That's a hard sentence."

"It was like a sentence," she said. "A prison sentence. Waiting and waiting."

"I'm sorry you had to suffer that." His voice was gentle, like warm rain. How good it made her feel, to find someone who understood. She'd not talked about Brian much to anyone beside her mother. So many men hadn't come home, their widows and mothers receiving the news in a cutting blow. At least when Brian had been listed as missing, she'd had hope. Oh, yes, she'd had hope. She looked up again and saw a hesitant eagerness in his eyes, anxious to know more even at the cost of pain.

"He was lost in the Pacific," she said at last, head high, shoulders straight. She'd not suffer again.

"It was fierce fighting there," he said.

"Fierce everywhere is my guess—were you in it?" She said it lightly so he wouldn't be ashamed of admitting to not having served.

"Yes, but often behind the fighting lines, in Europe." He looked down. "I don't like people to think I was in the thick of it when others experienced so much more."

Her heart went out to him. "It didn't matter what you did if you were there, Aaron!"

"But people like your husband, they had to face things every day, quickly, with no time to think."

Inwardly, she smiled. Yes, Aaron would have struggled with the lack of thoughtfulness in war.

Their dinners arrived, but before they dug in, he prodded her again to tell her story. She took a couple of bites and decided to get it over with quickly.

"We were just before he got the call up. He shipped out to the Pacific in '44, was missing in action six months later." She'd been a mere girl, just out of high school, into her nursing studies.

"When did you come to accept he wasn't coming

back?" He wiped a bit of grease from his beard. That small movement startled her. Brian had done that. Oh, not on a beard. His chin. He had a distinctive chin with a dimple in it, and he'd wipe it a lot when they went out for burgers or sandwiches.

"*Come to accept*—I don't know if I'd use that turn of phrase exactly. 'Forced to accept' is more like it. See, after a year went by and the war ended—I started having a different vision. I thought maybe he'd been taken prisoner. So I just moved on to believing in something else. But then he didn't come home with the other prisoners; he wasn't on those lists."

She'd never thought of him as dead. Never dead. Never a lifeless body. No, in a hospital somewhere swaddled in bandages, unable to speak. She'd said Novenas, bought Mass cards, prayed the rosary.

The end of the war—what a time that had been. The whole city one big party. And she'd thought: Bri will come home. Now it's over, he'll be coming home.

"So you were forced to accept it then."

She patted his hand, comforting him. Even he didn't like to think of how foolish she'd been.

"No," she said, "I'm mulishly stubborn. A couple years after the war, I read of some fellow in a hospital in California, burned real bad and unable to talk or use his hands or anything for a long, long time. They didn't know who he was until he fully recovered. And then I heard of some other guys who were hurt so bad—disfigured, you know—that they stayed away from home for a long time."

"And you thought that's what happened to him."

She nodded without looking at him. It seemed so humiliating now, pinning her hopes on all those stories, and selfish, too, to hope that Brian had been so grievously injured. But she couldn't help it. She remembered her ma just looking at her so sad when she showed her the newspaper stories. "Yes, Kate, I guess it's possible," she'd say. "But it's best to let it go." Let him go, was what she'd really been saying.

She'd even had a big fight with her mother after one of these talks. Her own faith had been flagging, and she'd needed her mother to be more enthusiastic about the wild scenarios she was envisioning for Brian. When her mother failed to deliver, Kate had accused her of giving up too soon, suggesting she'd done the same when her father had been in the hospital after an accident that had ultimately claimed his life. How could she have said that to her mother?

"I even thought. . .well, I'd heard a story of a friend of a friend of a friend…." She looked up, shaking her head, her appetite gone now. She put down her burger. "Her husband hadn't come home because he didn't want to be married anymore. He'd taken on a new name in another city. She found out from someone who ran into him."

"You believed your husband had done that, too?" He sounded incredulous.

"Yeah, pretty bad, huh? But I figured if Brian had wanted to move on, I would have told him that was okay. I just wanted to know he was still alive. I just wanted to be…right about him being alive and the army being wrong."

They both lapsed into silence. When she thought of this story now, it was only in snippets, not one long tale. It seemed much sadder as a whole. The little pieces were all noble. The whole added up to something pathetic and miserable.

"It took me five years," she said at last, her voice low. "An old army pal of Brian's came into town — Bob Brody. Big Bob, Bri called him in a letter home. Big Bob was such a cut-up that Brian said he would forget where he was from laughing so hard. Big Bob went through training with Brian, saw combat with him. And he was in town on some sales meeting—he lived in Pennsylvania, had a wife and two kids—and he called me up out of the blue and said he'd like to meet me."

She smiled at the memory, at how happy it had made her feel to hear his voice, this connection to Brian. She'd danced on air all afternoon. Her heart hadn't felt so light since before the war. She'd spent hours deciding what to wear, how to do her hair. It was as if she were going to meet Brian himself.

"I got it in my head that...see, this was just after I'd heard that story about the husband who'd changed his name. So I was kind of thinking about that a lot. And I got it in my head that Big Bob was going to break the news to me—that Brian was living near him and all. That's what I thought. I was sure of it. I felt it in my bones. I even knew what I was going to say to him, how I was going to tell Bob that all I cared about was that Brian was alive. And you know what? I believed I would have said that and meant it, too."

"But that wasn't why he wanted to see you. Did he come on to you?"

"No, no, nothing like that at all. Bob was a gentleman, happily married, just working hard to take care of his family. No, he wanted to see me because..." Even now, it choked her to say it. "Because Brian had died saving Bob's life. At least that was the way Bob saw it. It was some big ambush and Brian had provided cover for Bob and a bunch of guys. Bob says he saw Brian go down and then a big shell blew up the spot where he and a couple other stragglers had been.... Poor Bob. He didn't know Brian had been listed as MIA. He thought I'd been told outright he died."

She looked up at the ceiling, blinking. "I was a blubbering idiot the rest of the meal. I couldn't touch a thing. And he was paying for a nice steak dinner for the two of us, me in my gloves and crinoline and he in a fancy blue suit. Goodness, he must have been embarrassed."

She'd dissolved that evening. She couldn't even remember all of it, so dramatic had been her loss of composure. All that hoping—it had come crashing on her like a crumbling building. No digging out easy from that. The waiter had come by asking if she needed a doctor. And Bob had told him in a big, commanding voice to get her a brandy. Big Bob with the booming voice. She'd sat for another hour, staring straight ahead with a stupid half smile on her face, trying to listen to Bob tell stories about Brian he'd figured she would want to hear. But all she'd wanted to do was run screaming from that restaurant, out into the street, hoping a car would hit her.

Later, she realized she had been right in one aspect—the army *had* made a mistake. Brian hadn't been MIA. He'd definitely been killed. It was a strange but real comfort knowing they'd been wrong.

She'd faced the unpleasant task of getting in touch with Brian's family, asking Bob if he'd mind if she gave Brian's mother Bob's address in case she wanted to write to him. He'd said, sure, sure thing. Anything for Brian McClaren.

CHAPTER EIGHT
Acceptance

"ALL RIGHT, I've told you my story," she said, her voice's brightness covered as if by a scrim. "Now you tell me yours."

"Why do you think I have a story?" His hands clasped the beer glass as if it were a life preserver. He drowned in her gaze. He wanted her so badly. Even more so now that she had shared her tale. Of course Kate would hold out so much hope! How cruel of the army not to tell her the truth. How she must have suffered!

And yet...part of him recoiled from her because of it. He wouldn't have waited so long—five years. He would have accepted the truth, even though it had not been told directly. What kind of fool holds out for so long? But maybe that was because he'd actually been at battle scenes. She hadn't.

She smiled, real cheer in her face now, her composure completely returned. He was lost.

"Oh, let me see. You're maybe forty or thereabouts? A good-looking forty, mind you, but still...you're past the age most men would be married. So either some girl broke your heart or you're just not the marrying kind." She leaned in. "It's about time you told me, Doc. Don't worry. Your secrets are safe with me."

He grinned at her good-natured ribbing. This is

what he loved about her — how she said the obvious, the things other people would whisper about. Why isn't Aaron married? Is he not that way?

"I haven't found the right girl," he said.

"But surely you've found some girls — and maybe thought one or the other was the right one at some time before she broke your heart?"

She touched his hand while she talked, sending an electric shock through his body.

"Well, yes, I suppose..." He looked down. Here was the dark side of her frankness. It required frankness in return.

"Well, mister, I shared with you a whole decade of grief, so I think you can ante up a little of whatever heartache that's passed your way. Was she a nurse, another doctor? Someone you met in school or someone your parents fixed you up with? A sister's friend?"

"No. No, none of those." His mood changed. He didn't like to think about it. His divorce was such a small thing, compared to others' sorrows. And ever since the war, when he'd been forced to see things he couldn't bear to see — soldiers ripped apart both mentally and physically, and then, the evil that had been Nazi Germany — he had stopped looking at things that hurt him. He never listened to German music any longer. He'd been hard-pressed to find that concert to take Kate to, one without a German composer on the bill. But he couldn't bear it. Not after what he'd seen. He found it filled him with too much rage, too much frustration, too much pain. And he, of Teutonic heritage — his parents had emigrated from Austria when he was a boy, too young to remember. It had filled him with self-loathing.

And yet, he had no right to be so hurt. He'd not suffered personally. His suffering was purely empathetic, second-hand. Nothing had been done directly to him.

"Then who was she? Aaron, there had to be at least one special girl. If not, you can now tell me I'm your special one!"

She required honesty.

"I'm divorced," he said simply.

She looked down, suddenly sheepish. "Actually, I have a confession — one of the girls mentioned she heard you were divorced. I'm sorry."

"Don't be. It really wasn't that big a deal."

Her head flew up, her eyes widened. Divorce would be a big deal to her. And, yes, it had been a big deal to him, just eclipsed by the context of so many other bigger deals going on at the time.

"We married quickly," he explained. "Right before I went into the service."

She nodded. She'd understand that part of the tale. But maybe not the part about how unsure he'd been about Sharon, about how she made him feel somewhat lacking, and how surprised he'd been that she'd accepted him, she with her sophistication and beautiful looks, her knowledge of poetry and books and fashion. She'd been the only daughter of another psychiatrist — someone Aaron had worked under while doing graduate research at Bellevue. How small he'd felt in that household. It had seemed the perfect match, and then with the war — who wasn't grabbing quickly to something that would offer comfort? It felt right at the time. But perhaps only then, only in those whirlwind months before he donned the uniform.

"And when I was away — well..."

"A 'Dear John' letter? Oh, Aaron, I'm so sorry."

He looked down, embarrassed, and shook his head. "No, not that. We just hardly wrote at all. She had her own life...."

As he talked about it, he realized how petty it sounded, to have a wife who barely cared to write to her husband in service, but he'd not felt that way at the time. He'd been just as happy not to feel obligated to write her so much after a while. He wrote to his parents. He wrote to some college friends, a colleague or two. Those letters had meaning. But hers — she'd told him of the parties she was attending, the museums she'd visited, the new shows she was seeing, always with the addendum "I wish you were here to enjoy it with me, dear," but hardly ever a comment on anything he'd written to her.

He'd thought at first that their letters were crossing, and she was unable to respond to the stories he'd told her — stories of the mistreatment of Jews, of the death camps, of the irreparable harm done to...their people. He'd wept writing some letters. And only once had she written that it was all too horrible to contemplate, so far away.

So far away — she'd not wanted to identify with these Jews. Oh, at first he hadn't, either. He had told himself, even before the war, that he was more American than Jewish. More American than Austrian, even though his parents had taught him fluent German. He'd never felt he quite fit in anywhere, he with his foreign parents, his shyness.

Why, he hadn't "fit in" in the military either. He'd been relegated to a special unit of men like himself — immigrants or sons of immigrants who spoke German, Polish, French. They'd been trained at Camp Ritchie in Maryland and sent to Europe with special assignments. His had been as a translator of propaganda at first. Then, as they marched farther inland, his medical background prevailed, and he worked exclusively with soldiers and refugees. "Go get Aaron," his commanding officers would say when encountering German-speaking natives.

"Aaron speaks their lingo."

It was easy to tell himself he wouldn't have fit in in Nazi Germany, either, that he would have resisted, rebelled.

He'd told himself it would have never have happened to him. He would have fought back. He wouldn't have gone. But then he'd encountered a middle-aged man, a survivor, who'd felt the need to confide in him that he'd been a selfish rogue before the war, "deflowering" women and leaving them in anguish, extorting money from friends over small indiscretions, bribing officials for favorable treatment. And this man, who knew the darker side of a soul, said that even in the trains on the way to the camps, he fooled himself. He told himself they were going to work camps, nothing more. Who could have contemplated such inhumanity? It was beyond the imagination of decent people, even of bad people. This was evil distilled to its purest form. Thank God they hadn't known what it was before encountering it. How could one live knowing it existed?

"Don't be sorry. Believe it or not, I think I knew we weren't meant to be together shortly before I shipped out. And when I was in Europe, I didn't care to think how I'd face her when I came home."

She studied him, pondering this. At last, after she must have thought she'd comprehended, she said, "The war changed us all. Only some don't like to admit it."

He smiled. She was so kind and sweet now. Had she been less so before? He couldn't imagine. If the war had changed her, it had probably only made her better.

"Was it hard—when you came home? The divorce, I mean."

"It was awkward more than difficult. We tried to pick up where we'd left off, but, well, we hadn't been together that long."

They'd hardly fought. They'd just lived separate lives. He accompanied her to a few functions before begging off entirely. She showed no interest in his work. He felt like a...a patient, one of those put into insulin-induced comas in order to rouse them from schizophrenia. But he wasn't rousing. He was moving, trancelike, through life, inwardly sobbing out his sorrow at all he'd witnessed.

And Sharon — she'd wanted to buy a house in Connecticut, and he'd found himself agreeing...oh, yes, dear, a sunny study sounds wonderful, whatever you think best...mostly because he looked forward to the time alone in their New York apartment. That had been the epiphany. He wanted to be alone, without her. She had represented an entrée into a world where he hadn't fit in, a world that was disappearing. Her father, such a great psychiatrist, was subtly mocked in the articles he read in journals. Not by name, no. But his generation of doctors, they with their talking cures, their desire to meet a patient on common ground. That had begun slipping by in a stream he couldn't stop.

After the war, he realized he'd never fit in, there was no ticket. And if there ever had been, he was past caring about getting it. He'd been filled with despair, so much so that he'd seen a colleague about it and then let him think he'd helped him after it became clear his anger and hurt and fear weren't going away no matter how much he shared his war experiences, his ennui, his disappointment with his life. He'd ultimately decided time was the cure, and he set about passing it.

When he'd told Sharon maybe buying a home together wasn't such a good idea, she'd suggested getting her daddy's help. And he'd said, simply, yes, that was a good idea. That maybe she needed to do things on her own entirely.

She'd tilted her head and narrowed her eyes, absorbing his message. And then she'd nodded, saying, "Yes, I know. I understand. Aaron, I'm so sorry." As if she'd been waiting for him to realize what she'd accepted already.

There had been no rancor. Just sadness. It had been a quiet parting, and she'd even sent him a card when she remarried a scant year later.

"So she wasn't the love of your life?" Kate prodded.

"No, no. Not at all." He laughed softly.

"Hmm, that makes it sound like there *was* one," she teased. "Don't be coy now. Tell me—who was your big love? Did you break her heart?

"No, of course not," he said, still smiling. Normally, he didn't like people prying into his personal life, especially into areas he himself had not visited in years. But Kate made it all so easy, as if nothing was off limits. If only his colleague had made him feel so comfortable!

"Well, tell me the story, Doc. I'm all ears. Or should I ask you to step into my office and lie down on my couch?

His face lit into a grin, and he smiled at that open gaze of hers, one with no guile, no hidden cruelty, only acceptance. She would have made a fine psychiatrist. She wouldn't have needed a couch in her office. Just that smile.

"Well, there was one...." He saw a light dim in her eyes. She had hoped, after all her kidding, that there hadn't been "one true love." Oh, poor Kate. But she insisted on truth. "A girl I met in Europe when I'd done a year abroad...."

It had been in 1935. He'd gone to Austria to study with a disciple of Freud. He'd met Lena in one of the classes. She came from a wealthy family, was unhappy being a rich Jewess waiting for a banker or lawyer to marry her—her family pressed many upon her—and they'd had a romance. She loved poetry and hiking, and she had the darkest eyes and hair. His parents would have adored her. He had felt as comfortable with her as he now felt with Kate. And he realized how alike the two were. Lena had been disarmingly frank, seeing into his heart and saying things others politely avoided. How he'd loved her!

"What happened to her?" Kate whispered, suddenly serious. He could tell she was afraid.

"I don't know."

"Didn't you write to her?"

"Yes, for a time. But then, of course, one couldn't write."

"But after the war—Aaron, did she die in... the camps?"

He shook his head. "I don't know."

"Didn't you try to find out? Didn't you try to find her?" Although she spoke in a hushed tone, it didn't hide her shock. She sounded appalled, and her astonishment awakened his own.

Why hadn't he tried? Because he'd assumed she was gone? No, he'd known it in his heart. The mirror image of Kate. He'd been unable to keep any hope alive. And maybe, too, his hope for Lena had been tied up with his hope for his profession. It all seemed to be dying around him.

How could he explain this to her? She was so optimistic and sunny, so willing to believe the best. Even with her own sorrows, she remained confident in tomorrow's blessings. He'd lost that ability, if he'd ever had it at all.

He couldn't bear to look into the abyss any longer, not after dealing with soldiers who'd liberated camps, after seeing the destruction himself. He couldn't bear it. He knew in his heart she was dead. He'd accepted that. Just as Kate had ultimately accepted her husband's death.

"It was like your Brian," he said, looking up at her, a little anger igniting now. She shouldn't judge him. "She was dead, and I just knew it."

She sat back in the booth so swiftly that it rocked the table.

"Oh, no, you don't. I thought Brian was alive for a long five years after the war. I didn't give up hope until I heard from his buddy Bob. I actually believed he'd come home." Her voice trembled.

His false indignation vanished. What an insensitive boor he was, equating his loss to hers. She'd been married. He and Lena had been lovers, but not married. They'd had an affair, not made a commitment.

"I'm sorry," he said. "You're right. It is different. But—I had married."

"And divorced," she countered. "Right after the war, right?"

"Yes. A few years later."

"So, why didn't you try to find her after that?" she repeated, her voice still tremulous.

She sensed peril in this conversation. He could tell. Should he?

"Lena and I were not husband and wife. She might have moved on after me."

Kate snorted out a questioning laugh. "Aaron, no offense, but after the war she probably had a lot of other stuff to take care of, besides trying to figure out if some old flame might like to hear from her. *You* should have looked for her!"

He studied her. Was she pushing him away—was she afraid to love him?

"Lena is the past," he said.

"If she came walking through that door there—" She pointed to the front of the little tavern. "What would you do?"

"I'd say hello, how have you been?" he responded, trying to capture their earlier more jocular mood.

"No, Aaron, really." She looked down, shaking her head. "You wouldn't say that to someone who'd survived… all that…even someone you didn't know well."

He wanted to leave. He was tired. He had work left to do. A pleasant evening had taken a turn into something painful. He felt—he couldn't help smiling as he realized it—he'd made a particularly relevant discovery after a therapy session. But he was the patient.

"What do you think I should say?" he asked, seeing her as helpful Kate again, as more intuitive and courageous than he in her analysis.

She stared straight in his eyes with that penetrating gaze that would brook nothing but the most brutal honesty.

"I think you would say, 'Lena, I'm so glad you made it. Please, sit down, tell me what happened. Forgive me for not trying to find you.' That would be the compassionate thing, don't you think?"

He swallowed and nodded.

Their waitress came by, asking if they wanted dessert. The break stopped the conversation, and he had to admit to a feeling of relief. Kate ordered a milk shake, and they spent the remainder of their time together talking about Sister's case, with Kate providing what information she could on convent life, what she knew of it.

When he walked her to her car, he kissed her lightly on the cheek and squeezed her arm.

They both knew something had changed between them.

の心や

That night, as he lay in bed, unable to sleep, he kept thinking of Kate's question — what would he have said if Lena had walked through the door.

The compassionate thing — Kate had said it would have been compassionate to ask Lena her story. That had immediately triggered in him a feeling of intense guilt, even embarrassment — the thought of Lena telling a story of survival in front of Kate.

He sat up in bed and turned on the light. He rubbed his face with his hands, trying to wipe clear the slate of his thoughts.

Guilt — why, that was perfectly normal. Survivors' guilt. He, a Jew, had a tinge of it even though he'd not been in the thick of that particular struggle, only experiencing the aftershocks.

And, of course, he also had the burden, as did his parents, of not being able to do more to help relatives and old friends escape. One always wondered if there was something else one could have done, some door one could have knocked on, some letter one could have written.

Yes, that was it.

And the shame would be tied to that particular aspect of the guilt — he was embarrassed over his inability to help, so of course he'd be embarrassed, ashamed, in front of Kate as Lena would tell her story. . .

My goodness, just listen to yourself, assuming Lena is still alive! That Kate, she can make one believe in miracles, can't she?

Thoughts of Kate made him smile. Such a good woman, a loving woman. She should have been the psychiatrist — once again he found himself thinking her skills outshone his own. She had razor sharp inner vision. It was a gift. He thought he had it, too, but it wasn't nearly as well tuned as hers. Then again, his had dulled over the years. He felt its loss keenly. Maybe that, too, was why he was in such doubt about the future of his profession. He doubted his own abilities.

Yes, yes...but there was something more in the conversation about Lena, something else uncomfortable. It wasn't lifting, the way it should once he'd identified its source.

He rose, grabbing his robe, and headed to his kitchen where he placed the teakettle on to boil.

Why did the shame still bother him? The guilt he was able to shrug off as soon as he reminded himself of its origins? But he still felt a sense of embarrassment when thinking of Lena sitting at table, explaining to Kate what had happened to her.... Was it because they were both Jewish? Was that it—he'd be embarrassed by their parochialism, their race? It curdled his stomach to think that. No, no, that wasn't it.

He sat at his own table, closing his eyes, imagining the scene.

Lena, dark hair and pale skin, smooth as cotton, those eyes, just like Kate's, capable of saying so many things and seeing past his ridiculously clumsy attempts to hide what he felt. Lena had known he loved her before he'd admitted it. Lena had known he would go home before he told her. She'd known almost to the day when he'd leave. She'd figured out his heart and obligations before he'd even told himself....

She'd know.

The teakettle's sharp whistle opened his eyes. As he went through the motions of finding a tea bag, pouring water into a cup, waiting for the tea to steep, he recalled their last exchanges.

She'd written that her family was trying to get visas to travel to see relatives in Belgium, but he'd known they had no relatives there. He'd telegraphed her at that news, happy to hear they were trying to get out. He'd offered money for the trip. She'd responded quickly — a letter came within the week — thanking him for his offer but declining. A friend of the family — Herr Rosenblatt — was providing what aid and counsel they needed. She wrote how helpful he was, how friendly, how much her family admired and appreciated him.

Moshe Rosenblatt, a young man Lena's age. He'd met him once. With her description of the man's helpfulness, Aaron had assumed Lena had been telling him her family would expect her to marry Moshe once their escape was arranged.

Aaron had not written her again, sure that she'd been sending him a message that their relationship had no future. He'd been wounded to the core.

He sat at the table, the tea untouched before him.

Why had he assumed that? Why had he not written again?

Well, she didn't write to you again, either, now, did she?

What had Kate said — she probably had other things on her mind?

How could he have been so cold? He hadn't even tried to reach her after that letter. He had assumed she had been done with him. And the polite thing to do was to be done with her, not to expect her to return affection she was no longer free to give…. So he had gone on with his life. He had met Sharon. He had moved on to a new girl, just as she'd moved on to a new man.….

My god, what kind of man was he?

No, what kind of man had he always been?

If Lena had sat down at the table with them, she might have asked that question herself, or a variation:

Why didn't you try anymore to help me, Aaron? Why did you assume the worst about me? Why did you marry a woman you knew you didn't love as much as you'd loved me?

You don't really know who you are until you are tested.

He hung his head, in shame.

❧

"Kate, why are you up?"

Kate's mother appeared in the kitchen, yawning, tying her robe around her waist, hair frazzled and unkempt.

"I couldn't sleep," Kate said, sipping at some hot cocoa she'd made. "You want some?" She held up her mug.

"I can get my own." Her mother went to the stove, looked at the milk-skin in the pot and put it in the sink. She started to wash it, talking over her shoulder.

"You were in early tonight."

"Aaron had work," Kate said.

"You didn't have a lovers' spat, did you?" Her mother put the clean pot on the stove, and went to the icebox for milk. She turned to her daughter when Kate didn't answer, surprised to see tears running down her face.

"No, no spat," she said through tears.

"Oh, Kate." Her mother put the milk down and went to her daughter, hugging her and stroking her hair. "What was it?"

"He…he is in love with somebody else…." She said between sobs.

"Oh, Kate, Kate, sweetie." She knelt down and held her daughter's chin, looking into her eyes. "And he waited until now to tell you? That's not a good man, Kate. You're better off knowing that now. And you knew it might not work out. It's really for the best, honey. Really, it is. You know it is."

She pulled Kate into a hug, patting her on the back.

Kate soaked up the comfort, letting her tears roll. Her mother was right. It would have been a struggle to make something work with Aaron. There hadn't been a future in it. Not really. He'd not convert, and she wouldn't give up her faith.

That made her cry harder. She couldn't help it. She'd hoped— Why couldn't she stop hoping? It was so much easier if you just stopped hoping.

"There, there, Kate, you'll find someone. You're a very special girl, you know. There's somebody out there just for you. "

"I don't know, Mom. I don't know."

"Don't be silly! Of course there is. Someone just for you. Mrs. Bromley has a nephew, you know, who is just getting started with his own appliance store up on Belair Road. He moved here after going to business school. And I need to look at a washing machine.... We'll go see him. It will be a good day, don't you worry, honey."

CHAPTER NINE
Patience

THE NEXT morning, Aaron awoke tired and numb. Without realizing what she'd been doing, Kate had sentenced him to her prison—the waiting and wondering, the hoping. He knew he'd have no peace until he discovered Lena's fate.

He'd told her the truth, dammit. He'd believed in his heart that Lena was dead. Why should she, of all of them, be alive? Why should he be granted this blessing?

Because it's not just for you, you selfish bastard, he thought as he lathered up in the shower. Lena being alive or dead has nothing to do with you. It is an objective fact, one way or the other. The only thing subjective about it is which fate you prefer.

Life. Of course, life.

The thought stopped him, water streaming down his face, through his beard, pooling at his feet. Of course he wanted her to be alive. He wanted all of them to be alive.

He quickly finished washing and dressed. Knotting his tie, he studied himself in the mirror.

Have you always thought this, he asked himself silently. Have you always wondered if she were alive, wanted it to be so? And yet you buried it. It was like burying her. Get past the pain, move on. When had he become so heartless?

And what about Kate? He didn't have to stop seeing her, did he?

He remembered her face freezing in place when he'd revealed his history with Lena. She'd not expected that. She already knew its implications.

Stop being silly, he chided himself. *How can she know its implications if you don't? Just take it one day at a time. Kate and you...you're just beginning to get to know one another. That needn't be cut off.*

❧

His relationship with Kate might not be over, but it had certainly changed. That was apparent when he greeted her at the hospital an hour later. Instead of an open "hello," she smiled shyly, made some polite small talk, and then hurried to her duties.

More worries confronted him when he stepped into his small office before beginning his morning rounds. Dr. Emmett Carroll, a Phipps luminary, stopped in shortly after Aaron had settled in his chair to review files.

"Oh, you're in," he said, standing in the doorway. He was a tall, muscular man of noble good looks—a strong chin, piercing eyes, wavy gray hair. The kind of man people pictured when thinking the phrase "good doctor."

"I was going to talk with you this afternoon. This Sister Francis Marie—she's a candidate for Dr. Freeman. I'd like you to put her on the list."

Aaron's mouth dropped open. He'd been so careful with his notes, so meticulous in making sure each of his patients was safe from the surgeon. He'd even talked with some of their family members yesterday afternoon and last night about the upcoming visit, explaining the procedure in case Freeman tried to railroad them. Oh, he'd been careful and diplomatic, but he was absolutely sure none of them would agree to have their relatives go under Freeman's ice pick.

But Sister—ah, she had no family to speak for her really. Her brother and sister-in-law weren't responsible for her care. The convent was. They'd make the decision. Would they be eager to have this problem child calmed, persuaded by the lobotomy missionary that this was Sister's best chance?

"I have to disagree, Emmett," he said, in as agreeable a tone as he could muster, deliberately using the doctor's first name to telegraph he spoke as an equal colleague. "She's been making remarkable progress." This was hardly true, but he couldn't let them cut the life out of her without him first trying to unravel her puzzle.

"Aaron, she has a history of regression," Dr. Carroll insisted, condescension in his tone. "I've seen her file."

"Only one other hospitalization," Dr. Kaplan said. "Just one."

Dr. Carroll put his hand on the doorjamb and smiled. "She's a suicide attempt. She's only been in here once before, but she's been sent back to her Mother House five times over the years because she couldn't function. I strongly suspect she didn't receive much treatment there beyond an extra 'Hail, Mary' or two. Freeman could help her."

Damn it! Aaron now saw the wisdom of Dr. Remy's scant notes. Aaron himself had added the information on Sister's history to the file, filling in all the blanks that Remy had left. He'd been proud of his thoroughness. Damn.

"We don't know for sure it was a suicide. Her memory is blocked."

Carroll just shook his head. "If you hear hoofbeats…"

Think horses, not zebras, Aaron mentally finished. The mantra for doctors who grabbed for exotic diagnoses. That wasn't what he was doing. The zebra here was the lobotomy.

"A lobotomy wouldn't help her at all, regardless of the suicide attempt," he blurted out. "She wouldn't be able to teach. That's what she does. She's a teacher."

Dr. Carroll narrowed his eyes, his good will gone. "Not much of one, with these episodes. At least she'd be spared the debilitating depression, with Freeman's procedure. I'm sure this last incident must weigh heavily on her mind, just exacerbating her underlying condition. At least after it was done, she'd be stable, and I'm sure she could do something useful at her convent." He shifted his tone, sounding as if he were lecturing a slow student. "These patients sometimes can't be brought to a level on par with you or me, Dr. Kaplan. It's somewhat self-centered to believe they can, don't you think?"

Red-faced with anger and frustration, Aaron couldn't speak for fear of what he'd say. For a fleeting moment, he wished Kate were there. She'd know what to tell him—with the right combination of honesty, indignation and charm. Kate! A nurse! He was the doctor. He had to deal with this. He stood.

"I think Sister Francis Marie is capable of resuming a useful place in society, in her society, that is, a very quiet life to begin with," he said firmly, forcing collegiality back into his tone. "A place that would be denied to her with this procedure. One can't reverse it, after all." He saw Dr. Carroll redden a bit and knew he was now starting to get angry with this upstart's intransigence. Carroll could make life difficult for him, so Aaron forced a smile to his face. "But thank you for the advice."

In his heart, he shouted: "I'll not let you take a single patient and expose him to your torture, your cold, lifeless dissection of what it means to be human—do you hear me? Not a single one. Not as long as blood flows in my veins."

Yes, in his heart.

His mind told him he'd hide Sister in a laundry basket before he'd hand her over to Dr. Freeman. It shook him to feel so filled with purpose. And it scared him, too—would he end up disappointing himself and her?

❧

As Karol hurried his wife to the car that morning, his mind wouldn't settle. Paula had once again mentioned the idea of letting his sister stay with them while she recovered. She seemed so set on the idea that it made him suspicious. And now they were in the middle of a fight about it. Or about something. Margaret might be the subject now, but he always felt their disagreements were one step removed from something that would hurt them both in ways that couldn't be fixed.

"What makes you so damn sure she's going to be released any time soon anyway?" he asked as he held her door. Christ, she was so big now that she had trouble scooting into the seat. She shouldn't be going into town like this. What kind of husband was he to allow her to go in when she was so heavy with child?

"Get out," he said suddenly as she swung her legs inside.

"Wha—" She looked up, confused and afraid. My God, she was a looker. Those big blue eyes, that cloud-soft hair. That had been the end of him.

"You can't be going in when you're so far along. You should be at home. C'mon, Paula. Get out."

"Karol, I'm dressed and ready. I want to go."

"You're huffin' and puffin' every time you walk two steps. You might not care about that baby, but I do." He still held the door open.

Her eyes widened, and he saw tears pooling. Aw, shit.

"How can you say that," she whispered, placing a hand on her stomach. "I love this baby more than life itself. How can you say that?" A tear spilled out and dripped onto her pale blue jumper. Dammit, he felt like a heel.

"I don't mean it that way," he said, the gruffness fading from his voice. "I mean, I—I worry about you. That's all." He gave up and slammed her door for her, hurrying to the driver's side.

When he got in, she was still sniffling and weeping, but she'd taken a handkerchief from her purse and dabbed her eyes. He pulled away from the curb, and conversation ended. At least with each other. In his head, he was saying a million things. He just couldn't latch on to any one phrase long enough to make sense of it.

As he pulled around the corner of Broadway to the hospital, she finally spoke. Not looking at him and sounding defeated, she said softly, "If you want, I won't offer to have Margaret stay with us. You can tell your mother to come. I want to do what's right for you. For us." Then she glanced at him, her face afraid.

Geez, God Almighty. What—did she think he'd hit her? Christ. He wasn't that kind of man. Why was she so—aw, dammit. Dammit to hell.

"Go ahead and find out when Marge is coming home," he said, pulling up in front of the hospital. "We'll take her in. But would you stop with the visiting every day? It's making me..." He stopped, the words blowing away again.

"Worried," she finished for him. "I know." She smiled, placing her gloved hand on his arm and squeezing. She leaned over and kissed him lightly on the cheek. "Thanks for worryin' about me, Karol. It makes me feel..." But she just shook her head and didn't finish, the waterworks starting again.

When she got out of the car, he finished the sentence in his mind. *Loved.* It made her feel loved.

&ce;

Be patient with Karol.

Those had been Rosy's words to Paula, one of the last times she'd spoken with the girl. Paula breathed deeply, staring at herself in the ladies' room after sprinkling cold water on her swollen face and repairing her makeup.

I'm tryin', Rosy. At least he's worryin' about me now.

Sometimes she wished they could just talk about it and be done with it. Talk about ...what? How much they loved each other?

Or how little. Maybe that was why they avoided it. She knew he doubted her. And she wondered if he doubted his own rash declaration now. Maybe there was wisdom in not confronting questions neither of them really knew the answer to.

Because of Rosy, Paula knew Karol's history. He'd been a confident, happy-go-lucky kind of fellow, a take-charge guy who'd made sure they had food enough to eat after their father had died, Bernard had run off, and their mother's poor business sense meant the family store lost customers at an alarming rate. He'd stepped in, Rosy had said, and forced his mother to take chances, buying on credit. He'd also made sure they used some of that inventory to feed themselves, instead of subsisting on stale bread, dented canned goods, and nearly spoiled meat.

He'd been shaken by the war, though, she'd said, in more ways than one. He'd not had a steady girl since he'd gone off to fight. In fact, Paula, in many ways, was his first real relationship since then.

She sighed and forced a smile on her lips. She'd visit Sister, stop by and talk with Father Al again—she'd looked over the pamphlets he'd given her and was eager to get the baptism on the books—and then take the bus home. Maybe she'd stay home tomorrow, to show Karol she was trying to take his advice. It all depended on Father Al and how fast this baptizing could move along.

৵৶৽

Worried about her—of course he worried about her. Karol slammed his fist on the steering wheel as he headed to the gas company. He hated being made to feel like the heavy. He was a good guy, a decent guy. Hell, he took care of her pretty well. She didn't complain for nothing.

Still, he knew what she lacked, and he knew that he hurt her by holding it back. But she'd hurt him, dammit. He was no dummy. He'd known from the outset she'd not been so stuck on him as he'd been on her. And then...

He ran his fingers through his hair. And then what?

137

Things had gotten mixed up. Mixed up real bad with Rosy getting sick and the news about the baby and…

Why wasn't anything easy? In a straight line? Why was it all curved and bent?

Before he'd left for war, Karol had done his best to make sure his life was mapped out all nice and fine. He'd been young, yeah, but he'd had a fiancée, not just a girl. Beautiful Maria Cagliano. Luscious dark hair, a body as good as any pinups—no, better, even—and a willingness to do things with him despite her devout upbringing.

Oh, his ma had clucked her tongue and shaken her head at him going out with an Eye-talian girl. Why not someone from your own neighborhood, she'd asked, as if their street was a little Poland and Maria's the Republic of Foreign. His ma had made him squeamish, too, about the foreign food he'd encounter in Maria's house. *Don't be eating all that red sauce. Not good for your stomach. Too rich. Like blood.*

Like blood. And here she'd make pickled pig's feet and all manner of sausages for him on Sundays.

He hadn't listened to his ma, and he and Maria became as close as man and wife before even tying the knot. She was a fierce lover, with no inhibitions, not a shred of modesty when she was alone with him in his bed—the times he managed to get her there, that is, when both Ma and his sister Rosy were out of the house. Marge had been off to the convent by then.

When he'd enlisted in the navy, she'd cried up a storm, and he'd blurted out: "Marry me, honey. Say you'll marry me and wait for me."

To his surprise, she'd not answered right away. Her tears had stopped, and she'd cocked her head to one side and then smiled. Finally, she'd said, "All right," so softly he'd almost not heard her. He'd bought her a ring the next day.

So, at least he'd gone off to war warm in the knowledge of his Maria's love. Well, what he thought was love. She'd never uttered the word to him. She'd cooed up a mess of Italian in the throes of passion, but hell if he knew if one of them words was "love."

It lasted two years. Two years when letters came infrequently and then not at all, while he poured his heart and soul into letter after letter—four for her every one.

Finally, after a three-month gap in her correspondence, a really rough time for Karol and his ship, too, which made it easy for him to rationalize that her letters simply hadn't gotten through, he received it. Actually, he received more than one letter from home. He opened the one from his sister first.

Dear Karol, By the time you get this, you will have surely heard from Maria by now. At least she returned the ring. She and Johnny Paluzzi are getting married this fall. Do you remember him? He was always kind of sickly, but his parents own a couple stores and they're giving one over to him and Maria as a wedding gift. I hope this news doesn't upset you too much. Maria said she thought you'd have guessed by now anyway, and I do remember you saying in your last letter that she didn't write so much, so I figured you were figuring things out…

Figuring things out? He'd mentioned the lack of letters as a hint for Rosy to check on Maria!

And then the letter from the Bathsheba herself:

Dear Karol, I am heartbroken to tell you this, you are such a sweet man, so good to me, but I do not have the feelings I once possessed, and I cannot in good conscience lead you on to thinking that I am yours. I have given the ring back to your mother…

He'd crumpled the letter, thrown it away. He'd raged inwardly, not sharing the news with anyone, half hoping he'd die a hero. Johnny Paluzzi—yeah, he knew who he was, the skinny coward. Word on the street was his father had pulled strings to get him a 4F. Karol saw men on his ship with the same physique. Jackass Johnny

could have served, could have put his life on the line
instead of skulking at home stealing a fighting man's
girl. Damn him!

Karol fought hard after that, so hard, he'd damaged
his hand—yes, he'd done it, not some Jap winging him.
He'd been overzealous, grabbing a gun turret before it
was cool, burning his hand so badly he could have
gotten a ticket home then and there. But he'd stayed.
What was there to go home to? He wouldn't be seen on
the same continent with that shitass Johnny Paluzzi.
He'd serve his country and show up all the chickenshits
at home.

And when he finally did go back, after the bombs,
after the celebrations, he'd felt personally beaten, sore
and changed, the one constant in his life his anger.

The first thing he'd done after getting off the train,
before he went home to his ma and sister, was walk
down to the Paluzzi market store. And he'd boldly gone
in, watching Maria, heavy with child—obviously not her
first if the two ragamuffins pulling on her hem were
hers—working the cash register, her eyes bright and her
lovely body tired.

When she turned to pick up one of the kids, her gaze
caught his, and, after a moment's pause, she'd smiled at
him. Smiled! As if they were long-lost friends.

Come here, come here, she'd called to him. And then,
"Johnny, look who's home!" As if they'd never been
lovers, never shared intimacy.

His throat tight with irritation, he'd pretended to be
happy for them, shaking Johnny's hand, kidding him
about his war deferment, complimenting their kids. He
didn't say a word to Maria, and before he left, when no
one saw but her, he glowered at her, a look so dark he
was sure she understood. She'd quickly looked away.

He spent the next five years intent on making her
pay for her mistake. While Johnny worked her hard in
his store, Karol went to school and got a good job, an
office job as he studied bookkeeping and finance. The

little he contributed to the family purse left him plenty to save or spend as he desired. He bought a car—the young Paluzzis didn't own a car. He bought an expensive watch—the Paluzzis couldn't afford such luxuries. He took his mother and sister on a trip to Atlantic City—the Paluzzis hadn't even gone on a honeymoon.

Each time, he made sure that Maria heard of his success.

More satisfying than these displays of "what you could have had" was some gossip that came his way. Johnny Paluzzi was cheating on his wife.

Oh, how that stirred his heart. Now she'd know. Now she'd feel what he'd felt.

As luck would have it, he happened to be in a tavern a few weeks after hearing this news when she and Johnny came in. She looked sad and haggard, and he guessed that Johnny had probably urged her to go out with him regardless how tired she'd been.

Made bold by a few drinks, he invited himself to join them in a booth, and there he shared war stories that he'd not even told his mother or sister, horrible tales of lost lives and limbs. When Johnny had had enough, he excused himself to play cards with some fellows at another table, leaving Karol alone with Maria.

It was as if God himself had opened the door.

"You know he's running with Gina Terrabianca," he said over his beer, as casual as day.

When he looked up, he was surprised to see her face flaming and her eyes overflowing. She said nothing. And his anger dissipated into the emotion that had first fueled it—hopeless love, so strong it couldn't stop, so strong that even now he wanted to…

"You deserve so much more, Maria. You deserve…I can give you things he can't give you…he's a jackass, a cheat and a coward…why don't you let me…"

"Let you what?" she seethed. "Let you make me like him—a cheater? I am not that kind of woman."

"You were that kind of woman once!"

"I might not have been the most virtuous woman, but I was never a cheater!" She scooted out of the booth, and he followed, grabbing her arm. "And that man you call a jackass, he is the father of my children. I'll not dishonor him."

He could hardly believe his ears. She was defending him? Something inside him broke. She would stand up for a louse like Johnny but not for the love he'd thought they'd shared.

"Why did you do it—why'd you...?" He couldn't say it. Couldn't ask her why she'd left him.

She gave him the same look she'd given him when he'd proposed—as if she knew something he didn't know or wouldn't recognize.

"You always loved me more than I loved you," she said softly, the anger gone from her voice, as if she was glad to finally talk about this. "And I'd always had a thing for Johnny. He helped my mother once, when she had no money to pay the store. You don't know him at all."

With that, she went looking for her husband.

After that incident, Karol felt he couldn't show his face again in the old neighborhood. He was sure everyone knew of his shame, of being rejected once again by Maria.

He stopped spending money on extravagances and put it into savings. Within two years, he had enough for a down payment on a house. With Rosy's help, he found his little bungalow outside the city, promising both her and his mother he'd be back often. For his mother, it seemed as if he were immigrating, just as she had, to a foreign land.

But he stayed true to his promise and saw them every Sunday, going to church with them at St. Bridget's or letting Rosy sleep over on Saturdays to go to church with him at St. Benedict's.

That's how he met Paula—at St. Benedict's.

Paula, a real southern belle with a face like an angel

and eyes that sparkled when he talked. Paula, who made him forget about his parents' immigrant status, his war experiences, his aching heart. When he met her, his anger disappeared, and his love for Maria was replaced by a tender and somewhat nostalgic pity.

He'd felt whole and alive and worthy.

When Paula had let him into her bed, Karol had thought he'd finally realized his dream—a great girl, his own house, a bright future. And all on New Year's Eve, the very meaning of new beginnings. Just as with Maria, he'd felt old angers disappearing, old resentments fading away. Except this was better than Maria. Paula wasn't like her or him. Her family hadn't come over on a boat a mere quarter century ago. Her family didn't speak a foreign language at home or eat strange foods or feel different.

Her family had been here since, well, since the beginning. Paula Stevens, that had been her maiden name before her widowhood. And she'd married a Wop! She'd already demonstrated the openness of her heart and mind. My God, he'd hit the jackpot with her, yessirree.

But…it was a small thing, really, a tiny thing, probably nothing, probably just his reserve after being hurt by Maria, reading too much into every little gesture, every little look…

When he'd smiled at her and said, "I love you," she'd smiled back in that kind of funny way—the same way Marie had, damn it, when he'd proposed—and she'd said, "Me, too."

And never said it again.

The more he'd thought about it, the more it bothered him. And the more he realized…he could be getting set up for a fall again, something big, another Dear John, except this one face-to-face. He'd started probing her more on her past, and sure enough, he could tell. She'd had a thing for another guy, maybe still did. He thought it was her old boss, but he couldn't be sure.

Naw, he could be sure. The way she talked about him, it wasn't dreamy or anything, it was kind of sad. He knew what that meant. The fellow changes his mind and snaps his fingers, and she'd be back in his arms in an instant.

He stopped seeing her. He wouldn't be going through that again. Stupid of him to think he could have the likes of her. She was in some other guy's league, not his. She probably wised up after marrying the Wop. No foreigners for her. He'd looked up her old boss, he with his pedigree and his country club memberships and his big house in Guilford. Oh, he didn't know all the details. Didn't need to. He knew that the good doc was part of a different crowd. Paula would fit right in there, that's for sure. Not eating kielbasa and pierogi with Wojehedkis.

For all he knew, she'd made fun of him behind his back, probably drinking sherry with her pals from the old neighborhood. That should have tipped him off, too, that apartment of hers in the city up Charles Street. Jeez, he knew what types lived up there. The kinds that owned the companies but didn't work in them.

But then Rosy had gotten sick...and Paula had told him...

He'd felt afflicted with vertigo that week. Rosy dying and Paula pregnant. He'd told Rosy, as she'd lain half asleep in that iron lung, he'd stroked her hair and said, "I'm gonna marry Paula, honey, so you need to get well for the wedding." Rosy had liked Paula an awful lot and had tried to convince him he was wrong about her.

"I'm gonna marry her..." And she was having his kid.

A scintilla of doubt made its way into his mind about the paternity, but he figured if she was having the doc's kid, she'd be getting big money out of him. This terrible cynicism provided comfort.

So they buried Rosy and they married each other.

And every night he came home to his little house and his little wife, and he wondered why wasn't he as happy as he'd thought he'd be.

Why wouldn't she love him as much as he desperately wanted to be loved?

CHAPTER TEN
True love

ANOTHER UNSATISFYING visit with Sister, but now Paula had a reason not to come tomorrow—she'd be obeying Karol. The more she thought about it, the more she liked it. Everything about it. He wanted her to stay home because...he cared about her. He might not say it out loud, but he did. Thank God! She was trying so hard to be a good wife, the one goal she'd ever set for herself.

At least Sister had cheered when Paula had offered their home as a sanctuary when she was released. My goodness, the woman had come alive, sitting up straight, talking about getting permission, how she could do this because of her vows or something. Paula had hardly understood it all. She was glad to have brought Sister—Margaret—some good news, though. She'd brought her a book, too, just a novel she'd enjoyed, a happy story with nothing racy or wrong in it. Maybe that would brighten her spirits, too.

Now, on to Father Al. Paula had given a lot of thought to how to deal with Father Aloysius. She knew he wouldn't stop trying to get at why she didn't want Karol knowing about her baptism. But he was a clever rascal, so he'd probably try to get at the truth some other way, slipping some unexpected question into the conversation so that she'd reveal something she shouldn't. She needed to be on guard. But that didn't mean she needed to be quiet. No, she'd decided the best strategy was to appear—on the surface at least—as if she had nothing at all to hide, as if she wanted to tell him

146

everything.

She settled into her pillowed chair in his office as she had before, and she smiled at him, and he asked if he could smoke, and she said, "why, sure, Father."

He surprised her by being all businesslike and pulling out some more booklets with things about the faith. He went over them with her, and she was a good student. She already knew most of it from her own observations, even if it all hadn't been fully explained to her. Every once in a while, though, she asked a question, just to let him know his efforts weren't going to waste. Half the time, she knew the answers already.

When he was finished with the part on all the sacraments, she thought she might escape with no strategy necessary. She thought she could ask about scheduling the dunking, but was savvy enough to realize she had to handle that in a way that would get the darn thing on the books. The best option—don't ask, just tell him.

"I was thinking, Father, that I'm as ready as I'm gonna be, and with the baby and all, time's a'wastin'. So maybe we could do something simple at our next meeting," she said, making sure to keep her hands on her extended belly as a reminder of the need for haste. "I could come to your home church if you'd prefer to do it there and not here in the hospital chapel. I'll leave that entirely up to you, Father. I know this must be something of an inconvenience."

He raised his eyebrows. "It is no inconvenience. My 'home church' is the chapel at Loyola. But…"

He paused, took a drag of his smoke, looked beyond her to the window, then began slowly, "Mrs. Wojehedski, I would like to say something, and I've been struggling with how to put it without giving offense."

She felt on edge, not liking this interruption to the flow.

"You see, I keep asking myself why a wife wouldn't want her Catholic husband to know she's embracing his faith. I understand you have explained your reasons, but they don't make a lot of sense to this slow-witted priest, I'm afraid." He smiled a little, but she knew it was just to show her he wasn't angry, only confused. "You say you don't want to make a big 'to-do,' but the sacraments are something of a big 'to-do.' That's the point of many of them—to publicly acknowledge the redemptive power of God. The power to change. You seem to understand that, if our conversation is any guide." He stopped and stared at her. His eyes burned right through her. For sure he knew she'd been holding back on him.

"You say your husband will be happy with your conversion. If he will be happy, then it follows that he would consequently be sad that you denied him the opportunity to be present at this event that will make him so happy."

Her face flushed. She fanned herself with her hand, and he bent down to turn on the electric one.

"You don't know Karol," she said, grasping for something to say. "He's a good man. But he's not one for big fusses." This was true. "You'll just have to take my word on that."

He sighed and leaned back, his expression telling her she'd not fixed his struggling problem at all. She was already planning her next move—maybe going to a church down the road or something and starting over with another priest—when he surprised her.

Once again, he fixed her with a stare. She didn't look away because it felt like a test of some kind, whether she could hold his gaze. In a low voice, he said, "I suppose it is an act of great faith that you are taking these steps to be a member of your husband's church. After all, you could have continued saying nothing, and no one would have been the wiser."

He'd come as close as was polite to calling her a liar. She blushed and finally broke his gaze, sucking in her lips. It gave her no pleasure to deceive a good man. She'd told him most of the truth—most of it.

"All right," he said quietly, with a big touch of regret in his voice that hurt her to hear.

"We can schedule it for next week," he said. He pulled a calendar off the desk, put his cigarette down, and wrote something on a page. "What about a week from Friday? I'd be happy to meet you at the Loyola chapel. Bring your witnesses, of course. Is three o'clock suitable?"

She'd make it suitable. Her heart lightened. Her witnesses. She could ask Kate…who else? She'd have to work on that. But now that they were discussing an actual date for the baptism, anything seemed possible. Sure, she would have preferred something earlier, but she wasn't about to argue. She knew he was taking a chance on her, making a leap of faith by not giving her any trouble.

"Yes, that's fine," she said, her voice filled with happiness. "I'll make sure my witnesses can make it." And if they couldn't, they'd drag in a janitor if they had to.

He stubbed out his smoke and relaxed. "All right, Mrs. Wojehedski." But he wasn't done with her. He leaned forward, his hands between his knees, and he bent his head and…started to pray.

"Dear Lord, you have brought your servant Paula to the door of your church. Enter her heart as she enters into communion with you. Help her to be true to the faith and true to those she loves, that they might support her in her lifelong journey to know and love you with her whole heart, her whole mind, and her whole soul."

Be true to those she loved… When he opened his eyes and stared at her, there was no doubt what he was asking of her—to let Karol know she was to be baptized.

❧

As her bus bumped along Pulaski highway, Paula stared out the window wondering what to do. Should she take the chance and confess to Karol, ask him to stand up for her at this baptism? He might be touched by it. He might...love her more.

He'd not uttered the word since their lovemaking on New Year's Eve, the night they'd most likely conceived this child. She knew why. She'd had too much to drink, and she'd been thinking of Jack—my God, her heart had ached for him, had wanted so much to be in his arms, where she had been for nearly ten years. Not always on holidays, though. Not always when she'd wanted him.

So drenched in nostalgia for Jack had she been that she couldn't bring herself to murmur the words back to Karol. Those words had belonged only to Jack for so long that it had still felt like a betrayal to utter them to someone else, even knowing she couldn't have Jack, shouldn't have him.

She'd been at such a low point when she'd met Karol. For the first time in her life, she'd feared for her future. She'd known nothing but comfort at home in Percy. Her father had provided all she'd needed and then some.

When she'd landed in Baltimore with Ginny some ten years before and decided she didn't want to return to tiny, little Percy with its dead-ends and bad memories, she'd been lucky enough to secure a good position as secretary to Dr. John Waterston Wilson, orthopedic surgeon—Jack. He'd paid his staff well, but it was the gifts he'd given her, the things he'd bought for her, the bills he'd insisted on paying for, that had ultimately led to her feeling of being protected from penury. She'd still been so young then, even in her new widowhood, just a girl, really, a girl in her early twenties who'd thought she knew all there was to know about the world and the men who ran it.

✦

John Wilson's office on St. Paul Street had been her last stop for the day, and she was so tired by then that she almost didn't go in. Later, this only added to her sense that her affair with him was meant to be. After all, if some inner voice hadn't urged her on when she was dead tired, wavering, ready to turn back, she might never have met him. She might have packed up and gone back home to Percy, figuring that no new life awaited her in Baltimore.

When she climbed the curving stair in the big old building that housed several orthopedic surgeons' offices, she thought at first that she'd arrived too late and his office was closed. No one was in the cavernous waiting room with its Victorian furniture and marble fireplace. No one was at the secretary's desk set in a large alcove off the waiting room.

"Hello?" she'd called out tentatively, and when no one responded, she'd shrugged and turned, figuring she'd have to try a different list of offices the next day. This office, with its brocade furniture, its ornate moldings, its weathered Persian carpets, was probably too grand for her anyway. Then his voice called after her.

"May I help you?" He'd stood in the doorway of the farthest examining room—the one that doubled as his private office. He was lit from behind by the last golden rays of a late spring day, light pouring from the western window from which you could see the roofs of houses and offices stretching beyond. He had golden hair and a quick, sunny smile that made her feel at ease. And even though he wore a white doctor's coat, she assumed at first that he must be some sort of assistant, because in her experience, doctors were gruffer and less friendly than that.

When she explained why she'd come, he asked her in, and by the time they were finished they'd talked for nearly two hours. Only part of it had been about her qualifications—her typing and stenography skills, her past experience. Most of it had been about the war and life in general. He had a brother who had died just last year.

"In a training accident," he'd told her when she asked. "It's funny but some people don't seem as sympathetic when I tell them it was a training accident and not in battle."

Nodding her head vigorously, she'd told him about Tom, even though she'd taken her wedding band off that very morning. He himself hadn't served, a deferment due to his medical studies, he told her. How he wished he could have joined the cause....

He hired her that day and asked her out for a cocktail that evening. He was shy, or at least pretended to be. "I hope you don't think I'm too forward, but..."

Could I impose upon you to dine with me?

You wouldn't be in the mood for a drive, would you?

Are you too tired to go dancing?

Every invitation was coupled with an apology, as if she were doing him a favor by going out with him. They went to unique restaurants where he enjoyed teaching her about different foods. Calamari at Athenos, cannoli in Little Italy, Peking Duck ("not chop suey, Paula, dear, that's an American dish") at the Mandarin House. Dancing was at smoky jazz clubs, dark and blue. Drives were into the country, a yellow chiffon scarf tied around her neck.

The scarf was a gift from him, the first of many. Diamond earrings. Leather gloves. Even a red dress for New Year's Eve. Later, after they had been lovers for many months, he bought her new furniture for her apartment—a French Provincial boudoir set—and a rug for her living room. She sold all of them when she moved in with Karol. He didn't ask why.

She invited John to her bed late that first summer, on a night when fireworks lit the sky and horns blared in the streets, when the world breathed again at last. V-J Day.

She would have slept with him sooner—after all, it wasn't her practice to hold out for too long—but John was so different from any man she'd known that she was afraid he would think her too cheap if she offered herself too quickly. She was afraid she would be breaking some unspoken rule of etiquette—one shouldn't make love too soon to a wealthy and sophisticated physician, a waiting period of at least three months into the relationship before intimacy is customary.

Dream when you're feelin' blue…

That had been on the radio.

Intimacy with John was not like being with the other men, not even like being with Tom. It was, she decided, what real love must feel like. Satisfying and longing all at once, a perfect balance of pleasure and yearning for more, of appetites sated and expectations whetted.

A conversation with Ginny burst her happiness, three days after Christmas, the first Christmas of peace, when Paula showed Ginny the red dress Jack had given her. The dress flared below the knee and draped sensually down the back. She twirled around imitating a model, pretending to hold a cigarette while Ginny sat on the sofa and didn't smile.

Ginny: Do you think it's appropriate for him to give you a gift like that?

Paula: Like what?

Ginny: So personal. I mean, you're just his secretary.

Paula: He likes me.

Ginny: He's married, you know.

Of course. Of course. Of course she knew—how could it be otherwise? She'd wanted Ginny to go home to Fred so she could throw herself on her bed and cry.

Ginny had come over that day to tell her two pieces of news. First, she thought she was pregnant (this turned out not to be true). And second, Jack was married. Two blows. As happy as she was for her friend, Paula had the same feeling of unfairness, of being left behind, when Ginny told her she was expecting.

Fred was the one who'd told Ginny. When his wife mentioned that Paula was seeing her boss, an orthopedist on St. Paul's Street, Fred had asked who it was. Oh, yes, he knew him. Great reputation at Hopkins. Fantastic surgeon, a terror to interns. But he was married. Fred had been in his office at the hospital when he'd taken a call from his wife. "I tell her not to bother me," Jack had apologized after the call. "She usually doesn't call me at work."

Usually doesn't call at work. That was why Paula didn't know even though she did know. She knew when he told her he couldn't be with her at Christmas because he was on call. She knew when he showed up later that night smelling of brandy and pumpkin pie. She knew when she'd tried to reach him at home and a woman answered, not the maid, a woman who sounded as if she belonged there, as if she owned something.

-- *What are you going to do, Paula? You can't keep seeing him. Will you quit your job?*

-- *Of course not. I have to work. I can't afford...*

-- *I thought you were a gentleman! How could you lie to me? Did you think I wouldn't find out? Beating her fists against his chest.*

-- *It's not a marriage. Not a real marriage. She's...she drinks. I can't leave her right now. She's going to a sanatorium. I'll make her. And then we'll divorce. I was going to tell you. Please, Paula, don't. I love you. Only you. Kiss me, sweetheart. Oh, baby. I want you so.*

Over the next few years, Ginny shared other small tidbits about Jack that she heard through Fred. Rumor was that he'd not received a deferment during the war for his medical training as much as for his influential father, who'd pulled strings to keep him out of harm's way. His father hadn't been so fortunate with his other son, John's brother, who'd run away and enlisted before anyone had known what was up.

Ginny also told her that Jack was in debt, but Paula was able to excuse that, figuring it was his wife who'd run up bills. As to his war service, she found she couldn't ask him about that. She didn't want to get Fred in trouble for sharing these stories with Ginny. She consoled herself by rationalizing that he probably hadn't been aware of his father's machinations.

Oh, the stories she'd told herself! She'd invested in tale after tale, all lies, all put in a bank of falsehoods. She couldn't stop after a while. She was relieved when Ginny and Fred moved to Virginia, and Ginny's revelations ceased.

Being a mistress was another leftover, another hand-me-down. But all that first year, Paula told herself that maybe she couldn't have both love and marriage. Maybe she could only have one. She'd had marriage with Tom, but no love. She'd have love with Jack, but not marriage. She didn't know why she was asked to carry this special burden, but carry it she would. So in this sense, being Jack Wilson's mistress became a noble cause.

Ginny did not approve. They couldn't talk about it, so gradually they talked less and less, and Paula became more and more dependent on Jack for company and friendship. When Ginny had another pregnancy hope dashed, Paula was able to reestablish their friendship by consoling her. But they didn't regain their old level of comfortable intimacy, not as long as Paula stayed with Jack.

If Jack couldn't bring himself to be loyal to his wife, he was loyal to Paula, which made leaving him all the more difficult. In all the years they were together, he didn't stray from Paula, making her believe his protestations about his wife, his reasons for delaying divorce, his desire to be with Paula, his one true love, were real.

Holidays were lonely and quiet. One Thanksgiving she spent with Ginny and Fred, and Fred's family. One Christmas, she went home to North Carolina to see her ailing father. And another Easter, in '54, she went to the shore with Jack, their stolen holiday cut short when news reached her via his answering service that her father had died.

How like her father to beckon her away from earthly pleasures. Even his death seemed a reproach.

She'd stayed in Percy for three weeks sorting out his

things, putting the old house on the market, settling his estate. And here was a shock—he had some debts. He'd started providing medical services to a lot of poor folks for free. And the lack of income had made him late on some payments. The car belonged to the bank. The sale of the house only just covered what was left of the mortgage, with a little to spare. It had been a worrisome time, a dark time. Not once during that time did she talk with Jack. She couldn't call him at home. And the two times she'd tried to reach him at the office, he'd been with patients.

Her unspoken grief over Jack's marital status blended with grief over her father. She lay on her old bed and sobbed every morning and night, bookends to days filled with numbing activity. She could barely bring herself to eat. It was only the relentless claims of duty that forced her to function. She met with an estate manager. She talked with her father's lawyer. She met with the minister and received the condolences of countless friends and patients.

She shouted into the empty house: *Why couldn't you wait until I had a chance to say I was sorry?*

But she knew the answer. Because she wasn't sorry enough. She wasn't sorry for loving Jack, and she wasn't ready to give him up, despite the fact that he was married, with a wife named Emma.

❧

Emma Wilson was a refined woman with straight auburn hair in a neat pageboy. She wore expensive but nondescript clothes. A beige herringbone skirt and white silk blouse, paired with a brown corduroy jacket. And pearls around her neck, extravagant pearls, not the single small strand Jack had given Paula.

"Tell my husband that his son fell riding his bike and I think he broke his arm. I'll take him into the lab."

Jack had a son? Paula scurried to Jack's office where he was examining an elderly woman recovering from a fall that had strained her ankle. Tentatively, she knocked on the door. When he told her to come in, she stepped just in the threshold.

"Your wife is here, Dr. Wilson. With your son. She thinks he might have broken his arm. He's in the lab."

Yes, she said it very calmly, as if in all the time she'd worked for him, she'd not once exchanged more than an impersonal good-morning and good-evening, perhaps not even sharing holiday greetings, perhaps knowing nothing about each other but the lives they led in this office. But she had wanted to brush the files off his desk and hurl accusations at him in front of the old woman who surely admired him, in front of the room of waiting patients who looked on him with supplicant-like devotion.

You bastard! You've slain me now for good, Jack Wilson, not telling me you had a son. That must have taken some conniving! And your wife is no drunk. How could you. How could you break my heart? I thought I knew you. You bastard.

After she went back to her alcove, she heard the examining door open and shut, and saw him hurry to the small lab room off a hidden hallway, a room where they kept drugs and bandages, and used only for patients when the schedule was overflowing.

Ordinarily, Paula would have gone with him to help, to call the hospital and alert them that someone was coming in for an X-ray, or to comfort the hurting child. Instead, she sat at her desk, folded her hands in front of her and inwardly crumbled, shouting a dozen questions at herself, all variations on "what am I to do?"

Leave him.

Leave him leave him leave him. Don't wait.

But in the meantime, she had a job to do. No use making the child suffer. She pushed herself up from the desk and walked with exaggerated serenity, her chin held high, to the lab. She would walk in and ask if the doctor needed any help. She would soothe the child. She would give him a lollipop as they often did with fussy children. How old was he? He'd looked to be about seven. *Seven!* She'd been with Jack for ten years at least— that meant his wife had been carrying the boy when Jack was unfaithful. My god, Jack was a monster!

What kind of father didn't brag up on his child? Even Ginny and Fred hadn't found out this scintillating part of his history. A father. A father silent about his child. She felt sick.

Just focus on the child, the job, the child, the job at hand. Call the hospital. Yes, that was it. She'd probably have to call the radiology department. *A young boy, seven, his name? Wilson. His mother's bringing him by. And his father is Dr. Wilson. Yes, that's right. If you could be so kind.*

Outside the room, her courage faltered. She heard their voices, the camouflaged arguments of adults trying to hide their deeper disagreements from their children by fighting over inconsequential details.

You should have taken him straight to Hopkins.

He wanted his father.

If it's broken – and I think it is – it will have to be x-rayed first.

All right. We'll go there.

Why weren't you watching him?

I was watching him, Jack. I see more than you know.

Emma's voice had broken—*I see more than you know*—and with it, Paula's world collapsed.

She leaned against the wall, closed her eyes, and breathed fast. She couldn't finish the day. What was she thinking? He'd never intended to leave his wife. Not this woman, no drunk at all, a good mother, a good woman, beautiful and kind and sweet, a woman like her but not her, not Paula from a hick town in the South. How many women did he need?

Good lord, but she sank low, barely able to remain standing as it all became clear. She'd been somebody in Percy, a woman of a good family, a child of good fortune with a decent name, upstanding and respected. She'd been the upper class there. Not with Jack. No, he had Emma. Emma with her sharp angles and bright sophistication. Not like Paula, with her curves and backwater charm. Why, she'd let John school her in some things she'd already known—particularly music—because she'd enjoyed playing pupil to his wise mentor. She'd let him think she was low!

Emma was clean, while Paula was....

And sometimes men craved that kind of woman, the kind she'd become.

She pressed her knuckle into her mouth to suppress a sob. *I see more than you know.* Paula had seen but refused to acknowledge it. At least Emma Wilson had the strength of heart to look at the truth. What a pretty little fool Paula must have seemed to him, all decked out in his gifts, a Christmas tree every day of the year, a living, breathing present.

The door opened.

"Paula!" Jack stopped, surprised, staring at her mottled face. "They...I...he needs an X-ray. If you wouldn't mind." He handed her a slip of paper with instructions, and then he rushed away, a dog with its tail between its legs, the most unattractive she'd ever seen him.

How had she not known? Because Jack had a private line in the office. Emma must have reached him on that. Paula had seen it light up sometimes, heard it ring. She'd never thought...she'd not wanted to think...

A few seconds later, Emma Wilson herself appeared.

"My husband said you'd have some aspirin for him—to relieve the pain until it's set?"

Eye to eye, they peered into each other's souls, and she knew Emma could not forgive her. As much as Emma Wilson might be hurt by her husband, she must also believe that a willing woman abetted his worst predispositions. That, without Eve, he would not taste the apple.

"I'm sorry," Paula said, then brushed into the room

to retrieve the pills. "I should have come in earlier." Five minutes became a lifetime. Emma Wilson, Jack, Jr., and Paula stood in the tiny room, barely large enough to hold them all, while the boy swallowed the pills, gagging at first, then getting them down with both women coaxing him.

"A big gulp, honey."

"Pretend you're drinking a soda, Jack."

"Good boy!"

"That's it!"

Paula wanted to embrace Emma, to say she was sorry, to feel a sense of empathetic pain, but as soon as Jack, Jr. was ready, they tore out of the room, Emma calling over her shoulder that they could be at Hopkins in ten minutes. The dutiful employee, Paula hurried to her desk and made the call for them.

Then she put paper in her typewriter and tapped out her resignation. First, she wrote the letter she would not hand in.

Over the past ten years, I have loved you unconditionally. My love was based on a simple premise — that you loved me similarly in return. Without that assurance, I can no longer stay in your presence, neither as your lover, nor as your employee. I loved you...

And then she had to stop because she remembered the note she'd written to Mrs. DiGiacomo when Tom had died, the notes she'd written to herself in Tom's name, and it seemed that all her adult life she'd done nothing but fool herself, that she was the thief who stole her own happiness, not these men, that it was her own childish desires that led to her downfall, not their unscrupulousness.

After she regained control, she typed another letter, and in a few minutes, she handed him a note that merely stated her intention to leave because of personal difficulties, and she requested a good recommendation.

He accepted the letter in silence, yet one more blow to her ego and her heart. She'd prepared herself for an onslaught of protest. When none came, his coldness was all the more stinging. He didn't think she was worth fighting for.

Although she gave him two weeks' notice, she left the next day when she saw his letter of recommendation on her desk. Handwritten, barely legible, it said only that she had worked for him, been a responsible and punctual employee, and he highly recommended her for whatever post she sought. She cleared out her desk, went home and cried.

For five days, she stayed in her apartment, living off canned soup and toast, talking to herself, to her father's ghost, telling him how sorry she'd been, how stupid she'd been, how she wished she could take everything back and do everything over. Then she'd called Ginny and poured out her heart.

It was Ginny who set her on a new path. Ginny, who didn't gloat, who didn't let a breath of "I told you so" enter her tone. Good-hearted Ginny.

"Didn't you tell me about a job as a teacher that interested you?" Ginny reminded her on the phone later, insisting she phone Paula back so Paula wouldn't have to pay for the long-distance call.

"It was something a patient mentioned. I don't even know if it's still open."

A young woman who'd broken her wrist had talked amiably with Paula as Paula had readied the room. Such a problem, having a broken wrist because she played piano. Oh, Paula had said. So do I. My father made me take lessons for years. Never done anything with it, though, beyond playing at a few church services back home.

My children's school is looking for a music teacher. St. Benedict's. Too bad you've already got a job!

When Paula originally had mentioned the conversation to Ginny in a letter it was to show her friend that she really was thinking of moving on with her life, when in fact, she'd had no such thoughts at the time. Now she did. Why shouldn't she try something new? Maybe she needed another fresh start. How many was she allowed?

Sniffling, she promised Ginny she would call and see if the job was still open. And if it wasn't, she'd do what? Return to Percy? With her father gone, there was nothing for her there. Nothing. She would soon be destitute! She'd not moved forward in life at all—toward love, security, position, peace. She'd hurtled backwards instead.

In the morning, she'd called St. Benedict's, and two weeks later, after an interview with the principal of the school and the pastor of the parish, she had the job.

Although she had no qualifications to teach beyond some experience with piano students at her Percy home, the school was desperate for someone to help one of their nuns handle a children's choir and go from class to class giving music instruction. At first, this job didn't appear to offer enough pay—it was only part-time hours. But when Paula mentioned she was leaving a full-time job as a secretary, the principal had told her that was grand. They needed a part-time secretary as well, and she could combine the jobs if Paula was willing to consider it.

At long last, Paula had been in the right place at the right time.

※※

Tired and melancholy, she ambled up the road toward home after getting off the bus. Just as she made it to her street, a pinching cramp stopped her in her tracks. She held her breath and instinctively placed her hand on her stomach.

She waited. She worried. Then settled into a peaceful haze. Her time was getting closer. She'd call the doctor when she got in.

CHAPTER ELEVEN
The first day

AFTER THE conversation with Dr. Carroll, Aaron planned his afternoon session with Sister with meticulous precision. He had a list of questions to ask her, each designed to build on the previous ones' answers, each designed to elicit a memory until the final memory was unlocked—the day of her overdose. He had to believe in something, and he'd hitch his wagon to this—that this nun's problems could be solved if only she'd face hidden truths.

As he strode toward her room that afternoon, he wished he could just say frankly the reason for his zeal: she had to demonstrate forcefully she was not a candidate for Dr. Freeman's monstrous procedure. Oh, yes, he'd do his best to keep her from the man's clutches. But the best way was the truest way—to affect a cure, or to get her on the path to an accommodation with the world. To get her to admit she'd tried to kill herself. He didn't need to be a Catholic to realize the implications of such an act. He knew full well how difficult it would be for someone in Sister's position to own up to that transgression.

Really, all she needed to do was confess and ask for absolution! She should have practice at that.

Despite all his training, all the complexes and neuroses and schizophrenia discussions he'd read, listened to, absorbed, Aaron had come to believe that some patients, like Sister, merely had to find an "accommodation" with the world based on some kind of softening up of the rough edges of their personalities. He didn't believe they needed to be made completely whole or even completely happy. My God, the suffering he'd witnessed in Europe had taught him immediately that some people might never be whole again, through no fault of their own, and no drug or shock or surgical procedure would make it so.

This accommodation, he believed, could only come with an acceptance of the truth of their lives. Without that, they constantly struggled. They fought themselves, creating collateral casualties along the way. They waged war against the past—what they'd done or allowed to be done—a phantom adversary who never came out of the shadows enough for them to clearly confront the beast.

He had come to see his job as something of a private investigator, helping patients find the perpetrators in their past and face them. At least he could hang on to that role, he thought cynically. Drugs wouldn't replace that. Would they?

As he rounded a corner, he found himself glancing in doorways, searching...

He didn't see Kate. Was she avoiding him? Sadness swept through him.

But when he entered the nun's room, a pleasant surprise greeted him. Kate was there, and Sister was sitting in a wheelchair. At least, he assumed it was her. She was in her habit—a voluminous black robe and veil, with coverings around her neck and face. Only the oval of her face showed, and how different it looked to him. A little puffy and flushed. Less youthful.

"Oh, Dr. Kaplan, we were going to go for a walk. For some fresh air," Kate said in her lilting voice. "Sister was able to get dressed, but she's still awfully tired."

The nun turned her face up to Kate and smiled. "But I'm much better, really."

Her voice certainly sounded stronger. He sensed

something had changed. He wasn't sure whether to feel pleased or anxious.

"We can go later, though," Kate said, obviously reading his face. "I know your schedule is tight." She pushed the wheelchair to the side of the bed, close to the chair he usually sat in, and fixed the brakes.

"I'll be back when you're finished," she said to Sister, and then to him, "She has some good news to share."

Gone so quickly, her perfume lingering in the air, teasing him, cutting him. She'd seemed more professional than necessary—no wink in her eye, no sparkle in her voice. He could have been any doctor.

After Kate left, Aaron pulled up his chair and sat down, his previous sense of optimism gone. Kate triggered and deflated it. If she only knew the power she held over him.

He forced his thoughts away from her to Sister.

"What's your good news?" he began.

"My brother's wife—she told me that Karol has an extra bedroom. I can stay there while I recover. When you release me."

He sat back, relieved and a little confused. At least the burden of keeping her away from Dr. Freeman was lifted. All he needed to do was write her discharge papers. He could do it today if she seemed stable enough. And the woman sitting before him certainly looked capable of living peacefully and not doing herself or others any harm. But he distrusted this woman. She was so different from the Sister he'd seen before. She didn't seem…real.

"That's wonderful news, Sister," he said, honestly. "That certainly simplifies things."

"When can I leave?" she pressed. "Tomorrow?"

He smiled, wary. "It's good that you're eager. Why don't we do this—we'll talk today, and then I'll let you know tomorrow about release plans. I'll have to speak with your sister…sister-in-law and brother…and make sure everything is all right."

She nodded her head, her fingers folded neatly in her lap, most of her hands hidden under the hot robes. My God, the woman must be sweltering under all that fabric, he thought to himself. And Kate planned to take her out into the sunny afternoon....

"Have any memories returned—of the day you collapsed?" he asked, already knowing the answer.

"No. I really think that's because of the medicine, though. Nothing else," she said emphatically.

"That might be true," he said slowly. "But it is important to sort it out. You do realize why, right?"

She said nothing.

"We want to make sure it doesn't happen again." He stared in her eyes as he spoke. Her gaze didn't waver. No fear or apprehension showed in her glance. Her look was as placid as a frozen lake.

He sighed. She'd regressed. At the outset of her hospitalization, she'd been self-aware enough to grasp frantically for the explanation of *accidental* overdose. Her forceful embrace of that idea had told him how afraid she'd been of the alternative.

Now, with not a single memory of the incident returning, she'd convinced herself so well that it had been an accident that she no longer feared that it hadn't been.

"All right," he said, feeling defeated before they even began. "Let me ask you some more questions about your father, your family..."

And ten minutes later, he had nothing but the history she'd already given him. He sensed here that she was being honest—she had none of the usual "father complex" issues. She had loved her father, he had loved her, she had accepted his untimely death. Her frankness in discussing him was nothing like her obfuscation when talking about the overdose. Yes, she'd mourned his passing. Yes, she'd resented it for a brief period. Yes, there had been hardship and tension. She'd even told him of the upheavals and fights in the family, all with the appropriate amount of regret and embarrassment. All with normal animation.

Her dreams, too, were nothing out of the ordinary. Easily analyzed anxiety dreams—perfectly natural since she was, after all, anxious about being in the hospital and being released. No great puzzles there, no great clues.

Sweat beaded on his brow. He looked at his notes. Dammit, why wouldn't she just…

"Okay, let's talk about your days in the convent. You had a difficult time of it—"

"What makes you say that?" Her tone sharpened.

Aha—here she was, the Sister hiding from herself. "You were transferred numerous times.…"

"I had a sickly disposition. I…I…can't help that," she said, her voice rising.

So he was getting close to a truth she didn't want to face. Without realizing it, he leaned forward.

"You were to be transferred back to the Mother House—"

"I've already told you you're mistaken on that."

"Let's say, for the sake of argument only, hypothetically, that you were to be transferred back. Is there some reason you'd not want to go? Did you not like it there?" He knew for sure, from a follow-up call to Sister Fulgentia, that she was indeed scheduled to go back, and that the transfer had taken place later than usual because of a delay in getting a replacement.

"No!" she said, growing more agitated. "The Mother House—why, it's beautiful. A lovely retreat. I enjoyed my stays there. I loved my postulancy, novitiate…" She scratched at her face, where taut fabric cut into her cheek.

"Should I ask the nurse to come in and help you with that?" He pointed to her habit.

"No, I'm fine." She placed her hands in her lap, half hidden by the long sleeves. "I'm…tired."

"All right," he said, excited to feel he was getting

somewhere. He'd elicited unease, at least. "Tell me about that, then. You remember your early days?"

"Yes."

"What about your first day?"

She trembled as she sighed. She looked away and swallowed.

"I'm tired," she repeated.

Despite her discomfort, Dr. Kaplan couldn't help feeling his spirits rise. She was evading him again, which meant he was coming closer to some truth she'd rather not share.

"Why don't you get back into bed? I'll help you. Rest awhile. After we're done, you can go outside." He stood and helped her out of the chair, back into the clean bed. She lay down, looking as still as a corpse. "Very good, Sister," he said, encouraging her.

She closed her eyes. Good. She was relaxing.

"Sister," he began softly, trying to light on the truth that would convince her. "If you took too much Phenobarbital accidentally, perhaps it occurred because of a lapse—not remembering how much you had taken. Why did you experience such a lapse? We can't find anything physical that precipitated it. So perhaps there is something that is difficult for you to face that caused you to forget, to overdo."

"Difficult for me to face?" she murmured.

"We all have things that are hard to face," he explained. "There is no shame in it. When we discover what they are, though, we often find…we can go on, we can make decisions, we can think more clearly. You'd like that, wouldn't you?"

She said nothing. She wasn't falling asleep, was she? The room was warm, he was speaking softly….

No, she was allowing him to coax her, as if hypnotized. He'd considered hypnosis but had not yet reached for that therapy. This was just as good. She was being obedient!

"Humor me," he breathed on a sigh, not wanting to

break the mood. "I know nothing about your world. Teach me. What was it like—the first day?"

After a few moments' pause, she began to speak, her voice low and trancelike, her eyes still closed.

CHAPTER TWELVE
Refuge

IT WAS a warm September day, more like summer than fall. I rose early that day, much earlier than usual, much earlier than the days on which I'd gone to Mrs. Mallory's to clean, then on to school. Or the summer days when I'd ridden the trolley to her home and stayed all day. I thought of all those days when I awoke.

On this day, the sky was still gray-blue, and it was too early to tell whether it would be bright or cloudy. In the distance, I heard some trucks rumbling along city streets, and their growling engines and echoing brakes seemed to me the loneliest sound in the world.

I had stayed in bed as long as I could because I didn't want to wake my sister Rosalinde. When I couldn't stand it any longer, I'd crept into the kitchen of our basement apartment, and I'd stared up at the tiny patch of sky visible through the window that hugged the ceiling. I remember thinking that I should be praying, and I said a quick prayer, maybe it was a Hail, Mary. I remember searching the sky and thinking how it looked like a fall sky, despite the temperature. It was washed out, as if it were tired.

My mother must have heard me stirring because she came out soon, hugging her worn cotton wrapper around her body, yawning as she put on the teakettle.

But she didn't say a word about why I was up early or why this was a special day.

Karol came out a little while later, too. But he wasn't there to wish me well. He was opening the store that day and working it himself as mother and Rosalinde took me to the train station.

I was afraid to be afraid, lest it be interpreted as a weakening of my resolve.

I reminded myself of my calling. No longer did I have to wonder what the future would hold. I knew. No longer did I have to be afraid.

We had suffered so much that year after Papa's death. We had nearly starved.

How easy it is to say these things, as if in a dream, in this warm room, with the fans blowing, my future now secure....

Dr. Kaplan interrupts me, his voice melodious.

"What did you say your father died of?"

"Heart attack," I answer.

A heart attack. A broken heart. Bernard had run away from home and my father had died, losing this favorite son. Mother had tried her best, but there wasn't enough. We went without. We got by, but barely. Was it any wonder I was so afraid?

On the morning I left for the convent, I fought a desperate battle with fear, knowing that if I could vanquish it, I would be safe. If I could get to the other side—to the convent itself, to a new routine—I knew I'd be all right. It was the journey that was perilous.

I had worked in the store every day that week, as if working so hard would store up graces that I could use in my travels. I had finished the sewing I needed to do before leaving. Bloomers, slips, knitted hose—I'd checked and rechecked the list the sisters had sent to me. I checked it again on that morning, gently lifting up my neatly folded garments from the cardboard suitcase my mother had bought, second-hand, from a neighbor.

Karol was jealous. He wanted to go "into the world." He wanted to follow Bernard.

"Did that bother you?" Dr. Kaplan interrupts.

Dr. Kaplan is looking for the one thing, I suppose, that bothered me most of all. All right. This isn't unreasonable. But I don't know how to find it. I only know it's not in this story, which he's so eager to hear.

"No. It didn't. I thought it was normal. All boys want to run off somewhere and do something different. I was just afraid he would be unhappy because he couldn't. He had dropped out of school to help in the store after Bernard left."

"Is that why you think he married Paula, because she is something different? You don't seem to like her very much."

"I don't know."

"Go on. With your story. About the first day." I hear him shifting in his seat. It is so warm, and I am so drowsy.

"I had to take a train and I'd never been on a train before. It was exciting but, obviously, also frightening, as all first experiences are. My mother packed me a lunch, the largest lunch she'd ever prepared for me. I remember thinking how odd that was—that she scrimped so much while I was there and now that I was headed off to the convent, she was spoiling me. And the trip was only four hours. She packed a ham sandwich, and boiled eggs, and an apple, and a jar of tea. I didn't want to take the tea."

"Why not?"

"I was afraid I'd spill it."

I remembered how she'd been worried that I would get thirsty on the train. When she'd finally given in, she'd taken the tea out of the sack. "If you get thirsty," she had said, "eat the apple. It is very juicy."

I spent that morning in between. In between wanting to go and wanting to stay, wanting to move on and wanting to remain the same. Most of all I wanted to be at a destination, any destination, whether it was in that basement kitchen, or the moon.

About midmorning, Rosy gave me a gift, very shyly

as if she were afraid I would think her silly. I was sitting on my bed in the room that we shared. It was a dark room with no windows, its only light the glare of a lamp on the table. Rosy, two years younger than me, pulled out a present wrapped in the newspaper's funny pages.

"Here, it's a going-away gift," she said. Her voice sounded choked, and I looked at her face for signs of illness. But health was there at last, pink cheeks in her creamy skin, shiny golden hair, a halo of soft curls around her angelic face. She wore one of my old, plaid school jumpers, and it was too big for her. Her legs looked like scrawny sticks.

Unwrapping the present, I found a wooden statue of St. Francis, his hand cradling a bird, while a squirrel frolicked near his bare feet.

"You won this in the spelling bee! I can't take it," I said.

"No, I want you to have it. And it's something you should be able to keep, right? A statue of a saint." Impulsively, she rushed over to the bed and wrapped her arms around my shoulders. I smelled the strong scent of soap in her hair and the lavender powder I'd given her for her birthday. She was crying. "I'll miss you, Margaret. I wish I could go. I wish I was going."

Rosy was the one person I would miss from my family. She was my confidante, my supporter, my…

I break off, my lips trembling.

"That was very hard for you," Dr. Kaplan says.

"Yes. Very hard." I bite my lip.

Dr. Kaplan says nothing, but waits for me to regain control. At last, the storm passes and I am able to go on.

"She was never well. But that day she was radiant. She would have made a good nun. Far better than I am."

"Does that bother you?" Again, the question.

"No. It makes me sad. That she wasn't able to serve. It seems like such a waste."

"So you were frightened and sad when you left that day?"

173

Skittish, jumping at every sound, seeing portents in every gesture, every event. But this was only natural, as I said, because I was going away from home for the very first time, on a train for the very first time, and I was about to embark on a change that would affect me for the rest of my life. Really, it was only natural. Now, I look back and see how natural it was. But then...then I was afraid, as I said, that my fear would be misinterpreted.

My mother couldn't find her change purse an hour before we left for the train station. This seemed to me at the time hugely significant. I was transfixed by the fear that perhaps God was sending me a sign that I shouldn't go. Perhaps He was deliberately delaying us. I wondered if I would displease Him by going. I wondered if I should cry out to my mother to stop. I worried that if I didn't interpret this sign correctly, I'd be...doing something wrong.

But the purse had been nearby all along, just under my suitcase on the table. And Mother had nearly torn our apartment to pieces looking for it. Rosy was scurrying back and forth asking her where she'd left it last. And I'd sat at the kitchen table the whole time, silently praying, watching it as if it were a play.

When we finally took off for the station, my throat was dry. My mother kept telling me I'd get thirsty without the tea. I started to worry about that, too, about making myself sick. What would happen to me at the convent if I was sick?

This led to a whole new slate of worries. I thought of Rosy. I had always taken care of her when she'd been sick. I worried that mother and Karol wouldn't do it well enough. But every time this worry flitted through my mind, I'd look over at her and be reassured. She was so lively, with good color. Nothing would happen to her. I was sure of it. That thought got me to the station. It gave me a sense of peace which I was sure was grace.

We arrived at the station terribly early, at least an

hour before the train was scheduled to come in. But I'd insisted on taking the early bus there. I remembered a time when the bus was late taking Karol and me to Mrs. Mallory's.

"Mrs. Mallory?" Dr. Kaplan asks.

"I had a job cleaning her house."

"Was Mrs. Mallory ever unkind to you?"

"No." Poor Dr. Kaplan. Searching for villains.

We sat in the large waiting room together, I continue. Mother, Rosy, and me. Huddled on a bench. My mother reached in her change purse and brought out a precious coin. She told me to buy myself a lemonade. I think she was still worried I'd be thirsty. So I took the money to a nearby kiosk and purchased a drink, grateful for the excuse to get up and happy to have something to soothe my dry throat. On the way back to the bench, I looked up and saw my family the way others saw them. Mother in a brown print dress, shiny from too many washes and too many times worn. She sat straight and proud, her hair pulled under a net close on her head, her tight curls indistinguishable from one another. Rosy leaned against her. She was scrawny, undernourished-looking. Her head seemed too large for her slim body, and her jumper was grossly oversized. I realized I was ashamed of them, of us. We were so poor.

We sat in silence for most of the hour with Mother occasionally asking me about the rules. How often could I write home? Once a month. How often could they write to me? As often as they liked. Would I be able to visit? No. Only on the occasion of death—for either a funeral or at the deathbed. Not both. Would they be able to visit? Yes. For the ceremonies where I become a novice and a full nun. After that? I wasn't sure. I didn't think so. No family contact was the Rule.

I shared my lemonade with them and was glad to see Rosy eagerly drinking most of it. Finally, the moment came. It was a relief. Like waiting for death and wanting the waiting to go away even if the end is more fearsome than the waiting itself.

My train was announced, and I shot up, grabbing my suitcase. Mother and Rosy followed. Mother stiffly embraced me. Rosy hugged with more passion, wiping tears from her eyes when she pulled away.

"I'll write you as soon as I get home," she said. "I'll write to you every day."

(And she did write—not every day but nearly every day. I was her diary.)

Mother reminded me to eat the apple if I was thirsty. She swallowed and looked as if she was about to say something, but I was now afraid I'd miss the train, and, yes, I was afraid of what she would say, afraid it would be a hook that pulled me back when I was beginning to break free, that it would be temptation and I would be unable to resist. So I said a hasty goodbye and ran to the stairs.

On the platform below, I was shocked to find no train. Maybe it had come and gone and I'd missed it because of my farewells. For one second, for one harrowing second, a wave of relief flooded over me as I thought about going back upstairs and returning to my family. The train leaving without me—what sign could be clearer?

But the moment passed. The train pulled in with a whoosh of noise and air, and other people started filing down the steps, and my crisis of faith was lost in the jumble of ordinary movement. Some of the people had friends and family with them who were not boarding but merely saying goodbye on the platform. I felt cheated that I hadn't thought of that, that I'd left my family upstairs because I thought that was the rule of the train station. There were so many things we didn't know.

On the train, I sank into a seat by the window, and my fear started to lift. After all, I was on the train and it would take me to where I needed to go. Short of a derailment, nothing would stand in my way.

As we pulled away, my spirits lifted even more. Yes, I still had fears—whether it would seem rude to eat on the train, whether I'd miss my stop, whether I'd find my way to the convent once we arrived at the little Pennsylvania station. But I'd accomplished a great feat already—getting on the train. It gave me the confidence to handle these smaller challenges.

I settled in and watched the city of my birth recede, lampposts and backyards and streets all moving by slowly, as if the engineer were letting me enjoy a last long sip of home, then with more speed until they were memories, images from a postcard.

I was lucky—no one sat next to me, so I had the comfort of isolation. Although I'd brought a book to read—a religious book from Mrs. Mallory's store of them—it sat unopened on my lap for the entire trip. In fact, I was like a statue with my head turned toward the window, eager to see landscapes I'd never experienced. When I noticed no one else was eating on the train, I shoved my lunch into a corner of my suitcase. Hunger was pushed aside by excitement now, and joy. I was on my way—I was doing the right thing—I was on my way. The train's relentless push north sang to me.

Four hours later, I felt like a seasoned traveler. Oh, yes, I still had fears, but I was now able to answer them. What if I missed my stop? I would keep traveling to where God wanted me to go. What if I couldn't find my way to the convent? God would send a stranger to help me.

Once off the train at the tiny station in Pennsylvania, no strangers were about. No one seemed to populate this rural countryside with fields on either side of the road, a wooden fence extending on my right, and empty road before me. The conductor had told me that if I followed the state road north, I couldn't help but find the convent. It would be on my right and clearly marked by a sign on the gate.

Tired but hopeful, I started trudging that way, my

heavy dark shoes crunching into the gravel shoulder, sweat forming on my brow. From time to time, I'd stop underneath a tree and drink in the shade to cool myself. But I was afraid of being late. We were supposed to register by five o'clock that evening, and I had no watch. The train supposedly arrived at three thirty. I didn't know if it was on time or late. I was in a pastoral limbo surrounded by the rolling landscape of Pennsylvania with a dark strip of road beckoning me into the distance.

Later, my hands ached from carrying the heavy suitcase. I had no idea how long I'd been on the road. Maybe I had walked in the wrong direction. Maybe I had misread the sign. Maybe someone had switched it as a prank. I pushed the fear aside and retrieved my earlier sense of mission, summoning it from the depths of my heart like a spell or a curse. Even if I was lost and had to spend a night in one of these fields, I had my packed lunch for sustenance, and the soft air of autumn would keep me warm.

Just as I'd reconciled myself to being lost, I came upon some trees that then gave way to heavy underbrush, and out of a copse of bushes, a tall brick wall began. My heart light, I now increased my pace, knowing that my destination was at hand. Happy, wonderfully happy. That's how I felt. I wanted to cry, I was so happy. I'd passed the first test, and you mustn't underestimate how difficult a test it had been for me, a girl whose sole experience of travel so far had been to a neighborhood a mere three miles from her home, or into downtown Baltimore, the same distance away. The rest of the world was to me as America had been to Columbus. I was always sure the precipice began just beyond the toe of my longest stride. And on this day— this is the day, *haec dies*—I had stepped off the precipice and survived.

At last, the wrought-iron gate opened before me. To its right, embedded in the wall, was a brass plaque. Mount St. Agnes Convent. Sisters of the Blessed Name of

Jesus.

I stepped into the grounds, onto a wide, glistening gravel path. Serenity—that's what that campus embodies. Eden. Trees shaded me. Flowers greeted me on the well-groomed lawn. In the distance was a large, long building, and before it a marble statue of St. Francis—an exact replica of the smaller version Rosy had given me.

I stopped. Put my suitcase down. Fell to my knees. Said a quick prayer of thanks.

I was home at last.

CHAPTER THIRTEEN
Sacrifice

"KATE!" HIS voice first made her happy, followed by a quick reminder of what could not be, a little stabbing pain. She turned from the nurse's station and smiled at him.

"Did it go well? She seemed so much better today," she said, touching him gently on the arm. She smelled a tiny bit of his perspiration mixed with a minty soap. She liked it. It was him, all earthy and clean at the same time. But she had to turn her heart away from such thoughts. He couldn't be hers. The Lena story was a gift, she'd decided, a nudge toward reality.

"Yes, yes," he said. "She spoke for the first time about her first day in the convent. She really opened up. I'm hopeful…"

How good it was to hear him express hope about something. But then he looked down, and she knew what he was thinking—whether it was safe to discharge her.

"She has her sister-in-law's to go to," Kate said slowly.

He looked up at her. "Does that seem odd to you?"

Kate laughed. "Why, look at you, the expert on convents. Yes, it did seem odd. As far as I know, they don't get to live where they choose for any period of time."

"What if I wrote a note, a permission of some kind?"

She shrugged. "You could try it. Maybe call her Mother Superior again and ask. I bet she won't like it, though."

"I could tell her this is what is needed for her care. Not ask permission."

She smiled. He had to think about being imperious, plan it. It didn't come naturally.

"Maybe explain about Dr. Freeman?" she asked, and saw him immediately reject that idea. She didn't blame him. The nuns weren't worldly. They might not comprehend the implications and decide the procedure wasn't such a bad idea. Better not to mention it.

"Here's something," she offered. "She's not taken final vows yet." At his puzzled look, she went on. "They take the veil and then they go into the field to teach. And it's years before they make the actual lifetime commitment—the final vows. Each Order does it differently, but seems to me she should be coming up on that decision soon. Anyway, you could mention that to Sister Fulgentia, that since she's not taken final vows, this leave of absence shouldn't be a problem. Might make you look pretty in-the-know." And then he could be the imperious doctor, too. Sometimes that was necessary.

"Thanks, Kate. That's useful." He paused, and she could tell he didn't want to leave, that he liked talking to her and not just about Sister Francis Marie. She liked it, too.

"Have you… written anyone about Lena yet?" she asked in a near whisper.

"No, no. I was going to do it this evening."

"Don't wait too long, Aaron," she said, a frown dimming her mood. "You know you want to know." With that, she forced herself to say she had to get back to work, and she walked away, not sure what room she was headed for or which patient she should tend to, her eyes blurred by tears.

181

❦

A few minutes after Dr. Kaplan had left Sister's room, the nurse, Kate, came in, sniffling, suggesting they finally go outside. She helped her into the chair again and wheeled her out, the sun making her habit an oven. Already she felt the starch melting on the linen wimple, its flat surface creasing into untidy wrinkles. Her neck itched terribly, and she remembered that it was eczema, caused by the wimple, which had once sent her to the doctor at the first parish she'd been stationed.

Kate said little as she strolled with her, just a few pleasantries about the weather, how it was expected to turn bad soon, that she was glad Sister had a home to go to in order to recover sufficiently.

But all she could think of was the memories Dr. Kaplan had stirred up. Her first day in the convent. Her years of postulancy and novitiate. Peaceful years. Yes, peaceful, but...always afraid. Afraid she'd not measure up. Even though he was no longer around to hear her story, she told it to herself, reliving each moment, turning each one over in her mind, looking for something, whatever it was he'd wanted to find....

❦

Other girls were arriving as I made my way to the door. With growing excitement, I hurried past neatly planted blooms, pink and white flowers encircling a statue of Mary near one tree, the statue of St. Francis near another.

I felt blessed, as if I were walking into heaven. I could barely keep from laughing out loud. It was like a private joke between God and me.

A large black car drove past me up to the front door. As I approached, a woman stepped out and held the door for a girl who appeared to be her daughter. The woman and her daughter walked up the steps to the heavy wooden door which opened before they knocked. A nun shook her head, and the mother reluctantly let her daughter go without even embracing her goodbye. My heart went out to them, and I wanted to rush ahead and tell them it would be all right, that they just needed to go, to take the next step, that the key was taking the next step. The woman went back to the car and got in, but the car didn't drive away. It sat there, as if the occupants were waiting to see if their daughter would change her mind.

Several girls approached the door from the other side of the drive which seemed to lead to another gate farther up the road, beyond my sight. They, too, reached the door before I did and were ushered in the same way—with the door silently opening before they knocked.

And finally, I was there, ready to enter. But I must have come up to the door too quietly, and it didn't open automatically for me. After waiting a few seconds, I raised my hand and knocked.

It swung open immediately. A young nun, her face smooth as ivory and just as pale, pulled me in.

"Come in, come in, child. I didn't hear you! You must be tired. Did you walk from town?" She was tall and her hands were long and bony. Although her skin and eyes were clear, there were dark circles beneath her eyes. She grabbed a notebook from a nearby table.

"Your name?"

"Margaret Wojehedski."

She asked me to spell it, and her handwriting flew across the page, sloping and beautiful, with no extra adorning loops or swirls. She grabbed my suitcase and set it with a pile of bags along the wall of the foyer. As I watched her, I began to take in my surroundings. We stood in a large anteroom that stretched the width of the building. I could see to the back where lush, green fields glistened beyond a terrace. The floor was black-and-white tile set in a diagonal pattern, and against the right wall an enormous wooden staircase wound its way to the upper floors. It was like the vestibule to a palace.

"I am Sister Charles Mary," the nun explained. She

183

gestured to a door to my left, past the mountain of bags. "Go in and have some refreshment. You must be exhausted."

She opened that door for me, as well, and I stepped into a cheerful party, lit by hushed excitement. It was a dining room, not unlike the one at the Mallory household except perhaps twice as large and more spare. An enormous oval table was in the center, with a pressed linen tablecloth on it. Set about its surface were trays of treats—iced cakes, cookies, grapes, bread, and butter. At the end of the table was a huge, silver tea urn. A very old nun sat in front of it, turning its spigot to release the tea for any girl who wanted some.

Already, about fifty girls were gathered there. Later, I learned there were more than eighty in our class. They laughed nervously and talked lowly. Some were dressed as I was—in old school uniforms or obvious second-hand clothing. But others—like the girl I had seen step from the car—were dressed quite well. In fact, I caught sight of that girl. She wore a plain, gray skirt and soft-as-cloud sweater, and a beret topped her shiny, red hair. She was beautiful. I could see why her mother had waited. Who wouldn't want to see such a lovely girl go on to marriage and family?

I followed another girl 'round the table, filling a small plate with cakes and other things. My hunger overcame my timidity, and I piled my plate very high. I assumed this was our evening meal.

It was so crowded that there was no place to sit in the room, so I wandered onto the veranda. It was a glorious day, and now at last I could appreciate it the milk-warm air with its scent of leaves and grass, and the view. The view! I was used to cramped city streets; I was used to being hemmed in by houses and concrete and rows of steps. I was used to hearing bird songs echo, empty and metallic, off walls. Here they flew unfettered through blue mist, and their songs sounded all the happier because of their freedom. I was used to having to look up to see the sky. Here, the heavens stretched above and beyond, filling as much of my vision as the grounds of the convent, which themselves were rolling, graceful fields as far as the eye could see, with only trees and bushes, a cemetery, and gardens in between. If the foyer felt like the entrance to a palace, these fields were its fiefdom, providing the peace that only wealthy isolation can buy.

On the veranda, I ran into the redheaded girl again. She looked so forlorn that I introduced myself and began a conversation. This was normally not my way, but my travel adventure and my happiness had made me bold. I was in the right place. What could go wrong?

"Lillian," she said in response to my question about her name. "Lillian McRowan."

We found two chairs together and sat down.

"I'm from Philadelphia." She nibbled daintily at a small cake, and I felt clumsy and awkward around her. "Our Lady's High School for Girls," she said as if I should know its name. I said nothing, trying to pretend I did know. I wanted to know everything, to fit in, to feel at home.

It did feel like home, more than my own home felt, more than the Mallory household, where I'd felt so secure for a short time.

"My mother was upset," she continued. "She thought she could come in with me."

"We're on our own now," I said. I wanted to comfort her.

"My mother wasn't too happy about...about this." She looked awfully sad. Her chin quivered a little, and she bit her lower lip. I didn't want her to cry. It would spoil the afternoon, the perfect sense of peace I was feeling.

A small hand bell began chiming. Without being told, we knew what to do. We stood and went into the dining room again, placing our plates of half-eaten food and cups of tea on the table.

Sister Charles Mary stood just inside the room. Before her was a small but stocky nun with a glum face. Her mouth seemed permanently turned down at the edges, her eyes were sad, and her flesh pushed over the sides of the wimple, looking uncomfortable.

"Girls, this is Sister Ann, the director of postulants," she said to us.

We stared. She cleared her throat. We responded: "Good afternoon, Sister."

"Sister Ann will guide your first year here until you become a novice. Her office is on the second floor. We'll begin by taking a tour, then we'll show you to your rooms. Then we have chapel and finally we'll meet together again in the refectory downstairs."

She clanged the hand bell again to signal something. Some girls seemed to know what to do. They started lining up, side by side. I ended up next to Lillian. We tramped out into the foyer and up the stairs.

As Sister Ann took us through the classrooms, the chapel, the infirmary, the sewing rooms and kitchen, explaining what our daily routine would be, I kept thinking of how I'd describe everything to Rosy and hoped I wouldn't tire in the attempt.

Routine was a blessing. It allowed our minds to be free and empty for God's word. And after my home life, where we'd struggled so, I enjoyed knowing exactly what each day would bring, what each second would bring. There was never any doubt.

There was never any doubt even from that first day. It became so clear to me, then, that the way to squelch fear was to ensure comfort. My heart leapt when I saw the spacious lawns with their neat gardens, green hills, cropped hedges. I'd loved the outdoors as a girl and hadn't had much chance to enjoy it in a damp city apartment. The classrooms were bright, clean, and airy, with walls painted a muted yellow, the color of daffodils. In fact, everything felt new and quickening, like springtime itself, even though this was the fall of the year.

By the time we reached our rooms, I was giddy with joy. I had the overwhelming desire to fall to my knees and openly thank God in front of all my soon-to-be sisters and wondered if I was being called to that display. But there was too much to do. We were each assigned a curtained cubicle in one of the dormitory-style rooms. Each cubicle was the same—it held a simple cot and a plain, white, three-drawer dresser. We were told to place our undergarments and other things in the drawers and to change into brown gowns that were neatly spread on each cot.

As we all dressed, silence surrounded us. Occasionally a girl would cough. I heard someone say "oh" as if having trouble with her clothes. I had no trouble. I was glad to be rid of my old skirt and blouse, reminders of my poor past. The brown robe seemed rich in comparison, and it didn't carry the stigma of poverty.

A short, white veil was also on the bed, and we weren't told how to place it on our heads. After a moment of panic as I struggled with the strings, I finally managed to secure it and pat my hair under it. I worried that it would look disheveled. Mirrors were gone now.

Finally it was time to follow Sister Ann and Sister Charles Mary to the chapel. Again, my excitement bubbled over, and I could barely contain myself. There was a sense of peace, of beauty in that chapel when it was filled with sisters chanting the Hours that I can feel even now. If you have never heard it, you can't possibly know—how the music seems to come, not from the women, not from something human, but from the rafters, from the rosy windows, the altar, the hidden places in the marble carvings, all revealing their secrets in those notes one after another, primitive and elegant at the same time, that capture the purest form of yearning, the yearning to know and praise God. The melodies lifted and soared and rested. They entranced. Pew after pew was occupied with black-robed figures—the fully-professed sisters in all black, the novices with their white veils, and then we lowly postulants in our humble brown. I felt like a child again, like a child on her first day of school when everything is exciting and I am eager to learn, to absorb it all.

As we filed into our pews in back, I had to force my eyes away from the soaring arches of the church, from the still figures in front of me, from the glistening altar in the distance. The air was cool and damp in here, with just the tinge of incense left in the air, and the unmistakable odor of beeswax, a mellow soothing scent, the consoling scent of religion. It was all I could do to keep from reaching over to the girl next to me and squeezing her hand.

We knelt and opened our psalteries. The chants were familiar, but we were timid. Our mouths barely moved as the psalms floated around us. We breathed as one. I didn't want to leave that chapel. If all my life could be like those first moments there, I would be in paradise.

The service ended. I don't know how long it took. I was oblivious to time passing by then, swept up in these new experiences. Sister Charles Mary led us all back to the main building, into the foyer and down a flight of stairs to a bright, white room. It was the refectory, where all our meals were taken.

When we finally made our way into the cavernous room, I noticed steaming bowls of food were on each table. This must be the other nuns' mealtime, I surmised, still assuming that our earlier treat was to be our evening meal. But Sister Charles Mary led us to tables in the back of the room where a feast awaited us, as well. Bowls of potatoes, cabbage, corn, beans, stewed beef—I'd never seen such a spread, not even at Mrs. Mallory's. I was dumbstruck, which was just as well because the vow of silence, which was imposed if not yet sworn to yet, would have precluded us talking.

After we were all in place, Sister Charles Mary signaled for us to sit down. Way across the room, in the middle of a long head table, was a diminutive nun whose face did not betray her age. She stood and smiled at us.

"Welcome to Mount St. Agnes Mother House," she began. "I am your Mother Superior, Sister Margaret Mary. In honor of your first night, we will have conversation at dinner."

Sister Margaret Mary? Her name was the same as mine. What a glorious sign this was! Why, it was like the touch of God Himself. Tears actually came to my eyes. I wanted so badly to share it all with Rosy and that was the only sadness that shadowed me that day—that she was not there to enjoy it with me.

Voices began to murmur in the echoing room as sisters passed food to one another. Sister Charles Mary explained to us that it was customary to take more of a food one did not like. I noticed she placed an inordinate amount of cabbage on her own plate.

I had no such special tastes. After years of deprivation, everything was good to me, and I could hardly believe we were being fed again in such sumptuous style after the food of the afternoon.

I ate heartily and felt as if I were at a party—we were given permission to chat after grace was said. I talked more freely than I'd ever done before, asking questions of my table mates about their families, their origins. I was everything I'd never been before—outgoing, friendly, self-confident.

To my surprise, we were even fed dessert—a vanilla custard topped with a cherry. I was so full by the time we were led to our beds that I thought I'd be sick and embarrass myself.

Once in our curtained cubicles, we were told to say our prayers, and then we'd have a quarter hour before the lights were turned out. I hastily murmured thanks to God for the blessings of this convent. The words were a jumble, tumbling over one another, barely coherent. But I promised God I'd be more articulate in the morning.

First I had to write to Rosy in my remaining minutes.

I pulled out pen and paper from my top drawer and hastily scrawled a letter filled with exuberant impressions of my first day.

I'd filled three pages, and my hand was starting to cramp when I heard a noise from the doorway. Sister Anne was making an announcement.

"I'm sorry to disturb you, sisters," she said in her gentle voice. "But I must collect your personal things now."

Personal things? The letter from the Mother House had specifically said not to bring personal items, mementos from home, photographs, anything other than what we were told to bring. I was surprised to hear the sound of objects being dropped into a box. What foolish girls, I thought. Had they imagined they'd be able to get away with keeping a trinket or a souvenir from home? Now I felt pride in my poverty. We had no money for such extravagances.

I continued writing my letter as the box was taken around the room. When Sister Anne reached my cubicle, I smiled up at her from my perch on my bed, fully expecting her to move on quickly to the next new postulant. Instead she stared at me as if waiting for me to respond.

"Good night, sister," I said, thinking that was what was expected of me. Then I noticed her frown and followed her gaze to the top of the chest of drawers. There was Rosy's statue of St. Francis, her parting gift to me. Sister Anne was looking at it.

"All personal items must be given up," she said.

Even though it was a religious symbol, I still had to sacrifice it. Mortified, I placed it in the box and noticed that the objects it joined there were not frilly handkerchiefs or nostalgic photographs. There was a pearl rosary and an embossed prayer book. A gold crucifix on a chain and a Holy Card. A few books...

That was the true beginning of my postulancy,

giving up Rosy's gift.

❧

Back in Sister's room, Kate helped her out of the habit. The nurse was concerned about a rash on her face and how flushed she looked. Kate helped her don the hospital gown, then noticed a few purple spots on her right arm.

"What are these?" she asked. "It looks to be part of the rash."

No, just old scars. She used to prick herself to stay awake during meditations, only stopping the practice when a director at the Mother House suggested such a mutilation would be grounds for dismissal.

"You can have this," Sister said, handing Kate the novel Paula had left. They couldn't read books, except spiritual ones. A rule many sisters broke, but not her. She'd stayed true.

"Why, thank you!" She reached for it and smiled. "You take a nap now, Sister. You're doing very well. Father Al is coming by this afternoon to say the rosary with you—I thought you'd like that."

Sister's spirits lifted. Yes, she'd like that very much.

❧

Hours later, she awoke, drank some water and waited, rosary in her hand. In the hallway, she heard the hum and rattle of the hospital, carts moving down hallways, nurses murmuring to each other. From the jumble, she picked out this thread

"I'm so glad you could come by." Kate's voice.

"I'm happy to." The priest who gave her Communion in the mornings.

"Did you ever talk to Mrs. Wojehedski? Hope you don't mind me asking."

"Yes, we've spoken several times. I've scheduled her baptism."

"Aw, that's so nice. I know she wanted to surprise her husband...."

❧

That evening, Aaron called his parents. How would one go about finding a refugee from the camps? They wanted to know why. He made up a story, told them it was for a patient. Not a complete lie. He was the patient.

They gave him some phone numbers, some addresses—refugee organizations, Israeli groups, some people from their synagogue who'd conducted successful searches. Well, successful in the sense that they'd learned a loved one's fate, even if the fate itself was bad news.

They asked him who the patient was looking for. He described Lena—they'd never known of her. He'd kept their affair to himself.

"Oh, a girl like that—she'd probably have gone to Israel if she survived," his mother had said when he told her about her feisty nature. "Here, call this woman..." And she gave him another name, a doctor—a pediatrician who'd moved from Baltimore to Israel to work with orphaned children. "She comes home regularly. You can reach her at her mother's sometimes. Rachel Guildenstern."

Later, after making several sometimes frustrating calls to the numbers he'd been given, he sat down and tried Rachel Guildenstern.

"She's not here; can I take a message?" a woman said.

"No, no, that's all right." He was ready to give up. A strange ember started to glow. If he gave up the search...he'd start over with Kate. Or go on as before with her....

"Are you calling to try to find someone?" she asked "I can take the message. I'm her mother."

He smiled, wondering how many calls this Rachel received.

"Yes, I was." He proceeded to tell her about Lena, about himself, and this Rachel's mother was so well-trained that she asked some vital questions along the way, clearly writing down all his answers, hurriedly asking for his phone number, other contact information, when he was finished with his story.

"I'll tell her. She's in town now, just out tonight. If she finds anything for you, she'll give you a call."

He slept well that night, and he dreamed of Kate, an erotic fantasy that quickly shifted to a bittersweet parting. She was standing on a dock, crying as his boat pulled away. Instead of farewell, she kept saying: This is the day.

He didn't need a degree in psychiatry to interpret that scene.

CHAPTER FOURTEEN
Setback

IN THE morning, Sister was roused by movement at the door. There was Paula, impeccably dressed as usual and obscenely large with child. Her blue maternity top over black skirt did nothing to conceal her grotesquely protruding belly. At her ears were mother-of-pearl discs. At her throat, a pearl necklace. And on her swollen feet, white pumps. Sister noticed it all. And she remembered the overheard conversation of the day before. Paula was not Catholic. Sister had suspected it but now knew. What else had she lied to Karol about?

"Good morning," Paula said, almost as cheerfully as the nurse who'd just left. "I know I said I might not be by today, but I'm stopping in on a quick visit to my doctor."

Paula went to the wardrobe and grabbed Sister's robe. "Kate says she took you out once already, and I could help you get ready for another stroll!"

Her eyes immediately focused on the robe in Paula's arms. Scrunching it up like that would wrinkle it. It should flow smoothly, with no indication of pressing or folding, no sign that anything as earthly as ironing or storage had taken place. She never should have let Paula handle it in the first place.

Oh, yes, she remembered—Paula had taken it home the other day to wash it. The thought of Paula's impure hands on her habit made her wince. If Paula had just left the habit in the hospital, Margaret could have dressed herself the other day, without the nurse's help. She could have risen with the dawn and said her morning prayers, then dressed and knelt devoutly when the chaplain came around with Communion.

"Karol sends his love," Paula said as she brought the habit to the bed. "Do you think you can wash up by yourself, or do you need help with that? I thought doing this in the cool of the mornin' would be best."

"I'd do it on my own."

"Okay. Do you need help getting up and ...going to the bathroom?" Paula touched her arm. She almost recoiled but then allowed her sister-in-law's contact as a penance, offering it up, saying a wordless prayer. Maybe this would wipe out the sin of allowing her habit to be taken from her.

For an awkward moment, nothing happened. Then she realized Paula wouldn't go away until she got out of bed and started preparing for the walk. So she swung her body slowly to the edge of the bed and stood. She was still tired enough that she needed Paula's steady hand on her arm to guide her first to the bathroom, and then to the wash basin and mirror in the corner of the room.

The mirror. Again, a mirror. She'd avoided it when Kate had helped dress her. But with Paula here…

The winter morning she'd heard the news that Rosy had fallen ill, she'd caught a glimpse of her own reflection in a shiny copper bowl of daffodils in the convent parlor.

One event seemed to follow the other. She sinned. Rosalinde fell ill.

And then, the morning of the funeral—she'd looked again, in the bathroom mirror.

What did it matter? She was already sinning— without her habit, in a city where her family resided, breaking other Rules. She'd talked during Grand Silence the night before when a nurse had come in the room. She'd even forgotten it was time for Grand Silence.

At the washbasin, she sucked in her lips and stared at the sink. Leaning on its porcelain surface, she half listened as Paula offered cheering encouragement. Paula grabbed the bar of soap and turned on the water. She lathered up a washcloth, but when she offered to wash Sister's face, she took the cloth and began the process herself.

She looked in the mirror with grim determination.

Time did not stop. Instead, the action was seamless, with nothing marking it. She just stared in the mirror. A stranger looked back—a white-faced unkempt woman with reddish skin along her right jaw like a sunburn, some of it exploding into a weeping sore. Her hair was dull brown, spiky tufts protruding this way and that, making her look like the madwoman they thought she was. Her lips were almost the color of her skin; dark circles accented her eyes, eyes that were watery and blurred; her neck was scrawny, and dark creases along the side of her mouth told the tale of too many frowns.

And yet—and yet she saw the shadows of her former self there. High cheekbones, well-shaped nose, and eyes that sparkled like brown marbles when not clouded by illness, stray strands of hair that glowed reddish-gold. In a flash, she saw beyond the mirror to a deeper truth, that she had once been beautiful and hadn't known it, or had refused to believe it.

Paula's reflection appeared beyond hers.

"It will grow back," Paula said. Then, she laughed nervously. "Not that it matters. Under the veil."

She splashed water on her face and brushed her teeth. After drying herself, she turned to see Paula holding out a slip made of coarse black cotton. She took it from her and let it glide over her shoulders, then undid the hospital gown and slid it to the floor. Stepping out of it, she bent and picked it up, folding it neatly before placing it by the washbasin.

"We'll take a short stroll," Paula said. She handed Sister the white, starched wimple. "It's a beautiful day."

Sister pulled the wimple over her head and felt it cut into her cheeks. Where it squeezed against the rash, it hurt so sharply, she shivered.

"Then you can rest."

Be still, be still. Putting on the habit required silence and devotion. It was an act of self-diminishment, not a mere part of one's morning toilette. Sister reached behind her neck to tie the wimple, but Paula took the strings and pulled them for her.

"Kate says that fifteen minutes would be good." As she tied the strands, Paula's sharp nails accidentally scraped Sister's neck.

Clumsy woman. Full of her own preoccupations. And not even Catholic — hiding it from Karol!

"It's bright and warm this morning. Perfect weather for a short walk." As Paula tugged at the top ties, Sister winced. Her cheek felt on fire.

Too tight. Is she deliberately trying to hurt me? Is she...evil? Am I being called to resist? Is this a trial sent by God?

"I hope I'm doing this right," Paula said. "Tell me if I'm not."

As Paula knotted a last tie, Sister felt the wimple cut and gag her under her chin. She felt a dampness on her cheek. A sore must have opened.

She could bear it no longer. Surely God didn't expect her to die like this, strangled at the hands of a fool. "You're hurting me!" She yanked the ties from Paula's hands and whirled away from her, back to the bed.

"You've knotted them. You're not supposed to knot them." Tears fell from her eyes, making her even angrier. Why was Paula there? Where was Sister Fulgentia? Or Karol—Karol wouldn't have tied the knots. He'd have asked a nurse to do it. Or Rosy! If Rosy had been alive, she'd have been gentle. What was Paula thinking—

knotting them so Sister couldn't undo them? Foolish, silly woman. Not even a Catholic. If Karol knew... She shivered

"Stay away," Sister told her as Paula approached to help. "I'll do it myself." Yanking on the ties, one broke. "Now it's hopeless." The strand lay in her upturned palm. "I can't do it now."

Overcome with sudden fatigue, she couldn't move another muscle. Looking in the mirror had been a mistake. Where was Dr. Kaplan? Maybe he had been wrong. A walk was too much to do each day. She'd done one yesterday. That should be enough. She'd collapse, and then what?

Didn't anyone care about her? Sister Fulgentia hadn't cared. She'd made her go back to work when she was ill. She'd made it all worse. Perhaps the rash wouldn't have appeared if she'd been allowed to rest in the convent, just an extra day or two. Yes, she remembered. She'd been ill after Rosy's funeral and Sister Fulgentia had not been pleased. The day of Rosy's funeral—Sister Fulgentia had been angry then, too, telling her she'd spent too much time away. She had the right! She had the right to go the funeral.

She pulled her knees up on the bed and leaned on her side, the wimple half off, the sheath still on. When Paula came near, Sister rolled over. "I feel dizzy. I can't breathe." She couldn't fill her lungs. It was the wimple— even with the torn string, it was still too tight. It was choking her. Paula had tried to choke her. She clawed at the wimple, but it would not come loose. She groaned. Paula had done this to her.

"Here, let me..." Paula reached for the wimple's ties, but Sister's arm flew into the air and knocked Paula away, almost making her fall.

"No! Leave me alone! Leave me alone!" Her voice rasped into the room, sounding as if it had come from another being. Her tears streamed, dampening the wimple and making it tighter. Sobbing, clutching at the sheets, she buried her face in the pillow where darkness comforted her.

"Nurse!" Paula was calling from across the room. Soon one came in. Sister recognized her voice. It was Kate, asking Paula what was wrong.

"She became...she hit me," Paula said in a funny, trembling voice.

"You better leave. Here, I'll help you."

"I...I'm seeing my doctor anyway..."

Another woman's voice. "Do you need help?"

"Call Dr. Kaplan. Tell him Sister Francis Marie lost control."

"There's a standing order for..."

"Get some."

In a few seconds, a steel-cold pinprick pushed something into her body that uncoiled her breath and transported her three feet above the bed where peace resided. Paula was gone. Voices murmured. Someone removed the wimple and pulled the slip over her head, replacing it with a fresh hospital gown.

A man's voice came from below. They all talked. He said: "Sister, you've had some trouble, I understand." He shouted it at her from very far away, down below her cloud of peace. She merely smiled, then laughed at him. He patted her arm. "I'll come by later and we'll talk."

≪≫

He stood by the nurse's station, carefully folding the discharge papers he'd started to fill out just that morning. She wasn't ready. Dammit, maybe a drug would be better than this. Maybe he was useless, he with his questions and clever plans. Maybe Dr. Carroll was right about how self-centered this all was. He wanted to help Sister so that *he* would feel better about himself and about his profession.

Kate appeared by his side. She placed her hand over his, quietly, secretly. He held his breath.

"Don't worry, Aaron. I know you'll help her. She'll be well enough soon."

He couldn't look at her. He was afraid if he did, he'd break her spell—her confidence in him, her closeness, her...love? How he needed that—like an addict, he counted on it, now more than ever.

"She's..." He did look up. There were Kate's blazing blue eyes, startling him into action. "Dr. Freeman's visit is next week, Kate. Next week. She won't be ready to go home." His voice carried his despair. Despite his inner bravado, he had no idea how to save her from the man's clutches. He'd risk his career if he let her go too soon and she had another incident like this one, possibly hurting someone or herself. How could he do that to her family?

She squeezed his hand. "You'll think of something. You still have time."

Time. Not much of it. A few days. And what solution would come that hadn't already presented itself? The issue wasn't just Sister. He should stand up to Dr. Carroll, to them all. Not just for Sister but for the others. He was a coward. Oh, yes, he'd told himself he would. He'd started writing notes. He'd made preparations. But in the end, he'd not followed through.

"I don't know what to do," he murmured, just as much to himself as to Kate.

"Have you talked with her Mother Superior yet, about the discharge idea?"

"No."

"Why not start there? Get it all set up." She paused, sliding her hand away. He immediately felt its absence. "Do you want me to do it?"

Good Kate.

"It's my responsibility," he said.

"Of course it is! But I'm a Catholic. I think I'd know how to approach it.... Listen, Aaron, you'd not be putting it off, I mean, making it easy for yourself by letting me do it."

So she knew what he was struggling with—his lack of fortitude. When he didn't respond right away, she continued. "Look, she might just have had a bad morning. That's all. It's just a little setback. Let me call her Mother Superior and keep her discharge plan moving forward, at least."

A setback. He looked at Kate's pleading eyes. She didn't want Sister hurt any more than he did. He might not believe in himself, but he'd believe in Kate.

"All right. Tell her…tell her we expect Sister to be discharged within a week. She can't go to the convent—they can't care for her there. She can't go to Glendale—same thing." He grew in forcefulness as he spoke. "And she can't wear the habit. Not until we clear up the skin condition. We'll keep her informed, of course. As often as she'd like."

Kate nodded. "I'll do it today."

❧

In the white room, during the white part of the day, the white angel of mercy visited Margaret once more. Morning was gone. It was now bright afternoon, the shades open high, letting in the glorious light and a teasing breeze—it was sinful to stay in this cell.

"It's too beautiful to stay inside today," Nurse Kate said, snatching the thought from Margaret's mind. "My shift ends soon, and I wanted to help you get up."

Margaret's mouth was dry, and her head ached, but she didn't want to disobey. Wordlessly, she began to climb out of bed.

"Wait! Let me help you." Kate came over and put her strong arms under Margaret's. She positioned her upright and held her elbow while Margaret walked to the window.

"See? Isn't it gorgeous? I can get a wheelchair again and take you out." Kate turned and picked up some items she'd left on the foot of the bed—clothing.

"Dr. Kaplan says you're not to wear the habit until we get that rash under control. I found a few things for you in a bin we keep for patients." She snapped the wrinkles out of a gray skirt. "This should fit."

Gray skirt. White cotton blouse. She felt like a

201

schoolgirl. She still wore her black shoes, though, and insisted on holding her rosary. Within moments, Kate had her ready, seated in a wheelchair.

"I'm sorry if I upset things," Margaret said as Kate wheeled her through hallways filled with the scents of healing and decay—antiseptic, pine cleaner and soiled bedding. She heard patients moaning, nurses talking loudly as if they were coaxing children to do what they didn't want to do, trays being wheeled in and out, a telephone ringing, soft whispers in the background. She seemed to notice all these things more without the habit muffling the world.

"You just need to rest and get better," Kate said. "And talk with Dr. Kaplan. He can help you. You shouldn't feel...shy...about talking to him, telling him anything at all."

This wasn't the response Margaret had wanted. She'd thought the nurse would say, "Oh, you didn't upset anything at all. Paula overreacted."

"Paula was hurting me," Margaret felt compelled to add. "I was choking."

"She's all right. No need to worry about it. Dr. Kaplan will talk to you later, I'm sure."

Kate seemed determined not to yield anything but the wrong kind of assurances. Margaret would have to wait and talk with Dr. Kaplan some more, just as Kate said. But in the meantime, she felt unjustly accused. Yet another instance where her reaction was completely warranted, and she was judged unfit because of it. She had to get out of this place. She would try harder to be good, their version of good.

They made several turns, took an elevator, then another, until finally at the end of a long, wider hallway, she saw the sunlight streaming through open doors, creating a clear pathway outside.

"Here we go," announced Kate when they came to the door. "You want to try to walk from here?" The last time they'd come outside, Margaret had stayed in the chair.

Kate stopped the chair and kicked on a brake, then placed her hand under Margaret's arm, hoisting her up.

Kate matched her pace to Margaret's, slow and tentative, down the steps that led to a patch of grass with benches and flowers. Beyond that, a sloping hill tumbled to the street where cars streamed by. It was Broadway, the front of the hospital. With disappointment, Margaret turned to look back. The Christ statue. She'd been so focused on herself, she'd missed seeing the huge statue of Christ—the Divine Healer—that adorned the Hopkins lobby. Kate knew why she looked.

"You can see it on your way back in." Kate led her forward, not letting her stop. "There's a bench over there." When they reached it, Margaret slumped, out of breath, onto its hard surface.

"It's a beautiful day," Kate said again, looking out and not at Margaret. "Hot, though."

"Yes."

Silence, and then, as if she were trying to make conversation, Kate spoke.

"Your brother was in the army, wasn't he?"

Margaret nodded, and her lips twitched with defeat. What else had Paula told this woman that Margaret would have to correct or undo?

"She said they live in Rosedale. I come in every day from Hamilton. All those areas are really growing now. What kind of home does he have?"

"A bungalow," Margaret told her, seeing Karol's house on a shaded street with its big front porch and airy small rooms.

"My husband died in the war," Kate said, her voice sure and matter-of-fact.

Sadness touched everything, even here in this sunlit plaza.

Margaret knew the polite thing to do would be to ask questions, to allow Kate to talk about her husband. But now she wanted to go back inside where she could sleep again. Or pray the rosary in peace, alone. Her face itched where the rash had sprouted before. With a wavering hand, she reached up and rubbed it.

"After I...accepted his death...I thought of changing direction in my life." Kate stared at her hands in her lap, oblivious to Margaret's discomfort. "I took a weekend retreat, at the Mother House in Pennsylvania."

"Mount St. Agnes?" Margaret sat up straighter.

"Yes. It was lovely. I felt so at home there. I just don't know, Sister...how do you decide? I can't quite decide how to decide." She laughed a little, like a young girl.

"How old are you?"

"Thirty."

"You could still find a husband." Margaret tested her just as she had been tested, her vocation questioned by the nuns at her parish school. One had to be sure the calling was true. She had passed easily. She had been so sure that no temptation could shake her conviction.

Kate chuckled again, but Margaret could tell it was from discomfort, embarrassment. "I'm finding most men are already taken."

"There might be one for you." Nurse Kate was too easily distracted, Margaret thought. No wonder she'd not persisted in following a vocation. Thinking of entering, then not. Thinking of Margaret, then Paula.

The sun hit them directly, and even in the shade of a tree, heat intensified, making the itch more fiery and insistent. With all her self-control, Margaret refrained from scratching. Instead, she rubbed the sore spot again as if she were thinking of Kate's problems.

The nurse continued: "I don't know. I've begun to wonder if not finding anyone is a sign, a sign I should enter the convent after all."

Overhead, a seagull drifted and called, its lonely sound piercing the still summer air. Even the traffic was light. The whole city must have gone on a picnic, thought Margaret, because it was so hot. *What do I tell this child?* This child. She was about the same age as Margaret, who'd entered the convent only in her teens. Yet she felt two dozen years older, a generation older.

"I always wanted to be a nun," Margaret answered. "From the time I was a little girl."

Kate didn't press her further, and they sat another quarter hour in the afternoon sun before they headed inside. By this time, Margaret's rash was bothering her so much she could hardly appreciate the imposing statue of Christ with his outstretched hands, welcoming the ill to this healing place. All she could think of was getting past his arms, back into bed and out of the heat.

When they returned to the room, another nurse chided Kate for staying out so long. Dr. Kaplan had been looking for Margaret, the nurse said. When they helped her into bed, the nurse was even more critical.

"We'll have to put some ointment on this," she said, pointing to Margaret's face. "Is she allergic to anything?"

Kate said nothing, and now that Margaret was back in the safety of her room, her discomfort relieved, she felt freer to help Kate. Maybe that's why she was here, to guide this young nurse. She should have offered something, some wisdom or direction, when they were alone together, but it had been so warm, and her rash had been so distracting....

Why were the tests always foisted upon her when she was tired and uncomfortable? Later, she'd talk to her. She'd apologize. She'd explain.

As the nurses settled her in bed, Dr. Kaplan returned.

"You're still on duty?" he asked Kate.

"I was just leaving. I took her outside."

"Did you speak with...?"

"I was just about to do it, now that my shift is over."

"Thank you."

After this cryptic exchange, Kate left, and Dr. Kaplan stood next to Margaret's bed.

The sun cut through the windows at an acute angle,

its intense yellow shafts making Margaret squint.

"You had a bad morning." He pulled out a chair and sat down, balancing his clipboard on his knee. He was so heavily bearded that it was hard to see his mouth move when he spoke. From somewhere in that mass of dark and gray brush, a voice emanated.

"I was tired. My sister-in-law came. She hurt me."

"Why did she hurt you?"

"She doesn't like me. She doesn't like my family. Even her husband, my brother. She doesn't like him."

"You remember this?"

"Yes, I remember it! It was important. She only married Karol, my brother, because she's going to have a baby."

"So you know they don't love each other?" When she didn't answer, he tried another way: "Did she tell you this?"

Margaret couldn't conjure up the specific memory—the when, the where, the what that was said. She only had a feeling, a very definite feeling of what she knew. And it had seemed to her that the logic was so unassailable as to preclude any questions about it. Yet he persisted. And she must find a way...to obey. She shifted in the bed. Her mouth was still dry, and no one had given her any water. When Dr. Kaplan saw her reaching for the pitcher by the bedside, he poured her a glass and offered it to her.

"No. I don't know. I'm not supposed to know. No contact." She drank, almost all of it in one long sip.

"What do you mean 'no contact'?"

"It's one of the Rules. No contact with your family."

Dr. Kaplan looked at his watch. She was keeping him. He had come to see her special because of the morning's incident.

"Perhaps tomorrow you can take another walk with one of the nurses." Dr. Kaplan spoke tentatively, as if trying the idea out. "But you won't be able to wear anything around your head because of the rash. Was that explained to you?"

She couldn't wear the habit without the wimple. She'd look ridiculous! She just wouldn't go out.

"Do you have any clothes besides the uniform?"

"The habit. It's called a habit."

"Do you have something else?"

"No."

"We'll bring you more. I see Kate has already provided some." When she didn't protest, he went on. "I might need to keep you a few more days, too. For observation. But don't worry—we're working on your discharge to your brother's house. It's important that you try to be calm…in order for us to move that forward quickly. No more incidents." He cleared his throat. "In the meantime, I think it would be helpful if we could pick up the pace of our work. Trying to recover your memory of that day, that is." He handed her a notebook he'd had stashed under his clipboard. He also gave her a pen.

"When you are awake, it would be helpful for you to jot down memories—anything that comes to mind. It could be way in the past or just yesterday, just a second ago." He smiled and stood. "I know you're eager to get on with your life. I think if we work hard together, you can reach that goal."

An assignment. She was being given an assignment.

He left the room. He had found out that she was willing to wear something besides the habit—she'd not protested. She felt betrayed, as if he'd tricked her, and she wondered if he was a deliberate tempter sent to lure her into breaking her vows. But she was too tired to fight. What good would it do? She had become a habitual sinner, her fall from grace starting long before when she wasn't vigilant, and she was now experiencing its consequences.

The nurses came in with dinner, but her hunger had left, and she picked at the food. The sun faded, its earlier late-evening brightness now an impotent show, just like her own attempts at righteousness.

CHAPTER FIFTEEN
Mrs. Mallory

"YOU MENTIONED working for a Mrs. Mallory." He flipped through his own notes, since she'd hardly written a thing in her notebook. He was disappointed. He'd been sure her desire to be obedient would have had her filling the pages. And he felt he'd begun to unlock a more expansive Sister with her discussion of her first day at the convent. Today, she appeared nowhere near as open. She lay in bed, breakfast tray almost untouched. She was retreating again, and he had to get her to advance if, in good conscience, he was to release her.

Releasing her would mean she'd have to pick up that pen at some point, even if not to write memories. She had to write a letter to her Mother Superior, requesting permission to stay with her brother.

Kate had given him the news this morning that she'd spoken with Sister Fulgentia. The nun had been pleased to hear of Sister's progress but was troubled by the idea of Sister Francis Marie staying outside the convent. Kate had managed to make her understand that Sister's best chance of recovery lie in this unconventional approach. In the end, Sister Fulgentia had not opposed the idea, but she'd insisted on having Sister Francis Marie formally ask for the arrangement herself, at least to have the letter to share with her own superior.

Upon reflection, Aaron didn't blame her. She was

trying to be scrupulous with the Rule, with her own obedience. She had to be sure that Sister Francis Marie wasn't being coerced into breaking that Rule.

"Sister?" he prodded. She seemed to be staring into space.

"Mrs. Mallory," she repeated, as if finally listening to him. And she sighed, too, as if she were as tired as him at trying to solve this puzzle. "Both Karol and I ended up working for her. I was the first, though. The pioneer."

She smiled, and he relaxed. He'd chosen a good place to start.

❧

I'm guilty again—for not writing things down. But I'd been so tired the night before, after the outing, after talking with Dr. Kaplan, after....Paula. I wish they'd just let me go. But letting me go means living with Paula. Surely I can find it in my heart to forgive her....

Dr. Kaplan sits patiently, as patiently as a priest in a confessional, and I cannot avoid the feeling again that God devises these unusual opportunities for penance, simultaneously blessing and cursing me. Perhaps that is the reason I am here. Perhaps God has sent me here to tell him about our religion. A mission. I have been so deaf to calls from God. How can I not find the energy to respond to his simple questions?

I close my eyes. *I'm awash in distant memories, just not the one memory you require, Dr. Kaplan, the memory you hope to find in these byroads, these tangential explorations.* I have random flashes of recollection of the past few months and nothing extraordinary appears from the stream. Just the relentless routine of the convent, the slow turning of the season, the intractability of my Mother Superior as I struggled with illness, with everything. And Paula in the background. A constant reminder that Rosy was gone.

While those months are still a fog, my earlier days appear in crisp detail. In this hospital room with the

210

scents and sounds of home so nearby I become eager to touch those memories. My eyes still closed, I begin talking... He's asked about Mrs. Mallory, but I'll give him more. Maybe if I give him enough, he'll let me go, he'll realize that the one memory he wants is inconsequential....

My father had been a distant but happy man, goose-stepping around our small basement apartment making fun of Russian soldiers he'd left behind, to the accompaniment of our delighted giggles. "Shush," my mother would say to him, as if Cossacks were listening at the door.

She was always scolding him. You buy too many expensive foods. You give too much credit. You should make Bernard work on Saturdays instead of letting him go off with his friends. You give too many candies to Rosalinde.

And his answers always began "But, Marie..." But Marie, if we sell poor quality goods, no one will buy. But Marie, if we don't let them have credit, they'll go to Koslowski's. But Marie, Bernard is a young man and I know what it feels like to be a young man... But Marie, Rosy is our baby.

When Bernard left, my Father did, too. Bernard ran away in September of 1939, just after my father finally gave in to Mother's complaints and made him work Saturdays. My father died of a heart attack in November of that year, alone in the kitchen while the rest of us were at church, scrubbing the floors, polishing the wooden pews, all in exchange for free tuition at St. Bridget's. Rosy did little work. She was too frail that year, with a cough that wouldn't go away, and no money for the doctor.

Our lives were hard before my father died, but they were harder after. No high quality foods at the store meant no high quality foods at home. And whether it was because Mother's business ideas now ruled the roost or because times were tough all over, our finances dwindled. We rarely had enough food to fill our bellies. Thin broth. Old bread. The ends of meats no one would buy. One morning, there was nothing but tea for breakfast.

Rosy was always sick, coughing and feverish. I hated my mother for not being able to take her to the doctor. I was her doctor. I fixed her tea. I hid a can of stewed prunes under my jacket and rushed home early to warm them and feed them to her. I combed her hair and prayed by the bedside while she slept.

Christmas that year was grim, made sadder by the realization that what we had thought was deprivation in the past—our constant hunger and desire for nice things—was actually a better life than the one we now had.

I gave Rosy a scented soap, carved to look like a rose in bloom. It was something I'd found at the Christmas fair at St. Bridget's. I gave Karol an embroidered handkerchief—one of his own upon which I had stitched his initials. And I gave mother two new pencils that I'd bought at Woolworth's. She was always figuring things.

We had no tree, and our Christmas feast was boiled kielbasa, cabbage, and potatoes, served to Mother's admonition that we should be grateful for what we had because she'd decided to close the store early that week and these were left over. If she closed the store early, it was because no one was shopping there.

After dinner that evening, she told us all to sit down at the table. We had many responsibilities, she told us in Polish, now that Father was gone. We all had to do our part. Rosy would take in some mending. Karol would work more in the store and deliver newspapers. And I, I would have the distinction of being sent out of our enclave to work.

"I have spoken with the Dombrowskis," my mother said that night. "They know of a woman who can use some help in her house. It is only light cleaning duties, nothing unsuitable for a girl your age. But the pay is very good."

"Yes, mother." At first I was relieved. It wouldn't be so bad. The Dombrowskis lived only one block away. I hadn't realized they were wealthy enough to be able to afford hired help.

"Her name is Mallory, Mrs. Bennett Mallory. The house is in a good neighborhood. In Guilford. I have already found out. You take the #3 into town then the #22 up Charles Street—"

At the mention of Guilford, I stopped listening. Guilford was a foreign country, a name on a map. It was a small exclusive section of town just north of the city, well beyond our own nest.

"—you start the Monday after New Year. I think you should write a nice note to the Sisters explaining why you will be out two days a week. I will tell you what to say."

We were settling into our new routines, checking off each "first" that occurred after Father's death. The first holiday without him. The first report card without him. The first Christmas concert without him. Now, I faced a double first—my first job and my first job *without him*. Without him prodding me—"you are a smart girl, Margaret, the smartest of us all." Without him comforting me—"it is a good neighborhood and very rich people who will treat you well."

The night before I was to make my emigration to Guilford, I stayed up late, standing on a kitchen chair to look out the window that abutted the sidewalk. The night was cold, and snow was beginning to fall, the first real snow of the season. I watched it hopefully, praying that each flake would be larger than the last one so that an impossible wall would keep me home the next day, even though I knew our pantry was bare and an impenetrable wall of snow would have meant more deprivation.

When I awoke, however, no such wall greeted me. An inner struggle began. What if I ventured out into the slick, damp roads and had an accident, or the streetcars stopped running, leaving me stranded in Guilford? Would that fate be worse than staying home and facing mother's wrath if the weather cleared?

I dressed in my school uniform, the best outfit I owned, a navy blue sweater and plaid skirt. I walked to the streetcar stop on Conkling Street like a doomed prisoner to execution, preparing for my journey in lonely silence. My mother was already at the store. Rosy was asleep. Karol was still delivering newspapers.

I was used to the Conkling Street streetcar, having traveled on it into town to visit the department stores, so I easily made the first part of the journey, trying to pretend the trip was as exciting as a shopping expedition downtown. But my stomach churned with nerves and I thought I would be sick. In town, I found the stop for the #22 on Charles Street and worried that I had missed it. When it came after only five minutes, my next worry was finding the right stop in Guilford. The people on the trolley looked ominous, not like the strangers I was used to on the Conkling Street line. These were busy and important-looking people, cold, impervious. I was convinced they'd shun me if I fell into peril. Why should they help someone who wasn't one of their own?

Too nervous to trust myself, I got off two stops early and walked for five blocks until I came to the right cross street. Even though I had the address memorized, I still pulled out a corner of a piece of paper with the address scribbled in pencil, not trusting myself to get it right. I was on course.

I stood in front of it, a large two-story home of red brick and black shutters. The front door was hidden under an arched portico. Trellises leaned against the side walls, and huge shrubs, now capped with snow, guarded the lower windows. It all seemed to shout out, "Don't enter here, go back, we don't want you."

I quickly walked, almost ran, up the front walk, afraid that someone would look out one of those windows and think I'd made a mistake. As it turned out, I had made a mistake. A woman in maid's uniform opened the door a crack after my faint knock. "Around the back," she said, shivering. "The back is the door for us." So I trudged off and around.

This back door was hidden underneath an arbor overgrown with heavy vines. Although they were leafless in winter, they collected the snow and created a claustrophobic cubicle in front of a bright white door. Stomping the snow off my feet, I raised my hand to knock again, but before my fist met wood, the door opened.

"Margaret? Come in, come in. You must be so cold. Let's get you dry!" It was the maid, cheerful and welcoming now that I'd corrected my mistake.

She was young, with frizzy reddish-blond hair and small wire-rimmed spectacles. Her voice had a slight accent, and she pulled me into the mudroom next to the door with a friendly tug.

"I'm Hilda Diangelo," she said, while unbuttoning my coat for me. "I'm the cook. Here, let's hang this by the stove to dry. There are aprons and uniforms in the far closet. You can change there. Pull the string to turn on the light."

As I changed in the large closet at the end of the kitchen, I pinpointed Hilda's accent as German, like one of the customers at the store. Not a good sign. Just that past September, the Germans had marched into Poland, and all our neighbors cursed them. But I was obedient and afraid and willing to believe she was a benevolent captor.

When I came out of the room, I looked just like Hilda, in a plain, gray cotton dress and white apron. I smelled cinnamon and nutmeg and noticed that on the long wooden table in the center of the room two places were set, and an apple pie, steam still rising from its vents, was placed between them.

"I've made tea. I like coffee, strong coffee. But we

can have that this afternoon. Sit down, sit down. I'll tell you all you need to know."

I did as I was told and sat in one of the straight-back cane chairs. Hilda poured some tea and sliced the pie into generous portions, placing one on an attractive china plate in front of me. I was beginning to shed my debilitating nervousness as I warmed up in the homey kitchen. I didn't yet know it, but this was a world where my hungers were easily sated, where my gaze lit on luxury wherever I looked, and where kindness warmed me as much as the glow from the kitchen's big iron stove.

Hilda was indeed from Germany, married just a year ago to an Italian boy, a union which would scandalize her family in the old country, she laughingly told me as we enjoyed the pie. This set me at ease. She was different, swimming against the tide. She lived with her in-laws in Little Italy near the harbor, which was how she found this job because Mrs. Mallory's family was Italian. This cheered me, too, to think that a woman of foreign birth could have achieved such comfort.

"Mrs. Mallory is a good woman," she told me. "The best employer you could ask for..."

I could barely get a word in to answer Hilda's polite questions about my own background before the good woman herself appeared, pushing open the kitchen door so timidly that you would have thought she was an intruder in this home. I stood and wiped my hands on my apron, the nervousness returning.

"Margaret Wojehedski," Mrs. Mallory said slowly, sounding each syllable to get the name right. While she spoke, her long slender fingers fidgeted with a narrow belt. "Hilda will show you everything, I'm sure, but please don't be shy about asking for anything."

She paused, as if looking for something else to say, then smiled quickly before leaving the room. If it hadn't been for Hilda's description of her as a good person, I would have guessed her to be more a witch than an angel. She had been dressed in black, a nearly shapeless sheath that hung on her thin frame except where the belt pulled it in at her waist. Her dark hair had been pulled achingly tight from her long olive face into a thick bun at the nape of her neck. Her eyes were large and piercing.

As if reading my mind, Hilda explained her employer. "Mrs. Mallory is a good lady but very sad. I will show you what to do but it isn't very much. Bring your schoolbooks with you. You can work on them in the afternoon. I don't need much help myself. There isn't much to do."

"Is Mr. Mallory...dead?"

She snorted. "No. But he might as well be sometimes. He's often...very busy. A very important man in the law, often working very late."

Hilda showed me where to find supplies after we finished eating. I worked hard and fast all morning, eager to show the Mallorys and Hilda what a good cleaner I could be. I dusted and brushed and swept and scrubbed everything that looked like it needed it and most things that did not. Except for an occasional glimmer of fine dust, the rooms were already spotlessly clean.

They were lovely rooms, rooms that before now had only lived in my fantasies of rich ladies and their charming heroes. They were filled with the understated elegance of old wealth— faded Persian rugs of muted red hues, antique clocks, embroidered chairs. A shiny baby-grand piano caught the morning light in a front sitting room. How I was tempted to touch the keys and hear their sound—but I was too timid to even press hard enough on the dusting cloth to bring out a rough scale.

It wasn't noon yet when I began sweeping a cold summer room, where the furniture was covered with white sheets. I was wondering whether to congratulate myself on how much I'd done or worry about whether I'd been thorough enough when Hilda came in.

"Ach! You don't need to clean this room until

spring. Don't be foolish. It's time to eat."

Expecting nothing more than bread and cheese after the morning pie, I was surprised to find the kitchen table set with soup bowls. Hilda ladled a thick vegetable soup in dishes, then prepared a tray for Mrs. Mallory.

"Go ahead and start while I take this up to her. It's very hot!"

While Hilda was gone, I allowed myself the luxury of a relaxing sigh. I closed my eyes and breathed in the aroma of the beef-based broth. When was the last time I had soup like this? I couldn't remember. I tried to memorize every detail—every scent, every noise, every view—in order to share them with Rosy that evening, wishing I could also take her some food but not wanting to be perceived as a thief. Hilda returned shortly and immediately cut two slices of a crusty bread, placing one on my plate.

"You are so skinny. My mother-in-law she is always telling to me I am too skinny!" Hilda laughed. After a few questions about school, questions that were obviously asked out of courtesy and not interest, Hilda launched into a story about the Mallorys.

Mrs. Mallory's maiden name had been Antonia Lambogne. Hilda's in-laws knew the Lambogne family. They had come from Sicily when Antonia was just a baby. A Lambogne owned a successful restaurant in Little Italy where Antonia eventually found work greeting customers. It was there that she had met Bennett Mallory.

"Mr. Mallory, he was just a young man, I don't know that he maybe was still in law school or maybe just starting out, but he was like all young men, showing off, flirting with the girls, such a big important man——Mama Diangelo say he was probably on an adventure coming to our part of town, looking for the liquor and the girls."

He did more than flirt with Antonia and shortly afterwards they had to get married. Although I knew nothing about sex, I knew what having to get married meant.

"But just a month after the wedding, she lost it—the baby! She lost a lot of blood I hear. It was very dangerous for her. My mother-in-law says Antonia wanted to go back home after that. And Mr. Mallory— his parents wanted them to divorce. But my *Gott*, they were married in St. Rose of Lima's, in a small service to be sure, with none of his family there, but still it was in the Church!"

Hilda shook her head with indignation, then finished her soup and took her bowl to the sink.

"Do you want some more?"

"No, no. This is wonderful."

A door opened and shut upstairs. That noise and the interruption of the meal itself caused Hilda to end her story.

"I shouldn't be going on so much. We will have lots of time to talk. The upstairs isn't much. They only use a few rooms and the others are just dusty. In a few weeks, I'll help roll up the carpets and wash the floors. Oh, don't worry about making their bed. Mrs. Mallory always makes it."

I finished lunch and grabbed the cleaning supplies once again. By now, I felt comfortable. Hilda was so cheerful and kind, the food was good and plentiful, the surroundings beautiful. Even the sad Mallory tale was inviting. Like a storybook on a rainy afternoon, it moved me in a safe way, letting me experience sadness without having to live with its consequences.

Even without Hilda's narrative, the upper floor told a story all its own. Beyond the spacious bedroom suite of Mr. and Mrs. Mallory, three other bedrooms occupied the top floor. Cleaning the suite was easy, as Hilda had predicted. The large main room, decorated in soft mauves and rose shades, was spotless, and the bed indeed was made. A smaller sitting room needed a little tidying for which I was grateful. Here I could prove my worth, placing books back on a bookshelf, folding a cashmere coverlet and placing it neatly on the end of a white chaise lounge.

The other bedrooms were dusty from lack of use, but each felt haunted and I wanted to be done with them as quickly as possible.

They both were intended as children's rooms. Embroidered samplers decorated with animals and alphabet blocks hung on the walls. Had Mrs. Mallory sewn them herself? A rocking chair stood still and silent in one corner of the larger room. In the other, a bassinet lay empty, its lacy covering now beginning to yellow. Both rooms were cold; I shivered as I closed the door to the second one and made my way to another room on the back of the house.

This room, above the kitchen, was warmer and brighter, with large windows overlooking the snowy rolling lawn out back.

It was also occupied. Mrs. Mallory was in the room, kneeling at a *prie-dieu* against the far wall. Above her, a heavy crucifix hung on the wall. Startled because the room wasn't empty, I blushed and rattled mop and dust bin against the doorjamb as I tried to exit quickly.

Turning toward me, she smiled. "Go right ahead, Margaret. You won't disturb me." Then she turned back to her prayers, pearly rosary beads slipping over her fingers in methodical rhythm. I cleaned the room self-consciously, aware of my employer's presence, wondering if I should sweep longer, even though no dust littered the bare wooden floor, or spend more time meticulously dusting a shrine to Mary set up on an old dresser in the corner.

A worse decision loomed—an old crib was pushed against the wall by the door. Should I turn its mattress, shake out the blankets, or leave it be? A book rested near one of its legs. I bent to pick it up. At least if I pretended to be tidying up, I could think what to do about the crib.

While I debated my next move, Mrs. Mallory

finished her rosary, blessing herself with a smooth, graceful gesture that ended with her kissing the beads before slipping them into her pocket. She stood just as gracefully and walked to the door. Or rather, it seemed to me that she glided there in one uninterrupted motion. "Do you like to read?"

"Yes, ma'am."

"Have you read that book?"

I looked at the dust jacket. It was entitled *Beloved Queen*, a fictional account of the Bible story of Queen Esther.

"No, ma'am."

"Well, then, take it with you. I'm done with it. You might enjoy it. And, when you're finished in here, come into my room. I'll show you some other books you may have."

The room was easy to clean. No dust settled on the statue of Mary, nor on the two silver vases filled with holly on either side. The *prie-dieu* was spotless, its kneeler still warm from Mrs. Mallory. Even the crib, I realized in horror, was clean. She must keep it neat herself, I thought to myself as I closed the door and headed for Antonia Mallory's sitting room.

Mrs. Mallory sat on the edge of the chaise, taking books off a four-shelved case near the window.

"Come in. I've just pulled out these that I've already read. Hilda doesn't share my taste in books...."

All the books were on religious themes, either biographies of saints or meditations on Catholicism.

"Thank you, ma'am. I can't possibly take them all home."

"Not at once, no, of course not. But I'll leave them here in a pile. It will be like a little private library for you. Only you don't have to bring them back. Do you have any brothers or sisters?"

The floodgates opened, and I told her about Rosy and Karol and then about Bernard and inevitably about my father.

"I'll say a special rosary for your father's soul," said Mrs. Mallory when I finished. She put her hands in her lap, a signal that the book search was over. I thanked her again and left the room, my heart lighter than it had been in months, since my father had died. Thinking of Mrs. Mallory praying for my father was a relief, as if I needed someone like an Antonia Mallory offering prayers for his soul, as if my own prayers were inadequate.

Our work finished for the day, Hilda and I sat across from each other in the kitchen in the afternoon, listening to the "Dance Orchestra" radio program and sipping the strong coffee Hilda had promised earlier. Hilda pulled out a cigarette and lit it with a stove match. The radio played an old song, "Bye, Bye Blackbird," and memories of my father flooded over me. He had liked that song.

"You saw the crib, *ja?*" Hilda asked, slowly blowing smoke into the air. "And the rooms with the...."

"Yes, the baby rooms."

"She torments herself," Hilda continued. "Just like her mother did to her."

I desperately wanted Hilda to keep talking, to tell the full story, but I was afraid to interrupt even with a question. Yes, I wanted to know. Who doesn't want to know of the sadness of others when suffering beats at their own hearts? If Antonia Mallory's pain was deeper than my own, I could feel blessed that I wasn't afflicted as badly.

A quiet sleepiness fell over the room. Outside, the skies were gray. Inside, the room was smoky from Hilda's cigarette.

"Her mother wanted her to be a nun. When she lost the babies, Mrs. Lambogne said it was a sign from God."

"The babies?" Hilda had only mentioned one earlier.

Upstairs, I heard the soft closing of a door and imagined Mrs. Mallory in the shrine room, kneeling, kissing the rosary crucifix, blessing herself, and beginning the prayers for my father's soul. I held my breath, hoping Hilda wouldn't be deterred by the sound.

"Oh, yes, Gianni's mother—Gianni is my husband—she tell me everything she know about it." Hilda blew smoke again and poured more coffee. "Mrs. Lambogne went to church every morning when the baby was coming that first time. She prayed every day, just like Antonia now. She asked for forgiveness for her daughter, forgiveness for herself. But it was no good. The baby was born dead. Mrs. Lambogne was heartsick, beating her breast saying it was punishment for breaking the promise, the promise to send her daughter to the Sisters of St. Francis.

"And then Mr. Mallory and the talk of divorce—it was enough to send Mrs. Lambogne to bed, so sick the priest came and gave her Last Rites." Hilda blessed herself and then took a sip of coffee and a puff of cigarette.

"Antonia was without a child for ten years. That's when I came to work here, when she carried the last baby. I've seen women who are with child and I have never seen one like her." Hilda tapped the table with each word.

"I didn't even know at first. She was so skinny—like you—with just a little ball in her belly. No good was coming of that. No good. This time, Mr. Mallory wouldn't let Mrs. Lambogne near the house. And Antonia was so full of, what is it called—*sehnsucht*—longing for her mother. Even with all the talk of punishment, she wanted her mother near her. Who doesn't want her mother at those times, huh? Who keeps a mother away from her daughter?" Hilda muttered something in German that I didn't understand.

"She was in labor, oh, nearly three days, so much pain. She was so weak, so pale. I thought she would die. My mother-in-law, she didn't want me to come to work. She said Antonia would die and we'd all be arrested for murder. But I had to come. I couldn't leave her like she was.

"Mr. Mallory, he finally couldn't stand it. He stayed away. When the baby came, he wasn't even here. Huh! When I heard the cry, I thought, oh, thank *Gott*, it has a healthy cry. But it wasn't the baby. It was her, Antonia, letting out a wail when the doctor told her it was dead. Another baby girl, just like the first one. With little blue eyes...blue lips, blue fingertips. It was dead inside her all that time...."

Hilda trailed off, staring into space. She used the knuckle of her right hand to wipe the corner of her eye.

"As soon as she was out of bed, she moved the crib into that room and set it all up and then it was every day in there....

"Mr. Mallory can't stand that room. He never goes in there, never goes in the other rooms. For him, it is like nothing happened. Mrs. Lambogne came out to see Antonia just once after that and Antonia told her not to come again. Antonia wrote to the Sisters of St. Francis and found out their Rule. And I think she follows it, here in this house, as if this were a convent...."

Hilda slowly shook her head.

I said nothing. So Mrs. Mallory was living the life of a nun, even though she could no longer be one.

"I believe in prayer, for sure, but this..." Hilda gestured aimlessly toward the upstairs.

A news program came on the radio. Hilda got up and turned up the volume, listening intently to a serious voice talk about Hitler. She then lectured me on how hard the Germans had suffered after the Great War.

But I didn't listen. I pulled out the book on Queen Esther and stared at its pages, not reading but thinking about the story I had just been told. In a little while, Hilda told me to come into the dining room so she could show me how to set the table for dinner.

"Two settings," she said, pulling out wafer-thin china from the dining room breakfront. "Even though he won't be here."

On the trolley ride home, I longed for my father so I

could tell him about the Mallorys and Hilda and the wonderful and horrible things their household contained. I tried to imagine what he would have said. But the only image I conjured up was him dancing with me treetop fashion as he sang in his accented voice: "Pack up all my cares and woes..."

❧

I reach up to wipe my brow. I'm sweating, and a headache has started to form. I ask for water and some aspirin, and Dr. Kaplan tells me he'll have a nurse bring something in.

"That's a good start," he says, flipping pages back on his clipboard. "A very good start. I want to hear more. Feel free to write it down." He points to the notebook. "In fact, I need you to write something else, too. Very important." And he proceeds to tell me how I have to put in writing a request to Sister Fulgentia to stay at my brother's house.

My face reddens. This feels like a humiliation, a public shaming. But I'll do it. Another penance.

❧

In the hallway, he was disappointed not to see Kate. He had found himself wondering the night before if his interest in Sister's case was intensified by its ties to Kate. Every time he stepped onto Sister's floor, he found himself searching out Kate, looking in doorways as he walked by to see if she was in another patient's room, listening for the sound of her voice.

He'd turned the issue over in his head a dozen different ways. He had no clear answer. Or maybe, that was his answer, the truth he wouldn't face. He did come to Sister's floor half searching for Kate.

But there was no question Kate was helpful, and that alone was reason to seek her out. She'd taken it upon herself to deal with Sister Fulgentia. Maybe it was unfair of him to let her do those things. It kept them connected when it was becoming clear she no longer wanted that connection. And now he had one more favor to ask, an idea that had occurred to him in the dark of the night as he'd mulled Sister's case and Kate and his involvement.

Squaring his shoulders, he went to the nurse's station and asked about her.

"She went to get a patient a cup of tea," another nurse replied.

"Would you ask her to stop in to see me when she returns?"

They nodded their assent, and he walked on, nearly stumbling into the tall priest he occasionally saw doing rounds.

Mutual apologies, offered simultaneously, awkwardly.

But Dr. Kaplan decided this was an opportunity—

"I'm Aaron Kaplan, Sister Francis Marie's doctor," he said extending his hand. "Might I have a word?"

When the priest readily agreed, they made their way back to Aaron's tiny office.

∞ℰℴ

"I see you use the same interior decorator," Father Al joked as Dr. Kaplan removed a stack of papers from a stool. The doctor shyly gestured for the priest to sit down.

"I have another office on the third floor, but this is convenient for working on case files."

"No need to explain."

"Do you know of Sister's case?" Dr. Kaplan began. He seemed a bit nervous.

"I know she's here for possible depression. An overdose of some sort..." He waved the air vaguely. A possible suicide. Serious business. He'd offered to hear her confession, but she'd not been awake when he'd stopped by for it, and he was not one of those priests who made patients adhere to his schedule, awakening them for his visits. He should make more of an effort. He'd spent more time with the nun's sister-in-law, in fact. It was the nun who was in dire straits. How easy it was to look past deep pain, especially when it had come so close to his own.

"Yes. Very challenging. She can't remember the day of the overdose." He sat back, pulled her file from a stack. But he didn't look at it. "I'm discharging her soon—in a few days, I hope—but I don't want her back in the convent. I mean, I don't want her there now." He looked down, shaking his head. "I'm sorry. That isn't what I mean...."

"No need. I understand. She's not up to the rigorous routine yet." Father Al admired nuns but sometimes felt uneasy around them, as if he needed to apologize for having a somewhat easier time of it in the rectory than he knew they must have in the convent. Oh, not that they lacked for anything. But their schedule was far more regimented and restricted.

"Look, I don't want her case presented to Dr. Freeman, the expert on lobotomies," Dr. Kaplan said in a rush. "I don't think she's a candidate at all, and I don't want there to be any question about it. So I'd like to discharge her once she's physically able. That could be as soon as...as tomorrow. And then I'd continue to see her—have her come here, to my bigger office—" he smiled "—and I can't discharge her if she's to go back to the convent, because she's not ready for that yet."

"Ghastly stuff," Father Al murmured, patting his pocket.

"Go ahead and smoke, if you'd like."

After Father Al had lit his cigarette, he spoke. "I mean this Dr. Freeman. Very disappointing Hopkins is having him here."

"Yes. I intend to voice my objections."

"How can I help with Sister—keeping her from Dr. Frankenstein's clutches?" He shouldn't be so glib, but Dr. Kaplan seemed agitated. He wanted to make him feel at ease, to realize he had an ally.

"You could talk to Sister...give her...permission, in a way. Tell her it's okay not to wear the habit, for example—it causes a terrible rash on her face that I believe is related to her underlying condition. She's not wearing it now, of course, but knowing that it's okay, that might be a burden of worry lifted from her. Tell her it's okay to talk to me, to keep coming to see me. I do worry if I release her too soon that she won't come back for sessions. I think she needs to be reinforced in this regard."

Father Al blew out some smoke and sat up straight. "You have my word. It's her duty to come see you, really. She'll understand that. She'll obey. I'm sure of it."

"Thank you." Dr. Kaplan relaxed, visibly relieved. "Her Mother Superior might need some convincing, too. She's been agreeable, but I sense she struggles with whether she's doing the right thing."

Hmm...that was trickier. While a Mother Superior would be deferential to him, a priest, ultimately the Rule of her Order would prevail. But he should make the effort, especially now that he was aware of how he'd not put forth much effort in this case at all so far.

"Do you want me to talk with her Mother Superior?"

"If you wouldn't mind. It might help. We've already explained things—well, the nurse has. But one more voice would probably ease her mind and help us as we determine therapies..."

"Give me her name and number. I'll try to reach her today."

Dr. Kaplan immediately wrote the information down. Thinking they were finished, Father Al stood. So did Dr. Kaplan.

"One more thing.... I had an idea...well, perhaps one therapy could be of significant impact. Taking Sister to visit the convent, the 'scene of the crime,' where it happened. With me, that is. If we could talk about that day in the place where the incident occurred. Is that allowed?" He handed Father the contact information.

"I'm not sure." Even if it was, it might be a tough sell. But he should still try. He was eager to do all he could now that he was aware of his aloofness to Sister's travail. "I'll mention this to her when I call."

CHAPTER SIXTEEN
Fresh starts

"SAY, I just discovered that the father of one of my summer students works for Pan Am. I'm sure he could get you a discount." Pete stood in Al's doorway once again, ever helpful.

Al had to admit the news was timely. He'd not spent a single day since receiving the letter about his aunt's death without thinking about it. It was distracting him, he'd realized after getting off the phone with Sister Fulgentia a half hour earlier. He should have made a far greater effort to help with this case, instead of waiting to be asked. He'd not paid adequate attention. He'd given Communion to the ailing nun every day. He'd spoken with her sister-in-law about converting. And yet he'd not lifted a finger on his own to inquire about Sister's difficulties, to see if he'd be able to help. He knew why—her despair was so deep, to be pushed to the edge, that he averted his gaze. A rational response, but not a priestly one.

Maybe that was a sign that he should go back and deal with the estate, go back and settle...something. He shouldn't wait for an engraved invitation. Why was he so resistant?

"I'm still not sure about going," Al said. "But I appreciate the offer."

Pete quirked an eyebrow but didn't say anything at first. Al was used to his long pauses. They weren't for dramatic effect. The man was actually thinking of what to say. It amused Al that Pete was so careful with his words when so many were reckless, so casually hurtful. He felt he was always learning something from the way Pete spoke. He cheerfully awaited the next lesson.

"Sometimes it's hard to go back to the scene of the crime," Pete said.

Al warmed. Scene of the crime. How apt. The very same phrase Dr. Kaplan had used, too, when talking about poor Sister Francis Marie's overdose. And the phrase he himself had thought when first confronted with the news of his Aunt Beady's death.

"I mean, you have a new life here. What if you go back and it doesn't seem so good—this new life?"

"You think I'll fly the coop?" Al asked good-naturedly. "Get home and not want to return?"

Pete smiled. "If that were to happen—" here he did pause for dramatic effect "—could I have your desk?"

Al grinned. Pete had a wonderful way of deflating his self-importance.

An inexpensive plane ride to London—how could he turn that down in good conscience?

"Should I contact your student directly?"

"Probably better if I make the call. He might even be able to sneak you on a flight for nothing."

"He's a pilot?"

"His father is."

"All right. Go ahead. I only have a few things on my schedule." Paula Wojehedski's baptism was the only pressing thing. All others could be moved easily.

In a few minutes' time, he heard the priest's light steps racing up the stairs.

"Good news," he said breathlessly as he came into Al's room. "There's a flight next Thursday evening. Here, let me write down the info for you…"

So it was decided. Now he was the one wandering to the phone, leaving a message for Dr. Kaplan: Sister Fulgentia had said yes to the visit.

Oh, she'd been reluctant. But when he'd asked if there was anything in their Rule that prohibited the kind of re-enactment Dr. Kaplan was envisioning, she had truthfully responded that she didn't think so. All she'd asked for was some time to arrange things. She would want the other Sisters to be off premises, not desiring to upset them.

He felt better now that he'd helped with the case. Not entirely free of guilt, but he'd learned to set his mind to improving his actions the next day instead of bemoaning what he'd done or not done in the past. Now all he needed to do was reschedule Paula Wojehedski's baptism. He grimaced as he thought of that. But maybe it was a good thing to delay. Perhaps she'd reconsider and invite her husband to the event. Before he could make that call, Pete was beckoning him into the study where a group of priests had started a lively game of poker. Pete had been wanting to teach him how to play for some time.

❧⨾

"Thanks for agreeing to meet me." Aaron stood when she entered Beck's, the same tavern they'd had dinner at not too long ago—no, a lifetime ago.

She smiled. He'd made it sound urgent when she'd responded to his message at the hospital, going into his tiny office. *Meet me for dinner tonight. Beck's Six.* Before she'd had a chance to think, the head nurse was calling for her help with a patient, so she'd muttered a quick "okay," figuring she'd beg off later. But she hadn't begged off. Instead, she'd thought about what she would wear, how she'd fix her hair. She'd chosen a cream-colored dotted swiss. Her hair was loose around her shoulders. She'd even worn gloves, which she now removed as she slid into the booth.

"Is this about Sister?" she asked, hoping that it wasn't. Oh, what did it matter—she had no intention of continuing this...attachment...whatever it was. She'd rationalized that she had to meet him if only to break

232

things off completely. Their discussion about Lena had awakened her good sense. She and Aaron were not a match. Her mother was right. She needed to look to the future.

"No," he said, sitting across from her. "I wanted to see you."

"And that you are!" she said brightly.

A waitress came by, and they both ordered beers and burgers without even glancing at the menu. She knew he was as nervous as she was. Had he asked to see her for the same reason—to make a clean break of it? This made her want to hurry, to be the one letting him go.

"I'm glad you asked me to come," she said, looking him in the eye. "I've been avoiding you."

"I noticed."

"I—I realized…after our last encounter here…" She nodded toward the room. "We don't really have enough in common to go further. I mean, I really like you, Aaron, but…" Without thinking, she put her hand over his, a habit, she now realized, she'd have to break. How warm it was—how strong and comforting. She pulled her hand away. No, how strong and tempting.

"What I'm trying to say is I don't think we have a future together. You have this other woman—"

"Lena? That was so long ago!"

"Yes. Lena. And I have not completely figured out what I want from my life, even this long after Bri's death." Which was why she'd stupidly talked to Sister Francis Marie about the convent—what had she been thinking, burdening a sick woman with her own troubles? It was a sign of how unready she was for any relationship. Even now. Even ten years after the war.

"Lena might not even be alive," he said softly.

"But she is in your heart, no matter what you might say or think. I can tell. Have you done anything more to find her?"

"There's a friend of my family, someone who works

with refugees," he said. "She might be able to dig something up."

He leaned forward. "Kate, if Lena is alive, it's unlikely she'll want anything to do with me. I just want to know, that's all. There's no reason you and I can't..."

She reached across the table and put her finger to his sweet lips, lost among that face-hiding beard. "Shh...don't even think it. There's every reason in the world why you and I can't be close. I love my faith, Aaron. I love it more than life."

"You think that because I'm a Jew I'm not worthy of you?" he said, a voice filled with indignation.

"No, not that at all!" she said, quickly trying to reassure him, saddened by his assumption. "If anything, I'm probably not worthy of you. You're a good man, a wonderful man. It's just...well, I think that I'd want a man who shared the most important part of my life with me," she said. "And I'd certainly want a husband who shared it—especially if we were to be blessed with children." Now that she'd said it openly, now that she'd put on the table the bleak honesty of their relationship's chances, she felt lighter. Watching his troubled face, she added, "I know you never expressed those intentions—my goodness, we'd only been out a few times—but you're a gentleman. And a gentleman doesn't keep going out with a lady unless he's having thoughts about a future with her."

After a moment, she saw his face break out into a grin. Slowly—it was hard to tell under his beard—his lips curled upwards. "I'm glad you think I'm a gentleman, Kate. It means a great deal to me."

"If you'd had other intentions with our times together, let me cherish my illusions," she bantered.

After some sputtering conversation, punctuated by awkward silences, the waitress brought their beers, and that was the dividing line in their meeting. They were no longer tense. He relaxed and talked about how he'd penned a letter to the head of psychiatry objecting to Dr.

Freeman's visit. She told him that made her proud. He also told her of his talk with Father Al. That made her happy. He asked her if she'd participate in the re-enactment of the day Sister overdosed—right before coming here, he'd received a message that Sister Fulgentia would allow it. She agreed.

At the end of their dinner, even though she knew it would be their last together on these terms, she looked forward to a farewell kiss, the memory of which she'd cherish along with her illusions.

"Do tell me if you hear anything about Lena," she said, as he walked her to her car on the cusp of twilight. The air was still and warm. The city smelled used up and sated all at once.

"Of course," he said.

They stood in front of her car holding hands. A breeze lifted the hem of her skirt and blew a strand of hair into her face. With the tenderest of motions, he pushed it back into place, leaned in and kissed her. It was all she could have hoped for—warm and loving and filled with longing.

She said goodbye without looking at him, peace and sadness enveloping her as she drove away.

వా

When she heard a familiar car door slam shut, Paula rushed to the window. Was it that late already? Goodness gracious, but she'd lost track of time. Hadn't even tidied herself up, let alone started dinner. She'd been too involved in getting the room ready for Sister— for Margaret. She was determined to think of her as Margaret, just as Karol did.

"Karol, come look!" Paula brushed a damp lock of hair from her forehead and walked into the hallway just as the screen door creaked open.

It had been a tiring two days, what with Sister's— Margaret's—upset and Paula's own doctor's visit. At least that had been reassuring. Nothing to worry about, the doctor had told her. Things were progressing nicely.

235

She'd be delivering within a month. A blessed month—just enough time, she thought, to get Margaret well and on her way, just enough time to keep moving ever closer to Karol, to proving what a good wife she could be to him.

Karol appeared a moment later, and she thought she noticed him eyeing her face—which she knew was clean of makeup. "Look at Margaret's room! Let me go powder my nose."

She slipped past him, hoping he'd stop her for a greeting kiss, pausing just the tiniest fraction of a second, disappointed when, as usual, he held back. Paula always felt as if Karol were reminding himself not to love her. And she was always reminding herself that he did really care; she only needed to keep working on getting him to acknowledge it.

"Nice, huh?" she asked, coming back a few moments later, rubbing lotion on her hands. She'd finger-combed her hair and put on lipstick.

She was proud of the room. It was to be for baby—but baby would be in a bassinette with them for a while. And Paula hoped Sister—Margaret—would be gone by the time baby was ready for a crib. Now the room sported yellow curtains, a bed, a rocking chair and dresser.

"You shouldn't be moving furniture around," Karol said, looking at her with creased brow. I was gonna take that bed out of here...."

She stepped up to him and rubbed his arm, happy when he didn't pull away. "I didn't do much movin'," she said, glad he was worried about her again. "Just cleanin' mostly. I think she'll be real comfortable here."

He put his hands on his hips and continued to admire her handiwork. "Do we know when she's getting out?"

"Not yet." She'd not told Karol about Margaret's outburst. It made her uneasy, but she reassured herself that the doctors wouldn't let her go until she was suitably calm. And…the longer Margaret stayed in the hospital, the longer they'd have the house to themselves. The best of both worlds—no Margaret and no Mrs. Wojehedski.

"When she is released, I imagine she'll have to still see the doctor."

"I can take her in," Karol volunteered, his voice less wary. He turned to her and put his arm around her, kissing her on the forehead. "You done good. I appreciate it. Ma won't worry so much if Marge is here."

Sighing with relief, Paula closed her eyes and thanked her lucky stars it was all working out so well. She just needed to get through her Baptism—she'd be asking Kate, and maybe a mother from St. Benedict's and she wasn't sure who else, to stand up for her—then this Margaret business, then the baby…and finally, finally, peace and security would be hers. She went to the kitchen to throw dinner together, feeling happy and lighthearted.

∾≈∽

While Paula mourned the lack of Karol's complete devotion, she had decided at the start of their marriage that she would have to deal with that problem after the baby came. The baby was everything, the consolation for lacking other things.

In fact, if it hadn't been for her pregnancy, Paula wondered if Karol would have stopped seeing her altogether. And she didn't need to ask why. She had been in love with another man, and even if Karol didn't know the man's name, he knew that she wasn't his completely. Yes, she knew this, even though she expected him to look past it. She was faithful, after all. She was everything a husband should want.

But because they'd never openly discussed it, she couldn't reassure him. She couldn't say "Karol, I may have loved Jack Wilson, but I'm married to you now. And I want to be a good wife and mother, if you'll let me."

Their unspoken doubts kept them from talking about the things that bound them together. Everything was a possible trigger for heartbreak—even the good things, the things they enjoyed as a couple, because those moments always inevitably ended with a look in both their eyes, a look that asked: Why didn't you love me from the beginning?

In many ways, her marriage had become an instrument for the collection of comforts, she thought as she put a simple dinner together for the two of them. She picked them up wherever she saw them—in the glass display cases of a department store, in the smell and sound of a busy market, in the neat look of her living room when she returned from an outing. All these things were hers because she was a wife, a woman to whom the world offered these pleasures. They made her realize what she'd escaped after squandering her youth.

She usually did a good job of pushing all those feelings to the side and focusing almost exclusively on the present and the future. She had ten years' worth of practice, after all. That's what her move to Baltimore had really been about all those years ago—leaving her past behind, stepping out of it as if it were a shift lying on the floor.

"Chipped beef okay?" she called out to Karol in the other room.

"Sure."

He'd picked up a taste for the salty dish in the war, and she was happy to fix it. It was easy and inexpensive. She started making the white-sauce gravy to go on it, and popped some toast in the oven.

After Tom had died, Paula had stopped feeling fresh. She'd gone from man to man, all in the military, all getting ready to ship out. She'd even been with Ginny's brother before he went overseas. Maybe Ginny knew.

When she figured out that one fellow had lied and told her he was getting ready to ship out when he wasn't, she became choosier. But not quickly enough.

Her reputation had already been damaged in her tiny community where neighbors knew what you had for dinner the night before and quickly guessed your economic status by how many times you wore the same dress. She might as well have been wearing a scarlet letter announcing her sins. Women hadn't befriended her and only a certain kind of man had wanted to get close to her. She'd known things had slid downhill when her Aunt Claire had appeared again one weekend, and her father had made sure they had ample time alone with each other.

Poor Aunt Claire. She was so kind and she tried so hard. She'd talked to Paula about grief, about how hard it was to let go of a man's touch once you'd felt it, and how no one thought the less of her for craving that which was denied her. But in a small town, Aunt Claire had said, people begin to see someone a certain way and won't let go of it. And sometimes, she'd gone on to explain, the low opinion of townspeople begins to seep into your own soul.

They'd had this talk over coffee one morning when her father had told her she needn't come in that day but could spend it with her aunt. It had started pleasantly enough with her Aunt Claire asking her about what movies she'd seen recently, and they'd had a swell conversation about whether or not one could really classify Humphrey Bogart as a handsome man.

And then her aunt had subtly shifted the talk to the *love* lives of the stars—a subject Paula loved to discuss—and before she knew it, Aunt Claire was talking about reputations in general and her eyes didn't leave Paula's face for a single second when she spoke.

She was so subtle, in fact, that at first Paula hadn't had a clue that her aunt might be talking about her. But it was her eyes—dark, slightly downturned at the corners so that a smile gave her a look of happy surprise—that bored their message into Paula's heart.

Paula had stopped talking. She'd sat up straight.

She'd swallowed and looked away. She'd said nothing. And then her aunt had said:

"Have you thought of going away for a while? It would do you a world of good. Why don't you come see me in Atlanta, and I could introduce you to some friends, go shopping? It would be great fun, dear. I'd enjoy it."

What a generous offer, Paula had mouthed. I'll certainly consider it. Her aunt was kind, but she was intensely private. The only other time Paula had spent at her aunt's elegant home in the city had been an awkward visit punctuated by precisely scheduled moments of fun.

Nevertheless, she respected her aunt enough to think it over. And she was considering it when Ginny provided her with another way to get out of town, as her companion traveling to Washington to see Fred. The rest, Paula thought as she washed and dried lettuce for a salad, was history.

In many ways, Paula had experienced a streak of good luck after finally breaking off her affair with Jack over a year ago. Oh, it hadn't felt like luck at the time. She'd been in the depths of despair, seeing no future for herself, nothing to pin a hope on, and swamped with overwhelming regret—over her affair with Jack, her behavior in Percy, her treatment of her father, her lack of planning to take care of herself. She'd sat in her little apartment and wrote a long anguished letter to Jack she was sure would persuade him to be with her forever. And then she'd torn it up when she'd realized she wouldn't want him, even if he begged for her forgiveness.

She'd been so afraid. Afraid, for the first time in her life, that she wouldn't be able to provide for herself, that there was no one who could do it for her. She'd been the town beauty, the one who'd catch a beau easily. And she had nothing.

With grim determination, she'd calmed herself.

She'd let one day follow another and was pulled to safety by Ginny's admonition to try for the job at St. Benedict's. Even then, if it hadn't been for the small amount of money left over from the sale of her father's house, Paula would not have made it through the summer of 1954. Her new job hadn't started until that fall, and her last paycheck from Jack had come in the mail in June of that year, wrapped in plain paper but with no note, nothing indicating that it was her last compensation for years of heartache.

Although she owned a large and fashionable wardrobe, she used the paycheck to buy several new skirts and dresses, all modest and plain, things she thought appropriate for teaching in a parochial school.

Her duties would be simple. For four hours a day, alternating mornings and afternoons depending on the class schedules, she'd work in the small school office, handling correspondence for Sister Fulgentia, bookkeeping, and filing. For the rest of the day, she'd wheel a small electric organ from room to room, teaching first- through eighth-graders the elements of music. One afternoon a week, she was to work with a newly formed children's choir, with the assistance of a nun named Sister Francis Marie—Margaret.

Neither Sister Fulgentia nor Father Janacek had asked Paula if she was Catholic, and while it nagged at Paula that perhaps the school assumed she was, she'd pushed it aside. They were desperate for a new teacher and willing to overlook her lack of substantial teaching experience. Perhaps they were willing to overlook this, as well. Besides, in a way she felt her marriage to Tom had given her a pass in this regard. He'd been Catholic, after all.

Paula had only taught occasional piano students at her Percy home, but she had few qualms about her new position. As far as she could tell, she'd be expected to do little more than provide basic instruction. And she actually looked forward to working with the choir. It would be working with children! Darling little children, something she'd thought would not be her fate. Another fresh start, with fresh responsibilities. Perhaps that had been her problem in the past—she had not broken off completely with the remnants of her old life. She had tried to start a new one using leftovers from the past. Here there were no leftovers. Everything, from her clothes to her work, was new.

During her first week at St. Benedict's, she didn't get a chance to try out her music skills very much, however. Sister Francis Marie, the nun with whom she was supposed to work, was ill, and Sister Fulgentia asked Paula if she wouldn't mind substituting for her at the head of a second-grade class.

It was one of the best weeks of Paula's life. If the students thought she'd be a pushover, she proved them wrong by learning their names quickly, drilling them, giving out homework, and enforcing a strict code of discipline. She discovered she was good at teaching and wondered if her problem all along hadn't been that she'd gone into the wrong line of work.

She was so excited about teaching that she actually talked to Sister Fulgentia about it at the end of her first week.

The principal's small office was on the front of the school and caught the afternoon light. Hot from late summer's sizzling sunshine, the shades were kept low, warming the room with a parchment glow. Quiet, black-robed nuns came and went, dropping off notes and papers, asking to see Sr. Fulgentia for a few moments. St. Benedict's employed only two other lay teachers—an eighth-grade instructor, and a kindergarten teacher—but both kept to themselves.

Paula typed the small pile of papers Sister Fulgentia had left for her as fast as possible. She knew the nun would leave the school no later than four forty-five, and she wanted to talk with her in private before that.

After neatly stacking the last paper and entering the

last amount in her ledger, Paula scooted her chair back and knocked on Sister's half-open door.

The older nun looked up, her oval face squashed by the white fabric on her forehead, cheeks and neck. Behind frameless glasses, her gray eyes squinted, adjusting to the shift in focus. She folded her hands on her work and smiled at Paula.

"What can I help you with?" Her voice was soothing and even.

"I was wondering if I could talk to you about teaching. About how to become a teacher."

Sister gestured to the chair in front of her dark wooden desk, and Paula entered the nun's sanctuary and sat down. The room smelled of chalk dust and children's lunches, the scents of childhood. Happy smells.

Sister's desk was clean except for a planning book, upon which she was working, a green blotter, and a dictionary. Behind her a floor-to-ceiling bookcase held everything from Bibles to textbooks to safety regulations from the State of Maryland. To the right was a table upon which a new mimeograph machine rested, and next to it were neat stacks of papers that Paula had copied the day before.

"As you know, we don't require our teachers to have any special certification," Sister began. "But we do prefer they go to college. And preferably, a teacher's college."

"Is that what Mrs. Beacon and Mrs. Matusek did?" Paula asked, disappointed. She'd hoped they had entered teaching without further training. They seemed so ordinary. The only people Paula knew who'd gone to college were doctors.

Sister nodded. "Mrs. Beacon went to the teachers college in Towson, and Mrs. Matusek received her degree from St. Mary's College for Girls."

"I see."

"You might want to talk to them about it."

243

"I...I might." But it was difficult to find time to talk with them. They didn't eat lunch together, and while both of them lived in Rosedale, Paula still lived downtown. If she lingered too long, she'd miss her daily bus.

"I wish I could help you more," Sister Fulgentia continued, with a genuine sense of regret in her voice, "but we receive our own teaching instruction at the Mother House."

Before Paula could ask more questions, Sister Fulgentia changed the subject. "I've been meaning to remind you that all the teachers are required to come to the School Mass on Sunday. At nine o'clock. Since this isn't your home parish, I wasn't sure you would remember."

"Oh." Not only had she not remembered, she hadn't thought it was something she had to do. Yes, she had typed the notice and placed copies in Mrs. Beacon's and Matusek's boxes. She thought it was merely a suggestion. "Thank you. I *had* forgotten."

Sister picked up her pen, a signal that she didn't want to talk much longer. "I'm hoping Sister Francis Marie will be well enough to be there. You can finally meet."

"Yes, that would be nice. Although I haven't minded at all teaching...."

"You've done a good job. She should be pleased."

With that the interview was over. Sister Fulgentia might have wished she could offer Paula more, but she hadn't volunteered to get information on teaching colleges for Paula. She'd told Paula to go to the other lay teachers. And while she'd complimented Paula's handling of the students, she'd also indicated that Sister Francis Marie should be the one pleased.

Nuns were curious creatures. Paula sometimes had trouble telling them apart. When they spoke to her, it was in little more than a whisper, their eyes lowered, their hands hidden in their robes, and no more than was absolutely necessary passing their lips. Sister Fulgentia's interview was downright effusive compared to her other interactions.

Mass at St. Benedict's would present several challenges to Paula that made her stomach knot. She'd have to make special arrangements to get out to the little suburb because the buses didn't run there on Sundays. As it was, her commute during the week was barely tolerable, and she was already making plans to find another place to live. She had to catch three buses—one that took her from her apartment on upper Charles Street into town, another that took her from town out to East Baltimore, and a third local bus that deposited her on the doorstep of St. Benedict's. She scanned the newspaper daily looking for an apartment closer to the school.

And then there was the problem of not being Catholic. She'd have to follow the service as best she could. She reminded herself she'd not actually lied to anyone about her religion. She'd just never shared the information.

Sunday dawned warm and humid with the hiss of summer's end in the distance. Summer's end always reminded Paula now of the war's end, and it filled her with a melancholy made up of equal parts hope and fear of disappointment, like the singed smell of birthday candles after they'd been extinguished at celebration's close.

She dressed in a forest green suit with oversized buttons and corded edging. This she paired with beige shoes and gloves, and a straw hat whose sole decorative touch was a green band of ribbon. She'd already called a taxi and when it didn't arrive right away, butterflies flew in her stomach. She didn't want to make Sister Fulgentia angry or doubtful. If Paula didn't make it to this Mass, it would be as if she were advertising the fact she wasn't a Catholic.

When she reached St. Benedict's, she had just two

minutes to spare before Mass began. She should have been there early to sit with her class. Frowning, she paid the driver quickly and tipped him too much—this morning would cost her as much as a new pair of shoes by the time she was done. Rushing up the steps to the chiming of the church bell, she entered, followed the lead of another latecomer by dipping her fingers in the Holy Water font and swooping the air in front of her chest in what she hoped was the appropriate gesture.

The church was full, but she spotted the squirming children in her class and headed to their pews, where a pale sister moved over to make room for her. "You must be Sister Francis Marie," Paula whispered, discreetly holding out her hand. But the nun didn't shake it, nor did she say anything in greeting. "I'm Paula DiGiacomo. I've been handling your class while you were out. I hope you're feeling better." Again, the nun said nothing, but the corners of her mouth moved up in imitation of a smile.

Perhaps Paula should have sat with Sister Fulgentia, she thought as she sat back in the pew, allowing Sister Francis Marie to handle the second-graders on her own. Paula noticed all the other classes had only their one teacher sitting at the end of their rows.

Before she had a chance to correct what she thought might be a mistake, opportunities for new ones appeared. The Mass began as the priest entered, and Paula panicked as she discovered there were no prayer books, nor hymnals, nor any guideposts for her to follow. Most of the children had their own little prayer books with pictures of devout children on the covers and gold trimmed pages. Sister Francis Marie, like the rest of the nuns, had nothing. Her hands were joined together, palm to palm, pointed upward toward the heavens. Paula imitated her.

In fact, Paula stole glances at the nun throughout the service, copying each move as best she could. Unlike the services with which Paula was familiar, this one was heavily Latin and with little music, none of it anything she recognized. No sturdy angular hymns about O God Our Help in Ages Past, no metered songs about lifting high the cross. Only melodies that had no end, sung by the priest with a few responses from the congregation.

When Paula wasn't following Sister's lead, she looked around at the congregation. Some of them followed along with the priest. Others prayed rosaries, the long beads hanging in front of them over the pew ahead.

At Communion, Paula's heart beat fast. What should she do? What if she couldn't see what to do? Pews emptied up ahead and to the right. People knelt at the marble rail, the priest came by and placed a host on their tongues. He murmured a prayer. Was there a response? She couldn't see. Then, to her relief, she noticed the first- and second-graders weren't moving. They and their respective teachers—nuns like Sister Francis Marie— stayed put. The older children behind them did go up, and Mrs. Beacon and Mrs. Matusek joined them. But Paula felt safe, kneeling next to the closed-eye figure of Sr. Francis Marie who was fingering her own brown rosary beads now.

When it was over, a mere forty-five minutes after it began, Paula felt as if she'd passed a test. As soon as she was outside, children surrounded her, introducing their parents, giggling, telling her she looked pretty, and asking would they have a test on Monday.

"Sister Francis Marie will be back on Monday," Paula told them, scanning the crowd for the tall, thin nun. She didn't see her. She must have gone back to the convent.

The crowd milled in the cool shadow of the white church. Parents said hello, Mrs. Beacon came over to talk with her, her own daughter in tow, a gawky girl of twelve or thirteen.

"We never get a chance to talk, Mrs. DiGiacomo," Mrs. Beacon said, holding out her hand. A solid woman with a shelf-like bosom, she was dressed in a silky shirt dress of dark stripes. Her brown hair was curly and already showed strands of gray. Paula guessed her to be in her forties. "I'm Donna. This is my daughter Beverly." The girl half grimaced, half smiled.

"Call me Paula," Paula said to both of them. "How long have you been at St. Benedict's?"

"Only a year. It's a new parish. We moved here from the city. I wanted Beverly to live in the country."

Paula noticed that Donna said "I," and not "we." She knew what that meant.

"My husband died in the war," Paula prompted.

"I'm a widow, too!" Donna's face broke into a wide grin, completely at odds with the sad news she'd just shared. "You should come by for coffee some time. We have these school Masses once a month. Or come after school. I don't live that far away. Just a couple blocks over."

"Mom," Beverly whined. "I'm hungry."

Donna scowled at her daughter. "Just a minute." Smiling, she turned back to Paula. "I'll talk to you this week."

"Thanks. I'd like that."

Donna and her daughter walked away, not toward the parking lot on the side of the church but toward Old Philadelphia Road. Clearly, they had no car.

No car. Paula didn't have one either, and she'd been in such a rush when she arrived at the church that she'd forgotten to tell the taxi to come back for her. As the crowd thinned, Paula looked anxiously up and down the small street that ran in front of the church. No cabs would be out this way on a Sunday morning. She could call one from the convent—but the convent looked locked up as tight as the nuns themselves. She didn't want to intrude, nor give away the fact that she'd not made arrangements.

Standing straight, she decided to walk to Pulaski Highway, just a block away, and hope to find a taxi somewhere on the way into town. Surely she'd come across one in good time. All would be well. It was a pleasant day, with no threat of rain, and now that the Mass was over her heart was light. The walk would be good for her.

Leaving the cool embrace of the church behind, she trudged up the small hill toward the major thoroughfare. By the time she got there, she was already beginning to perspire. She unbuttoned her suit jacket and removed her gloves.

Traffic was light, so she continued walking west toward the city. Surely she'd see a taxi by the time she reached the bottom of the hill.

But a few minutes later, she began to think she'd made a mistake. No taxies were in sight, and her feet ached in her attractive pumps not meant for long walks. The warmth of her body steamed her face. She took off her jacket and folded it over her arm. A gentle wind buffeted the brim of her hat, and she had to hold it with her other hand. If she turned around now and went back to use the convent phone, she'd look even more foolish. Better to keep moving and hope for the best.

A couple cars went by, honking their horns.

"Good grief!" she cried out when a stone, kicked up by a tire, hit her on the leg. Her stocking was ruined.

At the bottom of the hill, she stared at the city skyline impossibly far away. She could walk all the way into town without seeing a single taxi, she thought. It was Sunday, after all. What had she been thinking? She was just about to turn around and face the raised eyebrows of Sister Fulgentia, when a two-toned Chevy slowed down and pulled up beside her. A dark-haired man was at the wheel, with a good-looking woman in the passenger seat. Ready for the wolf whistle or taunt that was sure to follow, Paula increased her pace.

"Where ya goin'? Need a ride?" his voice called out as he let the car roll slowly with her.

The best strategy was to ignore him. She stared

straight ahead and walked even faster.

"Hey! I'm from St. Benedict's!"

Paula turned and looked at them more closely. He was well dressed—in a navy blue sports jacket and white shirt, with a striped tie. The woman, with strawberry-blond hair in a cloud of curls around her face, was laughing uproariously. When she saw Paula's confusion, she managed to sputter.

"I'm sorry. I told him to call to you... *I* should have done it." Wiping away tears of laughter, the girl got out of the front seat and held the door open. Extremely slender, she had a childlike face and a cupid's mouth. She wore a white silk blouse and navy skirt. Paula could see her hat on the back seat.

"I'm Rose Wojehedski. This is my brother, Karol. We saw you in church. Right, Karol?" She seemed to be prompting him to talk to Paula.

"Yeah. You were sitting next to our sister." He didn't look at Paula and kept his right hand on the steering wheel. His left hand seemed curled in a fist in his lap.

Rose gestured to the car. "Come on, get in. We'll give you a lift."

Gratefully, Paula sat next to Karol while Rose slid in and closed the door.

"You have a sister in school?" Paula asked Rose. Rose smiled, then giggled.

"Yes, I guess we do. Right, Karol?" She laughed again, her hand fluttering to her chest as she struggled to gain control. Her laugh was infectious—girlish, light, kind, a ripple.

"Not a kid. Sister Francis Marie," he said. "Margaret. Her real name's Margaret."

"Oh! Your sister is Sister Francis. I've been taking her class while she was sick."

Rose grew serious. "She was sick again?"

Should Paula not have told them? "She seems better now."

"She'll be fine," Karol said. "She gets sick a lot."

"We're headed into town to go to the bakery for our mother," Rose offered. "She's back at Karol's place. But she likes the shortcake at Patuchi's and Karol promised her he'd pick some up. He's nice that way." She smiled mischievously, obviously taking pleasure in teasing her brother.

"You can drop me there, then. At the bakery," Paula said. Wherever this bakery was, it was in town, and she'd be more likely to find a taxi there.

"Where were you headed?" Rose asked.

"Home. My apartment's on Charles Street."

After a moment's silence, Rose turned toward Paula and Karol. "You should drop me off at the bakery, Karol. I'll pick some things out. Then you can swing back and pick me up after dropping off Miss…"

"I'm sorry. I should have introduced myself. DiGiacomo. Paula DiGiacomo."

"You from Little It'ly?" Karol asked, suspicious.

"No, no. My husband's family was Italian." How odd to refer to Tom's family as if they had been her own. The only contact she'd ever had with them was a letter from their lawyer informing her she had no claim to Tom's things since they didn't recognize the marriage "outside the church." That was after Paula had sent her consolation note to Mrs. DiGiacomo.

"My husband died in the war," she added.

"Oh, dear. I'm sorry," Rose said. After a pause: "Karol served. He was wounded."

Paula looked at him, but he stared straight ahead. His arm. It must have been his arm.

"We were all so relieved when he came home." Rose smiled gently at her brother, as if she were trying to nudge him into good humor. "He doesn't like to talk about it."

"No point," he said gruffly.

As they drove in silence, Paula stole glances at him. His skin was tan, and his eyes brown. He had a wide face, wild eyebrows, and wrinkles near his eyes. He wore some aftershave or cologne that smelled of cloves.

Before hitting the center of town, he turned the car onto Conkling Street and then down some cross streets until he was in front of the bakery.

After Rose exited the car, she leaned down and smiled at them both.

"Don't let him get away without saying anything, Paula. He needs to talk to people more!" She wiggled her fingers in the air in farewell. "See you in a little while!"

Paula smiled to herself. Clearly, Rose was trying to push Karol on her, and she could imagine what the conversation must have been like before he pulled over. *Look, isn't that the woman who was sitting next to Sister? Pull over, Karol. Ask her in. Ask her out!*

"How long have you lived in Baltimore?" she asked him.

"All my life. What about you?"

She told him about Ginny and Percy. He told her about living in Highlandtown but wanting to get away from that after the war.

"So I saved some money and I put a down payment on a house."

"Your mother must be very happy there."

"Mom's stubborn. She wouldn't move away from her neighborhood. She and Rosy still live in town."

By the time they reached her apartment, he'd opened up enough to laugh with her over how silly she'd been to try walking into town looking for a taxi.

"Must be tough going all the way out to Rosedale from here every day," he said, parked in front of her apartment building.

"There are buses. But the last one's at five. I'm looking for a place closer." Remembering her conversation with Donna Beacon earlier, she told him how it was impossible to get to know anyone at the school when she lived so far away.

Relaxed by now, Karol turned to her and grinned, a smile almost as open as his sister Rose's. "Hey, if you ever want to stay and meet with anyone at the school, just give me a call. I can drive you home. I don't mind."

It wouldn't have been right to invite him up for coffee, so she grabbed her purse and gloves and thanked him, then slid toward the door.

"Wait a minute!" He got out and came around, opening the door with his good right hand.

"Thank you," she said again. "I can't tell you how much you helped me. I don't know what I'd have done."

Impulsively, he blurted out, "Maybe we can have coffee next week. At my place. After Mass."

Again, she imagined Rose coaxing him in the car to ask this very question. *Go ahead, Karol. Ask her out.*

"I don't…" She didn't go to St. Benedict's every Sunday. He read her mind.

"Oh, that's right. You probably go to the Basilica," he said, staring at his feet, the broad smile already replaced by storm clouds.

"No, no. I'd like to go to St. Benedict's—to get to know people more."

His face flashed again at hers. "I could pick you up."

᳘

In many ways, Rose had been the glue that had held them together, filling their silences with conversation and jokes, nudging Karol to be Paula's beau. Going out with Karol was awkward because of his shyness, his embarrassment about his arm and his lack of social graces. On top of all that, Paula always felt a little diminished when he took her home. He made her ache for John simply because Karol wasn't at all like him.

All summer she'd managed to fight the impulse to see John, to talk to him, to miss him so badly she could barely think of anything else. She'd filled her summer with getting ready for her new job, writing Ginny, seeing movies—anything to keep busy. In a way, John's absence was like a respite, not a complete break. Something in her always thought a reconciliation was in the distant future if she only suffered long enough. She dreamt of him many times that summer, dreams that they were together, dreams that they were apart, but still dreams in which she felt she owned a part of him again.

But once she started seeing Karol, her separation from John became real and stabbed afresh. Karol's presence in her life was now a point of contrast. Where Karol was unsophisticated, John had been suave, where Karol was just getting started as a bookkeeper at Baltimore Gas and Electric, John was a respected physician from a family of physicians, where Karol was timid, John had been passionate. And John had been whole.

There was no difficulty in being chaste with Karol. He was too bashful to go beyond kisses and hugs, and she was now cautious. More often than not, during that autumn they started seeing each other, she ended up going home and crying for what she missed.

If anything, she looked forward to seeing Rose more than Karol. Rose was like a glass of champagne—bubbly and spirited, dampening inhibitions and bringing out the most cheerful parts of themselves. No matter what Paula's mood, she always found a smile creeping to her face when she was around Rose, waiting to see what the girl would do or say next. A natural wise-cracker, Rose would tease Karol out of Sunday grumps and make a party out of donuts and coffee after Mass. Rose baked Paula a cake one Sunday, and stood in the doorway with a paper hat on, blowing a cardboard horn when Karol brought Paula up to the door, telling her since she didn't know her birthday, she'd decreed this one the day.

If they went out with Rose, Paula could count on having a good time, laughing the night away at silly jokes and faces. Rose had several beaux but kept them guessing. She confided to Paula that she had a hard time thinking of settling down because she was having too much fun. "Sometimes I make lists," she told Paula one night after they'd had too many beers at a tavern in the old neighborhood, "you know—the good points and bad points of each of them. But I can't even decide what's good and what's bad. I mean, Henry Dominick is a good dancer. But maybe that's not good. Maybe that means he'll be a lady's man. And Joe Stefano is too quiet. But sometimes I like quiet."

There were many times when Paula wished she could confide in Rose, when she could sigh, "I wish I could love Karol, but I love this other man. Still! I love him still!" Instead, she talked about work at St. Benedict's. Rose was a teacher, too, at a public school on the west side of the city. She had put herself through college.

Paula spent Christmas with Karol and his family, including his brother Bernard who reunited with them after an absence of many years. There was no point in heading home to North Carolina now; Ginny and Fred were in Virginia, and her Aunt Claire was way down in Atlanta, too far for a comfortable journey.

Christmas at Karol's was a strained holiday, with Karol's resentment of Bernard simmering so close to the surface that even Rose had trouble keeping things cheerful.

And on New Year's Eve, Karol invited her to a dance at the Knights of Columbus Hall, and she wore her red dress and drank too much and thought of John, and ended up inviting Karol into her bed, where he told her he loved her, and she said nothing but "you darling" and an acutely insincere "me, too" in return.

But Karol—unsophisticated, uneducated, inarticulate Karol—he'd needed no translation for those words. He'd waited for more. She'd smiled and stroked his chin. But she couldn't tell him she loved him. She couldn't betray John. He'd waited. Seconds. Minutes. His smile had faded, his eyes registered heartache, then shame. He'd slipped out in the morning, before the doorman came on duty, telling her he didn't want to harm her reputation. But she'd sensed he wanted to be away from the scene of a defeat.

After that, he became estranged. He didn't invite her to his house after Mass the following Sunday. He didn't call. He knew he was just a substitute.

Months went by. Dreary winter. Finally, Rose did call. Feeling a little under the weather, she apologized for not being at Karol's house on Sundays. She'd been busy, and now she was coming down with the flu. Paula didn't tell her she hadn't been there either, that she hadn't been there for several weeks. It was the last time Paula spoke with Rose. And the last words Rose had said were, "Be patient with Karol. He's just afraid."

The thought of Rose choked her, and she stood at the stove, finishing dinner, with tears surprising her.

"What's the matter?" Karol said, coming into the room.

"Nothin', nothin'. Just a spec of dust in my eye." She willed the blues away and smiled. "You're just in time. Dinner's ready."

CHAPTER SEVENTEEN
Warned

THE RAIN, a cool night. Not the unsatisfying coolness of the whirring fan in the corner, but dampened breeze cool. Maybe it was because of the rain that she felt better in the morning—as if she truly were recovering.

She had written her letter to Sister Fulgentia. Maybe that was it, having that task behind her. She'd stated her case simply and briefly. *My doctor suggests I spend some time recuperating outside the hospital. My brother's house is available. I shall keep you informed of my progress. I hope to be discharged any day now, closer every day to full recovery.*

That should satisfy her. She knew Sister Fulgentia had already been contacted. What did she need the letter for, except to judge her lacking once again? All right, she would be judged. She'd done nothing wrong. She was trying to get better. She would prove how obedient she was, even if it meant living outside the convent for a brief period. Yes, just a short time, that was all. She couldn't expect Sister Fulgentia, with her hale constitution, to understand. She would have to show her how much she was trying. She would have to demonstrate humility and acceptance.

Motion at the door grabbed her attention. The priest with Communion.

"I can come back if you're not ready," he said quietly.

Mutely, she came forward and knelt by the bed.

She'd not broken the nightly fast. She'd not broken Grand Silence. She was ready.

The rain, the Latin words, the host on her tongue— peace settled on her. He blessed her but did not leave. Her eyes closed, she listened, obediently.

"Be as kind to yourself, Sister, as Our Lord is to you. Work with your doctors. They want to help you. Listen to what they have to say and try to help them help you. And, please, call on me or another priest if you need anyone to hear your confession."

Hear her confession? Her body warmed. Yes, she'd like confession, but she'd let him know later. Not now, not on a day when she felt the Rule of her Order wrapping her in its comforting cloak of routine.

After he left, she stepped to the window, pulling tight a blue-and-white seersucker robe Kate had given her. Peering outside, she tried to place her room. She knew that Hopkins sprawled along city blocks in northeast Baltimore. Its imposing front faced Broadway. But where was this room in its empire? Where was she in the hospital, in the city, in the world itself?

Below, traffic snarled. Cars moved slowly down a narrow street, the sun now glinting from their metal roofs and clear windshields. A street Arab blocked cars' way on the far side of the road, a muscular Negro standing by the side of his horse-drawn cart rearranging fruit so it wouldn't fall. Cars honked at him as they realized he was the source of the congestion, but he remained oblivious. He moved at the pace of heat, slow and deliberate, so that the exertion wouldn't cost him too much energy in the life-sapping blaze of the sun. When at last he was satisfied, he hoisted himself into the driver's bench and grabbed the reins. Margaret couldn't hear what he said, but she saw his lips move, perhaps with the horse's name. When he pulled out into traffic, more cars blared but again, he paid no heed. He moved to his own inner clock. A nurse scurried through the stalled cars toward the building and disappeared below.

Two policemen greeted each other and moved on, looking after the horse-drawn cart as if deciding whether to force him to move off the street or pick up his step. A delivery boy carried boxes into a building two doors down and over. A man in a gray suit and hat took long strides to the corner where a bus was ready to pull away.

And above them all, visible over the tarred rooftops, was the wan blue sky, its color bleached pale by the summer heat, now returning after the storm. A few seagulls swooped and cawed, their voices cutting through the buzz of traffic and the whir of the fan in Margaret's room. With the fan blowing air directly on her, she could pretend it was spring, not summer, the season of promises and hope and not that of fatigue and melancholy.

"I see you're up. How are you feeling?"

She turned to see Dr. Kaplan standing by the bed.

"I'm feeling very well today. When do you think I can be discharged?"

"If you continue to improve." He stood, awkwardly looking at the bed and at her. Ah. This was to be a session. She returned to the bed, and he sat in the chair beside her. "Does that make you happy?"

Margaret wasn't used to thinking of happiness. She thought only of comfort—the heat made her uncomfortable, her room at St. Benedict's was too small, her Mother Superior too demanding, this bed soft, the window inviting...

"Yes," she said, but her voice sounded unsure. Nervous, she began to breathe shallowly. She had to calm down. This was part of being obedient. Hadn't the priest urged her to work with the doctor? She had to try harder. But her desire to be obedient was so strong, her yearning to be discharged was so passionate...she could hardly contain herself.

"Are you often breathless?"

What did he mean by often? Once a day, twice a week? That was the problem with doctors. They gave no indication of what was normal. How was she to determine on her own what wasn't, when her only point of reference was the abnormality of her own life?

"No...yes...." She had to be honest and obedient. Yes, she'd been breathless. "At the start of the school day. As I began teaching. I was...excited." Her heart would palpitate, her face would warm, her palms would sweat.

"That must have been difficult," Dr. Kaplan said. "What about other times—did anything else trigger your nervousness?"

"The choir. We had a children's choir." It sprang into memory. Sister Fulgentia had insisted she start one. That's when they'd hired Paula to teach—when it became painfully clear that Margaret's musical skills were limited at best. Defeated again at the memory, she sighed so loudly that Dr. Kaplan looked up suddenly, his wide face shining toward her like a beacon.

"I don't want to exhaust you. But I thought if we could talk about your daily routine, perhaps something of that day would come back to you—the day you took the overdose."

She cringed at the word—overdose. The tears came, so swiftly that Margaret couldn't reach for the tissues fast enough to staunch the flow. Dr. Kaplan helped her, handing her water, silently waiting until she was able to control herself.

"I don't remember," she said at last. "Do I have to remember before you'll let me go?" This was the source of her tears, this utter blackness about that moment, the moment that now trapped her here.

He sat back down. "Have you written anything?"

She nodded, pointing to the drawer in the bedside table. She'd jotted a few notes before going to sleep the night before.

He pulled out the papers, reading silently.

"More about Mr. and Mrs. Mallory," he said, rubbing his beard.

"He's gone now," she said, another memory returning.

"Mr. Mallory—how did he die?"

"He was killed during the war."

"I see. Did he remind you of your own father?"

"No."

Silly question—why would he ask that?

"I saw an article about him when I was at St. Benedict's." The words came in a rush as the memory flooded in. "One of the Sisters has the newspaper delivered because she uses it in her history class. I read part of it when I was home one day with flu." Another sin, reading that newspaper. No contact with the outside world. No contact with family.

"That was recent? Reading the newspaper and seeing the article?"

She closed her eyes, trying to place it. "I....I think it was in the spring. No, maybe the fall. The weather was cool." She could see the newspaper. She could see herself looking at it. She couldn't remember the date.

"What was the article about?"

"A charity event. Something he'd endowed was having some sort of celebration." A suite of rooms at Sheppard Pratt. They'd been redone or something like that. The Mallory Suite. The article had talked about him and his commitment to the mentally ill. *Bennett Mallory, lawyer and philanthropist.* When she'd first seen the article, she'd thought it had said "philanderer." Lawyer and philanderer. Her heart had jumped, as if the newspaper had found out about a secret of hers— one of *her* sins— not his. She'd read it again, but it had only added to her unease. Bennett Mallory had provided endowments to several local charities, and had contributed a sizeable sum to St. Rose of Lima. He'd been killed in Europe. How had he managed to serve—hadn't he been too old? He'd stayed true to Antonia in his way. He hadn't been the man Sister had imagined.

"What happened to Mrs. Mallory—did the article

say?"

"I don't know." She didn't remember. Did it say she had predeceased him? She should know—why hadn't she paid attention?

"Maybe she did go to the convent…" she said timidly. She would like to think she did, that she recovered and made good on her promise.

"You said her mother was the one who urged that on her." He pointed to the papers in front of him. "Did your mother similarly encourage you?"

"No, I struggled for a way to tell my mother. And Mrs. Mallory—she obviously agreed with her mother and had wanted to go…" If not for temptation, in the form of Mr. Mallory.

"She changed her mind. And then back again. Why do you think that was wrong?"

She knew what he was hinting at. It would be so easy if she told him what he wanted to hear—that she'd not enjoyed entering the convent. But her life had improved immeasurably the day she'd entered Mount St. Agnes. She'd gone from poverty to plenty, an irony considering their vow of poverty. Sometimes she'd tried to give up things to satisfy the vow, lingering at a task so as not to come into dinner to eat. But always, someone found her and brought her to the table, and she was reprimanded more than once for that approach, even to the point of being warned.… It made her tremble. Warned. The council at the Mother House that decided quarterly during one's postulancy and novitiate if you were up to the rigors and attitudes of the Order—the council had warned her more than once that her devotion was extravagant. It had stunned her. She'd meditated on it at length. She'd decided that they were wrong, but that she must somehow show her willingness to obey. She'd pleaded with them once to give her another chance. And secretly, she'd wondered if they were envious of her ability to discipline herself in ways they couldn't or didn't seem to want to. She'd continued her regimen but became more secretive about it—the pinpricks to stay awake was one strategy. Eating only those things she disliked was another. Praying rosaries and novenas continually was another…

"God had asked of her one thing, only one thing. And she couldn't do that one thing for Him."

"You mean you think she should have divorced her husband and entered the convent?"

Margaret looked at him again, remembering he wasn't a Catholic and didn't understand.

"She couldn't divorce him. That would have been another sin. Her one sin compounded itself. She didn't keep her promise, and then it became impossible to keep it."

"So she was punished," he prompted.

Yes, she'd thought of it that way—that Antonia had been punished.

When she didn't answer, he pressed forward. "Sister, do you feel you've been punished?"

The fan whirred. The hospital murmured its life in small noises outside the door. The sun began to warm the day. Couldn't she rest? Couldn't he leave her alone? Maybe if he left her alone, she'd dress and…somehow find her way out of this hospital, out of all of this, especially these questions.

How could she not feel punished—Rosy was dead. But that couldn't be. He couldn't have done that just to punish her…

"I am insignificant in God's eyes," she murmured. Fatigue washed over her. She felt she hardly had the energy to breathe and again began to struggle for air. Dr. Kaplan noticed.

"Are you all right, Sister? You look pale." He offered her some water, but she waved it away, closing her eyes.

"I'm very tired."

"All right. We won't be much longer. Tell me more about the Mallorys."

CHAPTER EIGHTEEN
Omens

THE MALLORY house was always quiet. As I cleaned, I would daydream about what it would be like to live in a house like that, a quiet life, a peaceful life, a life without all the mundane worries of my own household that kept us from being able to dream beyond our next meal.

Even so, the Mallory story haunted the home, whispering from its empty rooms, its still, straight mistress, always at prayer. Hilda continued to tell me bits and pieces of the tale, filling in the missing places until a full portrait of the woman's heartbreak was painted.

"He has a cutie," Hilda said one February afternoon as we sipped coffee and listened to the radio. "He's had her for a while. I hear he's even had the nerve to bring her by Little Italy, not by the Lambogne restaurant, but still..."

"Who is she?"

"A clerk in his office, a woman studying the law. Can you think of it? A woman in law? It wasn't meant to be...." She shook her head in disgust and blew smoke in the air.

The radio was turned low so that the music show and afternoon serials were only a dull murmur. In the background, a clock ticked away the minutes. Hilda cut us each a generous piece of cinnamon coffee cake. Being well-fed and warm made the story seem even more unreal. Who could blame me—a girl of just fifteen—for being so heartless that I enjoyed hearing this story of woe? It made my own troubles less hurtful, so that I could think, deep in my heart where thoughts are only feelings, that God loved me more than this, that I had been good in some way and had thus escaped heaven's wrath.

"Mrs. Mallory, she should eat more, keep herself better. Do you see what she eats? Hardly a thing. She won't touch this cake. Lent is almost here and she'll even give up lunch. I've seen her do it. *Ja!* No wonder he sees this woman. Sometimes, he doesn't come home for dinner...that's why Mrs. Mallory makes the bed. She doesn't want us to see he hasn't slept in it."

When Lent began, everything in the shrine room was draped in purple cloth—the crucifix on the wall, the shrine to Mary, the pictures of the Sacred Heart and St. Francis. Entering the shrine room filled me with more awe than entering St. Bridget's. Something profound had happened here, whereas St. Bridget's was a place of mere ritual. Here was real evidence of sacrifice and punishment, a story of Biblical proportions recently experienced, not some long ago event covered over with the gilt of the ages.

Mrs. Mallory's Lenten penance humbled me, while I didn't know what sacrifices to make for the season. Giving up a treat at the Mallory household was the obvious choice. But Hilda took such pleasure in "putting fat on those skinny arms" that I couldn't bear to think of telling her that I wanted to forgo her special baked goods.

Hilda was a Catholic, but a convert; she didn't share the same devotion to the rituals of the Church. On Ash Wednesday, she showed up at the house bare-headed, no ashes staining her white forehead as they did mine and Mrs. Mallory's.

A week into Lent, I finally decided my Lenten

penance would be to get off the streetcar a few blocks early and walk the rest of the way to the Mallorys. But even this turned out to be more pleasure than pain. As winter waned, a thaw set in, turning the short walks into happy opportunities to smell the quickening earth, hear the first robins return to the trees, see the grass begin its transformation from brown straw to soft green carpet. Breathing deeply the unseasonably warm air one morning, I chuckled to myself. Just the night before, I had told Rosy about the walks.

"So you chose walking as your penance and now you're enjoying it? It doesn't sound like much of a sacrifice to me!" laughed Rosy. Rosy never judged me harshly, always accepted me as I was, loved me as I was. We were two conspirators together in our bedroom, carving out a bright space in the gloom of our household, making jokes when we heard Karol and Mother argue, just as we had woven fantastic stories and games of pretend when Mother and Father had clashed.

"Well, I was going to choose giving up cake but Hilda started making pies and strudels....so...."

"So no matter what you choose it turns into something fun. You're like King Midas..."

Rosy was sick that winter, very sick, so sick we almost lost her. To think of it is to lose part of myself again, to feel a clamp tighten around my chest. I can't think of it. It is another memory fogged by time and pain.

Eventually a true spring came, one that teased and flirted and eventually burst into a glorious summer soon enough. The world changed that spring, and not just because war threatened. It changed because we had passed through a cauldron and we had survived. We were living without Father and we were no longer starving, no longer afraid.

War was at the doorstep and I was no longer afraid! How oblivious I was to the valley of darkness just beyond my door. If the shadow passed us over, I didn't want to know of the doors it darkened. In fact, everything was a shadow, gray and unreal with no real pain in it, like fairy-tale knights who fall off their horses. If you have come through even a distant brush with catastrophe, even an incident where Death merely whispers from a afar– and yet it still passes by— you know what I mean when I say that nothing—not even news of neighbors' families in peril in the Old Country, of boys craving adventure enlisting early, of bombs exploding far away—nothing could penetrate the blissful isolation of One Who Has Been Spared. And I felt, that summer, that I had been spared, that we all had been spared, that our war was over while another one began far away in lands that didn't touch us.

With school out, Karol was free to join the Mallory household as a gardener while Rosy helped Mother at the store. I now had company on my thrice-weekly rides to Guilford. Karol fit in well, working hard at his assigned chores and flattering Hilda, who was a natural flirt, during his breaks. The three of us began listening to a slate of afternoon radio programs—"Against the Storm," "Ma Perkins," and "Guiding Light," sipping at lemonade or iced tea and eating short cakes and cobblers that Hilda was always baking.

We even had a respite from Mrs. Mallory and her sad past as well. (And this just added to my sense of well-being, that she, with her scent of death, was gone.) The Mallorys went away in June to their Eastern Shore home, not to return until September when cooler weather would start to blow back into the city. Hilda clucked and clucked as she helped pack Antonia Mallory's bags, sure that a trip would be too hard on her employer and unconvinced of Bennett Mallory's intentions.

"Why does he want to take her away there? He's got his own girl back here. He's up to no good, no good."

"Aw, Hilda, you've been listening to too many shows," Karol kidded her. I was happy to hear him joke.

His mood was lifting, too, and he wasn't arguing with Mother any longer.

On summer days after that, worry was somewhere beyond the city, in someone else's yard. With the veil of Mallory sadness lifted from the house, the three of us became lords and ladies of the manor, finishing our chores in the morning and filling the languid afternoons with laughter and chatter.

Even home life improved at this time. The store began to improve after mother had finally sought the advice of a neighbor, a man who owned his own business, a dry goods store. He gave her some of the same suggestions Karol and even father had tried to give her, but somehow, coming from this "expert," they seemed more credible. She followed the advice and began to prosper.

The only cloud in the blue sky of my days was the fact that I still had not worked up the courage to share my vocation with anyone but the nuns at St. Bridget's. My mother didn't know. Neither did Karol or Rosy. And Hilda wouldn't understand. Ironically, the only one who would was Antonia Mallory, and she was far away.

After that horrible winter when the store was doing so poorly and Rosy's health nearly failed, it was so easy to believe we were spared forever. I felt immune to tragedy, wrapped in a mantle of security, sure that my vocation was insurance against illness, death, or despair. If a prophet had come up to me and announced that I'd be drowning in sorrow soon enough, I'd have laughed him away, so sure was I that we were safe—or at least that no sorrow would be unbearable now.

One July morning, however, when the Baltimore heat settled on the house, like a warm blanket from which there was no escape, sadness visited the Mallory household again, and we were able to watch it unfold like a drama on a stage.

That morning the still heat made me as jittery as the crickets that buzzed unseen in the bushes. No amount of closing and opening draperies to catch the shade or breeze would adequately cool a room. Even the sunroom with its screened walls and light wicker furniture captured the heat and held it like a coal on the hearth. Karol was covered with sweat from the smallest exertion, and just that morning a dozen trees arrived from the nursery to be planted in a row at the back of the yard. I fretted about him, taking him pitchers of lemonade while he dug the holes and placed the trees.

Hilda didn't cook that day. Instead, she sliced cucumbers and cold chicken and made little finger sandwiches for us. We spread a cloth under the heaviest trees in the backyard and made a picnic. Clouds were beginning to roll in, signaling a welcome storm. But Karol worried he wouldn't get all the trees in the newly dug holes and they would fill with water. He hurried through his lunch to finish the work in the blistering afternoon.

He worked so vigorously, filling the air with the quick smack of shovel hitting ground, that we didn't even hear the gravel crunch on the drive as the Mallory car pulled in. It wasn't until the doors slammed and voices carried that we knew something was happening.

"Take these things into the house," Hilda instructed me. "I'll go see."

While I put the picnic things away, I tried to listen to what was happening elsewhere. I only heard doors opening and closing and the soft murmur of Antonia's voice and Hilda's, too. I thought I heard crying but wasn't sure.

When Hilda returned to the kitchen, I had a glass of tea ready for her.

"Thank you, girl. *Gott*, it's hot up there. I don't know how she'll stand it. I told her to come down to the sunroom, or to the garden, but she went in to pray right away...."

"Is that why he brought her home?"

Hilda laughed a little. "Who knows the real reason?

She doesn't look well, though. Her eyes...I've never seen them like that...so filled with tears. And she's so...nervous. She was almost crying when I begged her to stay out of the heat. 'You sound like Bennett,' she said to me. 'You're on his side.' I'm on nobody's side but the side of good sense, I told her. And then she said, 'Every time I try to keep up with him, I get into trouble...' She capsized a boat on the bay while they were there. At least I think that's what happened. A boat! He could buy her a thousand boats!"

With Mrs. Mallory back in the house, the mood darkened. So did the skies. Karol was planting the last tree when the clouds opened and a hard rain began to fall, thick drops slamming the earth and roof. He ran back to the kitchen as thunder cracked the afternoon, dividing the good times that had come before from what was yet to happen.

The rain brought only a short respite. Although it was cooler that evening, the next morning dawned with the same buzzing humidity of the day before.

"I can stand this heat if we get an afternoon shower every day," Karol said to me on the way to the Mallorys.

But no afternoon shower came that day or the next, just the relentless sun that punished industry and energy. Mrs. Mallory resumed her routine with increased intensity. She was in the shrine room now as soon as Karol and I arrived in the morning, and left it only for a short period to eat a very spare lunch. As soon as that was finished, she returned to the room.

With its broad, thinly curtained windows facing south, it was easily the hottest room in the house. Mrs. Mallory was, as Hilda said, not looking well at all. Her olive skin had taken on a yellowish hue. Her eyes were red and constantly watering. Sometimes I couldn't tell if she had been crying. Large shadows deepened under her eyes, her hair dulled, and she became so thin that her clothes hung on her. Any thought I had of sharing the news of my vocation with Antonia faded the first week she was back.

"She's taking medicine," Hilda announced to us one afternoon that week. "I knew he was up to something. Mr. Mallory had her see a doctor while they were on vacation—he tricked her! I think it's poison!"

"Hilda, I swear we're going to stop listening to that show. Your imagination has run wild." Karol shook his head and smiled at her.

As summer wore on, I confirmed my promise to the convent nuns. I wrote them a note and left it at St. Bridget's the next Sunday after Mass. That lifted some weight off my shoulders. Now all that was left was telling Mother. If only I could write her a note, too, and leave it as I went off to the Mallory house. *Dear Mother, I'm going to join the convent in the fall. I'll pray for the family every day…*

What had Bernard written, I wondered, when he'd left home? As Karol and I rode the streetcar to Guilford that Monday, I realized that my difficulty telling Mother was due to Bernard. Because he had hurt her so much when he left.

When we arrived at the house, something was different. The Mallory car, a big black thing, was parked in the driveway at a hurried angle. When we entered the kitchen, Hilda wasn't there and nothing had yet been done. No tea was made, no coffee brewing, no bread rising. Upstairs, we heard a man's voice, then Hilda's, then another man's, then Hilda's footsteps on the servants' stairs coming toward us.

She wasn't in her cook's uniform but in a silky yellow-and-gray dress, a tight-fitting cloth hat still on her head. Pale and disoriented, she seemed surprised to see us.

"Margaret." She said it as if reassuring herself that I was really there. "Mr. Mallory is here. I have to go with them." She opened the closet and grabbed her purse. Just as I was about to ask for more information, a man came through the kitchen door from the dining room.

271

Here at last was Bennett Mallory, the man to whom I'd attributed every bad impulse and character trait a brute could have. Faithless, cruel, cold. I had never seen his picture so I had imagined him tall and malevolently handsome with a constant smirk, dark hair and a wide face, muscled arms, and flashing eyes. A gangster.

Yet here was no rogue. Yes, he was handsome, and yes, he was tall but with wavy brown hair and spectacles similar to Hilda's own. He was thin, too, and...and beaten-looking, with slender fingers that he couldn't keep still. He wore no jacket, and his shirt was wrinkled and his tie askew under a half-buttoned vest. He looked as disoriented as Hilda, with a pale face and a long mouth turned down at the corners. If I had met him on the street, I would have thought him a kind man who'd known sorrow, a man to whom I could turn for directions or a small favor.

"She's ready. I'm going to pull the car to the door."

He turned and left, his movement awakening Hilda to the moment.

"Mrs. Mallory is very sick. Dr. Fallon wants her to go to the hospital. I'm going to help her get settled."

❧❧

Dr. Kaplan tapped his pen on the papers Margaret had given him. Part of the story was there, part of it she'd told him in the past twenty minutes when he'd questioned her for more details. And part of it was in her head, the small details and observations.

"Do you think she tried to harm herself?" he asked at the end of a series of similar questions. Margaret straightened and looked away. He hadn't been there. He hadn't seen.

"No, of course not." Mrs. Mallory had been deceived by her husband, tricked into taking a new medicine that did her more ill than good.

"You said she was looking worse..." He consulted his notes. "Not taking care of herself..."

Margaret said nothing. Dr. Kaplan was annoying

her with his know-it-all attitude, his smugness.

It was midmorning now, and the heat was returning. She was tired already, and she wanted to go outside again, as had been promised. Waiting until the afternoon was a mistake. She'd be too tired then, and she wanted to look more closely at the Christ statue this time.

"I don't know."

"What hospital did she go to?"

"I think she came here." Margaret knew she had come to Phipps, she remembered Hilda telling them where they were going. But she didn't want to tell Dr. Kaplan because he would scribble something, and she suspected he would draw a parallel between Antonia Mallory and her. It rankled her to think he would view her the same as Antonia, a woman who'd given up on her vow to be a nun, who'd spent her life trying to repent. Why, Antonia Mallory shared some responsibility for her fate, didn't she? How dare Dr. Kaplan...

And then her thoughts veered in a different direction, from the heights of indignation to the depths of humility. She wasn't Antonia, no. She wasn't Antonia because Antonia had lost two babies—two babies! Margaret had not suffered like that. Margaret's sorrows were tolerable. Her father passing—so many people lost their parents. And even Rosy—well, Rosy had lived to adulthood. And Margaret wouldn't have had contact with her even had Rosy lived. No, Antonia's suffering was beyond comprehension. It was only natural that such a woman would fall into despair and....

She was beginning to regret telling Dr. Kaplan so much. She had written down the Mallory story and answered his questions about it this morning because she had to start somewhere and Mrs. Mallory had been in her thoughts this year, and she'd not had a chance to figure out why or what to think about her. Ever since she'd seen the newspaper clipping at St. Benedict's, she'd been remembering her days at the Mallory household and trying to piece together the story as if it were a puzzle. She hadn't finished the puzzle, and Dr. Kaplan surely couldn't finish it.

"Later, she was transferred to Sheppard Pratt."

"Why don't you think she tried to harm herself?"

"Because she was very devout. It would have been a mortal sin." Margaret glared at him.

"Do you think she could have not known that was what she was trying to do?"

"Do you mean her husband gave her too much?"

"Perhaps. Or perhaps she took too much medicine and only part of her was thinking it was enough to end her life—and the other part of her mind was distracted?" He shifted in his seat. "What was she taking, anyway?"

"I don't know," she said calmly, in the voice she'd used to deal with difficult children in class. Her story voice, melodic, unemotional. *And now, children, I will tell you the tale of a presumptuous doctor.* "I only know that Hilda came back later that day looking hot and tired. I poured her a cup of tea and Karol gave her a sandwich. We both waited on her and fed her as she had done for us in the previous weeks and months. When we settled into our familiar positions at the table, she told us what happened."

"To Mr. Mallory?"

"No, to Antonia—everything I described." Margaret sighed heavily, as if Dr. Kaplan were a dolt who didn't understand the simplest lesson. "Hilda had come in as she always had that morning, and was going to put together the breakfast tray, to take upstairs. She knew Mr. Mallory wouldn't be there because he hadn't been there for many nights. Before she even had a chance to change, the phone rang. And it rang and rang and rang. Mrs. Mallory usually picked it up, so Hilda knew immediately that something was wrong. In the bedroom, Mrs. Mallory was still in bed, barely breathing, her mouth hanging open. Hilda thought he'd killed her."

"What happened after she was hospitalized?"

"Hilda told us Mr. Mallory would probably close up the house because he had a townhouse on Calvert Street closer to his office. She said he didn't need all of us, never did, that Mrs. Mallory hired people out of charity, not out of need.

"And Hilda was right. Mr. Mallory did decide to close the house, and it didn't take him long to come to that conclusion. By the end of the next week, we had received notice that we would no longer be needed, and he gave us checks, generous ones. He also offered to write references if we required them."

What an unsettled time. It had shaken her. Everything had been so smooth for a while, and then to have this eruption— It had opened the door a crack to doubt. But now, she spoke in a strong, fast voice so Dr. Kaplan wouldn't jump to conclusions that even she was unwilling to leap to.

"Karol was so happy with the money. It came to just about what he would have made there the rest of the summer. He told me he was thinking of enlisting that fall. Now he could take a trip somewhere before doing that. I tried to talk him out of it, knowing I was leaving. I didn't want to leave Mother and Rosy alone.

"Hilda and I spent another week covering furniture and packing away Mrs. Mallory's things. Mr. Mallory asked that the shrine room be completely dismantled. As I packed the crucifix and other statues in a box, I realized I needed to tell my mother I was 'enlisting' in my own way—and so I told her that night about my plans to enter the convent."

She'd thought that by telling her mother, somehow things would be made right and whole again. And it had returned to her some sense of peace, even though her mother had looked skeptical and a little afraid at the news.

"Mr. Mallory was an adulterer," Margaret said with no rancor. But even as she said it, she remembered how

275

he'd looked that day he'd come into the kitchen. His hands had been shaking when he'd given them their checks.

"You mentioned that you were struggling with telling your mother about your decision to enter the convent. So you made that decision before going to work for the Mallorys?"

"Yes."

"When precisely did you make the decision?"

"Earlier that winter. I'd always thought about it. I was getting to the age where one would apply."

"It wasn't influenced by Mrs. Mallory—or her behavior?"

She turned and smiled at him. "Not at all," she said calmly. "Although, I suppose working in her household just reinforced my decision."

"Because of her broken promise, you mean?"

"I suppose." How smug that sounded. But that was how she'd felt—that she wouldn't make the same mistake as Mrs. Mallory. She'd keep the promise she'd made in her heart. "But not in any significant way." She knew what he was looking for.

Dr. Kaplan capped his pen. "You've done a lot today, Sister."

"So, discharge isn't out of the question?"

He smiled. "Not out of the question at all."

❧

In the hall, Dr. Kaplan stopped and breathed out a tremulous sigh. It had been a long session, between reading her notes and talking about them, but worth the time.

He'd finally hit on something, and its obviousness made him want to laugh at himself. She'd been willing to talk of the Mallorys quite easily. But when he'd try to draw the clear parallels or ask questions that forced her to look at her judgment of Mrs. Mallory as judgment of herself, she'd pulled away. As soon as he'd started to prod her with questions of punishment and promises, she'd retreated, a turtle going back into its shell.

Unconsciously, he looked around. He was always looking for Kate. They'd parted ways—hadn't they? Had it been real, a dream? And yet he continued to ache for her, to want her. Oh, not just in the physical way. She had been his balance since arriving at Hopkins, his cheerleader. He'd been so close to...giving up. And she'd made him believe, with her little nudges, her questions, her smile, that he could still do some good.

He frowned. All this talk of vocations, of faith, with Sister brought back a memory of his evening with Kate that still disquieted him. She'd want a man of her own faith. How offended he'd been when she'd said that— honest Kate. How quickly it rose in him, the anger that he'd be cast aside because of his faith. His faith—as if he were devout. Did he have a right to this outrage? He'd pored over answers to that question that evening after they'd gone their separate ways. He didn't observe the Sabbath or go to synagogue. After his bar mitzvah years ago, he'd drifted inexorably away from any faith whatsoever. And his war experiences had killed whatever belief system he might have had, just as news of new drugs was killing his belief in psychiatry. But now, in the face of rejection because of his...tribe...he found a geyser of anger shooting up.

"Dr. Kaplan, can I help you with something?" A nurse stood in front of him, wide eyes questioning. My God, he must look like the patient, not the doctor, lingering outside Sister's door, thoughts akimbo.

"I'm considering a case," he snapped and was both satisfied and mortified when she walked away, head down in embarrassment.

To prove he was engrossed in a case, he studied his notes a bit longer. It was just as well. It grounded him. He had to remember his job. It was to help Sister and his other patients, not to solve his own puzzles. That was for his own time.

He'd been trying so hard to determine what father

issues Sister might have, what events in her past family relationships had pushed her to depression and ultimately a suicide attempt. And it had been staring him in the face all along, so close that he'd not seen it.

Whether she realized it or not, she had been on the verge of a breakthrough today. The way she'd reacted when he'd pressed her about God punishing her—here was a sore spot, something she had trouble facing. He knew if he kept working with her, he could help her look in that mirror.

Now he felt confident in signing her discharge papers. Confident that the truth she needed to face was within reach. He looked around, hoping to see Kate. He wanted to tell her. She'd understand. She'd celebrate with him. He'd have to content himself with calling Sister's family and letting them know she was well enough to leave the hospital.

Yes, Sister had father issues. But the father she was angry with was her God.

CHAPTER NINETEEN
Escape

"YOU LOOK wonderful!" Paula breezed into the room "Here let me take that." She grabbed the bag from Sister's lap. She was a rush of activity, even in her heavy state. Today, she wore a white cotton top, black skirt and black shoes. But her makeup and hair were perfect, as usual, and she wore bright red enamel earrings. "Karol is waiting in the car. He wanted to come up but I told him it would be better if he stayed right out front so he wouldn't have to park and then go get the car. Do you need help?"

"I'm fine. Do I need to sign anything?"

"What? Oh, no, nothing. Dr. Kaplan spoke with Karol already, and I signed some papers for you. So we're all set. I'll lead the way, I guess. But wait. We should do one last check of the room."

The nurse, Kate, came to the door, beaming a smile. "I heard you were leaving today. You look wonderful, Sister!" She entered the room, helping Paula make sure nothing was left.

"Don't worry about returning the clothes," she said, pointing to Sister's gray dress and light cardigan, the latest contributions to Sister's wardrobe. "We're always getting new things."

She swept around the room, pulling open the bedside table's drawer, even looking under the bed to make sure Sister had not left anything. But she had nothing to leave. Confident the room was bare of personal belongings, she turned to Paula.

"I can get her a wheelchair."

"I don't think that's necessary," Sister said.

"I can help her," Paula said, offering her arm.

Kate came over to her and grasped Sister's hands, her eyes watering. "I'm so glad you've regained your health. I'll miss you, though."

"Thank you."

Kate's face brightened. "But I'll see you soon, I'm sure. At the convent."

Sister's face clouded. "You're entering?" she murmured.

Kate's fingers flew to her neck, and she blushed. "Oh, no. Not that. I'll be at St. Benedict's when Dr. Kaplan goes with you to try to remember that day."

"Oh."

Her confused look must have given away her ignorance.

"I'm sorry. I thought he'd talked to you about it. Your Mother Superior gave permission."

Paula piped up to offer her approval. "Why, that sounds like a clever idea. I'm sure it'll help."

"Yes," Sister murmured, realizing she should appear pleased at this "clever" tactic to refresh her memory. But inside, the brightness of the day dimmed.

Despite an inner resistance, she gave in and allowed Paula to lead her. As they passed through the door, she took one fleeting look at the room that had been her cell. She was shedding a skin, like a snake crawling free. With sudden recognition, she remembered that this was precisely how she'd felt when she'd arrived at Mount St. Agnes.

❧❧

During the drive home, she sat with her hands in her lap, staring out the window, her thoughts flying by as quickly as the scenery. Joy followed by worry followed by irritation and then by joy again. Joy was the constant, drifting back in through everything else. She was going home.

Yes, Paula prattled at first—there was the irritation. But she didn't mind that too much because she was free! She felt like shouting. She felt like falling on her knees and kissing the ground when they arrived. Blessed earth, blessed Dr. Kaplan for letting her go. Everything seemed coated with grace.

Only twice had she been in a car like this—once when a parishioner had picked her up at the station to take her to St. Benedict's, and then the cab ride to Rosy's funeral. Today her heart was less encumbered, and she let herself enjoy the sights of her hometown, its smokestacks and office buildings trying hard to look like a big city, its tight, mean neighborhoods, its damp harbor scent.

Her happiness only dimmed when they rode down Chesaco, past the small boxlike convent jammed up against the rectangular school. Sister Fulgentia herself could stare straight at the car and not recognize her, though, incognito out of the habit, her short hair combed like a boy's just that morning. She needn't worry.

But she did. What had Kate said—they'd visit the convent, to try to jog her memory. Why was that necessary? Really, she was doing so well. She had an appointment with Dr. Kaplan next week. She would reason with him, tell him how silly that would be. When she imagined standing in those small rooms and narrow hallways, she shivered. How embarrassing it would be.

At Cane Road, Karol carried her bag into the home as if it were an expensive suitcase and she was arriving home after the Tour. Paula immediately showed her to the small room to the left of the front door, the one that overlooked the steeply sloping front lawn.

"Here, we did this up for you," she said proudly.

"Paula did it all herself," Karol added.

She stepped over the threshold, holding her breath.

The room was clean and spare, but it was hers, hers alone. Against the wall, near the window, was a narrow bed, a blue chenille cover neatly tucked in. To her right was a tall four-drawer dresser. Arranged on top were a comb and brush, and some luxurious toiletries—scented powder, hand lotion, a small vial of perfume. Things she wouldn't use but Paula liked. Next to a rocking chair was a table arranged as a desk. Pens and pencils were neatly stacked in a cup, and a notebook sat to one side along with a battered dictionary. She remembered seeing the desk in the living room when she'd been there before.

"I didn't know what you would need," Paula said. "So I just put in here a few things I thought you'd like. That is from your sister's room." She pointed to a wooden crucifix that hung above the bed, and she recognized it as an old cross that used to hang in her bedroom at home, the room she'd shared with Rosy.

Oh, dear. Tears burned against her eyelids, but she couldn't cry. It would frighten them, making them think she wasn't ready to be out, to be in their home. She wanted them to leave. She wanted to look at the cross alone. She wanted to let go, to sit on the bed and weep, to grab each tender item to her lips and kiss it—the bedspread, the writing paper, the pens, the cross.

"Thank you," she managed to whisper. "I'm very tired."

Paula moved out of the room, nudging Karol with her. "That's right. You rest now. I have some things to do. So does Karol. You needed to change the oil in the car, right, honey? And I was going to bake a cake."

They shut the door quietly as if she would be disturbed by loud noises. Now at last she had the opportunity to sit, and she slowly, lingering over every second, slid onto the side of the bed, crossing her legs under her. She smoothed the coverlet with her hands and did a visual inventory of all the things in the cheery little room that were now hers. She came to the crucifix and stretched to lift it off its nail. Fingering it, she stroked its polished wood and thought of her sister. *Rosy,* she murmured.

An unfamiliar noise caught her attention. Looking outside, she saw Karol down below at the street, with the car hood up, a rag in his hand. From the kitchen, she heard Paula turn the radio on low as she rattled pans.

She curled up on the bed, crucifix in hand, and fell asleep.

CHAPTER TWENTY
Rosy

ON THE morning after Sister's first night with them, Paula awoke early to go to Mass with Karol. Already at seven o'clock, the house felt surrounded by a moist, warm veil, where air didn't move. Just walking slowly created a thin layer of perspiration on Paula's brow. Karol was in a good mood that morning, whistling as he shaved, letting Paula knot his tie for him. It was going to be a blistering day.

"We better get Margie going," he said as Paula dusted dandruff off his shoulders.

"She's still sleeping," Paula said. She still had trouble thinking of her as "Margie."

"I'll go knock on her door."

"No," Paula said, grabbing his arm. "Let her sleep. She's probably really tired. Yesterday was a big day."

"But Mass—she'd wanna go."

She looked at him, surprised. This was a softening, too, toward his sister. It was a good sign.

"Okay. Let me check." Paula walked quietly to Sister's door. Gently knocking while opening the door a crack, she said, "Margaret? Are you up?" It felt strange to use the nun's given name, but Karol did, and she was beginning to think of her as Margaret.

Not only was Margaret up, she was dressed and kneeling by her bed, the rosary beads over her fingers. When Paula entered, Margaret turned slowly but said nothing.

"Oh—sorry to interrupt you," Paula said. "Karol and I—we're heading to church. Would you like to go with us?"

"I'm not feeling too well," Margaret answered. She looked down and pulled in her lips. "I don't think I will go. Dr. Kaplan said I should rest."

"Is there anything I can get you—some aspirin? Or bicarb?"

"No, no. I'll just rest."

"We'll only be gone a little while. There's toast. But Karol will go to the bakery after church."

Margaret's eyes widened a little. "Will Mother come?"

"No, she's cooking for a Sodality breakfast this morning. At her own church."

Margaret didn't look ill. Her eyes were bright, her coloring good. But should they leave her alone?

"I could stay here with you."

"No, please. You go along. I'll...finish my prayers and rest. I'm sure I'll be fine."

When Paula told Karol his sister was under the weather and wouldn't accompany them, he shrugged. "She'd probably feel funny. Going without her habit and all."

Of course. She'd see people she knew. It *would* be odd. Paula felt duped, as if Margaret had taken advantage of her by pulling pity from her for nothing more serious than embarrassment. And she would have understood—and even sympathized—had Margaret been truthful. But as she saw Karol shrug off his sister's excuses, she determined to do the same. The important thing was that Karol was being generous of spirit, that Margaret looked good. She was getting better. She'd heal, the baby would come, and life would begin at last.

❧

Rosary beads in hand, Margaret stood at the window of her room, behind the curtain, watching Karol and Paula leave.

It had only occurred to her last night— after a dinner that Margaret was convinced Paula had cooked to impress her more than to feed her— that Sunday Mass might present a problem. Paula had brought it to her attention. "We go to the eight-thirty," she'd said. "It's cooler in the early morning."

Margaret had lain in bed that night unable to sleep. She'd looked forward all afternoon to the moment when she could retire to her room—her own sanctuary, now with her small new wardrobe put away neatly in drawers, with her rosary on the bedside table, and her prayer book on the dresser. Her own room! How luxurious it sounded even when she thought it.

But that moment of luxury had been spoiled by Paula's offhand remark, and Margaret had felt as if Paula had snatched the moment away even though God wanted her to enjoy it. Eight-thirty Mass at St. Benedict's? With the possibility of running into her Sisters, schoolchildren she'd taught, their parents? It was one thing to pass them in a moving car. Sunday Mass would bring her face-to-face with them. She'd closed her eyes tight and scrunched her hands into compact fists. She couldn't bear to think about it. Yet it would be Sunday, and she *had* to think about it. She had to go to Mass on Sunday.

Well, she didn't *have* to go—not really, not if she were sick. When Sisters were ill in the convent, or at the Mother House, a priest would come by to give them Communion, just as the priest had done for her in the hospital. But most people didn't have that convenience. When they were sick—when, say, Paula or Karol fell ill—they just stayed home from Mass, without Communion, and there was no sin.

And she was sick, after all. She'd just been discharged from the hospital. If she had any right to abstain from going to Sunday Mass, surely this was it.

She so worried herself into a dither over this that she

had slept fitfully, her restlessness exacerbated by the cloying heat which left her damp from sweat even when she wasn't moving. When she awoke she noticed, with a pang of relief, that she had a headache. No need to lie. She had a headache. But it wouldn't have been a lie, she reminded herself as she washed up quietly before Paula and Karol had gotten out of bed. She was still recuperating from the hospital stay. With that thought, her tiny, cherished headache had begun to recede. That's when she'd gone back to her room, dressed, and begun her morning prayers, supplemented by a rosary to make up for her inability to attend Mass. Kneeling so long on the floor had brought the headache back. She'd welcomed it.

Seeing Paula and Karol take off down the street, Margaret turned back in the room and inhaled deeply. She now had her luxurious moment of satisfaction and peace. As was her custom when she was happy, she voiced a prayer of thanks.

Toast, Paula had said. Or she could wait for Karol to return with donuts and pastry. She remembered seeing Karol in church with Rosy some Sundays, with Paula others. Sometimes with Mother and Rosy. So this is what they'd done afterward—come back to Karol's house for cakes and coffee.

After going to the kitchen and pouring herself a cup of coffee, she decided to wait before eating. If she didn't partake of food with them, they might think she was acting strangely, or think she was being rude. Better to wait.

The morning paper lay open on the kitchen table. The room already was awash in heat and light. No shades at the windows, only thin, white cotton curtains. The back door was open, a screen door giving the false impression of cooling shadows beyond. The air smelled of grass and concrete and warm wood. Every object's scent was released in the heat, even the acrid smell of a neighbor's burnt breakfast.

No one had spoken to her about what she should do once she left the hospital, she realized as she sat down to drink her coffee. Oh, Dr. Kaplan and Kate and even Paula had given her instructions on the importance of her doctor appointments. But no one had said, "this is how you'll fill a day and this is how you shall remain faithful to your Order during this leave of absence."

Margaret would have to construct her own regimen. There was the journal writing—she would have to do that early, after she rose, after morning prayer before everyone else woke up. Morning and evening prayers would be easy. Grand Silence might also be possible if she retired early enough. Other routines she'd have to forgo. Daily Mass was out of the question. And Sunday Mass—what should she do about that? She couldn't go to another church—she didn't know of any near here. And she certainly wouldn't ask Karol to drive her.

She'd love to go to Mass at St. Bridgit's again, their old parish, the one where they'd worshipped as children, as a family. Where Rosy's funeral had taken place. But she'd like to do it alone—not with Mother or Karol or Paula. She'd like to wander in, anonymous, and sit by herself in the back of the long church, and pull out her rosary and feel the way she had as a little girl.

She shook her head. No, she couldn't ask Karol to take her there. Too many questions—why not go to St. Benedict's, why not go with Mother to St. Bridgit's?

Wherever she went, it would be easier if she went by herself. She'd go to another Mass at St. Benedict's. She knew there was a Mass at six-thirty in the morning. Next Sunday, she could slip out of the house on her own and walk to it by herself, leaving Karol and Paula a note. She was used to rising early. It would be no hardship. She sipped her coffee and read.

Six-thirty Mass—that was the Mass the Sisters often attended, all in a row in the front of the church. She couldn't...

But they wouldn't recognize her. Not if she sat in the

back. Or over in the east transept. She'd wait and go to Communion late. She wouldn't look at them. She could do it. She'd have to do it.… Oh, it was too much to think about. Alone—she'd go to Mass alone. Somewhere. Somehow.

She made herself useful by cleaning the coffee cups and percolator, then sat on the cool front porch for a few minutes reading the Psalms to herself. When a neighbor walked by and looked up, she scurried inside, fearful she'd have to explain to him why she was there.

When Karol and Paula returned over an hour later, baked goods in hand, she was in her room again, writing in her journal as Dr. Kaplan had instructed.

Paula poked her head around the open door.

"You haven't been in here the whole time, have you?" She waved a hand in front of her face. "Whew, it's hot! We're going to get some more fans this week." There was a small rotating fan in the kitchen but none elsewhere in the house.

"I had some coffee," Margaret answered.

"Come have a donut or something. We got cheesecake." Paula led the way to the dining room where two white boxes, tied with string, sat on the table. As Paula set plates and napkins out and put on more coffee, Karol came into the room from the bedroom. He wore light-colored slacks and a shirt open at the collar. But it was a long-sleeved shirt and Margaret's brow creased, as she thought how hot he must be. She herself wore a navy blue dress with short sleeves, a hand-me-down from Kate.

"It's too hot in the kitchen," Paula called out to him. "So I thought we'd set up in here."

"Is there any coffee left?" he asked, picking up an empty cup and staring at it as if it should be full.

"I'm making more." Paula folded the napkins and set them by small plates at each place.

Margaret realized she'd made a mistake by discarding the last of the coffee—that they must usually drink it when they came home from church.

"I'm sorry," she confessed. "I had some and then I cleaned up."

Karol started to say something, but Paula interrupted him. "That's all right. I appreciate the help."

But of course it hadn't been a help if Paula had to make more coffee.

"Are you feeling any better?" Karol asked. He sat down and peered at Margaret suspiciously before struggling with the knot on one of the strings around the boxes. Paula undid the other one.

"Yes. I...I rested." She reached over to help Karol, but he shooed her away and only succeeded in undoing the knot after knocking his coffee cup over.

"No harm done," Paula said too cheerfully. "Nothing broken."

Karol read the paper while they ate, and Margaret didn't want to disturb him so she didn't say anything. After a few awkward smiles, Paula offered Margaret sections of the newspaper. When she didn't take any, Paula herself began to read the society pages.

The pastry was good—flaky dough with a cheese filling, dusted with powdered sugar. She hadn't realized how hungry she was, and when Paula cut her a piece of nutmeg-dusted cheesecake, she didn't resist.

After one bite, she remembered. Her father had brought home a cheesecake like this on a Saturday many, many years ago. It was springtime, before Easter, and he'd placed it on the table and cut them all pieces while their mother carped about the expense, about it being Lent, about making cakes for them herself. And he'd told her he'd bought it because the bakery owner was a good customer and he thought he should return the favor.

Looking at her brother, Margaret longed to ask him: Was this the same baker? But Karol was absorbed in his reading, eating while clumsily trying to keep the newspaper in place with his good hand. She didn't want to bother him. Of course it was the same baker. Why would he go back to the old neighborhood if it weren't the same?

After their breakfast, Margaret helped Paula clean up, despite Paula's annoying insistence that she rest because she had been "sick earlier." Margaret couldn't help wondering if Paula was poking fun at her, trying to make it obvious she hadn't been that ill. So Margaret resolved to prove she didn't have anything to prove and dried dishes, putting them away according to Paula's instructions. She was about to retreat to her own room when Paula asked her to come into the back bedroom.

From the closet, Paula dragged out a brown shopping bag with rope handles.

"I remembered these when we were in church," she announced, pulling out clothes and laying them on the bed where Margaret sat, her hands in her lap. "Some of them won't be suitable, of course. But others..." She laughed when she pulled out a red dress, shiny baubles sewn at the neckline and bodice.

"Don't think you'll need this one!"

Then she found a blue blouse, with neat straight pleats down the front. "I wore this to my best friend's wedding," she said, a soft smile on her face. "With a gray tweed suit." She set it aside in a pile intended for Margaret.

More laughter as she pulled out a tattered rustic shawl in natural fibers. A dark skirt, another blouse, and then, finally, a dress, one that Margaret mentally assigned to the discard pile because of its color. It was lemon yellow, straight, with a shirt collar and matching belt. Svelte and sophisticated. Not at all something Margaret would wear in her present in-between circumstances. Really, what was Paula thinking? Had she brought Margaret in here merely to show off her wardrobe?

"I don't think these are suitable," Margaret said. "But thank you all the same—"

"Oh, you must take this one," Paula said, placing

the yellow dress on Margaret's lap. "It belonged to Rose."

"Rosy?"

"Mmm-hmm."

Margaret fingered the light cotton, not able to imagine her sister wearing it because she'd not seen her much as an adult. It was so hard to conjure up that image—Rosy tall enough to fill out this garment. What a sunny color—of course, Rosy would choose such a color, just like her disposition, all bright and cheerful.

"She didn't like the way it looked with her hair. She said it made her look jaundiced." Paula laughed again, and Margaret realized that laughing was a reflexive habit when Paula was nervous. "But it was expensive—an extravagant purchase, she told me—so she gave it to me."

"Oh." Rosy gave it to Paula, undeserving Paula, who wouldn't know what it signified. But Margaret knew. It was a sign that Rosy had stepped up and out of their world. And it was a reflection of her good humor. A hundred meanings were sewn into its seams.

"She had some great clothes, but sometimes she wore older things. You know, to church. Saved her good clothes for work, she told me. Here, wait a minute." Paula went to her dresser and opened a top drawer. Pulling from it a photograph encased in a cardboard frame, she sat on the edge of the bed next to Margaret.

"Look. This is her. At the Knights of Columbus New Year's Eve Dance. We went together. Wasn't she gorgeous?"

Paula pointed to the photo. Even in black-and-white, it was clear that Rosy was stunning in a shimmering dark gown that hugged her body. Her hair tumbled about her bare shoulders, and she held a drink in one hand and a cigarette in the other. Next to her was a dashing young man who looked like a movie star. He had neat hair parted on the side and a pencil-thin moustache. He was smiling and glancing at Rosy from the corner of his eye. On the other side were Karol and Paula, smiling into the camera.

"Who is that?" Margaret asked, pointing to the man.

"Robert. No, Richard. Richard Trentlock. I think." Paula shook her head. "Rose had an army of boyfriends waiting to take her out. I couldn't keep track of them all." Paula fingered the edge of the photo, lost in memory. She smiled. "Karol was always getting on her about that. He was worried about what folks would think."

Margaret's head shot up. "Rosy was a good girl."

"Oh, I know! I thought Karol was wrong," Paula hastened to add. "She liked to have fun. There's nothing wrong with that." Paula stood and put the photo away. "I can have a copy of this made, if you'd like. I'll have to go through Karol's other photos and see what I can find for you. We might have some Christmas pictures. And those were in color. She wore a flaming red dress. Brighter than mine—the one I showed you. Karol said she looked like a stoplight." Paula laughed hard at the memory, this time not from nervousness, but real mirth. "You should have seen them. Bernard was here. And Rose decided that the way to keep them from clawing each other's eyes out was to feed them highballs all afternoon. One after the other. She came into the kitchen and announced her strategy. But she was the one who kept drinking. By the time dinner was over, she was ready to dance on the table. Oh, Lordy, it was funny." Paula held her belly as she chuckled.

Margaret blushed. Poor Rosy. "She wasn't used to drinking," she said in her sister's defense.

"Oh, no. She could hold her liquor better than any man I knew. This was just a special occasion. It worked, though. Bernard and Karol were good boys."

Margaret's head began to ache in earnest now, the small headache blossoming into a dull throbbing. "Why do you call her Rose?"

"She said all her friends called her that."

"But we called her Rosy."

"I know." Paula patted Margaret's leg. "She said Rose sounded more grown-up."

"I think I need to lie down." Margaret stood, grabbing the yellow dress. "I'm not sure these other things—" She gestured to the pile of clothes on the bed.

"That's all right." Paula turned back to the clothes and began placing them again in the bag.

In her room, Margaret set the dress on the rocker and curled up on her bed. The Rosy Paula described was someone different, someone whom Paula must have influenced. Her sister wasn't like that—loose and silly. *Paula sees everything through her own experience of life,* Margaret thought.

Before she fell asleep, a memory returned of the past several months. Not a lost memory, just something she hadn't thought of. An insignificant one. A Sunday memory. Going to church with her Sisters. And looking for Rosy. Seeing instead Paula and Karol occasionally, but not Rosy. And searching for her as if she were still at home or away.

And the worst Sunday of all—Easter. Paula and Karol were there, with Mother and even Bernard. And still no Rosy! On that day of new life, of resurrections. She'd felt so strongly on that day that Rosy's death had somehow been a mistake, that God had made a mistake, and just as with Lazarus, he could correct it if only…

But when she'd seen the four of them standing straight and sad on that sunny Easter morning, she'd crumbled inside. Rosy was really gone.

With a terrible ache, she drifted to sleep.

❧

After Margaret went to her room, Paula stared at the New Year's Eve photo she'd just shown her sister-in-law. Although they'd only known each other a short while, Paula had felt comfortable and close to Rose, the same way she'd felt with Ginny as a girl. When Karol and Paula had gone out with Rose, Paula felt she didn't have to try so hard, the way she did now, to make everything work. With Rose around, Karol had been lighthearted, and Paula could look into his laughing eyes and see...promise. If Rose were still alive, things might be easier.

A sudden weariness came over her, as it did from time to time when she grew aware of how much effort she put in to making simple things right. She'd hoped to cheer Margaret with the clothes, but she seemed to have created the opposite effect. And Karol could be brooding in the other room, and Paula wouldn't want to ask why.

And she had to think about dinner—in this heat! If she complained or even mentioned it, Karol would tell her not to bother. But she wouldn't let him say that. She never wanted him to think she hadn't tried. There was cold chicken in the refrigerator. She'd make chicken salad. And tomatoes and lettuce, and maybe a coleslaw, if she had the ingredients. And leftover cheesecake for dessert.

The photo clasped to her chest, she leaned onto the pillows and dozed.

ॐ

When the phone rang, Aaron jumped from a nap on his sofa, newspaper on his chest. His heart raced, his mind on one thought—Lena.

Every time the phone rang, he found himself thinking that. It tortured him. Every time he checked the mail, he hoped to see news of her—even though it was preposterously early to get word on any of the inquiries he'd made. This was too painful.

Instead, he was surprised to hear Kate's voice. Disappointment quickly melted to warm affection.

"I'm sorry to bother you. I guess this could have waited, but it's been bothering me."

"Yes?"

"Well, when Sister Francis Marie was discharged on Saturday, I mentioned how I'd see her when we visited the convent at St. Benedict's together. I didn't know she didn't know...I'm awfully sorry...I mean, she looked real good and everything. She didn't seem too rattled or anything."

He sighed. He should have told Sister himself before she left. He'd been too caught up in the breakthrough he believed they were approaching, and he hadn't wanted to tip her balance. He had to admit Kate's news disturbed him.

"I'm supposed to see her early this week," he said. "Her first visit after discharge."

"Oh. I just started worrying about it, wondering if I should let you know in case you would think it's a big deal. I know these patients can be kind of fragile when they're released."

"She's with her family," he said, now eager to reassure Kate. While he wasn't thrilled with the news of the slip, he was the one who should have prepared Sister for the visit they planned. It was good of Kate to think of letting him know. She was so thoughtful, she noticed the small things and tended to them. "I'm sure they'd call if there were any kind of upset. Don't worry, Kate. I'll be sure to go over it with her when I talk to her next."

"Thanks. I did worry. I mean, not at first—it seemed like such an ordinary thing. But I'm the nurse, and you're the doctor. I started to think it could be a bigger deal than I'd imagined and you should know. I have a big mouth." She chuckled.

In that warm laugh was an embrace, and he found himself hurting for its lack. Why couldn't they continue as before? He almost asked her, but she begged off, saying she was about to have dinner with her mother and wishing him a good evening.

When he hung up the phone, he felt unsettled. Not just because of his expectation when picking up the phone. No. He still loved Kate. Yes, loved her. If their relationship had progressed, he had no doubt he would have been professing that love before too long. But he'd also been not insignificantly disappointed when he'd discovered it was her on the phone and not Rachel Guildenstern or one of the other contacts he'd reached out to trying to find Lena. Kate, in her wisdom, was right. Part of him still belonged to Lena, and he couldn't expect Kate to wait until he figured out how deep that feeling ran.

CHAPTER TWENTY-ONE
Rehabilitation

IT WAS Tuesday, the day of her first appointment with Dr. Kaplan since her discharge.

Nervous, Margaret had to keep swallowing so she wouldn't gag. That led to a fear of retching, embarrassing herself at her brother's house. One fear added to so many others. Today, she had to learn to ride the bus home from downtown. Karol could drive her in, but she'd not wait for him all day to pick her up—he'd insisted she take the bus. Paula had offered to go with her, but Karol had also insisted she stay at home because of her pregnancy. She'd not resisted, which had made Margaret wonder if all her previous visits had only been for show. She hadn't needed Paula's help then. Now she did, and the woman turned away.

The knowledge she'd have to make this trip on her own had colored yesterday, as well. She'd known she had to go in for the appointment—it had all been mapped out in the discharge papers—but somehow she'd not thought about transportation. Paula had brought it up at breakfast Monday morning, leading to a back-and-forth between Paula and Karol on how to handle getting Margaret to the hospital. Since her appointment wasn't until midmorning, Karol had actually started by suggesting she take the bus in as well as home, a prospect that had chilled her. Paula was the one who'd urged Karol to give her a ride in—"You can wait in the lobby or the cafeteria," she'd told Margaret—

and he'd eventually agreed.

She'd spent the rest of the day trying to be helpful and unobtrusive, succeeding too well at the latter, sabotaging her efforts at the former. She'd wanted to wash the breakfast dishes, but Paula had tended to them before she'd had a chance. She seemed always to be late with her desire to help—coming out to the yard after Paula had hung the wash, going into the living room after she'd swept the rugs.

Finally, she'd given up entirely and spent most of the day in her room, praying, meditating, dozing…being. She loved the room. She walked around it, touching its objects, staring out the window to the summer streetscape, sitting in its chair…smiling. She purposefully pushed aside thoughts that might disturb her, or she came up with easy solutions to vexing problems.

Now she faced the morning of her exile—that's how she'd begun to think of it. Karol would drop her off on his way into work. She'd sit and read quietly—or pray—in the lobby somewhere, head to her ten o'clock appointment with Dr. Kaplan—another challenge since she had to find his office, the one where he saw patients—and then she'd catch the bus home.

Paula had told her over dinner last night that the afternoon bus was less crowded and the schedule better. She'd nodded enthusiastically, that bit of comfort allowing her to eat Paula's appetizing dinner. Her sister-in-law was a good cook, much better than the nuns at St. Benedict's. She cooked with abundance. No one ever would feel they could not take an extra helping for fear of leaving nothing for others. Last night, Paula had baked biscuits even in the grueling heat, and sliced cucumbers and tomatoes for salad, and served a chicken salad with grapes and celery. This morning, she'd made sandwiches for Karol and her with the leftovers.

After dinner, Karol had sat in the living room on the edge of the sofa, patiently explaining to her where to catch the Number 5 or 15 to the Rosedale bus line and which bus to take from there, on the "Green Line." She'd felt exhausted listening to him.

So exhausted that she hadn't heard all of what he had to say. She'd kept imagining things—that she would miss the bus, get lost, become hysterical, collapse, get sick.

To make matters worse, it was raining now. So on top of everything else, she worried about looking bedraggled, like a wet dog.

And more worries— Karol was late, rushing out the door with his raincoat over his arm, barely aware of her straggling behind him, trying to stay under his umbrella.

He didn't seem to know what to talk to her about, so their conversation was in fits and spurts, which was just as well. She was focusing on contingency plans. She opened her bag, borrowed from Paula, for the third time, making sure the slip of paper with phone numbers was in it.

"If you're up to it, I was thinking we'd ask Ma out to dinner next week. I know she'd want to see you," he said.

She nodded but wasn't happy. She'd feel like a failure around their mother, out of her habit, recovering from…whatever this was.

At the hospital, he dropped her off, giving her a quick reminder of the bus numbers.

"You'll be fine, sis," he said, and she slipped out of the car, running through the rain to the door.

Inside, she felt relief. At least she was alone now, alone in a sea of strangers. They wouldn't notice if she didn't do something right. She decided to look for Dr. Kaplan's office first, and after an elevator ride and several wrong turns, she felt confident she'd locate it again at the appointed hour. She then found a nearby lobby on that floor and settled in to wait. She'd not brought anything to read—it was against the Rule anyway—so she began the rosary, using her fingers to keep track of the decades.

✍✍

When she walked into his office, he smiled at her. What a beautiful office it was, spacious and filled with lovely objects—a carved desk, a leather chaise lounge and chairs, photographs of great doctors, a bust of Freud, a plant. She breathed deeply, savoring the air of this dispassionate temple.

"You look wonderful!" he said, coming around the desk to sit in a chair across from her. "That's a beautiful dress."

"It was my sister's," she told him. "Paula gave it to me." She didn't want him to read anything into it. Yes, she liked thinking of Rosy. But really, she had little else to wear.

"I only have a few things," she rushed to add. "I should be able to wear the habit again soon." Her rash was almost completely gone now.

She saw a slight crease in his brow, and he tapped a pencil on some papers. That reminded her. She opened her purse and pulled out some neatly folded pages to hand to him. Pages from the notebook. She'd written more memories down.

He thanked her, nodded and read while she waited. When he was finished, he looked up.
"You wrote about your first days."

"The postulancy. I thought— you seemed interested in all of that."

"I am, I am." He stopped and the crease returned. She had the impression he was struggling with how to put something. She sat, on edge.

"In fact, I'm glad you chose to write about this, because I'd like to talk to you some more about the Mother House and why you don't want to go back there."

"It's not that," she said, easing a little. Maybe this was all that bothered him—his continued misunderstanding of when transfers occurred. "The

301

Mother House is beautiful. I just won't be heading there when I'm better." She said it patiently.

"But here's the thing, Sister," he said, leaning forward, staring at her. "I double-checked, thinking I did have it wrong, and Sister Fulgentia assures me you were to go there. There is no mistake. When you are well enough, you will go there. Is there something at the Mother House that...disturbs you? I know I've asked before, but your insistence on not being assigned there forces me to repeat my question."

She shook her head as tears came to her eyes, tears she didn't understand. She felt persecuted. Here she'd just been released from the hospital, just found rest and respite in her brother's home, and he was already talking about ending it?

"I thought I'd have some time to...to recover," she murmured, sniffling and willing herself to regain control.

"Of course you will! No one is suggesting you go back to your former life until you're ready. Until *you* feel you're ready." He sat back, continuing to study her.

"I—I still think Sister must have made a mistake," she muttered at last. It had to be a mistake. "Who would teach my classes?"

"She has someone, another Sister, I believe. The transfer had been delayed, and that's why it was taking place at an unusual time."

"My things—my classroom things—are probably still there."

"You should feel free to contact your Mother Superior about those issues. Are you afraid to talk to her?"

Of course she was. She was afraid that Sister Fulgentia's reluctant agreement to the recovery plan would be shattered at the slightest breath of controversy, of challenge.

"I'll handle it," was all she offered Dr. Kaplan. Somehow. She'd write her a letter, another one, asking about the mistake, assuring Sister Fulgentia she was capable of resuming her teaching duties. Why, just last night at dinner, Paula had prattled on about how fast the parish was growing, how she'd heard that this year's first grade class had at least eighty children enrolled and more might be in the offing. Surely the school would need more help, regardless whether Sister Fulgentia had secured another Sister to teach. These thoughts calmed her, and she determined to logically point out the necessity of keeping her at St. Benedict's...when she wrote Sister. When she was better.

"This makes you very uncomfortable, talking about your Mother Superior, going back to the Mother House, doesn't it? Do you think on the day of the overdose that discomfort boiled up into something...larger?"

She sighed, suddenly tired, now afraid she'd be too tired to make her way home on the bus. She could always wait here for hours, calling Karol to pick her up after work.

"No! I mean, I don't know. I just don't know." She shook her head back and forth slowly. "My mind is still a blank about that day. I'm sorry," she said.

"Don't apologize. You've made tremendous progress, Sister. You've regained your physical stamina. You've regained an equilibrium that allows you to function. These are big steps forward."

Yes. She had. His words didn't just comfort her. They roused her from her stupor. She wouldn't allow this man, this doctor who didn't understand her faith, let alone the life of a nun, to stall her now. Maybe this was a gift, his obsession with that one day. Maybe it was a test, to see how strong her own devotion and faith were.

"Why do I have to remember that day? Why do you insist on this one memory when I have so many others?" Her head shot up, defiant. "If I'm healthy, what does it matter if that one day is lost to me? Couldn't it be because of the medicine itself?"

He smiled again. Her feistiness must have pleased

him.

"Do you really believe that is the reason?"

Her hands balled into fists in her lap. "I don't know! But it seems as if we're trying to find a needle in a haystack, a needle that might not be worth anything at all except as a...a curiosity, an oddity. Something with no significance or meaning. My life as a nun has meaning. My recovery has meaning. Going through my other memories, dealing with my sister's death, with the fears of my youth—that has meaning. It has helped me. You have helped me."

Calmer, she stared at him and tried to sound reassuring. "You said I'm making tremendous progress. I'm doing that without remembering that day. Maybe that's the way it will have to continue. With your help, eventually I'll be well enough to resume my routine."

His eyes narrowed. She sensed he was coming round.

"All right," he sighed. "You can be very persuasive, Sister. But I want to try something. An experiment. Sister Fulgentia has given us permission to visit the convent— when all the other Sisters are out. You and me and a nurse. We'll walk through and relive that day, see if it prompts anything."

Yes, just as Kate had mentioned. Now that she'd had a chance to grapple with this plan, she was less upset hearing him describe it. If anything, it sounded silly, like something from a detective story. But if it reassured him, she would go along to make *him* feel better.

"And if it doesn't? Is that the only memory that can prove my sanity?"

"If it doesn't, and you continue to improve..." He shrugged. "We'll see..."

≈≈≈

For another half hour they talked. She expounded on the memories she'd written down for him. She could tell from his questions that he was still searching for some horrible hidden secret of the Mother House that kept her from wanting to go back there.

But the Mother House wasn't horrible.

The prospect of leaving St. Benedict's, however, was. St. Benedict's with its too-small rooms, its too-small chapel, its walls pressing in on her. She wanted to stay there because it was close to…Rosy.

With a stabbing pain, she realized this as she boarded her first bus home. It was Rosy she couldn't bear to leave, and for the past year, Rosy had been at St. Benedict's. Even after Rosy had died, Sister could still imagine she might yet be alive even if she weren't in church on Sunday. She could still see her, feel her. St. Benedict's had given Sister her family back, and she was hard-pressed to say goodbye to them again.

She'd have to pray for guidance, for courage, for strength. She'd have to beg for mercy from Sister Fulgentia. Just a little more time. A little more time to say goodbye.

❧

Dr. Kaplan stepped to the window, Sister's papers still clasped in his hand. Maybe she was right. Maybe he was looking for a meaningless needle in a haystack. The woman had suffered a sad loss in the spring, made all the more piercing since her sister had passed away from a disease on the verge of eradication. Her early life had already been hard. Didn't she have the right to be depressed, even desperate? Why would that be considered abnormal? She'd survived hardship, and she was on the road to recovering a peaceful acceptance of her losses. Why did he want more?

He remembered his work with refugees at war's end. Pitiful stories, pathetic creatures, so painful to see and talk to that he had to force himself to greet them every day. He'd had to play a trick on himself to face them. He'd decided that his goal really should be to document their woes, their treatment, their outcomes, and write a paper, maybe even a book, about it all after he returned home. He kept copious notes. Before he set about his day, he'd review and refine them. At the end of the day, he'd do the same. He'd congratulated himself on how this helped him remove personal feelings from his care. So as he heard tale after tale of unspeakable horror, he'd mentally felt miles away, visualizing himself giving presentations to colleagues on his findings. He even ran through several permutations of possible titles, eventually settling on: Displacement of Mind and Body: The Symbiosis of Survivorship and Refugee Placidity.

It had helped up to a point. Until one day, a young man who'd lost his entire family, including a newborn he'd seen murdered with his own eyes, looked at him with obsidian eyes, dark with an eternal sorrow, and said: "I have a right to this grief. I refuse to surrender it."

He'd torn up his notes that evening. He would not profit from those poor souls' suffering.

Sister, too, had suffered. Oh, not the ghastly torments of the Holocaust survivors. Nowhere near their level of pain. But why should anyone expect her to be cheerful, happy, even accepting of her losses?

Whether or not her overdose was a conscious or subconscious act was irrelevant. She had a right to her grief. Her psyche had responded in a normal way—by trying to escape it. As far as he could tell, she was no longer in that frame of mind. She was learning accommodations, acceptance.

With a sigh, he turned from the window and threw her papers on his desk, scanning them while he picked up the phone to prod Sister Fulgentia about setting a date for the re-enactment, now wondering if it was truly necessary.

❧

All morning, all weekend, all day yesterday, the memories smothered me. And yet, to share them with Dr. Kaplan seemed to rob them of their power. This is what I wrote for him, and for me:

The gowns were stored in a basement room down steep narrow stairs. As soon as you opened the door, the damp, fusty smell hit you, reminding you that this chamber was a step back into the convent's traditions and cultures, as sacred a place as the chapel.

An old nun, hard of hearing and vision— Sister Geraldine—sat at a small desk just at the foot of the steps, her hands folded in front of her. Her features were carved in stark contrast by the cruel light of an overhead bulb, and it was hard not to think of her, so silent and still, as a frightening gargoyle, set in that room to keep evil spirits at bay. She said nothing as we filed in, in quiet nervous groups of five, to select gowns from this store of leftovers. The wealthier girls were having dresses sent to them. The rest of us chose from this underground trove.

Three walls were packed with musty dresses, old satins trimmed with yellowed lace, silks whose exuberant first impression was marred by a closer inspection of ripped hems or torn sleeves, and plain cotton sheaths sewn in simpler times. Despite the eerie light, the mildewed smell, the less-than-perfect dresses, nothing dimmed our pleasure as we looked through the racks, like shoppers searching for bargains. Some of the gowns were completely ruined by mildew and rot. Not that we would have chosen those anyway. We were still close enough to the world to know that those gowns were hopelessly out of style. No one wanted to walk down the aisle looking like their grandmother on her wedding day.

I chose a plain, white satin with a wide ribbon bodice, tight sleeves with a row of buttons at each cuff. Our veils were to be all the same—a long piece of sheer lace held in place by a garland of fresh blossoms.

On the Saturday of the ceremony, we were like girls going to a dance. We still had enough sense of ourselves to know how lovely we would look when our families saw us. This was another source of excitement—our families coming to the Mother House. The first time in nearly a year we would see them before never seeing them again.

I had already written to Rosy, and she had promised that she and Mother would be there.

Nothing—not even the war which was so distant and unreal—could sadden us that day. And it was as if God had ordered the day especially for us, which only heightened our sense of being chosen.

You see, cold, piercing spring rain had swamped us all week. But Saturday dawned bright and clear, not a single cloud to be seen even beyond the fields, a perfect May morning with a sky of blue silk and sun that kissed our cheeks as we tramped off to morning prayers. Flowers seemed to have opened overnight, a result of the drenching rain, now viewed as a blessing we had been too ignorant to appreciate during the days it pummeled our souls.

After morning prayer, we listened to last-minute instructions, a quick rehearsal, and then— the moment we'd been waiting for—we marched back to our dormitory rooms where our gowns hung on rods in each of our curtained cubicles.

A novice was stationed in each room to help us with the now-unfamiliar zippers, buttons, and clasps. The silence we'd learned to observe was gone, and no one chastised us. Chatter, laughter, even a scream of delight split the air.

With shaking hands, I put on my dress. I had to ask the novice to button up the sleeves for me even though I was perfectly capable of doing so myself. My hands shook. I couldn't look at her. All I could see was the dress, its milky softness hugging my body. Even though I couldn't see myself in a mirror, never had I felt so beautiful.

She helped brush my hair. All during our postulancy, we had kept our hair pinned back under our short veils. Now, it was allowed to fall free down our backs. My hair was my best feature—rich, thick, and dark. Rosy had loved to braid it for me. I had two hairstyles at that time, the time before I entered the convent. In one, I'd pull the hair off the sides of my face and secure it at the crown of my head in a tiny bun, letting the rest of the wavy mass cascade down my back. In the other, I'd weave it into two thick braids secured with dark ribbon. I wore the braided style when I'd entered the convent. But today, on my "wedding" day, I let it hang loose. Even the novice said it was beautiful.

At last it was time to line up in the hallway. There were sixty of us left from the original eighty who had entered in the fall. Over the year, girls just didn't show up for morning prayer or an evening meal, and we knew, even though we didn't speak of it, that they had decided to leave. Something was the matter with them, some character flaw or defect. How could they not find happiness in this glorious place, this gift from God Himself?

In that cocoon of smug contentment, I descended to the ground floor with my sisters. My feet did not touch the ground. We formed a line of chaste brides, or ghosts of brides, the white of our gowns fading into our pale complexions, our eager gazes darting up at each other, then down again, afraid we'd be caught staring at the only mirror we had—each other.

Outside the chapel, the morning air grew warmer. We could hear the numinous voices of our Sisters beginning to chant the Alleluias that would accompany our walk down the aisle. Hearts racing, we demurely looked down at our feet. Stepping into the chapel, I felt all eyes on us and knew they were admiring us and regretting our lost beauty. This was heaven. This was communion.

After such a long fast from human contact, I could hardly keep my gaze from drifting to the sides where people in all sorts of clothing pressed in the pews. Purple dresses, rich brown wool coats, green silk, pink cotton— all of it tempted me to look. But I followed the slow steps of the bride in front of me, clasping my rosary and psalter to my chest. I was so excited, so distracted, so overwhelmed, that the images of that day now all blur together like the voices of the choir, one mass of sound and impression, a union of many, creating a single, stirring, yet utterly indescribable, elation.

The Mass began; the Bishop intoned the Introit, the Kyrie and Gloria. Then, the Gospel was read and he preached a sermon, not a word of which I could repeat on this day. I don't even remember sitting in the pew. My mind was focused only on the one moment when I'd approach the altar.

At last, at last. Two by two we walked up. Our names were called.

Margaret Marie Wojehedski.

The tile floor was cold. It roused me to the moment. It made the too-fast morning slow down and move to the Chapel's usual languid pace, where time crawled by no faster than the speed of a priest's procession down the aisle. The floor even smelled cold, sharp and tart like steel. My eyes closed, and I heard my heart thumping, and at some point an inner voice told me it was time to rise, to walk beyond the altar rail to the altar itself, a cloud of gold and white and glowing candles.

Before the bishop, I kneel. In Latin, he blesses me. I feel the air brush my face when he sweeps his hands in the sign of the cross. He slips a ring on my finger. And calls out my new name.

Sister Francis Marie.

Then our Superior beckoned me to the side, where I was handed a pile of folded clothes—the dark robe of a novice, with its long, white cotton veil. No longer would we wear the little half veils that only came to our shoulders.

I was led to the sacristy behind the altar. The small room had been transformed for the occasion into three cubicles, divided by screens. In the first cubicle, I was instructed to sit on a stool where a close-mouthed sister took the pins from my lace veil, removed the garland of blossoms and began to cut away my hair with heavy shears. My hair. The luxurious mass that was me, that called for recognition and embrace. The hair that Rosy had braided, that I myself had twisted into attractive styles.

As Sister cut, I thought of Rosy brushing and braiding, and how sorrowful she'd be to see this sacrifice.

The whine of those scissors as the Sister brought them close to my ear and my neck caused me to flinch.

After handing my bridal gown to another Sister's outstretched hand, I slipped into a black cotton sheath. Over this I pulled on the loose, flowing robe of dark jersey wool of such a deep brown, it appeared almost black. I could feel my personality retracting, hiding under the heavy folds.

Then I walked to the next cubicle where another sister instructed me on how to place my head in the wimple that would now forever encase my face in public. She tugged at the strings, tying them so tightly that my head began to ache. Over this she placed a white bib, and then she set the veil on my head, gently pinning it to the wimple at the top and sides and again at a pleat in back. She handed me a corded belt and helped me slip it around my waist, then gave me my rosary and psalter, first draping the beads over the belt.

Through a side door that led to the other side of the altar, I walked back into the chapel and took my place again. No longer a radiant bride, I was now an anonymous nun, my individuality sheared away with my hair, the auburn locks that had enticed Rosy to touch. Margaret Wojehedski lay on the floor of the sacristy with my shorn locks. Sister Francis Marie was in the chapel pew.

As the last of the postulants took her place with the rest of us robed novices, our fellow sisters pealed out in their girlish voices a *Te Deum*. My eyes blurred. I could not read my psalter. I could not even focus on the words being chanted around me. I shut my eyes and tried to meditate. As we had been taught so many times, I tried to empty my mind in order to allow God to enter. The only thing that entered my mind and soul, however, was anticipation. Excitedly, I imagined Rosy and Mother's reaction to me when we would meet after this ceremony. I could hardly keep myself from turning around to see them.

But a little while later, I was disappointed to see my mother and sister glancing this way and that on the sun-dappled lawn, not recognizing me. I had to call out to them as they looked around outside the chapel. Even though Rosy was changing from a child into a young lady, I recognized her bright smile always on the verge of a laugh, her bounce as she shifted weight from one leg to the other. She never could stay still. She was wearing an unfamiliar dress, something beige and light that tied in the back and made her look slender, almost svelte. Her hair was a mass of untidy curls as usual. And Mother—she never changed. She was still as tightly wrapped as always, this time in a navy blue dress, shiny at the elbows, her hair in the usual stiff curls.

"Margaret!" Rosy cried out to me and ran across the lawn to catch up. I started to correct her, to remind her of my new name, but was strangely embarrassed and said nothing.

"Look at you! Turn around," she commanded. Shyly, I slowly moved around as she fingered my veil, the edges of my sleeve, the bib. "Isn't it hot under there?"

It *was* warm. Even though it was a perfect spring day with affectionate sunshine brushing our shoulders, I was beginning to perspire under the heavy robes. The wimple also made hearing difficult. Sounds were slightly muted.

"Margie, you're *beautiful*. The vision of a saint!" Rosy said and embraced me. Mother hugged me, as well.

"The Mass was so *Piekna*. Everyone was beautiful,"

Mother said. While Rosy spoke in English, Mother reverted to her comfortable Polish.

"Did you see me—when we walked up the aisle?" I asked, wanting to know their reaction to the way I'd looked in the wedding gown.

Rosy looked down at the ground and giggled. "Oh, Margie, we had such a hard time seeing. We were crammed between this giant of a man and a woman who kept leaning over. Was it a satin dress?"

"Yes, that was the one," I said. With a pang of disappointment, I realized that the moments I had imagined them admiring me had not existed. "With long sleeves and buttons at the cuffs..." I stopped myself. It was unbecoming for a novice to be discussing fashion, even the fashion of her own bridal gown.

"Oh, I wish I could have seen it up close," Rosy said. "We had to sit way in the back. We just got here in time."

"Where did you get the gown?" Mother asked. "Do I have to pay for it? It looked expensive."

"No. The gowns were here. From other sisters. From other years." Every time I talked, my chin cut into the wimple. And my voice sounded strange to me now that my ears were covered. It was as if I was under water. Everything seemed far away and covered by ocean depths of separation.

"Would you like a tour?" I asked. We had been told that we could take our families on tours of the convent as long as we did not show them our rooms or the refectory.

"Yes, I'd love that!" Rosy said, linking her arm in mine as if we were girls. I did not resist. Her slender hand on my arm was a tiny piece of home, tugging me back into a world that was receding with every second.

We trudged off through the brilliant sunshine, and by the time we were finished seeing the grounds and buildings, my face and arms were covered in a patina of sweat while Mother and Rosy looked fresh and free.

A bell clanged in the distance. Families started to

move inside, into the foyer and dining hall where refreshments were set up. I accompanied Rosy and Mother and made sure they were comfortable.

"Aren't you going to have any?" Rosy asked. She stood leaning against the veranda railing, a plate filled with crustless sandwiches and little cakes.

"No. We will have lunch in the refectory," I said. "In fact, I should go there now. I'll rejoin you in a little while. We can meet by the tree out front—where you first met me."

Dining was an act of intimacy. From now on, we would only share it with our fellow sisters unless we were traveling.

Usually when I walked into the refectory, I was happy. No longer did I have to fear not having enough to eat, as I had as a child in Baltimore. But today, the possibility of filling the gnawing hole in my stomach did not make up for the other hole that had begun to appear in my heart. I had only occasionally missed my family since coming to the convent. And even then, it was the companionship of my sister I missed, not the routine of my own household, not even my mother or brother. In fact, Rosy's letters and the occasional missive from my mother kept me in touch with home in a way far more comfortable than actually being there.

Having Mother and Rosy in the flesh before me today, however, made my loss real. There was something different about them. They looked more prosperous.

For the first time since arriving at the convent, I ate quickly and distractedly, eager to leave the table. I can't even recall what we had for lunch that day, but I know it must have been a festive meal for us. It may have even included a tiny sip of brandy, just as we were given at Christmas and again at Easter. This day was like Easter, filled with new beginnings, joy, poignant reminders of loss. *Haec Dies quam fecit Domino...*

While we ate, I looked around at the other novices,

trying to determine if they, like me, were experiencing difficulties with their habits. If they were, I saw no evidence on their faces, which were as serene as statues. I wondered if I looked the same and if some sister was scrutinizing me searching for the same clues.

At last we were dismissed. I tried to hide my eagerness by forcing myself to walk up the refectory steps with a studied pace. But once at the top floor, I let myself go, striding quickly to the front lawn, disappointed not to see Rosy and Mother there.

Patiently, I waited in the shade. Other families were strolling together around the grounds. Some sat on the benches in the gardens. Where was my family?

After a quarter hour, Rosy appeared at the front door, holding Mother's hand as she made her way down the few stairs. When they came over to me, I let my impatience show.

"Where were you? Did you forget the meeting place?" My voice was stern. Every minute with them was precious.

Rosy laughed. "We were inside, finishing up. We met some people from Maryland. Their daughter's name is Julia. Do you know her?"

"We don't make friendships. It's discouraged. I was waiting nearly a half hour."

Still smiling, Rosy grabbed my arm. "I didn't realize you'd be done so soon! Come on, let's walk some more."

Mother was tired, however, so we only walked back to the veranda, where we sat at a table together. Rosy went to get herself some more cakes, while Mother sat stiffly, staring across the rolling lawns.

"Karol enlisted," she said flatly without looking at me.

"But he's so young," I murmured, not wanting to think of sad things.

"And he has a girl," she added, not sounding as if she approved.

Rosy returned, plopping down across from me,

three delicately frosted petits fours on a plate in her hand.

"One for each of us!" She popped one into her mouth and offered the plate to Mother, who took one as well. Then she held the plate out to me.

"No, thank you," I said. At the sight of the smoothly glazed cake, my mouth watered. But I couldn't eat with them.

"Okay," Rosy said, her mouth still filled with cake. "If you insist!" She gobbled up the other one, gleefully licking her fingers after she swallowed it. "Do you make these here?"

"I think they order them from a nearby bakery. But the cooks here are quite good."

"You don't look like you're starving." Rosy grinned.

I blushed.

"I don't mean you're fat!" she hastened to add. "I just mean you don't look like a skeleton. I was worried that you wouldn't get enough to eat."

"I worried, too," Mother added. "I know they try to fast, don't they?"

"We fast during Lent and Advent. And only eat at meal times. But then the food is very good. And plentiful."

For an hour, we talked. Rosy was the major domo, leading the conversation, asking questions about my studies, what I would like to do, what my next few years would be like. She volunteered a little about her own life, her circle of friends, her own aspirations.

"I want to be a movie star," she said, smiling. "But I think I'll settle for teacher, right, Ma?" She patted Mother's arm and Mother smiled back at her.

"She is so bright," Mother said. "She would make a good teacher, no?"

"Yes, I'm sure she would." Rosy was still a girl. It was hard to imagine her as a teacher, especially then. She seemed drunk with life, not at all the sickly girl she used to be. They were both so different, so…happy.

Rosy looked at her watch. "Oh, no. It's getting late. We have to catch the train. The McMullens offered to drive us but we already have tickets."

"The McMullens?"

"Julia's family. Remember, I said we'd met them and they live in Maryland? They offered to drive us home. They have a car. But we already have tickets, so we're going to take the train. Besides," Rosy said, "I think Mother enjoyed the ride."

My mother looked embarrassed, but she smiled. She *had* enjoyed the ride.

"I can walk you to the gate," I said, standing.

It was late afternoon. And yet the moment that I'd walked down the aisle in a bridal gown now seemed an epoch away. Perhaps it was being with Rosy. I'd felt lighthearted before she'd arrived. But she was filled with so much joy that my own pleasure paled in comparison. She was too bright a sun.

"I am sure you could get a ride to the station," I said. "You could call a cab inside."

"Too much money," Mother said. "And it is not that far."

"Just a quarter mile or so," Rosy added.

We passed the statue of St. Francis. "Look, Rosy, just like the one you gave me." I pointed to the larger sculpture.

Rosy's face clouded, then realization dawned as she recalled the wooden figurine she'd given me the day I'd left home. "Oh, yes. I'd won it in a spelling bee, I think." She could barely remember.

At the gate, we looked at each other one last time. From this point forward, I was never to see them again.

But like many big moments, it was filled with petty discomforts. I was tired. My wimple cut into my face. I needed time alone to digest every part of the day. I strained to feel the momentousness of it, to memorize it, to find words to memorialize it. Rosy's golden hair in the sun. My mother's tight-lipped smile. The smell of the macadam, the distant lowing of a farmer's cow. How could I keep all this fresh?

"Tell Karol to write. Be sure to write and tell me how your trip was." I embraced them each in turn, their cheeks rubbing against the layers of cloth that now shielded me from the world. I wanted them to say something —*we will miss you terribly, we love you, we never wanted you to go.* I wanted them to say my given name—Margaret—one last time.

Instead, they left shyly, as if leaving was rude and they had to get away before I noticed their breach of etiquette. Rosy looked over her shoulder once and waved.

"Sister Francis Marie!" she called out, her giggle melding with the silver whisper of the leaves rustled by breezes.

I stood waving at them and stayed until their figures disappeared over a hill.

For a long afternoon, I wandered the convent grounds as the crowds of families thinned. I searched faces, scouring each smile, each frown, each vacant stare for something I couldn't even define. Then, as I grew tired and headed back to the main building, I heard someone saying goodbye to "Julia."

Julia McMullen, whose convent name I'd taken no note of. I didn't look at her. She was just one more anonymous nun, one more blackbird flitting around the grounds that day. Instead I stared at her family as they gathered next to their big shiny car—a tall, skinny father with thinning hair and thick glasses, a slender mother in a flowered dress and black hat, strands of her wavy brown hair coming loose from a bun at the nape of her neck, and a girl, a little younger than Rosy, impatient to leave, her eyes squinting into the late-day sun as if she wanted to be any place but here.

I stared so much at this family that Mrs. McMullen glanced at me with an odd look, and I was forced to turn away. When I heard them voice their final farewells and the doors slammed and engine started, I turned to look again. Her back to me, Julia waved, and as she moved her hand I noticed her shoulders tremble ever so slightly, like a willow touched by a gentle summer wind.

CHAPTER TWENTY-TWO
The copper bowl

MARGARET LEANED back, her head on the bus window, remembering the last bits of her conversation with Dr. Kaplan before the session had ended...

"I fell ill the next winter. Many sisters were sick with coughs and fever. I came down with it too, but I soldiered on. I kept thinking of the nuns, the nuns who...of Sister Beatrice, Sister Lucia, Sister Michael Ann..."

Dr. Kaplan flips through pages of notes while I talk. He's looking for their names, so I help him.

"In the cemetery. The sisters who'd died young."

"And you thought that was your fate, as well?"

"I thought I should accept God's will."

"And what happened?"

"Lillian, the postulant I'd befriended my first day, left. She and I took a walk one Sunday afternoon. It was bitter, bitter cold and even the wimple didn't keep my ears warm. The whole time we walked all I could think of was getting back to the warmth of the convent. She poured out her heart. She even cried. Her mother was sick and had written asking her to come home. Her mother had never wanted her to go in, you see. And Lillian was having doubts if she should stay and she was beginning to wonder if her mother's illness was a sign she should return. She wanted my advice."

"What did you tell her?"

"I...I don't remember. I don't think I told her much. I might have said she should pray on it. I was so cold I couldn't think. My ears ached from the cold."

"But she left."

"I only found out months later. After I was released from the infirmary. I had pneumonia."

And every day I'd waited, thinking God would call me. Every day, He'd disappointed me.

"Sister Margaret Mary was not pleased," I said, more to myself than to Dr. Kaplan.

"She was angry at you for getting sick?" Dr. Kaplan was incredulous, and I knew he would like to think that here at last was the person upon whom to affix blame.

"No. She was angry because I hadn't gone for help sooner. She came to see me as soon as I could sit up, after the fever broke. She scolded me and lectured me on how no one, least of all Our Lord, expected us to be foolish with the gifts He had bestowed on us. She told me that occasionally Sisters let themselves 'go' thinking it was God's will when, in fact, it was nothing but self-will."

I remembered her voice and her talk almost word for word. I'd burned with a new fever, the fever of embarrassment, made doubly worse because I'd thought she'd come to visit me to encourage me and offer me comfort.

"She told me that whenever I was ill, I must tell my Superior."

"And that's when she told you about Lillian leaving?"

"No. I noticed she was gone myself when I finally went back to Chapel." And we'd prayed for the repose of the soul of a Mrs. Dorothea McRowan. Lillian's mother had succumbed to her illness.

"But by then everything was messed up and I could hardly find time to think about Lillian, let alone miss her. If anything, I was hurt that she left." I'd waved the air in front of me, trying to brush away the clutter of thoughts that now bombarded me.

"You see, I started out in the nursing track. We had two tracks—nursing or teaching. And I was good at biology and science, so they put me in the nursing track. After I recovered, they felt I'd lost too much time and couldn't make it up, that it would be easier for me to make up time in the teaching track.

"Even if it was easier, I had months of material to make up—the month I was sick, and the months I'd been taking nursing courses. I was always behind. And Sister Margaret Mary wanted me to do even more. She'd heard I had a good singing voice, so she suggested I take music lessons. Schools can always use music teachers, she'd told me.

"Although I was a good student, I did poorly on tests that year. I was failing my music course. There was even the possibility I would have to stay back a year, a humiliation for a good student such as myself—to be in a class with new novices, instead of advancing with my own group. Sister Margaret Mary told me she'd give me a probation, she'd allow me to study during the summer with a tutor, Sister Lucy.

"I liked her. She was kind and patient. She was a fourth year novice, ready to be posted to a parish in the fall. But the last week of my lessons, before autumn classes began, she wasn't there."

"She was sent away early?"

"No." I looked down at my hands, still remembering how sad and betrayed I'd felt when I found out. "She left. Like Lillian. Her brother had been killed in the Pacific."

"You felt she was abandoning you."

"She was abandoning all of us."

৵৶

Before she'd left Dr. Kaplan's office, she'd asked him a question. When do you think I will be cured?

Cured. He wouldn't use that word, he'd said. He would stick to "recovered, able to function well."

She was able to function now. Proudly, she thought

of how she'd managed the bus trip. She'd quelled her anxiety, she'd found her way through the city. She was tired, yes, but still strong. She could go back to teaching....

She'd have to write that letter, convince Sister Fulgentia to let her stay. What had she ever done to that woman to make her dislike her so? How could she prove to her that she was worthy, capable of fulfilling her duties, deserving of a second chance?

Ideas, plans, panic roiled her stomach as she approached Karol's house and opened the door. Paula called out from the kitchen, and everything in her seemed to change, going from hard-won serenity to anxiety in the blink of an eye.

"You made it! Did everything go okay?"

"It was fine." She didn't feel like talking. She'd done enough of that. She needed to think, to write the letter.

"I have some iced tea, if you'd like. It's awful hot out."

"Thank you. I can get it myself." She wanted to be alone, couldn't Paula see that? "I'm...I'm going to rest now." Margaret rushed to her room, closing the door quietly and leaning against it.

A pressure in her chest built to a crescendo. She needed to be alone, to think things through! She didn't need Paula here, a reminder of her loss and her current failure.

Fat, heavy tears. They rolled down her cheeks with no warning. She strained to keep her weeping quiet as she gulped back sobs. Memories of Rosy's death thundered over her, a torrent of rage held at bay for months. Sister Fulgentia had no right to dislike her. But Margaret had every right to be angry at her!

Sister Fulgentia –the hypocrite! Punishing her, yet not reflecting on her own need for punishment! The lying hypocrite! If only Sister Fulgentia had let Margaret go to Rosy.

At the deathbed or at the funeral. Those were the

choices. No family contact. Only exception—at the deathbed or at the funeral for immediate family members.

Margaret had chosen the funeral.

No! Her inner voice screamed again. She did not choose the funeral. She chose faith. Faith in life. Faith that God would provide life for Rosy. But instead she was given death.

She sank to her knees by the bed, like a child again, her hands clasped together in a fist of prayer. Her head bowed onto the warm bedspread, she prayed. Or rather, she felt. Rage. Pain. And the searing yearning of someone who does not know precisely what she yearns for. All was a dry, aching desert. No solace. No rest. No answers. She was alone. Her connection to the world was gone. To the life she'd left behind. To life itself.

"Why did you take her from me?" Between her untidy sobs, the question shouted itself in her mind. Her lips tightened. She bit her teeth together and held her breath as sobs drenched her face and wracked her shoulders.

When she could cry no longer, she grabbed notebook and pen. But she didn't write to Sister Fulgentia. She wrote more notes for Dr. Kaplan. Or maybe just for herself.

∼∽

I saw myself in a copper bowl. I stared. I sinned. She died.

No, no, no. That wasn't enough sin to justify this. Not nearly enough.

So a catalog of sins spreads before me. My inability to perform my duties. My constant illnesses. My posting to St. Benedict's, near my family. My promise not to have contact with them. The small contacts I did have with them. Week after week, seeing them in church, sometimes after Mass. Rosy turning and smiling to me. Paula telling me when they would be there. Paula telling me what they were doing, when Bernard was coming home. Paula describing their gatherings, laughing, offering to take messages back and forth for me like a spy crossing enemy lines. Paula telling me they would be at Christmas midnight Mass—Bernard included. Paula asking if I could arrange to be there.

And I had been there.

Oh, my God. I had been there. I'd broken the Rule. Over and over again. Paula had tempted me. I had sinned. Rosy was dead.

A soft knock at the door is followed by Paula's low voice.

"Margaret? I'm going to talk to a neighbor. There's more tea in the fridge."

"Thank you," I mumble. I relax back onto my heels and stare at my bony white knuckles. Then I wipe my tears away with the back of my hand. I sit on the bed, pen poised over the notebook.

I compose a response. Not to Sister Fulgentia. Her heart is ice. To Sister Margaret Mary at the Mother House. Surely she will understand.

Dear Sister Margaret Mary, I write…

In March, my sister died…

My letter is part confession, part narrative.

My sister died of polio.

Young and beautiful. Like the other young nuns whose graves I passed. God whispered her name, and she walked toward Him.

I was home in the convent when I first heard she was ill. I was ill myself, having caught the flu from one of my students. I had been in bed for two days and was beginning to feel better and to regain my strength. So, I had taken it upon myself to help the sisters who were assigned to cooking and cleaning duties that week. We are a small convent and share these responsibilities instead of assigning them to one sister.

I went to the kitchen in the morning, after the other sisters had left to teach in the school next door. I remember the day vividly. It was unseasonably warm, and I opened the kitchen window, letting in a balmy breeze. The convent is so close to the school here—just a walkway separates us—that I could hear the first bell of the day. In our small walled yard, the grass even looked a little green. This was the third day in a row where warm weather had teased us, and I was beginning to think winter was truly over.

For an hour, I labored over a cake. In the midst of my preparations, the front doorbell rang, and I went to answer it. It was a mother. I didn't know her. Her daughter was in fourth grade and I teach second. But she had a bunch of lovely, not-yet-opened daffodils with her. She and her husband owned a greenhouse, she explained, and she thought we would enjoy an early taste of spring. I thanked her, making sure I had her name correctly so I could tell the other sisters. Then, I took the flowers into the kitchen where my cake began to perfume the air with its homey sweet smell as it baked.

And here is where I sinned, dear Mother. I reached into a cabinet for a copper vase. When I went to fill it with water, I noticed that I could see myself in its smooth surface. At first, I looked away. But when I arranged the young buds in the vase a few seconds later, I could not stop myself from looking again. I didn't just look. I stared.

Please forgive me, Mother, for this show of vanity.

I saw myself for the first time in over a decade. I saw myself the way my students saw me. And I liked what I saw. It was a good feeling, knowing that I did not look ugly, that I did not look unattractive in the habit, all squashed and shapeless like Sister Fulgentia. It was a good feeling to know that when my students looked at me they saw something pleasant and sweet and pure.

I stared at myself for the entire time I held the vase. After I finished arranging the flowers, I took them to the parlor. It was with great reluctance that I left them and the vase to tend to my cake. I enjoyed seeing myself. I had no sense of sinning at the time. It felt so fulfilling, so right, to see myself. At the time, I thought it was a gift—this chance reflection—to help me as I lay ill. It revived me. I even thanked God for it!

But later that evening, I reaped the consequences of my act.

We were in our evening Recreation, Mother. Our Recreations are boring affairs. Poor Sister Fulgentia struggles so to keep them interesting. But they often end up being silent gatherings. That night, Sister Catherine talked of a St. Valentine's Day project she'd had her first graders work on. But Sister Barbara pointed out that these students had done the same project in kindergarten. Sister Fulgentia said nothing, even though I could see that Sister Catherine was disappointed. She had been so proud of her ideas. Sister Fulgentia had been consumed in sewing at the time. Perhaps she was distracted. But she was sewing lace on the wrong side of a handkerchief. When I pointed this out to her, she snapped at me that she knew perfectly well what she was doing.

Then the phone rang, splitting the air like a slap. And I looked again at the copper bowl. I remember I blushed, fearing my other Sisters would see me. Sister Fulgentia took a long time to answer the phone. It must have rung ten times before she picked it up. We were all silent while she spoke. Our convent is so tiny we could hear her quite clearly, even though her office is across the hall from the parlor. I heard her say, "Yes. Oh, dear. We will pray for her. I will tell Sister Francis Marie."

When I heard my name, my heart raced. Phone calls can only mean bad news. I already knew it was bad news. I knew it was Rosy.

Sister Fulgentia didn't even tell me until she was fully back in the room, seated in the rocking chair by the far window. We were all crammed in the room with hardly any air to breathe. The day had been warm.

"I'm afraid your sister Rosalinde is in the hospital," Sister Fulgentia told me. "That was Mrs. DiGiacomo calling. She said she heard it from your brother."

The other sisters offered me their sympathy, their prayers. Before I had a chance to ask, they posed the questions for me. What was her illness? Would she be all right? What had happened?

Rosalinde had polio, Sister Fulgentia said solemnly. She had been ill with what they thought was the flu, but it had worsened.

I can barely remember now the rest of that evening, only that we ended Recreation early so we could go to the tiny chapel in back of the parlor and say a rosary together. The chapel opened onto the parlor, French doors dividing them. We arranged our chairs into pews. The words of the prayers did not penetrate my numb soul. I confess that I did not pray, I did not think. I was frozen. Mother, you must understand, surely you understand, surely you have had moments, or perhaps just one moment, in your life when things go terribly wrong and you feel like you've been sent to the train tracks to stand alone and stop the locomotive and you are filled with clenching fear, blood-stopping fear, knowing that you could fail and all would be disaster. That you have no way of stopping anything. That you don't have it deep within you, the courage or strength or whatever is needed. That you were the wrong person to call.

This is how I felt at that moment, that I was called upon to pray with an unswerving faith and devotion, that my prayers, alone among those of my family, would stop tragedy, would save Rosy from paralysis...or worse. And I knew I was incapable of doing this.

After the rosary, Sister Fulentia dismissed the other Sisters and called me into her office. We were violating Grand Silence, so she hurried through her explanations. I could go visit my sister, she said. I could go see her in the hospital. I nearly wept for joy. I started asking her questions. Could I go the next day? Would I travel alone? Should I arrange for my brother to pick me up or take a taxi?

Sister Fulgentia smiled. I could even go that night, she told me. She would call a taxi for me if that is what I wanted to do. I was about to tell her to make the arrangements when she reminded me of what I had learned long ago. I could only make one visit. It was the Rule. I could visit now as Rosy lay dying. Or I could go home for the funeral. Not both.

Hadn't Sister Fulgentia just told me she was ill? She hadn't described her case as terminal. People contracted polio and lived! Why, look at President Roosevelt—he'd survived the summer plague. I was angry. And I confess, dear Mother, that I said things in an angry tone of voice. I accused Sister Fulgentia of hiding this information from me. I told her she should have immediately told me that Rosy was so desperately ill. As soon as she got off the phone with Paula, she should have told me. And, yes, I thought that it was wrong—that it was a betrayal of faith—for Sister Fulgentia to even suggest that Rosy would not live.

She did not answer those accusations. Instead, she again explained my choice. Either. Or. Not both. Go now. Or go later. I asked if I could call my brother. When she didn't answer right away, I again accused her of not letting me find out the truth for myself. How could I trust her to tell me what was really happening? Perhaps I would be better able to understand my own brother. Reluctantly, she let me call Karol's house. In fact, she excused herself from the room, wanting to observe the Grand Silence. She allowed me the use of her office and only asked that I tell her what I wanted to do—if I wanted to go that night to the hospital.

She closed the door behind me, but I knew my voice would carry throughout the convent. I dialed the number. And Paula answered. Paula! Paula explained how Rosy had suddenly become much worse after suffering for several days with flu symptoms. I asked her why my mother had not called a doctor, and she said that Rosy wouldn't let her. Rosy had told her it was nothing, just the flu again. Rosy was getting sick a lot, said Paula, from her students.

Paula asked me when I'd be able to come and if I needed Karol to pick me up. Or Bernard could come get me, she said, on his way into town. I was almost ready to say yes, he could certainly pick me up. But then she told me that Bernard would stay with Karol until "it was over." *She* had called him. Not Karol. Not my mother.

She had given up on Rosy, too! They all had. They were all just waiting for her to die. And it was as if God was presenting me with a challenge, to be the only one who believed, to carry on my shoulders the full weight of everyone else's faith, to make up for their doubts.

I told her I would have to call in the morning, that I might not be able to come. I explained to her that the Rule is very strict. I explained that we were not allowed to go to the sick bed of our relatives. I would have to receive special permission.

So I hung up the phone and went back into the Chapel. I prayed for hours, saying rosary after rosary, offering to God this sacrifice—*I will not go to Rosy's bedside now because she is not dying. I will deny myself this visit as an offering of faith.* I confessed my sins to God, promising to do so to the priest that weekend. I only went to bed when Sister Fulgentia came down to fetch me. She asked me if I'd made up my mind, and I told her I would not be going to the hospital. She nodded and said she'd make arrangements "when need be." Did I not tell you that she, our convent's leader, had no faith? How was I to flourish under such a woman?

I went to bed that night with a peaceful heart. My conscience was clear. I was doing my part. While everyone else gave up, I would remain true. And I was surprised at how easy it was to accept this burden.

But it got harder. The next day, I went back to teaching, but I was tired now from both my previous illness and my late hours. Faith is so much easier when one has energy, and the commitment is fresh. All day I had to remind myself that I had to be the one to keep hope burning, to believe, and to continually voice my belief that God would cure her. Over and over I prayed that day, while I waited for the children to finish assignments, while they ate lunch, while they played at recess, while I cleaned up the classroom at the end of the day. It became automatic, uncontrollable, this prayer. I believe you can make my sister well again, O Lord. Say but the word, say but the word.... Over and over. If I slipped, if I stopped, I was sure that would be enough to send her over the edge.

Each second of that day and the days that followed were broken into a million shards to be crawled over at an agonizing pace. And I confess that I faltered. I became ill again and had to stay at home where I prayed continually, some days better than others, some days filled with hope and peace and the sure knowledge that she'd be better, and some filled with despair, the kind of despair that makes you feel carved out inside because you know this is what life without God feels like.

In the evening of the final day, we gathered for Recreation, and no one spoke of my sister. Instead, we talked of spring. In the copper vase, the daffodils had opened already. Their yellow blooms' reflection now obscured my own. Temptation gone, I easily handled the task I'd brought with me—looking through artwork my students had done to decide which to display. But Sister Fulgentia reprimanded me for bringing schoolwork to Recreation. I had to put it away and retrieve some sewing or knitting instead.

We retired for the evening after prayers. I did not sleep. I lay staring at the ceiling, listening to the wind, blowing cold and rain back into the region, rattling our windows, encasing my heart in fear. I tried to pray. I could not.

The phone rang.

Nothing existed except its whir. Once. Twice. Again.

No one got up. I didn't ask permission. I didn't wait. I rose and ran down to Sister Fulgentia's office and answered it myself. I just said "Hello," knowing as I put the phone to my ear that it would be Karol, knowing what the news would be, and knowing that this thought revealed my faith for the charade it really had been. I'd not believed. I'd been pretending. I knew she was gone before Karol even uttered the words.

When he heard my voice on the line, he whispered, "Rosy passed away a few minutes ago." I sank into a chair in front of Sister Fulgentia's desk, leaning forward into the phone, pressing it hard against my ear. I was a failure. I had not believed. God knew. Of course He knew. Why had I thought I could fool Him?

Karol was giving me details. The likely funeral time and day. The plans for a wake, a prayer service, rosaries, novenas, Masses. Nothing registered. All I could hear was the drumbeat of my own dismal fraud. You lied. You lied. You lied. And then, more insistently: He would know. He would know.

Sister Fulgentia came into the room, pulling her shawl around her shoulders, and I hung up the phone, explaining to her what had happened. She offered her sympathy and told me she'd awaken the sisters so that we could pray together for the repose of Rosy's soul.

In the Chapel later, I made no attempt to even move my lips. I was through with lying. I had felt the wrath of God, and I didn't want to risk more punishment. So I behaved like a good girl, kneeling noiselessly, with no movement, afraid even to breathe too hard lest I anger Him more. Stunned, I went to bed, grateful for the dark cocoon that wrapped us all in silence. I could not teach that day. I told Sister Fulgentia I was ill. Nothing touched me. I lay on my bed staring at the ceiling, trying to re-create the day, the weeks, the months, the years before, listing all my sins. And they became so clear to me then. The times I'd not offered help to a Sister. The times I'd let my mind wander at Mass. The times I'd forgotten a student's paper. Sins I had been unaware of. They bombarded me like demons, nipping at my soul, eating away at my heart until I was just a shell, no longer really alive.

That day before the funeral, I indulged myself. I read a newspaper left by Sister Barbara in her room. She used them for her history classes. I ate between meals. I said none of the regular prayers. I sat in my room at my desk and looked out at the parking lot where the children screamed and laughed during recess, and I cried. I wanted to go home. I wanted to wander like a ghost through the alleys and streets of my childhood. Maybe I'd find Rosy there.

I did not go downstairs for dinner that night. I stayed in bed. And the next day I went to the funeral, staying well past the time I was supposed to be back at the convent, spending time with my family that I know I shouldn't have. I was deliberately breaking rules, flaunting my fall. I wanted, I think, for God to punish me again. I wanted, at least, for Him to notice me.

Forgive me, Father, for I have sinned... I am convinced that He did punish me, that He sent me the illness which led to the accident with my medicine.

∾ళ∾

By the time she was finished writing, she had filled a dozen pages. Achingly tired now, she forced herself to breathe deeply and write the letter. She kept her tone matter-of-fact—she wanted to demonstrate how well she was.

Dear Sister Fulgentia,

I am happy to hear that St. Benedict's is doing so well that student enrollment is reaching record levels. I realize my illness made it difficult for you to make class assignments and adequately staff each grade level. But now I'm nearly fully recovered and am extremely confident that I can handle a class again. Dr. Kaplan, my physician, will attest to this recovery. I will ask him to

333

contact you.

In fact, I don't think it's an exaggeration to say that I am actually much better than I was before. This incident seems to have restored me fully to good health and spirits, and I am eager to use the skills I've been blessed to learn working with the children and with you.

My obedience and willingness to serve are more powerful than ever. I will be returning, I'm sure, within a week, no longer than two, and I can do my lesson planning here while I finish my recuperation.

I look forward to being under your tender care and guidance again.

Sincerely,

Sister Francis Marie

Satisfied with the hopeful, obedient, yet purposeful tone, she squeezed the pages into an envelope and addressed it. She wandered into the dining room in search of a postage stamp, finding one in the drawer of a table by the kitchen door. She set her envelope with a small pile of mail she knew Paula or Karol would post the next day.

It was the golden time, when the sharp light of day cut across the horizon to caress and beckon. Karol would be home soon, yet Paula was outside. She could hear her talking to a neighbor in the backyard. Margaret didn't know what Paula planned to cook for dinner, so she went to the front porch where she rocked contentedly, dozing until Karol returned home.

"Hey, sis," he called out gently when he trod up to the porch. "You survived, I see."

She opened her eyes and smiled. "No problems. Thanks for the help."

His jacket slung over his shoulder, he walked into the house, letting the door slam after him.

"Paula?" She heard him walk back through the house, then Paula's voice answering from the backyard.

After some muffled conversation, Paula must have wandered out to the kitchen. She could hear the pots and pans rattling as Paula started dinner.

Lazily stretching her legs straight out, she stood and went in to offer to help. But Paula shooed her away.

In an hour, they were all seated at the table. Karol said a perfunctory grace, and they began to eat. While he prayed, she stole a glance at Paula. She had her eyes closed, her fingers folded over each other, the vision of piety.

∾

It was trash night, and Paula stuffed the red dress, with its sparkling sequins, in a bag in their bedroom bin. It was about time she threw that thing out. All it did was remind her of Jack, and he was over, long over.

She'd spent the day cleaning while Margaret had been in town, and it had felt both holy and fine to be able to breathe easy while the nun was away. Yes, she'd looked tired when she'd come home, and she'd holed up in her room for hours after that, but at least she'd made the bus ride with no difficulty. In Paula's book, that was a big step forward, and it lifted her spirits to think that this recuperation plan might be working in so many different ways, especially when she'd experienced a disappointment.

When Sister was out—thank goodness—Father Al had called to tell Paula he had to go out of town this week, so her baptism would have to take place when he returned—a week from Friday. He'd been all over himself apologizing about letting her know at the last minute, and he'd been so sincere in his discomfort she couldn't help but reassure him it was okay.

A week from Friday—all right, she had to accept it. No point in starting over with another padre. They'd set a date, and she'd gone on with things. But it bothered her to have to put it off, especially now when things were going so well.

"Why you throwing that out?" Karol's voice startled

her, and she clutched her stomach where baby jumped, as she looked up at him. He was pointing to the red dress.

"It's seriously out of date, for one thing," she said. "And I doubt I'd fit in it again, for another." And it had been a gift from another man, one who was out of her life for good.

He scowled. "Perfectly good piece of clothing. You could have given it away." He came in the room and picked up the bin, to take it outside to the cans.

"It was worn, Karol. Had a hole near the cuff." Where John's cigarette ash had dropped.

"It looked good on you."

Then she realized its significance to him—this past New Year's Eve. The night they'd made love for the first time. Her eyes met his.

"Thank you," she said in a hushed tone. "I'm glad you remember." She went over to him and gave him a quick hug and kiss on the cheek. "After baby comes, don't you worry—I'll find something that'll sparkle like the stars, and you can take me out dancing."

He smiled at her, put down the trash can and embraced her, returning her peck with a passionate kiss. Her heart raced. Tears came to her eyes. Finally...he was relenting, letting go, just as she was trying to do, of the past.

"Thanks for being so good to Marge," he whispered in her hair. "I...Paula, I..."

She held her breath, waiting to hear him say "I love you."

But the phone rang, breaking the spell. He squeezed her arm and headed for the kitchen. She overheard him answering, calling for his sister, and then, after her phone conversation ended, Margaret's voice drifting in after Karol asked her who it was.

"It was Dr. Kaplan. He's arranged for me to meet him at the convent on Friday. To talk there."

CHAPTER TWENTY-THREE
Storm

WHEN SHE saw the weather forecast the next morning, Margaret rejoiced. Drenching rains, high winds for the next few days—surely Dr. Kaplan would have to cancel their meeting on Friday at the convent. Ever since he'd called with the news of the time for the "re-enactment," her stomach had churned, her head ached, even her face had begun to itch as if she still wore the wimple.

He'd been quick to reassure her that the convent would be empty—Sister Fulgentia had told him she'd scheduled a meeting with all the sisters in the school hall, and they could have up to an hour alone in the convent—but that hadn't been enough to calm her.

It wasn't the fear of regaining the memory of that day that roiled her. No, she was absolutely convinced that the memory loss was due only to the overdose, nothing that preceded it.

Instead, her apprehension sprang from a fear of embarrassment. What would they think of her poor little dwelling with its cramped spaces and odors of cooking? Would they pity her? And how would she react to the visit herself? What if she were overcome by buried emotions? Would she shame herself? Or worse, would she collapse again and be forced back to the hospital?

She prayed fiercely all day, rosaries following each other like waves on a shore, different only in the pleas

337

she followed them with—*please, let the visit go smoothly, please, let Dr. Kaplan realize I'm cured, please, help me to be strong, please, let the visit be canceled...*

Her fingers cramped by day's end, she retired early, sitting by the window, willing the storm to wash away her troubles.

❧

A hurricane was whipping up the coast, making Father Al nervous. But still he packed, stopping every few moments to stare out at the evening sky, its strange, orange light seeming to presage something ominous.

He shook his head as he put another neatly folded shirt into his bag, wondering for the tenth time if he was taking too little or too much. What did one need for an airplane trip? When he'd come to the States nearly two years ago, he'd traveled by ship. That leisurely crossing had required clothing for the journey itself. But an airplane would deposit him in London within a day. He only needed to pack clothing he'd need while in London.

He was surprised to notice his hand shaking as he took a puff on his cigarette.

Maybe this was a mistake. Maybe he had grabbed too quickly for the free tickets Pete's friend offered. He felt bad about rescheduling poor Mrs. Wojehedski's baptism and worse still for neglecting to call her as soon as he'd agreed to the trip. He'd been distracted right after saying he'd go, and then it had slipped his mind entirely until just yesterday. Probably a sign of how on edge he was about the journey. Although she'd taken the news with grace, he could tell it worried her to put it off. Maybe he should have moved it up. Now it was too late. And then there was Sister Francis Marie, now released to that family's care. He could have stopped by the house to visit them both. He could have been a shepherd to their tiny flock.

He stubbed out his smoke and ran his fingers through his hair. What time did he need to be at the airport, anyway?

Buck up, he told himself. You'll feel better in the morning. And you'll see to your sheep when you return. Now that you've realized they are your sheep!

Resolution back in place, he marched down the hall to Pete's room, catching him as he was headed out.

"How early should I be leaving tomorrow?" he asked, matching his stride to Pete's as he hurried down the stairs, obviously intent on a destination.

"For your flight?" Pete asked. He'd agreed to drive Al to Friendship Airport. "Oh, we should probably leave an hour or so before its departure."

At the bottom step, he stopped and turned to Al. "But I'm pretty sure it will be canceled, with this weather blowing in." He shrugged and smiled. "Don't worry. I'm positive you can catch another flight within the coming weeks."

The coming weeks—the semester would be starting by then. That would make scheduling difficult. Perhaps it would be best to postpone until next spring. It wasn't essential he go now.

A strange relief flooded through Father Al after he wished Pete a good-night and went back to his room. He wouldn't have to go. My God, he'd been dreading it more than he'd known.

With a terrible sense of guilt, he realized Pete might have been right all along. Maybe he wasn't eager to go back because he didn't want to confront the decisions he'd made that had led him here.

He stood at the open window, now enjoying the wind as it made tree limbs tremble and leaves fall.

He'd go back, he swore to himself and God. He wouldn't be afraid. Still, he was glad he didn't have to do it at this moment.

✌︎✍︎

Two days of it so far—the coming storm. Now, on Thursday, Kate hurried through the last of her shift, watching the weather blow and the rain pound as she passed each window. She'd be drenched by the time she went home. And she realized that her coming days off would be ruined by the hurricane. She'd hoped to go shopping after the trip to the convent with Aaron tomorrow. And on Saturday, she and her mother were both getting their hair done. She wondered if they'd be able to make it. Streets were starting to flood and lights flickered.

As she rounded a corner to grab her raincoat, umbrella and purse, she nearly collided with Aaron.

"I was looking for you," he said, a smile on his face. "I figured you were on duty. Let me drive you home."

She warmed from his thoughtfulness. She would have to take the bus otherwise, not a cheerful prospect on this rainy afternoon. But being in the car with him...alone...she wanted to avoid that.

"I won't bite," he said. "I promise."

"All right. I'm game." She strode with him through the hallways.

"It's awful out there," he said. "And you always seem to be here."

She smiled at him. "I actually have a couple days off coming up."

"I'm glad to hear it. You work too hard."

"I love it, Aaron! It's..." She had wanted to say "my life," but stopped herself when she realized how pathetic that might sound. "It's good to love your work."

"Won't argue with that."

A few moments later, he said, "Had some interesting news this morning. Dr. Freeman's visit was canceled—due to the hurricane."

She laughed quietly. "Glory, hallelujah!" she said. "And you went to all that trouble to keep Sister out of his reach."

"It was worth it. And she was ready to be discharged."

"Oh, I'm not doubting you."

He held a door for her as they made their way down a stairwell, her shoes squeaking from the damp marks left by other travelers.

"I ended up writing to the psychiatric chairman about the visit. I hope they don't reschedule."

"I'm glad." She stopped. "And I'm proud of you, Aaron. It's always hard to go up against authority." She relaxed now. They would have something to talk about on the way home, and she wouldn't have to think about what might have been between them.

&

In the muted light of the landing, Kate's face looked pure and soft, as if lit by soft inner glow, and her simple words—*hard to go up against authority*—took on a weight that impressed them into his heart and soul. Yes, it was hard. Even when the consequences were not life and death.

Despite the gloom outside, a strange resentment lifted off him, lightening his spirit.

Not a day had gone by since he'd begun his search for Lena that he hadn't thought of her fate and then the fate of…them all. Kate had set him up for torment with her suggestion to find Lena. First, the torment of wondering if he'd find her and if she'd respond. Every phone call brought hope and disappointment. Every mail delivery the same.

But more than that, he'd found himself thinking constantly about the refugees he'd seen and treated, the lost souls, the survivors—if you could call them that, they with the hollow stares and empty hearts. Trying to find Lena had resurrected those memories and the despair he'd felt when dealing with survivors.

No, more than despair. Anger. Fury! How could they have allowed themselves to be…victimized! How could they, how could they not resist? Over the years, his anger had turned more and more to the victims and not the victimizers, to those who'd let themselves be led away, like lambs to the slaughter.

Of course, they'd let themselves be led away…to the camps, to torture, to death. Of course they hadn't fought... How could they have known? How could they have resisted? Why had he expected more of them than of himself?

Swallowing hard, placing a smile on his face, he opened his umbrella as he pushed the door to the outside forward to the pattering rain.

"I'm parked around the corner. If we hurry, we won't get too wet!"

❧

"Are you all right?" Karol asked in the dark on his side of the bed.

"Sorry, honey. I must have heartburn or somethin'." She stood, grabbing her light wrapper. "I'll go get myself some milk."

Rain hushed the house as she padded out to the kitchen. One hand on her stomach, she pulled the milk bottle from the fridge and poured herself a glass.

After washing up, she was surprised to see Karol standing in the doorway watching her, a tender look on his face that touched her to the core.

"You okay?" he asked quietly. Sister slept in the other room.

"Yeah, I guess so." She patted her belly. "But I've been havin' a few more twinges."

"Twinges?" He stood up straight. "Should we call the doctor?"

"Naw, it's too early. He told me these things happen. Not to be alarmed." She waved the air in front of her. "Besides, I go see him next week."

"I'll take you."

She smiled. He'd offered before, but this was the first time she felt he offered out of true desire to be with her and not out of duty.

"Thanks. I'd like that. I'm getting a bit tired this stage of things."

"You should take it easy. Ask my sister to help out more. She's got a lot of time on her hands, and she probably had to do cleaning and cooking in the convent."

Paula wasn't so sure, but she nodded happily, just glad to hear Karol so openly expressing his concern for her.

"She has that appointment tomorrow morning at the convent," she said. And Paula would have the house to herself for a glorious hour! Not that Margaret was underfoot a lot—if anything, she kept to herself almost to the point of rudeness. But Paula always sensed her presence, always knew she was there, and she couldn't help feeling that Margaret might be judging her in some way.

"She can help out when she gets back," he said.

And then he paused, looking shy and uneasy, as if he wanted to say or do more, but his reserve held him back. Looking at him in the bright yellow light of the kitchen, she saw the strain on his face, the struggle there, and felt such a surge of sympathy for him that she stepped toward him and embraced him before her own fears of rejection held her back.

To her surprise, he hugged her with equal fervor, stroking her head as she rested it against his chest.

"I was thinking, Paula," he said in a near whisper. "Maybe asking Ma to live with us isn't such a good idea. When Marge leaves, I mean. Ma's been doing okay on her own, and she has her friends and church. I don't want to be taking her away from all that."

Paula held her breath to savor the moment. Her eyes closed tight, she silently prayed a thank-you. He might be telling her that he was just looking out for his mother's interest with this change of heart, but she knew it represented something deeper, something brighter, something she hadn't been sure she'd win.

"I'd love to have the place to ourselves for a bit, honey," she said at last. "Just you and me. And then baby."

❧

The next day, rain pummeled the house, a thousand

drops hitting with such force that Margaret thought they'd cut through at some point, breaching their little fortress. The wind pushed gusts of rain against the windows.

Surely they'd cancel.

She sat in the dim living room, hands in her lap, waiting.

Today was the visit to the convent. Nine o'clock. Dr. Kaplan and the kind nurse would pick her up, she'd been told, at 8:45.

Karol was off at work, Paula in her bedroom folding clothes.

Margaret had hardly slept. And when she'd awakened, she'd been irritated to see the eczema had returned as a faint blush along her jawline. Irritated at first, then relieved. If they did run into one of the other sisters, she could point to the rash as the reason she couldn't yet wear the habit.

She'd hardly eaten breakfast, either. Paula had chided her a bit, telling her she should make sure to eat something, "lest you get light-headed." A good point. She didn't want a fainting spell sending a message to Dr. Kaplan that she wasn't well. She'd resented that—that Paula had made a good point. She'd forced herself to eat some toast, even though it tasted like cardboard in her anxious state.

Karol, over his coffee, had suggested that perhaps this excursion would be canceled. How her heart had leapt at that possibility! And even now, part of her hoped...

Paula came into the room, folded towels in her arms.

"My goodness, I think we'll be needing an ark soon, don't you?" She crossed to the front window. "I think they're here. I'd recognize Kate's hair anywhere!"

Suddenly in a hurry, Margaret stood. "They shouldn't have to come up here—in all this rain." She rushed to the door and grabbed the waiting umbrella there. Paula put her towels on a nearby table and hastily pulled out her own raincoat.

"Here, you can borrow this." She held it out, but Margaret shook her head. "I'll be fine. I have this." She held up the umbrella. She noticed Dr. Kaplan getting out of the car. "I have to go. Goodbye!"

"Good luck," Paula said, standing back as Margaret hurried through the front door, waving to Dr. Kaplan to get back in the dry car while she hastened down the steps, the umbrella barely shielding her from the rain.

≈≈≈

They stood in the vestibule. It smelled of chicken soup and coffee, and Margaret felt as if she should apologize for it.

Sister Fulgentia, mercifully, had been true to her word, leaving the place vacant for their visit. A school janitor had let them in. Poor fellow had been standing in the rain waiting for them.

"Why don't we start by you showing us around?" Dr. Kaplan urged her.

This relaxed her a little. She took them on a tour, explaining their routine, showing them the small parlor where they could barely all fit for evening Recreations, the kitchen, the dining room, even Sister Fulgentia's office, which she'd left open, a gesture that touched Margaret in an unsettling way.

Then it was up the stairs. They creaked under their tread.

Then they stood in the hallway, the bathroom at the far end on the front of the house, the bedrooms along the hallway.

"The floor above is just like this one," she told them, gesturing to the stairs going up another flight.

"But this was your floor?" Dr. Kaplan asked.

"Yes." She took them to her room, the tiny space she'd shared with Sister Imelda, with its two neat beds, its desk under the window, looking out to a corner of the school building and a patch of the parking lot beyond, where children played at recess.

345

"This is cozy," Kate said at last, as if she felt the need to join the conversation in some way.

"This was my bed," Margaret said, pointing to the one to the right of the door.

"The records show you were brought into Hopkins around nine in the morning of the overdose," Dr. Kaplan said. "Why don't we go through your routine—walk through it, that is—until that time."

With a trembling sigh, she obeyed.

"I would have risen before six, observing Grand Silence," she began. And she took them through the morning like a tour guide walking them through a museum. The museum of her life.

She walked through the steps to the bathroom where she would have washed up, back to the bedroom where she would have dressed, down to the chapel for morning prayers, over to church for Mass—this, because of the rain, they left out—back to the dining room for breakfast and then...

"And then what?" Dr. Kaplan asked.

They stood in the dining room at the doorway. Really, the room was almost too small to allow the three of them to stand in it comfortably, with its huge table and many chairs pushed in. She noticed, for the first time, that a sliver of wallpaper was peeling away in a corner. She heard a clock ticking from the parlor.

"And then..." She held tightly to the back of a chair. The nurse came to her and put her hand on her arm. She closed her eyes. And then what, what? It was black, nothingness. From the moment she'd awakened that day...it was all gone. The routine she'd described for them was the routine of a hundred different mornings, not that morning. She couldn't remember that morning.

"Are you all right, Sister?" the nurse asked gently.

"Yes, yes," she said, swaying a little.

"Perhaps you should sit down." Dr. Kaplan stepped forward and pulled out a chair for her. She drooped into it. He and Kate took seats across and beside her, Kate folding her hands over Margaret's and leaning forward as if to comfort her.

"What are you remembering?" Dr. Kaplan asked softly.

"Nothing!" she burst out. "Nothing! That's the problem. I still don't remember anything, not even the parts I told you about—the waking up, the prayers, the breakfast—I can't remember them *on that day!*" Even though she'd been apprehensive, skeptical, of this tactic, she now realized that a part of her had hoped a memory would return, a benign memory that would have assured them all she was perfectly fine, that her overdose had been a mistake.

"Don't you see?" she said, sniffling. "I *want* to remember."

Kate handed her a tissue, and she wiped her eyes with it, slowly shaking her head. "I'd not realized how much I wanted to remember, until I came here." She gestured to the rooms beyond.

Dr. Kaplan sat back, his face wrinkled with thought. Eventually, he said in something of a defeated tone, "We have time to walk through it again."

She looked up, suddenly sorry for him. He, too, had pinned a lot of hope on this visit. But while her hopes had been hidden, even from herself, his had been clear and in the open.

"All right," she said, scooting her chair back.

And so they did it again. This time, she was more relaxed, her thoughts and feelings going back to poor Dr. Kaplan and his dashed expectations for the visit. She genuinely tried to remember at each stop along the way, closing her eyes, breathing in the silence of the house, recounting little details from previous mornings, explaining more about their routine, what most likely had been on her schedule that day—preparing for school opening, helping clean the convent or classrooms.

And yet, at the end, in the dining room once more, she still had no more memories than at the outset of this exercise.

"I'm sorry," she said. Now she was the one doing the comforting.

"Don't be," he said with false cheer. "You tried. You did very well, Sister. You're progressing well, that is."

She could tell he was grasping at straws, trying to find justification for this visit.

"It could just be the medicine," she offered, going back to the explanation she'd put forth before. "It wiped out that one memory. Just that one."

"Yes, yes."

A gust of wind pelted the windows with rain, making them rattle and startling them all.

"At least this will be good for gardens," she said to break the tension.

Kate laughed. Dr. Kaplan smiled.

And then, they left.

⚜

Swallowing his disappointment, he held the car door for Kate, then went around and slipped in the driver's side. They dropped Sister off at her brother's house, not exchanging more than a few pleasantries, if you could call complaints about the weather pleasantries, along the way.

Not only had this visit to the convent not triggered Sister's memory, she'd been remarkably poised throughout, showing little but reasonable strain under the circumstances. No unbearable unease. No histrionics. She'd seemed uncomfortable at first, yes, but it was an uncomfortable situation. The fact that she'd not hidden her discomfort was telling, too.

Maybe she was right. Maybe the medicine had caused the memory lapse. She was doing so well. He actually had begun to think of her as happy by the time they'd finished. Maybe all this fuss was for naught, and she had just needed some time away to recover. She'd suffered a blow with her sister's death, after all, and with her...Rule...she'd not had a chance to absorb the loss, to deal with it. Maybe that was the only phantom lurking in her past.

He voiced these concerns to Kate as he drove her back to the hospital.

"I'm thinking of discharging her from care entirely," he said.

"So soon?"

"I can't justify continued treatment if she's stable, functioning well."

"Where will she go?" Kate asked. "They'll send her to the Mother House, I suppose."

"That was the original assignment."

"But she never accepted that, did she? She's still convinced we have that wrong."

"She is writing her Mother Superior about setting that right. I guess she'll find out soon enough where she goes, if I do discharge her back to her Order." He was proud of himself for mastering the right language to use.

"Maybe then you'll know—once she learns she has to go to the Mother House. If that still upsets her, could it be a clue?"

He snorted cynically. "A clue, yes, but to what puzzle?" Sometimes he felt as if he were working a completely different problem than the one she had. He'd used the standard techniques. He'd felt embarrassed the number of times he'd raised father issues. It had felt so clumsy, so off the mark. Even when he'd figured out that her father issues were with God Himself, he'd still stumbled trying to connect her current anxieties with her very reasonable questioning of faith in the face of loss.

It had left him feeling even more unsettled about his ability and his profession, more questioning if he was right to so steadfastly cling to analysis. Was he like the doctors of yore who'd insisted on bleeding their patients? Was that what he'd become, a historical curiosity?

Sister's struggle with depression might be within the bounds of normalcy, at least, and obsessing over her one forgotten day was a sort of egotistical pursuit designed more to make him feel better, not her.

After today's experiment had failed, he was starting to wonder if forcing the woman to examine issues and memories that had no significant impact on her future or even her current attitudes was more a form of voyeurism for him. He'd become something of a Peeping Tom, looking over the sill into the convent world.

"I'm beginning to think I have no right to keep prying into her life," he admitted to Kate as they drove slowly through the pounding rain. His wipers could barely keep up. "I already know roughly, from talking to Sister Fulgentia, what happened. They spoke in Sister Fulgentia's office about the transfer, Sister Francis went upstairs to pack, one of the other sisters helping her....and then....at some point...the overdose. What more do I need to know?"

"Oh, Aaron, it's your job! Of course you have the right to pry." She gasped as the car slowed almost to a stall in a massive puddle across a low-lying stretch of Pulaski Highway.

"We're almost there," he murmured, gripping the wheel tightly. Then he realized "there" meant the hospital, not her home. She had off today. "I should have dropped you off!" he exclaimed, now irritated at himself for being so preoccupied. "I'll turn around."

"No, don't be foolish. Keep going. I'll catch a bus in town."

"No, you won't. Not in this." To mollify her, he continued. "I'll just run in and grab my mail, then we'll head out to your place." He wondered if she'd ask him in, if she'd introduce him to her mother. He'd like that, being able to visualize her in her home. Even though they'd been out several times, he'd never been in her home or introduced to her mother. He looked forward to it as he struggled with the car through the remaining blocks, pulling up to the curb beside a fire hydrant. It would be a consolation, to be able to think of her and her mother in their little house.

"Hold on—I'll be right back!"

He raced in the door and hurried to the mailroom to pick up his posts. He grabbed envelopes from his slot, just glancing through them with no expectation of anything surprising—a few letters from colleagues, a notice about a professional dinner, an advertisement for a psychiatric journal, and…

A blue envelope with a return address both familiar and different. Rachel Guildenstern. His parents' contact. The woman who'd not been home when he'd called but whose mother he had spoken to. With shaking hands, he stopped, ripped it open, read and reread, skipping ahead, taking it in. The driving rain outside, the whispering bustle of the hospital, Kate waiting for him in the car…it all faded to a muffled background as he read:

Dear Dr. Kaplan,

I'm sorry I wasn't in when you called and spoke with my mother, but she gave me your request. I tried to call you with the news of what I found, but I'm afraid Mother took down the wrong numbers. I hope this reaches you…

This search had been an easy one, she wrote, just one call. She'd only had to make one phone call….

He hurried into the hallway. Jamming the other mail into his pocket, he was oblivious to the rain as he ran to the car, skidding into his seat, facing Kate, water dripping down his nose.

"You're drenched," Kate exclaimed.

He laughed. "I have a letter! Lena's alive. You were right—she's alive!"

He saw her face register excitement and then a kind of serene but distant joy.

"Aaron, I'm so happy for you," she said, lightly touching his arm, looking into his eyes. He could read clearly what hers were saying. She was happy for him, yes—she was no liar there. But he saw, too, the dashing

351

of whatever hope she'd held, despite their drifting apart.

"Tell me what you found out," she prodded. "Is she here, in the U.S.?"

"No. She's in Israel. In Israel—clear as day, easy to find," he said, repeating some of what Rachel had written in the letter. Rachel had called and spoken to her—so easily. He could have done it. He should have done it! His mind raced. He was trembling from excitement.

"She lost her family—all but a younger brother, for whom she is now completely responsible. She was. . . married. . .and had a child...."

Kate put her hand to her mouth. Without telling her, she knew. "Oh, no," she murmured.

"They were lost."

"But she made it."

"Yes, yes. She was very sick at the end. She thought she'd die right after liberation. But she pulled through, in a refugee camp. She lives on a kibbutz not far from Tel Aviv."

"You have to go see her, Aaron."

He stopped. When he'd imagined her alive, he'd thought of a slow warm-up to a reunion, perhaps letter-writing at first. Then maybe, asking her to come to America, offering to pay her way, of course. What a selfish fool he was! He should ask nothing of her. No one should ask anything of her. He was the one called upon to make sacrifices now.

"Yes, you're right. I have the work, though." He gestured to the hospital.

"Oh, Aaron, it's the perfect time to go. Dr. Freeman's out of the way, your patients can be handed over to someone else for a short time. Even Sister Francis is recovering nicely, as you just said yourself. Now's the time to go, Aaron. This is the time. If you delay, something might come up!"

He looked at her and saw only kindness, nothing but sweet, untainted kindness. He knew she cared for him still. He himself had feelings for her that had not completely resolved. But she loved him—she loved all—unconditionally. If his happiness was in Israel, thousands of miles away, with another woman, she would let go gracefully because ultimately it was what was best for her, too. She knew all this, even if it hurt to accept it just now.

Impulsively, he leaned over and kissed her.

"Thank you, Kate. You are like no other woman..."

"Shh." She put her hand on his cheek. "Don't say that. It's such a cliché. It's like my mother telling me there's a guy out there for me somewhere. Maybe Mrs. Bromley's nephew."

"I think I dislike him already. But you deserve..." He held her hands. She deserved someone other than him, someone whose heart was all hers.

"We should get going," she said, her voice sounding overly cheerful. "Before we need a boat."

He laughed, glad to have the mood broken, and he drove back east toward her home, now confident and sure, unafraid of the storm as they traveled again through its torrents, deftly scooting around puddles and delivering her safely to her home.

A home he knew he'd not be invited into.

"Thanks," she said when he opened her car door, holding the umbrella for her as they raced to her steps. Once there, she squeezed his arm. "Get going, Dr. Aaron Kaplan. Go book that plane ticket and get Dr. Ashton to take over your rounds. Go do it, buster, before you lose courage, and I never speak to you again. This is the day!" With that, she turned and stepped inside, calling to her mother that she was home "safe and sound."

❧❧

That evening, Kate allowed her mother to put her in touch with Mrs. Bromley's nephew. So speedy were her mother's matchmaking skills that within a half hour of giving her mother the go-ahead, Kate was on the phone with James Bromley himself.

She was on the phone a long time, in fact.

To her surprise, she liked talking to him. He made her laugh. Made her laugh so hard at one point, that she actually cried. Brian had done that to her, too, she remembered when she finally hung up the phone. God, it felt good to laugh, to really let loose.

"Well?" her mother asked casually, coming down the stairs as if she'd not been waiting eagerly for Kate to finish the call on the kitchen phone.

"Well, what?" Kate teased, a bright smile lighting her face.

"Well, nothing. I've already got my answer," her mother said.

"He's asked me out," Kate said, relenting. "But I've not said yes yet."

"Oh, of course not. Of course you'd not go out with him right away!"

"Mother!"

CHAPTER TWENTY-FOUR
The anniversary

"COME ON, honey, We're gonna be late!" Karol called from the living room, jingling his keys for effect.

"I'll be right there." She turned and grabbed her purse, feeling...happy. Ten years ago, the war had ended. Ten years ago, she'd spent the evening with Jack celebrating. For the first time in ages, she didn't pinch with longing thinking of him.

The rains of Hurricane Connie had gone, and now they waited for the next onslaught coming up the coast—Hurricane Diane. She was glad she wasn't down in lowland Percy anymore. Although it wasn't a coastal town, it was close enough. And her little nest in Baltimore was a good ways from the harbor, set up on a hill, too, where they needn't worry about basement flooding.

Now that they had a respite, though, it was as if trouble had blown away with the storm. Margaret had come home from the convent visit Friday distracted and sad, but Paula had expected as much. Both she and Karol had asked her how it had gone—Karol had come home early due to the storm—and she'd only told them that it had not brought back her memory.

"You poor thing," Paula had cooed in sympathy. And she'd meant it, too. It must have troubled Margaret something awful to still not be able to recall that day.

Saturday had been better, with Margaret making

more of an effort to join in, to help out. She'd snapped beans for dinner, and she'd cleaned up broken branches with Karol. She'd even spoken with her mother on the telephone, something Karol set up, dialing the number, talking to their mother first, making sure she'd done all right in the storm. And then Margaret had spoken, quietly and lowly, to her mother, assuring her she was doing fine, answering questions, telling her she would be better soon.

Soon.

It made Paula downright hopeful. Margaret was recovering. She'd be going back soon. And not a moment too early. Although she'd not confided this to Karol, the baby was giving her indications he—or she—was itching to make an appearance.

She came into the hall, pulling on her gloves.

"Where's Margaret?" she asked Karol, looking around.

He shook his head. "Not feeling well."

Again. The second Sunday Mass she'd missed. Paula frowned. That didn't bode well. Mass should have been mighty important to the woman.

"I think she's still a little…embarrassed," he whispered, nodding toward her closed door. "You know, she might run into students or something."

She smiled in agreement at him.

Impulsively he grabbed her and kissed her on the cheek. Kissed her as if he meant it. She flushed with warmth. She'd forgotten how wonderful it felt to be loved. *Oh, Karol. I can love you if you'll let me.*

She responded with her own peck on his cheek and squeezed his arm. No matter how uncomfortable Margaret made her feel, it had been worth it taking her in. And this coming Friday she'd be getting herself baptized, hurricane or not. Things were finally looking up.

"We should get your mother out here, to see Margaret," Paula said as they walked out the door and down the stairs to the car.

❧❧

Margaret watched them leave from the window of her room, rosary in hand. She'd thought, after her visit to the convent on Friday, that she'd be ready to face the school crowd, the parents. She'd told herself the night before—a wonderful night of rest after a day working with her brother—that no one would recognize her, that she could leave church quickly at the end of Mass, even walking home ahead of Paula and Karol if they wanted to linger.

But in the morning, courage had vanished. Just one more Sunday, she'd thought to herself as her stomach had churned after breakfast. One more Sunday at home. Next week, she'd try again…

Next week…

Next week she would see another doctor. Dr. Kaplan's secretary had called her late on Friday to tell her that Dr. Kaplan had been called out of town unexpectedly and she was to see Dr. William Ashton to check on her progress, but it would have to be at a different time than her original appointment with Dr. Kaplan.

Where had he gone? The call had set up a quick flicker of panic, followed by an equally quick sense of repose. Dr. Kaplan going out of town—he must have felt confident she was improving. Maybe he was letting go of his relentless search for that one memory. Good. She wanted to let it go, too.

But sometimes it popped up in the strangest way. Even in the midst of happiness. As she and Karol had been clearing the yard of fallen tree limbs yesterday, she'd been filled with a sense of grace, of the joy of helping her brother, of being active and alive and…content.

And then, like a quick shower from the branches overhead, thoughts of that day rained on her good spirits. She should remember it. Why couldn't she? It had rattled her to stand in that convent hallway and not remember, to have the memory gone, like a page ripped from a book. It seemed unfair. What horror lie in that day?

She shook her head. No horror. Just ordinariness stolen due to the effects of the medicine itself.

She sighed and went back to her praying. She'd finish her rosary and perhaps a litany and read the Gospel. She'd meditate. She'd do all those things a good nun should do. She'd open her mind to God.

ᴄᴠᴄ

Two hours later, Paula and Karol breezed back in, laughing and toting a box wrapped with string. Bakery goods again.

"We made a quick visit to Ma," Karol explained to Margaret, who came out to greet them.

Paula put the box on the table and unpinned her hat. "Karol says this is one of your favorites." She pointed to the box. "Go ahead and have some."

She called over her shoulder as she went into their bedroom. "And that's not all—he's treating us to lunch today!"

Margaret looked at her brother as she opened the box. Cheesecake! The one she'd liked so much.

"Taking us out will be expensive," she said to Karol. She didn't want to be a burden.

"I can afford it," he said, cutting a piece of cake for himself after she returned with a knife.

Paula came back into the room, her hand on her stomach. "I'm a wee bit tired," she said, shooting Karol a knowing look. "So my darling husband is not going to make me cook."

"I could cook," Margaret offered. She felt uneasy, as if she were intruding on a secret.

Paula laughed and waved the air. "I'm sure you could. But I'm not going to let that stand in the way of a nice steak supper."

"But nothing will be open on Sundays," Margaret

demurred.

"Phil-Mar is on Old Philadelphia," Karol told her. "They make great burgers."

"When will we go?" Margaret asked. She realized that part of her discomfort was the same she experienced when thinking of going to church. She might run into parents, families who knew her.

"In a few hours," Karol said. "No rush."

"A late lunch," said Paula. She and Karol both disappeared to change and then set about doing Sunday things—reading the newspaper while they ate cheesecake, tending to a few household chores, napping.

During those hours, she fretted. Just as with the decision on whether to go to Mass, she veered back and forth between going and staying, calm and brave one moment, paranoid and scared the next.

She practiced what she would say if she should run into someone—how nice to see you, I'm doing well, recovering from an illness, I'll be back to teaching soon—determining that not mentioning why she was wearing regular clothes was the best strategy. Who, after all, would want to hear of her eczema problems over a dinner out?

She even wondered if perhaps Karol and Paula were wrong, and this restaurant was closed on Sundays, after all. What a blessed relief that would be—saving her from making a decision about it.

In the end, when Paula and Karol both wandered into the living room, where Margaret had spent most of the afternoon pretending to read while distracted by her worries, she still had not made a decision.

"I'm gonna change into something nice," Paula said, looking at Margaret's gray skirt and plain white top. "I think your yellow dress is clean," she hinted.

At that, Margaret focused her worry into annoyance. "It's not my dress. It was Rosy's," she said, irritably.

Paula laughed to break the tension. "Well, yes, you're right. Your habit is your dress. But the yellow dress looks nice on you." She came over to Margaret and patted her on the shoulder. "You wear whatever you're comfortable in."

Margaret's face flamed. Was Paula rubbing in that she couldn't wear her habit?

Before Margaret could figure that out or think of a reply, Paula vanished again into her room, ostensibly to change. The more Margaret thought about it, the more she realized it would be a mistake to go out with them. She hadn't gone to Mass this morning. She was living outside the Rule. She should at least try to live modestly. Why, she shouldn't have even considered going with them—that's how far outside the convent thinking she'd strayed.

She stood and walked to the window, brow creased, arms crossed. She really had to be more careful. She'd allowed herself to be tempted—by Paula, with her cheerful invitation. Paula—urging her to wear a dress because it was pretty on her. No, she had to remain true to the Order's Rule, even as she lived outside it. This was temporary. The convent was her life.

"You going or not?" Karol's voice, coming from behind her. She turned. He wore a short-sleeved shirt open at the collar and neatly pressed trousers.

"Thank you, but, no." She forced a smile. "It's really nice of you to ask me to join you. But I shouldn't go."

He didn't object, and she suspected he was relieved. He wanted to go out just with Paula. This realization pricked her, that he was happy she wasn't going with them. But she offered up the small pain. It was a trivial hurt.

Paula breezed back into the room, opening her purse to place a handkerchief there. She wore the blue maternity outfit Margaret had seen her in several times before—it certainly brought out her best features, making her look soft and pretty. And she'd accented those good looks with makeup, a cherry-red lipstick and some blush. Her eyes shone.

"Oh, dear. I forgot," she said, pulling an envelope from her bag and handing it to Margaret. "We saw Sister Fulgentia at church this morning. She said she had something for you and asked if we'd give it to you instead of her mailing it and all."

Margaret took the envelope. They left.

She stood, numb as a statue, with the unopened note in her hand, until the car had disappeared from view.

❧❦

Dear Sister Francis Marie,

I'm heartened to hear of your recovery. It is an answer to all our prayers. I'm also touched at your strong desire to return to teaching. I am sure you will find the right teaching position soon.

Unfortunately, St. Benedict's does not have a position for you now. Our scheduling and classroom assignments have been made for the year.

But even if they were not, I still believe you should return to the Mother House as originally planned. Finish your recovery there, and then accept God's will, in the form of your next assignment, as peacefully as possible. I fear for the worst if you cannot perform this duty. I hope you will give it much thought and ultimate acceptance.

I hope you will stop in to see me and your other Sisters before you return to Glendale.

Yours in Christ,

Sister Fulgentia

❧❦

God's will! What do you know of God's will?

I can't stay here. My skin feels as if it's bubbling. The rash is gone, but my face itches.

Paula—had she read it first? Had it been opened? I can't remember. Wonderful—another memory gone? So fast? I took the envelope…oh, yes, I ripped it open. It had been sealed. But still…Paula must have known it contained….

I dash out the front door quickly.

361

I plot my course up Old Philadelphia, choosing the east side of the street for two blocks where old maple trees throw off deep shade, and the west side for a block and a half when the maples give way to a sunny desert of concrete, macadam, and dewy lawn.

This walk is an offering to God as I seek his counsel.

After nearly a mile, I see a store, a white clapboard house converted into a small deli and market where I'd walk with other Sisters to buy small items for the convent. Closed now, it still reminds me...reminds me of going inside on warm days, inside where it would be cool from a buzzing and humming air conditioner mounted in a window on the back. I wish I could go inside now. I wish I could step back to those days when the cool of the air conditioner brought blessed relief from the heat trapped in our sweltering habits. I wish....

A black-robed figure, her back to me, walks along the shaded path. I know her. I know from the slope of her shoulders, her build, the thin white fingers I see flicking back her veil. It is Sister Imelda.

Memory, precious memory... She is my age, a kind woman, a fellow prisoner. She'd prayed with me that day, the day Sister Fulgentia had told me I would be leaving...

I remember that!

I see her kneeling with me by the side of my bed and I feel...

I remember. If only Sister Fulgentia had let me talk to good Sister Imelda. Surely she would have helped me remember....

My heart races. I stop and lean against a tree. She mustn't see me. Should I go back? Oh, God, can't decide. Can't....breathe. Meeting with Sister Fulgentia, seeing Sister Imelda...

I remember!

The details skip away like dry leaves rustling down a road on a windy day. And I am grateful! Yes, I feel gratitude that they are gone, relief! Dr. Kaplan...why?

Sister Imelda turns. Mustn't see me. She might wonder. She might...remember before I do. And then what? Then...blackness. I step behind the tree. I wait for her to pass on the other side of the road, her afternoon walk finished. Had she been praying? Had she been meditating?

She's kneeling beside me and talking to me. By the bed. Telling me to have faith.

Can't think of that. Have to stay out of sight. She can't see me. I'm not ready. It's not fair to her. It would be awkward. She'd have to tell Sister Fulgentia. She'd be punished. My hands grow clammy.

She's kneeling beside me. She's telling me how hard it was for her when she was transferred. She is telling me to have faith.

A girl calls out down the street: *Susan! Susan!* Trying to rouse a friend. Do I recognize that voice? Will this student know me? Oh, no. Trapped. No, Sister Imelda is almost at the corner. Soon she'll be far enough away. I can go on...

Go on where?

Blessed relief. She's turning the corner toward the convent.

I hear Dr. Kaplan's voice in my ear. "And then what happened? When Sister Imelda—is that how you say her name—when Sister Imelda prayed with you that day?"

She prayed with me, Dr. Kaplan, I imagine myself saying, and I imagine I say it with a condescending note in my voice and this helps me confront the memory, it gives me the distance I need to see it and not feel it, not completely feel it. She prayed with me, just as she prayed with me when Rosy was ill....

CHAPTER TWENTY-FIVE
The awakening

"I HAVE to leave! I have to pack!" I had said, running into my room. I was crying. Yes, *Dr. Kaplan, I cried. Nuns do cry. You have seen me cry. And I cried in front of Sister Imelda.*

Sitting on the bed, I grabbed a pillow and hugged it.

Sister Imelda followed me. She sat beside me and patted my hand."I'll miss you. I'll pray for you."

I sobbed. Silent, convulsive hiccups of tears. For a few moments, we both sat caught in time, without saying a word. Maybe if I didn't breathe, nothing would happen.

"I can't leave," I managed to whisper through chapped lips. "I cannot get on that train."

"You have to, Sister. We must obey." Sister Imelda stood. "Here, let me help you. Where is your valise?" She went to the closet by the door and pulled out my old black bag. "Is this it?"

I nodded. I wanted to be good. But I was so tired. Tired of trying to be good.

Placing the bag on the bed, Sister Imelda began packing for me.

"I know how hard this is. The first convent I was posted to was in Newark. And I'd grown up just outside the city. It was so hard to leave there to come here. I thought I wouldn't survive it. I thought I'd never be happy again. I had to pray a great deal my first year here. It was very hard."

She didn't understand. Going back to the Mother House meant...talking to the council, having them evaluate my worthiness, finding me lacking. I knew that's what awaited me. And Sister Fulgentia must have known, too. She'd informed me I was to leave this day. The very day she told me I was to be transferred. No preparation. *I've determined there's a train this afternoon. I have withdrawn enough travel money for you, and Sister Mary will pack you a small lunch. It's easier this way. Sister Helen arrives tomorrow, and we are, as you know, cramped for space. Go with God, Sister.*

Pray a great deal. I'd have to pray. That was it. Prayer. Lose myself in prayer. Just as I'd done before. Before, when Rosy was ill. No, not this last time, this time of betrayal. But that other time, the time when He'd listened and answered....

I slipped down to my knees, folding my hands together. When Sister Imelda saw, she stopped what she was doing and joined me in the same position next to me.

"Let's pray together," Sister Imelda said in that soft, reasonable voice of hers, that voice that wouldn't be denied. She began a Hail, Mary. My mouth moved, but no words came. I swayed from the heat, from the news, from the medicine.

I was so tired, Dr. Kaplan. You have no idea. It seemed to wrap around me like cords of rope and anchor me to the floor. Every movement was a struggle against that force.

The prayers—yes, something I'd done a thousand times, something that kept coming undone. Like mopping a floor that an hour later is covered in muddy footprints. That's what the praying felt like—tedious and ultimately useless work, a task I was required to perform that would just as quickly be undone and it would have to begin again. I was so... So. Tired.

I looked up and saw the bottle of medicine. I'd yet to pack it.

Blessed art thou among women. And blessed is the fruit of thy womb, Jesus.

The bottle was only an arm's length away. *This convent is so small. So small!*

Didn't I tell you this, Dr. Kaplan, how small the convent was, how miserly. It's no wonder it was a bad place, like "badlands" in the West, places where no good can happen, where demons whisper in your ear so often you cease to think of them as demons and only think of them as the insistent hush of an afternoon breeze, nothing more, nothing dangerous. It's no wonder they are able to do their work so easily. They mask themselves in ordinary things. In copper bowls. In newspapers left sitting around. In the smallness of a convent. In the convenience of a bottle of medicine just within reach when your soul is shattering.

Holy Mary, Mother of God, pray for us sinners...

Sister Imelda's eyes were closed in devout supplication. I reached out and grasped the bottle without her noticing. Oh, I was careful about that, not letting her notice. I didn't want her to be an accomplice, by her witness, to this....

...now and at the hour of our death, Amen.

Yes, at the hour of our death. Do you know that sometimes, as a girl when I was frightened in the dark of the ghosts under the bed and in the corners, I would leave out that part of the "Hail Mary?" I would simply pray "now and at the hour." Or even just "pray for us sinners now." It seemed to me that saying "at the hour of our death" tempted death, made those dark spirits come closer.

Did I say "at the hour of our death" that night years ago? Was that what made the difference, that I left those words out?

I'd prayed them years before this, the night I felt called to the convent. I confess—I'd not told you that whole story. I was afraid to. Afraid of how it would sound. Yes, I'd always thought of being a nun. But there had been a tipping point, something that had pushed me from idea to action. One night. A dark night.

I was praying that night, too, praying with every cell in my body. Praying for Rosy.

A voice from the present calls me out of my dreams. The little girl calling her friend. It awakens me and I move on, ambling forward…

Another memory, the one I should have shared earlier, but, in my defense, it was hidden from me, too, with only glimpses and flashes coming out of the dark….

Years ago, years before my "accident," the very first night I came home from the Mallorys, I had no worries. By the time I got home that night, the snow had changed to damp rain filling the night air with the smell of summer in the midst of winter. I had accomplished great things that day. I had found my way across town, on two streetcars, I had found my employer to be kind and her household to be full of plenty. I thought all worry was over, Dr. Kaplan!

But Karol was in a sour mood, sitting at the kitchen table studying when I arrived. He didn't even look up to say hello, and the happiness in my heart evaporated, a drop of water in a hot saucepan. Mother was sitting there as well, writing on a scrap of brown paper bag, her forehead creased in deep worry wrinkles.

In addition to the book from Mrs. Mallory, I brought home a loaf of bread that Hilda had given me just before leaving. Mother sniffed at it as if to say she had smelled better. Karol was not as fussy and immediately cut himself a piece, eating it with such voraciousness that I suddenly remembered how poorly they had probably eaten that day. Not wanting to make my brother envious, I told them only spare details about the day, assuring mother that I was up to the job and looked forward to the next day there at the end of the week.

I found a more attentive audience in Rosy, who sat

up in the bed we shared and pleaded with me to tell all about the Mallory house. I smiled and stroked her frizzy curls.

"You're hot. Are you sick again?" I asked her.

"No. Just a little warm. Tell me, tell me, tell me. Do they live in a palace? Do they have lots of servants? Does Mrs. Mallory have a mink coat?"

I described each room in the house, even the baby rooms and their story. I told Rosy about Hilda and the food she made for them. I told her how we listened to the radio in the afternoon and how Mrs. Mallory gave me the book and promised to pray for Papa's soul.

"Let me see," Rosy said, pulling the book to her. "Let me read it when you're finished. Do you think I can? Do you have to give it back?"

"No. No. She said I could keep it and there are lots more. She likes to read and pass them on.... She's a very good woman. I think she's like a...she's really almost saintly."

We talked together for nearly an hour before Rosy drifted off to sleep. I, however, was restless. Too many new things had happened that day; too many thoughts crowded my mind.

I quietly crept out of bed and wandered into the dark kitchen. Karol and Mother had gone to bed, and the room was dark and still. I got a glass of water and sat at the kitchen table to read the book. I loved the quiet of the apartment when everyone else was in bed, the sense of delicious privacy that made me feel self-confident and at ease with myself.

On the table, mother had left the brown papers she had been figuring on when I'd arrived home. I pulled them over as I sat down. Neat columns of figures, each with its one-word explanation scribbled in Polish, filled the page.

$20 – casket
$10 – priest
$5 – music

$35 – grave
$10—flowers

And more, much more—for food, for the funeral parlor, for a coat for Karol to wear at the funeral. The list was a gruesome accounting of the cost of burying my father. He was buried lavishly, making up for any poverty he had felt in life. I remembered wondering who had sent the large bouquets of red and white flowers and how we could afford the glistening coffin with its brass handles. Now I knew. I also knew, from the notations on the page, that $10 had been paid off from some unknown source. But $200 of debt remained.

Two hundred dollars. When Rosy and I fantasized together about wealth, our dreams rarely soared above the one-hundred-dollar mark. We would make up stories about a rich uncle appearing and giving the family that exorbitant amount. Even in our dreams, we didn't have enough money to solve this problem.

The next day I rose determined to work so hard and long for Mrs. Mallory that she would raise my pay. I also asked Mother if she would allow me to work all five days a week instead of two. Mother stared at me with narrowed eyes; I wasn't sure if she was angry or pleased.

"I will talk to the Sisters," she said.

But I didn't wait to hear whether Mother made arrangements at the school. That Friday, when I showed up for work again at the Mallorys, now feeling like a comfortable old hand, I immediately spoke to Hilda about my plan. Hilda was supportive, although she laughed at first.

"She will hire you for sure as long as you make it clear it is all right with the Sisters," Hilda said.

"I can do other things, like polish silver and wash the laundry...."

"She sends the laundry out... Don't worry, girl. She will hire you for more time. It is so much better to give people money for work than just to give them money...."

Hilda was right. Mrs. Mallory was very concerned

about me missing school. Even with the promise of a note from the Sisters, she still insisted that I work only three days a week, but she would raise my pay during those days.

I settled into a comfortable routine. I looked forward to the Mallory household and preferred it to my schoolwork and the spare life of home. The Mallory home was a refuge, a quiet clean place with good food and cheerful companionship when I wanted it, privacy when I didn't. This was the kind of life I wanted, I daydreamed as I scrubbed floors and dusted walls, this peaceful even life where no storms buffeted me or disturbed my equilibrium.

My own home was now filled with anger as well as sadness. Karol became increasingly surly as mother continued to scrimp on food at the store and home. When I came home from school or work, I often found them in heated discussions, even arguments, over how the store and the house should be run. Mrs. Mallory's house, in contrast, was as quiet as a church. Quieter still during that Lent when I couldn't decide what sacrifices to make, when Mrs. Mallory's sacrifices seemed enough for the whole world.

Mrs. Mallory stopped eating her regular lunch of soups, stews, or fish that Hilda prepared. Instead, Hilda set her tray with a piece of bread, a cup of weak tea and a tiny square of cheese. The last item was Hilda's own idea; she insisted that Mrs. Mallory eat something with the bread.

That was when Rosy told me I was like King Midas, with a golden touch, because every sacrifice I chose ended up not being a sacrifice at all.

I did feel lucky at that time, as if nothing could hurt me. I was safe in the cocoon of the Mallory household most of the week, and the rest of the time I stole every moment I could to read the books Mrs. Mallory gave me. The Mallory house, in fact, with its gloomy past and air of sacrifice, was a bulwark against grief. By being close to her pain, it was as if no other great pain could touch me.

Great pain did not touch me, but constant irritation did. At home, Mother and Karol barely spoke with each other. Food became scarcer and less palatable—bread with the mold cut off, stale cheeses, overripe fruits, all leftovers from the store. When Mother caught Karol offering to let an old customer buy on credit, she cuffed him after the customer left the store.

That evening, just a few weeks into Lent, Karol brought home some prime pieces of fruit, cans of vegetables, and new kielbasa. He threw it on the table in defiance of Mother who stood at the stove, heating up a weak broth.

"Let's eat like human beings for a change and not like dogs," he said in a low angry voice. "I'm tired of eating the garbage from the store."

He opened a can and poured its contents, peas and carrots, into a saucepan to heat, oblivious to Mother's physical presence next to him. Then, he sliced the kielbasa at the table.

"Should I put this in with the vegetables, Margie? Is that how to cook it?"

I sat at one end of the table trying to study. Rosy, who was not feeling well, was in our room napping.

"Just in some water..." I murmured, afraid to displease Mother who stared at the wall above the stove. "Or with the vegetables...it doesn't matter."

Karol put the slices in the saucepan with the peas and carrots, then he turned back to the table and began opening a can of stewed plums.

"Rosy!" he shouted as he punctured the can lid. "Here's some plums for you."

"She's sleeping. She's not well." Mother spoke in Polish.

"I'm not surprised," he said. "No wonder Bernard left."

From the sound of the bedroom, Rosy could be

heard coughing. The coughing and Karol's remark were too much for Mother. She turned off the broth and silently left the kitchen, walking slowly to her room where she shut the door.

"Karol, you hurt her feelings."

"So what? You don't know what it's like here day after day. I wish...I wish I had a place like the Mallorys to go to...to get away from this...." He gestured toward the apartment, dim, cold and damp. Near the window, a bucket sat on the floor, collecting water from a slow leak. Empty shelves lined the walls above the sink. Rosy's coughing started again in the other room.

We ate dinner in silence, Mother still in retreat in her room, Rosy still coughing in bed. As Karol cleaned up the dishes, I took a bowl of warmed plums to her, along with a cup of strong tea.

Rosy was tossing in bed, barely dozing. Her face was flushed and covered with a thin veil of sweat.

"Rosy? Rosy, wake up and eat something. Look what Karol made!"

I set the dishes down on the dresser by the bed and then roused her. Rosy seemed confused. She didn't speak. She ate a few spoonfuls before closing her eyes to sleep again. I was afraid. Rosy had been sick in the past but not like this, not dazed and drained of...life.

"I'm so sleepy," she murmured, each word a struggle as she gasped for air. I felt her forehead. It was so hot that I pulled my hand away, not from fear of burning myself but from fear of learning how sick Rosy really was. I thought of calling Mother, but when I went into the hallway and saw the bedroom door still closed, I couldn't bring myself to knock on it. I put on my own nightshirt and crawled into bed with Rosy.

I was determined to wake up regularly and check on her, an easy task as Rosy's raspy breathing, her coughing, her restless movement, made sleep elusive. Finally, near midnight, I got up to make some tea to soothe Rosy's cough. I slipped out of bed and went into the kitchen.

Karol had put the food from the store on the shelves. The sight of the now-full shelves cheered me, and I noticed that honey, Karol's favorite sweetener, was among the hoard. I worked quickly and quietly, brewing the tea and stirring in the thick golden honey. I found a cup and saucer from Mother's wedding set, a delicate rose pattern decorated the rim.

"Rosy," I whispered as I entered their bedroom. "Rosy, drink this. It will help your cough."

She didn't respond but continued to thrash in the bed. She wasn't coughing any longer, but she was gasping for air in long wheezing breaths.

"Rosy?" I turned on the electric bulb in the center of the ceiling. As the light flooded the room, Rosy winced, but other than this movement, she seemed unaware of me or anything else.

"Rosy, Rosy, wake up!" I shook her gently to no avail. Rosy remained caught in her delirium, struggling for air. She was still feverish, possibly even hotter than before. I was petrified. I couldn't wake her—Rosy just murmured nonsense in a half sleep. I ran from the room to fetch Mother.

"Mother, Karol, Rosy's sick!"

Mother appeared in her door, long hair streaming around her shoulders, her eyes wide with questions. Karol came into the hall a few seconds later.

"Rosy's sick, very sick. You must call a doctor! Please!" I spoke in Polish.

Mother rushed past me into the room.

"I'll pay for it, Mother. I'll work an extra day!"

Karol disappeared back in his room and came out a few seconds later in pants and shirt.

"I'll get Dr. Kozlowski."

"Tell Karol to get..." Mother knelt by Rosy's bed, feeling her forehead.

"He's already going."

"Get me another pillow and a cloth, a cold cloth."

I did as Mother said in a numb trance of lost sleep and fear. Did it take five minutes to get the pillow and towel or an hour? I lost a sense of time. I handed the items to Mother and watched her prop up Rosy's head and wipe her brow.

"Get a bowl of cool water," Mother instructed. Again, I obeyed, grateful to have something to do.

Another decade passed as Mother bathed Rosy's body with the cool water, wiping down each arm first, then her legs, then wringing out the cloth and wiping her face. As she worked, her lips moved, and just as Karol returned with the doctor, I realized she was praying.

Dr. Kozlowski, a middle-aged man gone prematurely gray, entered the tiny room. With a crisp, no-nonsense manner, he shooed us out to examine Rosy.

We waited in the kitchen, standing like passengers waiting for a train.

"No wonder she's always sick," Karol said.

"Karol, don't...not now." I was embarrassed for Mother, afraid the doctor would hear them arguing.

"I do the best I can," Mother said in Polish. "As good as your father. Do you think he would do better? Do you think the store would still be ours?"

"I think..."

"Karol, please, please..." I was almost crying.

He heeded my plea and said no more; he went to the stove and lifted the teakettle. "The water's still warm." He reached to the shelf and pulled down the tea bags. But he didn't make a full pot, only one cup for himself. We watched him as if we had never seen anyone make tea before, as if we had been called into the room to watch him perform this mundane task and had to memorize his movements.

Dr. Kozlowski appeared at the kitchen archway, his bag in his hand.

"Pneumonia," he said flatly. "Very serious too, far advanced." He spoke in accented English even though

Polish was his native tongue. I angrily translated for Mother, afraid that she wouldn't understand the diagnosis.

"She should have been in hospital days ago. Do you have transportation? Of course not. I have my car outside. I suppose there is no telephone, either. Well, bundle her up. I'll take care of it at the hospital."

Karol leapt into action.

"I'm dressed. I can go with her."

"No, I will..." Mother was already making her way to her daughter's room.

"We'll all go," I said. "I'll pack a bag for Rosy. You get dressed, Mother."

Within a few minutes, we were all ready. Karol and Dr. Kozlowski carried Rosy up the stairs bundled in a heavy blanket.

The journey to St. Joseph Hospital in downtown Baltimore was a silent trip through an eerie landscape. A tavern was happily lit on one corner, sounds of music and laughter penetrating the night. On another, our church was dark, looming and ugly. It was our first trip in an automobile and, despite the circumstances, Karol attentively watched the doctor's firm hand on the gear shift, envy in his gaze.

At the hospital, Dr. Kozlowski and Karol filled out the necessary papers while my mother and I followed Rosy to the charity ward where the nuns, Sisters of St. Francis, made sure she was comfortable. Her bed was in a row of twelve; only six others were occupied by sleeping patients. Karol came into the ward, carrying a piece of paper.

"It says here that patients can only have one visitor at a time."

"I will stay," Mother and I said in unison.

Mother shook her head. "You go home, Margaret." She looked at Karol. "What did the doctor say?" All in Polish.

"He said she's very sick, like he said before. He says

they'll take care of her and if he's needed in the morning, he'll be by to see her." Karol folded the paper and put it in his pocket as he spoke.

We said goodbye to Mother and to Rosy. I bent to kiss her head. As I did so, Mother slipped a rosary into my hands.

No streetcars were on the road at that time, so Karol and I walked home in silence. I began praying as soon as we left the bright hospital, fingering the beads in my pocket as we jumped over puddles and ran past scary dark alleyways. At home, Karol headed immediately for his room, turning only when he reached the door to offer some words of comfort.

"I think she'll be all right now, Margie," he said with simple confidence. "She's got doctors and nurses taking care of her and all."

I was not so sure. As I went into my room, empty and large without Rosy, I remembered what Karol had said about the doctor, how he would come by in the morning, "if he was needed."

Of course he would be needed, I said to myself, taking off my old woolen jacket and scarf. Of course he would be, of course he would be. I sat on the edge of the bed. Why wouldn't he be needed? Rosy wouldn't be well enough to go home in the morning. She would need more care, more medical attention. Wouldn't she? Wouldn't she?

"Oh, God," I whimpered, not as a prayer but as a curse. I began to cry, big, heavy stored-up tears in silent sobs. I didn't want Karol to hear so I clenched my fist into my mouth to stop the noise. "Oh, God, please." Now it was a prayer. I dropped to my knees by the bed, like a schoolchild, and pulled out the black-beaded rosary.

"Hail, Mary..."

I stopped and thought of my mother by Rosy's bedside. Mother wouldn't pray in English.

"Zdrowas Mario, laskis pelna Pan z Toba, blogoslawionas

376

Ty miedzy niewiastami I blogoslawiony owoc zywota Twojego Jezus; swieta Mario, Matko Boza, módl sie za nami grzesznymi teraz i w godzine Smierci naszej."

Over and over, I said it, the decades passing quickly under my thumb and forefinger, the Our Father's and Gloria Patris barely a ripple in the rhythm of Hail Mary's. I grew sleepy and prayed with my eyes closed, but this was too tempting, and when I felt my body sway against the bed as sleep crept over me, I looked up and stared at the wall where a picture of Mary hung. The Virgin Mother was standing on a cloud, her feet resting on the fluffy white vapor like a pillow. Cherubs smiled up at her and flew around her feet. Golden rays came from her head. Her lips were dark, her eyes sad. She understood. Of course, she understood. She knew suffering.

Swieta Mario I mentally shouted at the picture. *Swieta Mario.*

As the prayers became a subconscious monotone, my mind wandered. The sisters taking care of Rosy...what Order was it? The Franciscans. Ah, yes, the Order for whom they collected pennies in school. The Franciscans ran the hospital. The Franciscans, that was Mrs. Mallory's Order.

An irrational fear consumed me. Maybe we would lose Rosy just as Mrs. Mallory had lost those babies. Maybe Mrs. Mallory was cursed, and I had somehow entered her sphere of influence. I prayed even harder.

But Mrs. Mallory had prayed too, hadn't she? Maybe she had knelt at the bedside when the second baby was coming. Maybe she had prayed like this, had asked for mercy, had asked to have her little girl spared. What good was it?

No, no, the Wojehedskis were different than the Mallorys, I thought, desperately searching for that difference. The Wojehedskis, Rosy and even me, we had not...made mistakes. No, we had not sinned like Antonia. Antonia had to get married, after all. She was supposed to enter the convent. She had promised. Her mother had promised. They had broken their promises. What promises had the Wojehedskis broken? None! None!

Swieta Mario

I thought of Karol and his unflinching faith. He snored softly in his room. Where was my faith? I had to be careful now, very careful not to fall into the Mallory trap, not to lose my faith, betray my promises...what promises, what promises? I thought of my silly Lenten sacrifice. It wasn't enough, I realized with horror. He wanted more! I thought of my mother praying. I had promised Mother I would pray, hadn't I? Yes, by taking the rosary...that was a promise. I prayed on with renewed intensity, starting over when I couldn't remember if I was saying the words in the right sequence.

What about my father? What had faith done then? What had we done to deserve his death?

Tears came to my eyes, but I wouldn't wipe them away, I wouldn't take my fingers off the beads. The room blurred before me. I sank back on my aching knees in despair as my concentration began to slip. Why should we lose Rosy just because Antonia had lost her two girls? How could we lose her when we had already lost Papa? How could that be fair?

Swieta Margaret

I stopped, listening to the inner voice that had said those words, the wrong words. My tempo broken, I was aware of the darkness of the night and the silence of the house. I sighed, the tears dried on my cheeks.

Swieta Margaret.

What had the gospel said—Simon's mother-in-law in bed with a fever. And He touched her. And she served them.

Served them.

That was the promise that must be kept.

In that instant, I felt called to be a nun.

CHAPTER TWENTY-SIX
Sin

I'VE WALKED for so long I don't know where I am. I'm near a school. A park bench beckons. I sink into it, next to an old Negro woman. I stare straight ahead, seeing nothing.

I kept my promise that night, Dr. Kaplan, and God kept His, at least then. Rosy recovered. But now, years later, she is dead.

I sit on the bench, and I don't feel anything. Not the heat. Not the bench. Not the air against my cheek.

I can't keep the memories back any longer. I remember...

...that other bedside prayer vigil, when Sister Imelda pleaded with me to pray with her, when she tried to console me. I see myself on the floor beside her. I feel what I felt that day—absolute loathing.

I hated Sister Fulgentia. I knew why she was sending me back to the Mother House. It wasn't to recover. It was to stand before our council and be remonstrated, to be told to leave. I knew because the last time I'd been there, the council had suggested I was close to being asked to leave, that my zeal in serving God was not done in the healthy spirit of the Order. And I'd managed to persuade them I was healthy. I'd managed to convince them I should stay.

But I knew if I went back this time, I'd not be able to conjure up those arguments again.

I hated Sister Fulgentia. I hated that convent. I hated my Order. And at that moment, I even hated poor Sister Imelda who was trying so hard to help me. I hated—

I cover my mouth with my hand. The woman next to me turns and stares but says nothing.

Yes, I hated God.

And my act of revenge against those I hated?

I reached up to the shelf and grabbed my medicine, unscrewing the cap and draining the bottle in one deft movement. All of it. *All of it.* Now and at the hour of *our death*, Amen.

Sister Imelda, lost in prayer, the noise of a whirring fan nearby obscuring my sounds, didn't notice at first. No, not until dreams and blurs and shadows crept up and loosened my hate from me, and with this weight lifted, the cords snapped, and I was able to fall free...

She started shouting my name. She started crying. But from that point on, Dr. Kaplan, I was not there, I was somewhere outside of myself, watching from a few feet away, and a few feet became a few yards in a short time, as the scene became ever more distant, and the voices ever fainter.

Let me get Sister Fulgentia. Sister Imelda left the room. I tried pushing up from the floor, intending to walk out of the convent, away somewhere, somewhere peaceful where I would lie down and rest. They wouldn't find me. I felt my heart race and I needed to catch up with it. I would walk to Karol's house. Rosy was there.

❧

I swallow hard.

Perspiration drenches me. The woman on the bench is gone.

It wasn't an accident.

I look down the road, trying to orient myself. I'm lost. I turned down a street, maybe another...

I should confess! It's a *mortal sin!*

I start walking in what I hope is the right direction. My pace quickens despite the heat as my thoughts tumble wildly one over the other.

Dr. Kaplan must have known. He must have figured it out. He, with all his talk of not providing answers, had the answers all along. He talked with Sister Fulgentia, after all. He made the arrangements! He with his white coat and glasses and constant note-taking, incessant questions. It was all a show. The charlatan, the fraud!

But of course he wouldn't let me know. He's not Catholic. And Paula—she's not Catholic either.

Paula knew. She's the one who helped make this little arrangement. She and Dr. Kaplan. Both conspiring against me. Here I am living under her roof and she didn't tell me. She should have told me. I should confess! What if an accident befalls me on the way home? I can't die in sin!

But I can't go to St. Benedict's. I'll have to find another church and walk to that one. Even if it's miles and miles away. It will be a pilgrimage. Isn't there an Immaculate Heart of Mary parish nearby? Didn't one of the Sisters mention that once? In Hamilton, they said. Where was that? Is that where I am now?

I walk and walk. The heat bakes under my clothes, sending warm waves up my neck. I don't know where I am. I don't care. How can I go back to that house, the house where Paula lives?

She is a temptress. She is the one who provided contact with my family. She is the one who made the arrangements with Dr. Kaplan. She is the one who became Rosy's friend—

Oh, my God! She became Rosy's friend. Perhaps, perhaps....

Paula is a devil. She bewitched us all. First Rosy. Then me. And now Karol will be hurt by her. She's about to break his heart and then will snatch his soul.

I stop and can't breathe. I lean against a lamppost.

Give me strength. Help me, Lord. Help me fight this devil. Help me rid her from our lives. Help me, dear Jesus. Please.

کوبی

It takes me a long time to orient myself, and by the time I make my way back to Cane Road, I've doubled back twice through unfamiliar streets, crying like a lost child. An old man out clipping shrubs asks me if he can help me, and I tell him the address. He points in a direction toward the sun and tells me I'll hit Old Philadelphia if I keep walking that way. But when I get to the familiar road I don't remember which way to turn. It takes me several blocks to ascertain it's the wrong way. By the time I reach Karol's home, sweat has made clothes and skin one damp coat of sadness.

Paula and Karol are still out, thank God.

No time to lose. No time to rest. I straighten, walk to the dresser in my room and pull out some writing paper. I must take care of this. I must make it right. Do something. Save...myself, Karol. All of us. I was too late to save Rosy. I sink to the floor and use a chair as a desk.

First, Dr. Kaplan. On tear-stained pages I scribble and scribble. Since I cannot talk to Dr. Kaplan now, these pages are my substitute.

My first pages are a diatribe. How could you not tell me, you sphinx in mariner's garb? You phony doctor—for wouldn't a real doctor tell the truth? Wouldn't he see the truth as a pathway to a cure? Surely *veritas* is part of the Hippocratic Oath. You are a dangerous man, Dr. Kaplan. Do your administrators know how shrewd, how devilish you are? Do they know that you act in conspiracy with another temptress, the woman to whose home you have so slyly sent me?

Another page. Another letter.

Dear Sir or Madam, you should be aware of the fact that on your staff is a dangerous man. While being treated by him for an accidental overdose of Phenobarbital...

Dear Lord. Oh, God. My hand goes to my mouth.

Not an accident. Yes, an accident. They'd said so. Sister Fulgentia had said so. So she was the one who'd lied. But she, too, has been influenced by Paula, and by Dr. Kaplan. She is a naïf. She doesn't know. Dear, dear Lord. You never told me it was to be so difficult.

Scrunching up the paper, I start again.

Dear Dr. Kaplan, how could you break my heart like this did you think it would help me to find out this way that I'd be lied to that you'd lied, and I'd lied too? Is this what your treatment is: a hide-and-seek game?

I'm not a game!

Scrunching it again, I start over.

Dear Dr. Kaplan, while on a walk today

On a walk! You let me find out on a broken pathway, between the trees and the girl calling her friend, on this ordinary of ordinary days, I discover I was a sui—

I cannot write it. It's a mortal sin, a mortal sin. I must confess. But there is no priest.

Another rip, another effort.

Dear Father, I'm sorry to write you this letter but I am being held captive in a stranger's house so I do not have access to the Sacraments. Bless me Father for I have sinned. It has been several weeks since my last confession — yes, several weeks, right before, before…the event — and I must tell you that through an accident I came to take too much medicine and I might have tried — you see it's all so unclear that I cannot see — I might have accidentally thought — but not really truly intended or I would have remembered it all — I might have taken too much — and how could I have known, really, what was too much, so perhaps it was an accident — I might have taken too much medicine thus overdosing myself and letting myself be diagnosed as a suicide!

Father, forgive me, I knew not what I did. When I reached for the bottle I wasn't thinking this is the end — or was I, or was I, dear Lord, was I — I was only thinking I couldn't stay there where I was in that house where a witch of a woman controlled my life and made me miserable and kept me from my sister on her deathbed. Who would do such a thing, Father? Perhaps she has confessed to you already and been forgiven. Her voice is soft and sometimes like gravel, as if she has to clear her throat. Perhaps you know who I mean. Who would force you to choose between living and dying? Who could be so cruel?

And how was I to know that my act of faith was a choice of the dying. How was I ever to know that. And even so, I still stayed and did my duty, did I not, I stayed and cleaned and was a good Sister, trying so hard to be good, I thought for sure she would tell me I was good, but she didn't, instead she sent me away, or wanted to send me away where they would tell me what a bad Sister I was and then it would all be over and I would be...humiliated. Who could stand for that? I wasn't supposed to stand for it. I had to stand against it. I didn't mean to fall, to take the bottle. Why, it could have slipped from my hand, I'm sure I intended it to, I'm sure I intended to just take my dose but it must have slipped and then, you see, I ended up, well I'm confessing now, aren't I because I have to. I can't have this stain on my soul, not this one. Not this one.

I fill another two pages—with information about Paula.

❧

Margaret raised her head. She'd fallen asleep by the side of the bed. Her neck was cramped, and she stretched it first this way and then the other. Music came from the front room. They were back. Paula must have turned on the radio. She got her bearings, looked at the letters she'd just composed, felt a twinge of panic, then scooped them all together and stood. She placed them in the top drawer of her dresser, under some clothes.

She was warm and felt a headache igniting above her eyes. Honesty. She'd been honest with herself. She'd uncovered the truth. She needed to share the truth, all of it. She needed to talk to Karol. She needed to warn him about Paula, to let him know she wasn't who she said she was.

She paced the room, wringing her hands together, mentally rehearsing what she would say. There was the problem of getting him alone, too. She would have to find a way. The Lord would help her. Trust in the Lord.

Maybe she should confront Paula. Maybe that was what was required of her.

I'm not strong enough. Don't ask that of me.

Her eyes lit on Sister Fulgentia's letter, on one phrase—if Margaret didn't go back to the Mother House, she "feared the worst" for her.

She fears the worst? Margaret held the letter to her chest. The worst was excommunication. A laugh tickled at her throat. And here she was worried about not going to Mass. Not going back to the convent was the worse fate! It was all so clear now.

She smoothed her skirt. Looking in the mirror—it was second nature now—she brushed the tears from under her eyes. Sister was right. She needed to go back, to get away from here, this den of iniquity ruled by non-Catholics and tempters. Back to the straight path. Back to salvation. God was pointing the way, showing her the true path. She could return to the Mother House now. She wasn't afraid. She would face the council. She would assure them she was healthy and good and worthy. She knew what she was called to do.

❦

Margaret stood at her door, hand on knob, eager to rush out and warn Karol against his wicked wife. But when she heard him softly talking with Paula, she held back. Although she couldn't make out all the words, he sounded worried. She withdrew her hand and stood stock still, trying to figure out what to do. She voiced a prayer asking for guidance. Within a few seconds, Paula's voice came from just beyond the door.

"Margaret, we'd like to talk to you." Her voice was

silky and insincere. Margaret's flesh crawled at the sound of it.

Margaret leaned against the door, prepared to bar Paula's way should she try to enter. She breathed fast, her gaze darted around the room, lighting on the window. Perhaps she should escape? No, she had to help Karol. She had to get him alone. That was the goal. She had to focus on that.

She heard Paula walk away, heard her tell Karol that "she would lie down," heard him mumble something about "coming to check on her," and then Paula shuffling away.

With a sense of mission she'd never felt before, Margaret grabbed her chance. She opened her door and strode into the living room where Karol sat on the sofa reading the Sunday paper, the late afternoon sun glinting at such a sharp angle through the open front door that she had to squint to see him. Glancing over her shoulder to make sure Paula wouldn't reappear, Margaret stood before her brother, arms at her side.

"I have to talk with you."

Karol looked up. His eyebrows raised and he frowned.

"Yeah?" He put his cigarette to his mouth and pulled in some smoke. "I'd like to talk with you, too." He patted the seat next to him, and Margaret eagerly joined him, sitting near the edge of the cushion, angled toward him so that she wouldn't have to raise her voice. But before she had a chance to issue her alarm, Karol spoke.

"Paula's feeling kind of poorly," he said. He didn't look at her, but his voice was confident, as if he'd rehearsed this. "We're thinking we might need to call the doctor. Nothing to get excited about. She thinks she'll be okay if she rests."

"She's having the baby?" It sickened her to think of Paula having his child. But maybe this was a test of her fortitude. Maybe she needed to press on in spite of this news. Maybe it was important for Karol to know...

Karol smoked, then continued. "But anyway, if it is her time... Well, soon, we'll be needing the room. Maybe sooner than we thought. Now, we were real happy to help you out, but Paula says you're doing real well. The doctor says so, and she thought maybe that letter from Sister Fulgentia was about getting back to work or something...."

Blush warmed Margaret's face. Karol was getting ready to ask her to leave. Disappointment, hurt, anger all washed over her in quick succession. *It's Paula – she is a bad influence on him.*

He leaned forward, his hand between his knees, the cigarette in his hand, its long cylindrical ash ready to fall onto the floor. She reached beyond him and grabbed the ashtray, placing it beneath him.

"Thanks," he said and started to go on, but she stopped him.

"I'm going back. Don't worry," she said, waving the air in front of her as if this was a nuisance, not something serious. "I'm going to contact my Mother Superior tomorrow and make arrangements. I have something else to talk with you about."

He looked at her, relieved. "Okay. Shoot."

"Paula isn't—"

A shadow caught her attention. Paula, pale and disheveled, stood in the hallway near the living room. As soon as Karol saw her, he rocketed from his seat and went to her.

"Honey? You okay? You don't look so good."

"I—I'm feeling kind of woozy. And...I think I'm bleedin'," she said in a soft, troubled voice.

❧

"She's not Catholic," Paula heard someone say far away. Margaret, Sister. Why on earth would she say that now? What would Karol think? Lordy, what was going on? Her mind wouldn't clear.

"I'm gettin' baptized," she whispered. Had they heard her? "Father Al and me..."

387

She couldn't say more. Something was sucking the breath right out of her.

Her mother—she'd died this way. Cold fear, followed by warm peace. Maybe Stevens women didn't live through pregnancy. Maybe she should have thought of that....

✎✐

"Paula, Paula! Answer me! Paula, stay awake!" Margaret called out.

Hands touched her. Voices spoke somewhere far away. Her eyes flickered open and she saw Karol's face come close, very close, his eyes wide and watery, panic in his voice.

"Hang on, honey, hang on! We're going to the hospital."

✎✐

Margaret said nothing. She sat in the back seat with Paula's head cradled in her lap. "She can be baptized at the hospital."

"What?" He shot her a dark look. "Jesus Christ, Margie! Why you talking about that now?" He veered in front of another car onto Pulaski Highway.

"Because she's...she's not Catholic. She pretended to be...." She wasn't sure he'd absorbed her truth yet.

His hand gripped the wheel, and his jaw muscles moved. She saw him blink fast and had to call out to him to keep him from ramming a braking truck up ahead.

"Are you all right? Can you drive?"

"Fine." He said it so fast she wasn't sure she'd heard him, but she didn't press.

"You know something about this stuff," he said at last, in a little-boy's voice, a voice that wants so badly for everything to be all right. "Didn't you used to be a nurse? In the convent?"

"That's how I started, yes."

"She'll be all right, right? It's going to be all right? Nothing out of the ordinary?"

Inhaling, Margaret was about to tell him the truth—

that, in fact, Paula might not be okay, that the baby might be lost as well, that mothers and babies died in childbirth even today— but she stopped. She looked at his face, haggard in the bright, white light of sunset cutting straight at them as they drove west into the city.

"She'll be all right."

They rode the rest of the way in silence. At Hopkins, he parked illegally and carried his wife so fast to the emergency room that Margaret could barely keep up.

Nurses took over. Paula was put on a stretcher, ghostly pale, already looking like a corpse. Margaret went to a nurse and spoke to her privately about summoning "Father Al" or whoever was on duty.

When she saw Karol, he punched the air and muttered a strangled curse.

"You don't understand," he said like a madman, talking to himself. He ran his fingers through his hair, looked around wildly as if he would commit an act of violence at the wrong word, the wrong look. "She shouldn't...she...I need to tell her...."

"I'll pray for her. I'll say a rosary"

"A rosary!" He snorted. "Yeah, go ahead. Pray a rosary. That's great."

"Karol," she said softly, touching his arm. "Maybe you should pray, too."

"You think I'm not?" he shouted at her. "Sheesh. Almighty. You always thought you were holier than us."

"Us?" Margaret didn't move, waiting for the blow. "Rosy?" she whispered.

"Yeah, Rosy."

"No..." she whispered.

Karol went on, as if he'd not heard, directing his fear and anger at her. "She said she couldn't have been a nun because it would have been so hard for her to play by the rules. It was easy for you—because you're so fucking afraid of everything!" He stopped, his voice choking.

"Rosy?" Rosy had said those things.

"I can't talk about this, okay? I got other things on

Libby Sternberg

my mind. Crap." He paced away, patting his pockets for smokes, not finding any.

All those years, all that time when she'd thought Rosy knew, when she'd thought Rosy appreciated what she'd done. For her. All for her.

A movement behind them both caught their attention and diverted Margaret's pain.

A grim reaper in black robe, kissing his purple stole as he advanced down the hall, silently murmuring Latin. Father Aloysius.

"You must be her husband," he said, holding out his hand. "I'm sorry to meet you under these circumstances. Paula was coming to me for counseling, for preparation for baptism. A wonderful woman."

"You can't go in," Karol shouted. "They're going to operate."

Father Aloysius moved his head ever so slightly. He was carrying a prayer book, a vial of Holy Water, a container of chrism. "They'll let me in."

Margaret's throat went dry, her tongue sticking to the roof of her mouth, making her voice thick.

"Baptism," she said to comfort Karol.

Karol's face whitened. He knew.

Not just Baptism. Baptism as part of Extreme Unction – for Paula as much as for the baby.

Father Al opened the door and was greeted by a nurse.

Margaret heard a muffled sound, like someone grunting. It was Karol, turning, leaning against the wall, his right arm above him, his eyes closed tight. When she walked over to him, her arms extended for an embrace, he turned away again.

There was no place for her there. Not here. Not outside an operating room where Karol's wife was dying, the wife Margaret had resented, that Margaret had wanted to betray.

Her feet carried her through the hallways, through the hurly-burly of hospital life. Nurses rushing by.

390

Doctors standing, talking. Talk. Laughter. Trays rattling. Nothing was real except the pounding of her heart. Up a flight, over and around, through a passageway, up the stairs. Dr. Kaplan's office.

His door was locked. No one would be there on a Sunday. And he was out of town anyway, she realized in a daze.

"Miss, can I help you?" a nurse in the hall asked.

"No, no. I'm fine." She turned away, embarrassed that a stranger noticed how addled she must have looked.

I'd always wanted to be a nun, she heard herself telling the nurse. No, she hadn't said that out loud. *I always wanted to be a nun, ever since I was a little girl.*

She walked out the broad front doors, not looking up at the Christ statue.

I always wanted to be a nun....

I loved their robes, their serenity.... They never looked afraid of anything. And why should they be? They'd dedicated their lives to Christ, to God, their Father. They'd made a bargain, a sweet bargain. I give you my life. And you give me...peace, rest, safety, plenty.

And yet, the Father had betrayed her, hadn't He?

Here, I'll give it again if that's what it takes. Is this what I must do to make Karol's world whole again—go back to Mount St. Agnes, put on the habit again? Is that what you want? *Take it, take it, take it! I was going to give it to you anyway! Why couldn't you wait – just one more day?!*

Outside the hospital, the evening heat encircled her. But it might as well have been frozen tundra and not sweltering streets she walked along. She was numb, as removed from the world as a cloistered sister. That had been her mistake, not seeking out a cloistered Order. She'd selected her school's Order, a natural choice, yes, but a mistake. She should re-enter, but perhaps another Order, one with absolutely no contact with the outside world.

Rosy didn't appreciate what I'd done for her. She hadn't cared. All those years... And neither had He! *He'd not appreciated it either.*

She walked, breathing hard, step after step, into town, through empty streets and bad neighborhoods, just as she'd walked with Karol that night long ago.

※

Who called you? Paula wanted to ask, but she was so darned tired, she couldn't say a word, could barely blink. She was floating, and everything was good.

After kissing his purple stole, Father Aloysius bent close to her ear and whispered: "Don't worry. Your husband knows, Paula. He's fine. Don't worry..."

So Karol knew she wasn't Catholic, and it was okay. Don't worry, she thought, as he began to murmur the Latin. It was so beautiful, the sound of those pure syllables running into one another like a song. They just flowed over you, like the baptismal water itself.

Don't worry...of course I won't worry...

Karol must know, too...

As the gurney jolted over a doorway, Father Aloysius gamely stayed with their little battle party.

A flash of panic hit her.

Karol has to know...I love Karol, with my whole heart. I do love him. Now I know...

Her lips moved, but no sound came out, none that she could hear.

I must tell him!

Father traced the cross on her forehead and leaned down.

"We're almost ready, Father," an unseen nurse whispered. "You'll have to leave."

But good ole Father Al, he wouldn't be ordered by a nurse, not when he had a mission of his own to fulfill.

"Yes?" he asked her, the bare minimum of a question. He knew not to dawdle.

"I love him," she whispered.

He nodded, stood and continued with his prayers.

She closed her eyes, listening to the Latin, to the doctor, the nurses, the rattle of surgical tools on metal, the hiss of a breathing machine, the drip of fluid somewhere.

Someone was telling Father to leave again. He refused.

As she started to tumble again into unconsciousness, she comforted herself that Karol would now know. *I do love him.* Wasn't the baptism the sign of that?

But will Father know? Will he think I was saying I love God?

Love Karol. Love God.

❧

The Basilica looms, rooted to the corner of Mulberry as if defying even God to shake it loose. I rush up its steps and enter, bitter and angry, wishing I was in my habit so that I would be visible as a living sacrifice to all—to Him!—who see me.

Cloying air greets me, stale incense, candles, even the faint odor of perspiration. Clocks run slower here. But I race against time, eager to make a new promise, a fresh bargain.

Let her live and I will give up my life again. I'll do it tomorrow. No, today! Let them both live – mother and child! I'll seal myself off entirely. Let them live.

It is late in the day, but a few other penitents pray in pews. I rush past them into the dim church, up to the altar rail and to the right. Realizing I have no head covering, I reach in my pocket and pull out a lace-edged handkerchief. That will do. I place it on the crown of my head, holding it still while I walk to the votive candles in the corner, glistening in their red glass holders in front of the statue of Mary.

I drop some coins into the offering box and use a wooden stick to light a candle from another. Although I voice no prayer, I think a name. "Paula." I kneel in front of the bank of candles.

"Let her live," I say out loud, not caring who hears me. I stare at the statue—Mary with outstretched arms looking down on me, a mother herself, a woman who'd labored and delivered. "Let her live," I say to the stone. "And I'll go back. Just let her live. Please let her live."

I bury my head in my hands.

Behind me, in the distance, I hear the church doors open and close as supplicants enter and leave. I hear murmurs and coughs, kneelers clacking down, shoes on stone floor. I kneel and I pray and I remain silent. I don't tire, nor do I feel the need to retreat. It is a test of wills. Mine against God. I will not leave until He answers me.

Twilight creeps in the windows, throwing soft streaks of red and blue across the pews and onto the altar. Altar boys tidy up for a late Sunday service, lighting the two candles that signal a Low Mass. Kneelers thud against the floor. The door opens more frequently. But still I wait, my mind empty, my soul waiting waiting waiting.

I'm waiting for His voice. But He doesn't speak to me. I'm waiting for His response to my offer of sacrifice. Instead, silence.

A breeze flows up the aisle, and with it a thought as cold as ice.

Going back to the convent will not save Paula or the baby.

And most importantly, it will not save me.

It is not within my power to save them.

The priest enters from the sacristy and intones the Introit. The Mass begins. Stiff and sore, I stand and move back to a pew where I whisper the prayers, accept the blessings, listen to the cadences and rhythms of a ritual I have always loved. I walk to the altar rail and kneel at Communion, accepting the wafer on my tongue as if it were manna itself.

No prayers. No struggle. Just peace. Silence and peace.

At the end of Mass, I take a deep breath, smooth my

blouse and skirt, and walk toward the sacristy behind the altar. The priest is removing his surplice while altar boys put away candleholders. He looks up, surprised.

"May I help you?" he asks.

"I need to talk to you," I say. "Alone."

"All right," he responds with some trepidation, probably trying to evaluate my sanity. "We can go to my office. What is it you'd like to discuss?" He shoos the boys away, so we are alone.

"I'm a nun. I want a dispensation from my vows."

CHAPTER TWENTY-SEVEN
Atonement

FIFTEEN MINUTES later, I sit in a narrow room beyond the reception area. Across a wide expanse of empty desk is Father Lawrence Neale, the middle-aged balding priest who'd looked so uneasy when I'd encountered him in the sacristy. Sunset has faded and the hush of blue twilight makes the room feel like a secret place. It's bare except for our chairs and the huge desk that separates us. The only light comes from the tall narrow windows to the right. But it's light from streetlamps flickering on, and the windows are heavily draped in dark green brocade to keep the heat at bay. A small rotating fan whirrs beyond the door, sending an occasional breeze into this oversized confessional.

Father Neale has introduced himself, bade me to sit, and then calmly led me through a series of questions. I have had to explain my odd circumstances, why I am not wearing the habit, where I am living. He nodded at each answer, saying nothing.

"Do you mind if I smoke?" he asks, patting his hip as he looks for his pack before I even say yes.

"Go ahead."

He lights up, then looks around the room for an ashtray. Seeing none, he opens a desk drawer, reaches far in and pulls out a cheap metal dish that he sets on the desk in front of him.

"Have you spoken with your Mother Superior?" He sucks in some smoke.

"She has urged me to come back."

"Perhaps a retreat would help. How long has it been since you've been home?" He folds his hands in front of him, the cigarette poking through his fingers.

"I am home," I answer, confused. Baltimore is my home. Then it dawns on me. He means the Mother House in Pennsylvania, my spiritual home. "Oh... I haven't been back for a year. Last summer I was there. To take some courses."

"You've been working, teaching, for all the years since your novitiate ended?"

"Yes."

He purses his lips. They are thin, long lips and they nearly disappear as he presses them together. "I recommend, Sister, that you consider returning to the Mother House for a month or so. To pray, to reflect. And then we can talk again. I can arrange for a confessor in the area to visit you, to offer you guidance. It's Mount St. Agnes, right?"

"No!" My voice cuts through the dead space. It startles him. He sits up straight. "I mean, yes, that is the name of my Mother House. But I don't want to go there. I'm sure. There is nothing that will dissuade me now."

He sighs heavily. "You have to understand," he says almost apologetically, "I'm required to try to make you think this over." He lifts his hands in the air, spreading them on either side and shrugging his shoulders. "But you've already left, haven't you? This is just an exercise to see if I ask the right questions and you provide the right answers."

I look down at my gray skirt, my stockinged legs. *You have already left.* This is true. I was only pretending to be a nun.

"You're a lay person now in every sense except for the piece of paper from the Church that says so." He even laughs a little. "I've counseled many priests and nuns thinking of leaving, Sister. But never have I spoken with one who did it backwards—leaving, then asking for permission to leave."

I relax. I know he won't fight me, nor make me choose between the Church and leaving.

"Then what do I do now?" I ask softly.

"There are some papers. I must contact your Mother Superior, talk with her. In your case, I suspect this will be pro forma."

"In my case, I expect she will be relieved."

He grimaces. "Don't underestimate the sorrow these events cause superiors. They often take it as a personal failing."

"There's nothing she could have done," I murmur.

"I suggest you write to her and tell her that."

"So, now what?" I keep expecting him to pull a ream of papers from the desk, legal documents I will have to sign. But he remains with his hands in front of him, the cigarette half smoked now.

"I'll call your Mother Superior first thing in the morning. I'll have the papers drawn up and notify you of when they're ready. You'll have to come in to sign them." He gives me paper and pen to write down my brother's address.

"Thank you," I say, relieved that it is almost over.

He stands. The interview, such as it was, is finished. "This is where you are living now?" he asks, pointing to the paper I'd just handed him.

I nod.

"Do you have a way of getting home?" He starts to pull open a drawer.

I shake my head. I'd not even thought of it. I'd thought I'd walk. But it would take hours.

He unzips a bag and pulls out some money, handing it to me. "It will be hard this time on a Sunday, but you should be able to get a taxi."

I start to refuse, but his serious look stops me. This is no time for meaningless sacrifices. I take the money and thank him, promising to pay it back.

"Best of luck, Sister."

"Thank you."

Outside, a summer rain has started falling, gently kissing the city with its cool vapor. As I walk down the front steps of the Basilica offices, I look ahead, not below. Each step is like a step into a chasm, a void of unknown things and experiences. And I realize that this is the one thing I never offered God—this fearless step into the unknown. It was a favorite son, an Isaac, held dear to my chest, embraced and loved, never offered for sacrifice. Trust and you can be disappointed. So I never trusted. I never offered my faith as a sacrifice and I never felt the whisper of His voice in my ear. I offered instead the gestures, the words, the crawling years of pretense. My faith had not been a gift but a bribe—or sometimes a dare.

Now, I hear nothing but the noises of the everyday world. Car horns in the distance. The comforting pummel of summer rain, the muffled slam of the Cathedral door. I see a woman rushing with a perambulator to find cover from the rain, so I pause to watch her, oblivious to the soaking as I stand and stare. A scarf tied tight around her head, she leans over and reassures the baby. She coos and throws kisses at the unseen infant, but I hear the music of her affection even from a distance.

Heaven is when people come home, Rosy had said. Heaven is a sun-drenched room. Inside, I feel as bright as sun, and now my mind is finally empty—empty enough to let grace in.

I am as light as air. I am air. I can breathe.

CHAPTER TWENTY-EIGHT
Reconciliation

AARON LEANED back into his seat and stared out the window at the Sunday evening twilight. Kate—that was the only cloud in his own serenity. Would he return to her and try to win her over again? He didn't know. He almost laughed at the admission. He simply didn't know.

After he'd read the letter from Dr. Guildenstern the other day, Aaron had taken Kate home, then raced to his own apartment, heart thrumming with both excitement and anxiety. He had to reach out to Lena—but how? Rachel had included a phone number in her letter but with the caution that calls were difficult because the phone was in a communal area, and Lena might not be able to return his because of the cost. But, yes, Lena was willing to talk to him.

He'd sat at his desk and immediately begun composing a note. A note he'd crumpled as soon as he'd written the greeting. He'd laughed out loud as he'd thought of what Kate's reaction to that strategy would be: *Writing her, Aaron? Really? Dr. Guildenstern says she'll talk to you. You have her number, for goodness' sake. Use it!*

So, with shaking hand, he'd picked up the phone,

connected to the operator and begun the arduous task of getting through to the Tel Aviv number.

It had taken several tries. On the first, he'd been disconnected. On the second, a man with a thick accent had answered and told him Lena was out and... And he hadn't been able to understand the rest. Confused, a little embarrassed, he'd told the fellow he'd call back.

And he had, within the hour, telling himself he'd write a note if he didn't get her this time.

But he had gotten hold of her! She had been there on the second try. Her voice—my God, to hear it had been to hear angels singing.

He'd stumbled, he'd laughed, he'd cried. He'd told her a white lie. He was headed to Israel "on business" very soon and wanted to see her. She'd agreed, and he'd immediately made the plane reservations after getting off the phone. Thank you, Kate, he'd whispered to the air. Thank you, blessed Kate.

Now, on the plane, he wondered what the future held. Perhaps he'd find Lena changed and unwilling to accept him. Perhaps he would not want to accept her, except as a dear friend. And then what?

Then he'd return to Baltimore and...court Kate again?

No.

It was as if a voice said it aloud. No, he and Kate were finished. She'd always known, and he'd come to understand, that she wanted a man with whom she could share her faith.

That pinched him, thinking of how good she was, how deserving of happiness. She didn't see sacrifice as a choice. She accepted it when it was called for. As soon as she'd learned of Lena, she'd urged him to find her. Not one second of hesitation.

How did one become like that? How did one find

that goodness within?

To distract himself, he pulled out the newspaper he'd picked up at the airport. August 14—the day the war had ended.

Ten years ago on this day, he'd hardly been aware of the news. He'd been immersed in following a thread of a story, desperately trying to find at least one parent alive of an emaciated and forlorn fifteen-year-old Jewish girl who had touched his heart—touched him because she'd looked so much like Lena in her haunted eyes, and she'd told him she was ashamed to admit she longed to hear Schubert again but was afraid to ask. He'd thought he'd located the mother. He'd been on fire to reunite her with her daughter. He'd spent the entire day going from refugee camp to administrative office to his own headquarters, every bone in his body aching as he fought off a summer flu. He'd wanted to lie down, to rest, to give up.... But he'd kept going, in a fever during his fever to at least solve this one case. Even if it meant he had to tell the girl her mother was among the lost.

But she hadn't been. One good story among the thousands of bad ones. One tiny blossom among the barren soil. At last. As sunset painted the skies pink and orange, as his fellow soldiers celebrated, as his fever broke into a cooling sweat, he found her—as thin and near death as her daughter, the only one of seven children she'd borne, the only living relative left of their once large family.

And even now, tears came to his eyes as he remembered their silent reunion, the mother stroking and kissing her daughter's head, whispering, caressing, thanking the Almighty...the daughter saying, over and over, "I never gave up, Mama, I never gave up..."

He blinked fast and swallowed hard.

≈≫

Kate snapped a sheet over an empty bed and started tightening the corners with military precision. She refilled the water pitcher on the nightstand, fluffed the pillows, opened the window and went back to the nurse's station, ready to look at the schedule for what the night held. She was starting a week of evening shifts on a Sunday—she liked being busy.

She noted with satisfaction that it would be a full night. Except for the empty room she'd just attended to, they had patients in every available bed. While she wished no one ill health, she was glad for the work. She didn't want her mind to wander.

If it did, it would go to Aaron and his flight to Israel. She knew he was in the air now and murmured a silent prayer for a safe journey. She also included a prayer for Lena, that she would be healthy in mind and spirit and able to give Aaron what he needed—whether that was a renewal of their love affair years ago or the sense that they were both better to have moved on.

Oh, that wasn't an easy prayer. She felt herself going through the motions more than feeling it. But she knew if she did petition God for this peaceful ending to Aaron and Lena's story, she might eventually begin to feel, somewhere deep in her heart, that it was the right thing for them, and for her, as well.

Oh, come on, she urged herself. *Get out of the doldrums. You've got this Jimmy Bromley to get to know. Darned if your mother wasn't right trying to get you together with him. She knows you well...*

With shock, a gulp of sorrow engulfed her as she felt the weight of her pretense. Stop kidding yourself, Kate. You loved Aaron, and now he's gone. She quickly headed for the ladies' room and closed herself in a stall, regaining control, breathing more steadily.

She heard two women come in talking.

"He never really recovered. It doesn't surprise me he's..." a forlorn voice muttered.

"The doctor said he might go home today, Mom."

"But he'll never be the same. Never. Ten years ago he came home. Everybody else was drinking champagne. We were in a hospital..." She tailed off, obviously crying.

"Aw, Mom..."

Ten years ago. That was true—it was the anniversary of the end of the war today, the day the Japanese surrendered.

Ten years ago—she'd been just starting as a nurse then, and after work, she and Mom heard the news on the radio. To Kate's surprise, her mother had found an old bottle of whiskey. Whiskey—they never drank. She'd never remembered her mother having anything but Communion wine.

"Your father's," Mom had explained, twisting the cap off. She'd wondered whether they should drink it with something. Eventually she'd settled on some ice and a little water—the former because it was so hot, the latter because of another memory of how her father drank it.

It had burned going down and immediately made them both tipsy. For the first time in ages, Kate had laughed with real joy as her mother found some old LPs of Irish songs and demonstrated her dancing skills for her daughter. She'd pulled Kate off the sofa and tried to teach her, too, but Kate had fumbled and fallen, her side aching from so much laughter.

It had been a blessed relief, and later, she'd wondered if her mother had planned it to keep her from thinking about Brian too much. If so, it had worked.

It hadn't been until late at night, when she'd awakened for some aspirin to soothe her whiskey headache, that the pain of not having him had overwhelmed her.

She'd gone back to bed, but leaned on her window sill above it, breathing in the humid night air, listening to revelers blocks away, giving in to her own personal sorrow, weeping silently as she stared at the black sky.

Brian, she'd whispered, do you hear me? Are you there? It's over, beloved. It's all over. We won, darling. We won.

She'd continued like that for some time, having a conversation with her absent mate, and when she'd finally had her fill of telling him all he'd missed while away, she'd grown drowsy and lain her head on her pillow, spent at last.

In the morning, she and her mother had gone to Sunday Mass—the Feast of the Assumption. A Mary holiday. How peaceful she'd felt that day, as if the world's peace had entered her heart at last.

Tomorrow was that feast. She'd go to Mass again. She'd say a rosary for Aaron and Lena. She'd call Jimmy Bromley and tell him, yes, she'd go out with him.

❧

By the time I get home, the rain has stopped and stars sparkle in an evening velvet sky. It was a long, tiring journey from downtown. Father Neale had been right about few taxis being about. I'd walked nearly back to Hopkins before catching one.

As it turns onto Chesaco Avenue, I look out the window at the convent that had been my home, wondering if I should attempt to see Sister Fulgentia. Whereas she once had seemed so cold and cruel to me, now I think of her as shy and uneasy. Remembering what Father Neale said about superiors suffering when they lose a nun, I decide not to throw salt in her wound by standing in her presence and announcing my exodus. I will write instead, a conciliatory note expressing my gratitude and, yes, even my admiration for her patience with me.

I tell the driver to stop there, and I stare at the building that had been my home, before walking up Chesaco to Karol's place.

As I go inside Karol's darkened house, I pick up the faint copper odor of blood. Paula's.

First, I clean the house. I wash and put away the dishes. I mop the floor in his room with its bloody stain. Then, I go into my room and pack my things. I have no suitcase, so I neatly stack the few folded garments on the bed, then go to the kitchen for a paper bag in which to place them. I will go to Mother's. I'll take care of her. Find a job. Perhaps I can teach, like Rosy did, in a public school. Perhaps Karol will have pity on me and drive me to Mother's. Otherwise, I will have to wait and take a bus—or call a taxi—in the morning.

Hours pass, and it is past midnight by the time I am finished.

As I come out of the kitchen, Karol walks through the front door. He is looking down, so he doesn't see me at first. His face is ashen. His shirt is stained with sweat. He pauses, then looks up.

I can't speak. I can't ask.

His shoulders tremble as he starts to talk. He bites his lower lip, looks up at the ceiling. "Paula's all right. It's a girl." He shakes his head, laughing.

"A girl, Margie. A girl!" Laughter has turned to tears of relief.

"Thank God," I murmur. "Thank God!"

EPILOGUE
Home

August 1968

MORE THAN ten years—it had taken him this long after the first canceled trip back to London, to make the reservation again. Something always got in the way. Classes. A paper to finish. Patients to visit. He'd become more vigilant about his duties over time. He'd become, he hoped, a better priest.

He'd taken pains not to neglect a single sheep in his ever-growing flock, including the Wojehedskis—Paula and Karol, their lovely daughter, Marie Rose, and Karol's sister, Margaret. He'd recently been present at Marie Rose's confirmation, in fact. And, although he knew they were eager to send her to college, he wondered if she wouldn't be swept off her feet by a young man instead. She was beautiful in a lively and angelic way, with light hair and a quick smile. She reminded him of his own sister Anne.

Being a better priest had made it harder to schedule what felt like an indulgent trip to his past, but he'd managed it at last.

By the time he'd gotten around to making the arrangements, though, Pete wasn't available to offer tips and discounts. No, Pete was now dean of students at a Jesuit university in the Midwest, a position for which he was well suited. Al missed him. But Al had never forgotten Pete's teasing question about doubt—would he doubt his decision to leave England if he were to go home again? Many times he'd analyzed that question and its deeper implications. Would he doubt entering the priesthood? Had he run to it the way he'd run to the fire brigade, seeking glory and action?

Maybe it had taken him these ten and more years to answer that question sincerely. He was reasonably sure he'd not doubted his vocation or his path in general. Reasonably sure. And sometimes, that was better than zealous confidence that masked doubts one couldn't face.

And now—he couldn't stop himself from laughing once he was off the plane in London. The flight had been an ordeal for him, making his heart race so fast, he'd had to fortify himself with a few drinks.

All these years after trying to get into the RAF, he'd discovered he had a fear of flying! He'd never flown before, never had the need or opportunity. Not getting into the RAF had spared him this embarrassment.

Ironically, what had also helped calm him during the flight was rereading a letter from Margaret Wojehedski. She'd done well after leaving the convent. She'd become a teacher and had lived with her mother until three years ago when the poor woman had succumb to cancer. He had seen Margaret occasionally over the years, once at a retreat, other times at some Wojehedski gatherings, another time in a class he'd taught at Notre Dame, where she had taken some special courses. She'd always seemed happy to him, or at least content, and her self-confidence had soared. Now Margaret was making a momentous step.

"I'm re-entering the convent," she'd written to him. "If you can't send me encouragement, please send a long list of challenges so that I can test my new vocation's strength…"

The fact that she could joke about it seemed to him

good evidence that her heart was in the right place.

"All these years, I have felt something missing from my life. And I realized after Mother passed that perhaps I'd been right in my action long ago but wrong in my motivation. Now I think I have them synchronized. Everything's changed now, of course—no long habits, more lenient Rules—but this just means I have nothing but real faith to prop me up and keep me going.

"The one thing that was the same—the new Mother Superior asked the same questions of me, about why I wanted to 're-up,' how I was sure this was for me. But there is no way to make sure, is there? I only know that I love God and want to serve Him with my whole heart, my whole soul, my whole mind. In the years that I've been separated from the convent life, I've taught, I've worked with the poor, I've rejoiced in my family's happiness and grieved in their sorrows, and throughout it all, there has been this pull, this voice that keeps saying, sometimes gently, sometimes insistently, sometimes even with humor and always with grace: *This is the way you can love and serve me best.*

"So, Father, I've awakened to my calling, maybe a little later than usual. I prefer to think of it as a gradual awakening, though, beginning with that day that I awoke years ago, in a white hospital room in my native city, filled with terror and grief...."

Yes, Sister, he thought to himself as he made his way to a rectory in *his* native city, there is no way to be sure, is there? You just put one step in front of the other, and you hope for the best.

He was hoping for the best, too, hoping Pete had been right when he'd suggested that he "go home to say goodbye," knowing he was settled in the U.S. for good. Hoping this visit wouldn't shake anything loose from his own commitment to the religious life, which sometimes faltered, particularly lately when the world seemed in chaos again. A new war raged, this one in Vietnam. Two Kennedys were dead, as was Martin Luther King, Jr. His students asked him questions that he often struggled to answer...

To be honest, he might not have planned the trip at all if not for the news that the small cemetery where his family was buried in London was being dug up and moved, part of a bustling renovation of his old neighborhood. He'd chosen a new resting place for them—in the country on the outskirts of his aunt's village—and was going home to pray over their new graves, presiding over a ceremony should anyone show up for it. He suspected he'd be alone.

❧

And alone he was a few days later, on a wind-swept hill in his long cassock, his prayer book pages flipping in the breeze, an annoyance that rattled his concentration.

The distraction sent his mind wandering, back to his visit with his mentor at the rectory—still alive but very frail—his tour of his old, favorite haunts, his nostalgic and somewhat painful trip to his parents' old neighborhood, now inhabited by ne'er-do-wells and hoodlums and a huge pre-construction hole that looked too much like a bombed-out patch of earth for him to feel comfortable.

When Father Gregory had heard of his intention to stay in America and even become a citizen, he'd nodded and said the same thing as Father Pete, "Well, it's a good thing you've come home to say goodbye, then."

But, in reality, he'd said goodbye years ago. He'd done that when he'd entered the seminary. He'd said goodbye to his old life, then, a life of drifting and sham heroics, of the grasping for large gestures and the ignoring of small acts of mercy. He was glad now that he'd come back. There had been no pull away from his decision long ago, nothing to be afraid of. He felt settled and peaceful. This trip had turned out to be more affirmation than test.

Réquiem ætérnam dona ei Dómine...

He prayed for his mother's soul—

410

You were the true, Jesuit, Mum. It was in university that I felt called to the priesthood, finding God through finding knowledge.

Dad, why didn't you share more of your wisdom? Maybe your silence was your wisdom, like the silence in that church...

Anne...innocent Anne...

A loud squeal rent the silence, sending his heart racing. Turning, he saw a sheep being roughly nudged back over the western ridge by a no-nonsense collie. Its annoyed bleats echoed dimly after both animals disappeared from view.

Startled by the noise, his heart seemed to jump, too, then settle, jump again.

Pages stirred in his prayer book. A cloud covered the sun, then drifted away, bathing the valley in bright sunlight in a jewel-blue sky.

He wondered if he should book a passage on a ship, instead of flying home. Flying might be the death of him.

Another jump. Another settling.

I only know that I love God and want to serve Him with my whole heart, my whole soul, my whole mind.

Yes, Margaret, I only know that, as well. Maybe it's all I need to know.

Pain pierced his chest and jaw, as if a hand were squeezing his upper body in a too-tight embrace. His prayer book falling from his hands, he crumpled to the ground, seeing in his mind his father do the same so many years ago when a heart attack had felled and ultimately claimed him.

There was no one to call out to for help. Even the sheep were out of range now.

As he gasped through the torture, peace embraced him, a sweet loving calm that felt as blue and bright as the sky. The peace strengthened as the pain intensified. He felt drenched in a forgiving, unconditional love. A love he returned in full as he mouthed silently the words to the Last Rites. He added to its litany: Forgive me.

Forgive me for wasting the love you showered on me early in my life.

Forgive me for my stubbornness, my bitterness.

Forgive me.

Go home to say goodbye, Pete had suggested—he couldn't help smiling.

Yes, Lord, I've come home. I've come home at last.

A LETTER TO READERS
And an extra chapter!

Dear Reader,

First, about the extra chapter: If you'd like to receive an extra chapter, telling you what happens to some of the characters in this novel, email me at **Libby488@yahoo.com**, put "ATW extra chapter" in the subject line, and I will send you a short "episode" that takes place in the weeks after the epilogue! (If the email doesn't work, go to my website at **www.LibbySternberg.com** for directions.)

Now…on to some thoughts on *After the War*…For many years, even before I started thinking about devoting myself to writing, this story called out to me. At first, it was Paula and Margaret's story alone, two women whose approach to life and whose histories were almost direct opposites. Paula, despite her good upbringing, was to be a Mary Magdalene character, while Sister was something of a zealot for whom faith and religion meant rigid adherence to a set of rules. I wanted the book to be an exploration of their approach to faith, Paula's springing from a desire to be loved and love in return, and Margaret's coming from a desire to feel safe.

As I thought of who they were, their lives became populated with other people: Margaret's family, Mrs. Mallory, the sisters in the Mother House, and for Paula, her cousin, her father, the doctor who hires her in Baltimore. I couldn't let these backstories go, and they became as real to me as Margaret and Paula.

But as I wrote it and rewrote it—I started it years ago and returned to it over time—other characters called out to me to tell their stories, too. The nurse Kate, for example, had always been a part of my tale but way in the background, her struggle with what to do with her life after accepting widowhood playing out only in relation to Margaret's travails.

Dr. Kaplan's point of view hadn't been in early iterations of the novel, and Father Al hadn't made an appearance at all.

As I included more about Kate, however, I realized I had to share more about Dr. Kaplan. And I also realized I couldn't very well write a book that touched on faith issues and not include something about the priest to whom Paula goes for baptismal instruction.

This is when the book's overarching theme deepened and diverged from my original goal. My initial objective, in fact, became less attainable for me as I realized I didn't want to write a theological discussion on faith and certainly didn't feel qualified to pen one even if my inclination was there. I wanted to show how ordinary people dealt with the doubts and assumptions about their faith, if they had any at all. I wanted to show them wrestling with their beliefs as many do today.

Each had had their faith tested, in large and small ways. But in some way, each test was related to...the war.

All the characters had, in some significant way, been affected by the war. As I wrote their stories, the book became about that effect and their reactions, their accommodations to life after the war. Intertwined is the story of faith, but binding it all together is that "after the war" theme.

When I realized this was what I was writing, I thought, "of course." As a Baby Boomer, I grew up in a time when World War II was still a tangible event, still something that hung over my parents' lives and that of my friends' parents, as well. My father's army uniform (he served in the Philippines after the bombs were dropped) hung in our basement. He'd met my mother when he was stationed at a camp near her Indiana home. My friends' fathers had served, some in combat. I often felt, in fact, that my early years were like a long, warm summer after a bitter cold—and deadly—winter. I might not have experienced the war, but I lived through the collective sigh of relief afterward.

So the "after the war" theme felt natural and real to me, as much a part of this story as Paula's struggles with love or Margaret's wrestling with her vocation.

Although I only covered the lives of Margaret and Father Al in the epilogue, I do have ideas of what happened to the rest of our cast of characters...*and you can see them in the extra chapter!*

A few words about Margaret's convent life: I researched the life of nuns in various convents as I wrote this story, and I'm very grateful to Sister Ann Marie Slavin, OSF, for her insights into convent life. My research provided me with bits and pieces of the convent in which I wanted to place Margaret. But the Order of Sisters in my novel, as well as their specific Rule, is entirely fictional, and not based on any particular one.

As to the life of an immigrant family, my own father and his family inspired me there. The son of Polish immigrants, he and his family lived in a Baltimore row home in Highlandtown when he grew up.

I'm extremely grateful to Jerri Corgiat Gallagher, a fine novelist, for her suggestions and thoughtful edits, and to my family, especially my husband, Matthew, for his unwavering, continued support of this writing habit of mine.

Libby Sternberg

ABOUT THE AUTHOR

Libby Sternberg is the author of young adult and adult fiction. Her first book, a young adult mystery, was an Edgar finalist. She writes romantic comedy under the name Libby Malin. Visit her website at **www.LibbySternberg.com** for a complete list of her books, especially new releases! Visit her blog at

www.LibbysBooks.wordpress.com for interesting short essays on books and life.

Did you like this book? Love it? Not so much? Consider posting a review at Amazon!